IN A WORD...
SUSAN HILL'S SIMON SERRAILLER MYSTERIES ARE—

"Superb."
—P. D. JAMES

"Stunning."
—RUTH RENDELL

"Elegant."
—NEW YORK TIMES

"Atmospheric."
—NEW YORK JOURNAL OF BOOKS

"Somber."
—WALL STREET JOURNAL

"Timeless."
—WASHINGTON POST

"Chilling."
—NEW YORK TIMES BOOK REVIEW

"Gripping."
—STRAND MAGAZINE

"Compelling."
—KIRKUS REVIEWS

"Electrifying."
—SAN FRANCISCO REVIEW OF BOOKS

"Gritty."
—BOOKLIST

"Ominous."
—ENTERTAINMENT WEEKLY

"Outstanding."
—LIBRARY JOURNAL (STARRED REVIEW)

"Taut."
—PUBLISHERS WEEKLY

"Intelligent."
—TIME OUT

"Brooding."
—WASHINGTON TIMES

The Comforts *of* Home

A SIMON SERRAILLER CASE

SUSAN HILL

THE OVERLOOK PRESS
NEW YORK, NY

This edition first published in paperback in 2020 by
The Overlook Press, an imprint of ABRAMS
195 Broadway, 9th floor
New York, NY 10007
www.overlookpress.com

Originally published in hardcover by The Overlook Press in 2018

Abrams books are available at special discounts when purchased in quantity
for premiums and promotions as well as fundraising or educational use.
Special editions can also be created to specification. For details,
contact specialsales@abramsbooks.com or the address above.

Library of Congress Control Number: 2019930869

Printed and bound in the U.S.A.

1 3 5 7 9 10 8 6 4 2
ISBN: 978-1-4197-3895-1

ABRAMS The Art of Books
195 Broadway, New York, NY 10007
abramsbooks.com

For

HRH The Duchess of Cornwall

'Simon Serrailler's greatest fan'

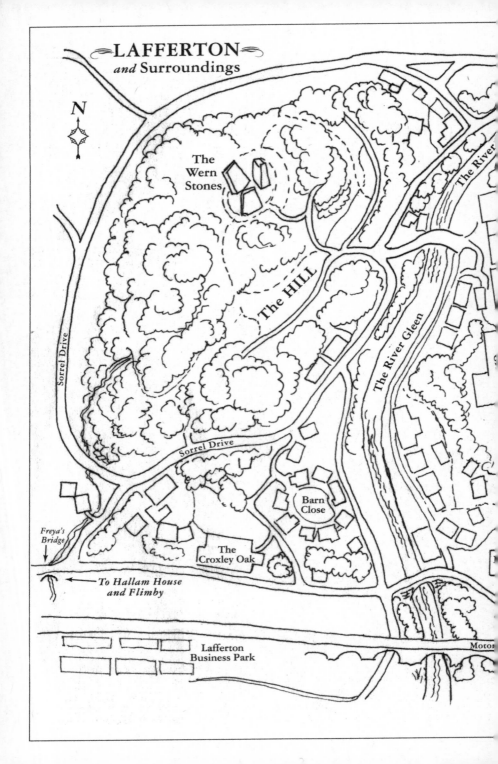

Prologue

For a long time, there had been blackness and the blackness had no form or shape. But then a soft and cloudy greyness had seeped in around the edges of the black, and soon, the images had come and these had moved forward very fast, like the pages of a child's flip book. At first he could not catch any, or distinguish between them, but gradually their movement had slowed and he had made out faces, and parts of bodies – a hand, a thumb, the back of a neck. Hair. The images had begun to pulse, and balloon in and out, like a beating heart, the faces had swirled together, mingled then separated, and once or twice they had leered at him, or laughed silently out of mouths full of broken teeth. He had tried to back away from them or lift his arm to shield his eyes, but he was stiff, his arm heavy and cold, like a joint of meat taken out of the freezer. He did not know how to move it.

The faces had split into fragments and begun to spin uncontrollably, and he had been looking down into a vortex.

A flash of light. Inside the light, millions of glittering, sharp pinpoints. Another flash. The pinpoints had dissolved.

Simon Serrailler opened his eyes.

It was surprising how quickly things had fallen into place.

'What day is it?'

'Thursday. It's twenty past five.' The nurse turned from adjusting the drip to look at him.

'When did I come round?'

1

'Yesterday morning.'

'Wednesday.'

'You're doing very well. How do you feel?'

'I'm not sure.'

'Any pain?'

He considered. He moved his head and saw a rectangle of pale sky. The roof of a building, with a ledge around it. Nothing seemed to hurt at all though there was a strange heaviness in his left arm and neck. The rest of his body felt slightly detached. But that wasn't pain. He remembered pain.

'I think I'm fine.'

'That's good. You're doing very well,' she said again, as if she had to convince him.

'Am I? I don't know.'

'Do you know where you are?'

'Not sure. Maybe a hospital?'

'Full marks. You're in Charing Cross ITU and I'm Sister Bonnington. Megan.'

'The nearest hospital isn't Charing Cross . . . it's . . . I can't remember.'

'You're in west London.'

He let the words sink in and he knew perfectly well what they meant. He knew where west London was, he'd been a DC somewhere in west London.

'Do you remember anything that happened?'

He had a flash. The body parts. The hand. The thumb. The mouth of decayed, broken teeth. It went.

'I don't think I do.'

'Doesn't matter. That's perfectly normal. Don't start beating your brains to remember anything.'

'Not sure I've got any brains.'

She smiled. 'I think you have. Let me sort out your pillows, make you a bit more comfortable. Can you sit up?'

He had no idea how he might begin to do such a thing, but she seemed to lift him and prop him forwards on her arm, plump his pillows, adjust his bedcover and rest him back, without apparent effort. He realised that he had tubes and wires attached to him, leading to machines and monitors and drips,

2

and that his left arm was in some sort of hoist. He looked at it. Bandages, a long sleeve of bandages, up to his shoulder and beyond.

'Is that painful?'

'No. It's sort of – nothing.'

'Numb?'

'Not exactly. Just . . . I can't explain.'

'Not to worry. The consultant will be in to see you at some point this evening.'

'Who is he?'

'Mr Flint. And Dr Lo is the senior registrar. He's been looking after you these last couple of days, but we're a team.'

'I have a team?'

'You do indeed, Simon. Is it OK to call you Simon? We always ask, you know, but you haven't been in any state to answer. What do you prefer? Mr Serrailler? Superintendent? Chief Superintendent?'

'God no. Simon's fine.'

The door opened slightly.

'Here's a visitor, so I'll leave you. The buzzer's there, by your right hand. Press if you need anything.'

'Hey, you.' Cat bent over and kissed his cheek. 'You're awake again.'

'When wasn't I?'

'Most of the last three weeks.'

'Three *weeks*? Until when?'

'Yesterday. You remember me being here?'

He tried to sort out the confusion of images in his head. 'I don't . . . no.'

He saw his sister's fleeting look of concern which she masked quickly.

'I'm told the consultant is coming in soon. Did you know I had a "team" of my own? Are you on it?'

She smiled.

'Did you bring me grapes?'

'No. But you don't really want grapes, do you?'

'I want to know what happened and why I'm here. Talk to me.'

3

'Listen, Si, you have to know everything but I'm not the one to tell you the whole story, because I wasn't there. Kieron's coming down again tomorrow, and if they think you're ready to hear, he'll tell you.'

'The Chief's been here?'

'Of course he has. He brought me down the day it happened, and he's been in a few times since, whenever he could make it, and I've kept him briefed every day.'

'You have? Why you?'

'Because I've been here most days and I talk to the medics so I can translate their jargon for him.'

'No, I meant . . . I don't understand how you even know him.'

'He's been a rock, Si . . . when there wasn't anyone else looking out for me.'

'Ah.'

'Ah nothing.'

He tried to read her expression but he couldn't concentrate on that because he was aware of a pain in his left arm, which was getting worse by the second, in waves which crashed over his arm onto his chest and up and down his body, pincers and gashes of pain.

'Si?'

'Jesus.' He looked at all the bandages and the hoist that kept the arm up. If it had been in flames he would not have been surprised. It felt like that.

Cat was on her feet. 'It's OK. I'll sort it . . . hold on.'

She did not return for an hour. A night. The rest of his life. He was wrapped in pain and pain was all he was aware of. He heard himself cry out so loudly he was afraid they would come and punish him. The faces. The blackness was no longer simple dark, no longer soft-edged, it was scarlet in the centre and the centre was spreading out and out.

'God . . .'

'It's all right. Someone's coming.' Cat was holding his right hand tightly. She was touching his face and then wiping the tears from it, but he didn't feel shame or embarrasment, he felt nothing beyond the pain.

4

'Let's get this sorted out now.' A man this time, looming over the bed.

'Hold on.'

He couldn't hold on but there was no escape route. He lay convulsed with pain. Cat was wiping the sweat from his forehead with a damp cloth. Angry. She was angry too. Why was everybody angry with him?

A swirl of activity, people coming into the room, people leaning over him.

'Here you go, Simon . . . any second now.'

And the infinitely gentle easing away of pain, so that his body relaxed, his head felt cool, his arm seemed to have disappeared.

'That's it. You should have pressed the bell. You should have said –'

'No,' he heard Cat say, and he recognised her tone though it was one she used rarely. 'No, it has nothing to do with him, it's to do with everyone else. There's a meds regime, and it has to be stuck to or this happens. And it took me far too long to find someone who knew anything at all about him and his case, and then get them to come – and don't, please, tell me it was shift changeover.'

'It was shift changeover. I'm sorry.'

'Christ's sake.' The man. He was young and bearded and his eyes were full of concern, compassion and anger.

'Simon, I'm Dr Lo. Tan. I know you but this is the first time you've been awake to see me. Is the pain easier?'

It was like lying on a bed of down. He felt nothing but gentleness and ease. He smiled beatifically at everyone in the room.

He knew that he had slept again and then floated on air and finally on water, but the hands of the clock on the wall opposite his bed went slowly backwards so that he lost all sense of time and even of day. It was light, then it was dark and still he floated.

'It's Friday,' someone said.

He surfaced.

There were two of them, and Cat was there as well. He was propped up and drops of silvery rain slid down the window-panes.

'Friday.'

'We'd like to talk you through what we plan to do, if you feel up to it?'

He recognised the younger doctor but not the older one with very little hair and small round spectacles.

'I'm Mr Flint, Greg Flint. I'm an orthopaedic trauma consultant.'

'Is this a conference?'

'More or less. I'm glad Dr Deerbon is here actually . . . if you're OK with that? I'll try to be clear but she'll be able to translate our jargon for you if I'm not and you can ask her anything you need to. I filled her in briefly while you were still away with the fairies.'

'I'm here now.'

'And I apologise that you were left in so much pain – shouldn't have happened and it won't happen again. How is it now?'

'Numb. If you mean my arm.'

'And the rest of you?'

'Fine, I think. I've had some bad headaches.'

'I'm not surprised – you had a terrific blow. I'm amazed your skull wasn't fractured.'

He frowned. Blow? Skull? What? He looked at Cat.

'It's OK,' she said. 'You can't remember. It's normal. It'll come back. Or maybe not but there's no brain damage, your scans were fine.'

'I had scans? The things that have been happening . . .'

'We're not worried about your head or the rest of your injuries, they're mending nicely. If it weren't for the arm you'd be out of here.'

Simon felt his mind clearing. 'So . . . what exactly happened to my arm?'

'Essentially, it was mangled in the bin machinery.'

Bin? Bin machinery? But he nodded.

'We did what we could at the time, but we've had to wait to see exactly what's salvageable. You need to go for another scan and when we look at that things should be clearer – these injuries do settle down. I want to be able to save your arm, Simon,

6

and having looked at the last scan, I'm pretty sure I can, though until I actually get you on the table we won't be certain. Even then, sometimes things look good and then halfway through there's a problem. But I don't anticipate that. I never anticipate problems.'

'When you say "save" my arm . . .'

'Yes.'

'You mean it'll be as good as new?'

'That does depend. I'd hope we can get 80 per cent or possibly even 90 per cent restored function – time and a lot of physio will tell. It's unlikely to be 100 per cent.'

'Right.'

'Physio is absolutely crucial and your never failing to do the exercises, not even once. I'll do all I can and so will everyone else, but after that it will be down to you.'

'That doesn't worry me. It was the thought of losing the arm.'

'I'm confident. But we'll get that scan and when I've seen it I can plan. They'll have to take off the bandages but we'll get you down straight away and then you'll have a new dressing. They've been doing that every day anyway.'

He remembered suddenly. They had given him so much pain-killer he hadn't felt anything and she had said, 'Don't look at it, that's my advice. Turn your head. Injuries always start to hurt when you look at them.'

He had turned his head. But everything had been numb.

'After the scan, how long before you operate?'

'If it all looks OK, probably Monday morning. I need to clear my list. This sort of reconstruction takes a while.'

It took seven hours, or so they told him, but seven hours which had meant nothing, and now he was back underwater, floating, blissful. His life passed quietly by.

The door opened and he saw a man in dark chinos, pale blue sweatshirt. Dark wavy hair. He thought of his own blond hair and realised that he hadn't needed to push it back from where it always flopped over his forehead for some time. What time? Maybe for years.

'Where's my hair?' he said, to the man with so much of it.

'They had to shave it off to do the repairs, I think. Don't worry, it's growing back.' The man had taken the chair beside his bed. Simon knew him. Knew him fairly well.

'Hi,' he said, to give himself time.

'Cat sends her love and she's glad things are looking good but she had to cover for a colleague – there wasn't anybody else apparently. She'll be here tomorrow.'

So the man knew Cat.

'I wish my bloody brain would get its mojo back. Sick of thinking through cotton wool.'

'That's the drugs.'

So he knew about those too.

The bolt shot backwards and the door fell open. 'Chief . . .' Simon said. He ought to sit up but his body was covered in lead weights.

Kieron Bright smiled. 'Me,' he said. 'Don't worry, that's the drugs as well. How do you feel?'

'Weird. Listen, they haven't told me much. What happened?'

For the next half-hour, Kieron told him. Serrailler thought he was sparing him some of the detail, perhaps only for the time being, but the broad outline of what had happened to him was clear, and as the Chief spoke, now and then a glimmer of something came and went on the horizon of his mind. He remembered but he did not quite remember, and yet it seemed familiar, it made some sort of sense.

'I can't tell you much about your injuries but the docs have done that.'

'Not really.'

'They have told you – you probably didn't take it all in, which is understandable.' He leaned back in the chair, arms folded. In casual clothes, the Chief looked younger, but that was usually the case. Gold braid lent gravitas and with gravitas came age. He was only four years older than Simon.

'Thanks for coming down here.'

'I've been before but you were out of it. It's good to see you now. We were worried.'

'I'm invincible.'

'So it would seem. Your sister wasn't so sure.' He crossed one leg over the other, then recrossed them. Simon was aware of some sort of tension about him, or else an anxiety – he couldn't tell, even though the mists that had swirled around his brain were clearing again. And his arm was hurting.

'I've taken her out a couple of times.'

'Cat?'

'Cat. Hope that's all right with you.'

Simon laughed. 'Nothing to do with me – her life's her own affair.'

'You're close though.'

'Yes . . . we always have been. Strange – you'd have expected it to be me and Ivo but it never was. He was always the odd one out. Ivo's quite different.'

'Cat says the same.'

So, they had talked in that way, which Cat rarely did. She had never been an especially private person about herself, her marriage, career, children, doings, but about the three of them she was, and so was he, come to that. He didn't know about Ivo. Australia had beckoned for Ivo even before he had qualified as a doctor, and the moment he had, it had claimed him permanently. He had never been back.

When Kieron had left, and before the next lot of painkillers kicked in, he had a lucid interlude in which to think, about the man, as Chief Constable and therefore his own boss, and also as someone in a relationship – whatever that turned out to be – with his sister.

He turned the thought round, looking at every side carefully, the idea of the two of them together was like a globe he was holding.

Nothing looked wrong. Nothing worried him.

'How's it feeling?' The brisk, unsmiling sister. Unsmiling but not unfeeling, he thought, but she wasn't going to be caught out in any display of sympathy. A bit like him.

'Actually, even when the meds need topping up, it isn't so bad – a hell of a lot better than before.'

'Good.'

'When can I see it?'

'Mr Flint will decide. Perhaps tomorrow.'

'When will I be able to start using it again? No – forget that. "Mr Flint will decide." But, dear *dear* Sister, couldn't you be Mr Flint, just for now?' He raised an eyebrow. She threw the used syringe in the sharps bin, peeled off her latex gloves, threw those away too. On the way out of the room, she said, 'Don't push your luck.'

Simon thought she might just have been smiling.

The following morning she was holding his right arm and another nurse was pushing his drip stand as he took his first walk, slow steps down the hospital corridor. His legs felt uncertain, as if they were waiting to be told how to move forward, one and then the other, but by the time they reached the junction with another corridor, it had fallen into place.

'I can go on.'

'What was it I said?'

'Don't push your luck?'

'So don't. But that was very good and you can have another jaunt later.'

Simon felt as pleased as a child with ticks all over his homework.

Two more walks down the corridors and speeding up. Walking felt normal again. All the bruising and contusions he had noted on his body, legs, right arm, were fading and healing well. He saw in the mirror that his hair had now grown back over most of the scarring and stitches on the front of his head. Would they shave it again when they took them out? Would they take them out? He meant to ask but the nurses had gone. He felt suddenly exhausted, then very cold. There was so little in the way of bedding. He needed a duvet but hospitals did not have duvets.

'Supper.'

The tray with the tin lid on top of the plate. A side dish of what looked like tinned fruit salad and custard. The young man lifted the lid with a flourish and the smell of cauliflower wafted up. Cauliflower. A slab of quiche. Three small potatoes.

'I don't think I'm hungry actually. Could you take it away?'

He smiled and said, 'You must try now.' Polish? Romanian? 'Eating is right. Not eat not get well. OK?'

And he swung out of the door. The trolley wheels screeched on the corridor floor and the tin lids rattled on the dishes.

He could not eat. He could not have swallowed anything, though he drank the glass of water and tried to lean over to the jug on his side table and pour another. But he couldn't reach.

He was so hot he felt ill. He felt ill from the smell of the food and the heat and a headache and the throbbing in his left arm.

After a long time of lying still, feeling increasingly worse, wondering if someone would come, wondering what to do with his food tray, wondering, in the end, where he was and why, he noticed something on the bedcover. He was confused by what it was but he reached out his hand and found that there was a button that he could press.

'Altos, you're still not together. I know it's tricky, but once more please.'

It was tricky. They had been rehearsing the John Tavener piece for a month and they were barely getting to grips with it. The altos were struggling. Cat was struggling. The Mozart Requiem, which the St Michael's Singers were performing in the same concert, was smooth sailing by comparison.

'It's no harder than the Britten we did at Christmas – now come on, focus.'

'It's way harder,' Cat's next-door neighbour in the altos muttered. 'Honestly, we're not the London Philharmonic Choir.'

'No, Nancy – we are aiming to be even better. Right, back to page four please.'

Andrew Browning, the conductor, was a hard taskmaster, far more exacting than his predecessor. He was becoming known in the ranks of singers as Browning the Cruel.

'One two three AND . . .'

Cat's phone vibrated in her pocket. She ignored it. It continued to vibrate every few minutes and she continued to ignore it. If Sam had forgotten his front door key yet again he could wait in the garden shed.

They hit a rich singing seam and suddenly things clicked into place. Perhaps Tavener was possible after all.

They broke for drinks and Cat checked her phone. Sam's name flashed up on the screen. No, she thought, one time too many, Sambo, this will now teach you to remember your key. She pictured him, huddled in the shed, waiting for her to get home.

'Cat, someone wants you.'

She looked up. Sam was not in the garden shed, he was walking down the hall towards her and his face told her that this was not about a lost key.

'How did you get here?'

'Kieron. I could only think of him because you weren't answering. You've got to come, the car's waiting.'

'What car? What for?'

'Simon. The hospital rang. Mum – hurry up.'

Kieron was not like her husband, Chris, in more ways than she could count, but in two, and the two mattered greatly to her, they were the same. Chris had been calm and unflappable. So was Kieron – probably more so. She realised the second similarity on the way home very late that night. Kieron did not ask her how she was feeling, did not try to put a good face on what had happened, did not once say, about Simon, 'Well, at least he . . .' He sat beside her in the back of the car, he held her hand, and he said nothing until she did. They travelled swiftly and smoothly, but there was no race to get to Simon now. It had happened. They had arrived in time to see him being wheeled out of theatre and back to his room. Coming out behind him, still in his scrubs, the surgeon had beckoned them to follow him into an empty bay. He and Kieron stood, Cat sat in the one chair.

'I'm afraid I couldn't wait for you to get here. Time is crucial – the infection in his arm was spreading fast and if I hadn't got to it he would probably have died of sepsis. It was bad.'

'So you had to amputate.'

'I had no choice. It is absolutely maddening because I was pretty sure I'd saved the arm. It took a long time but it worked. Things went my way and it was looking better than I'd dared hope.'

'Then this.'

'Sepsis is always a risk, no matter how careful we are.'

'I often tell people that as far as infections are concerned, they're safer out of hospital than in it.'

The surgeon shrugged. He looked exhausted, his face grey, dark circles beneath his eyes. It was well past midnight.

'You can go in and see him briefly but he probably won't be aware you're there.'

'But he will be all right?' It was the first time Kieron had spoken.

'Yes. The source of infection has gone and he's being pumped full of the strongest antibiotics we have, the ones we use sparingly. His temperature's down. Yes, he'll be fine. Not sure when I can let him out of ITU but there's no reason why he shouldn't be ready to go home in a couple of weeks. Then it all starts.'

'Physio?'

'Yes, but mainly fitting up for a prosthesis. They'll want to get going as soon as it's safe. I'm referring him to the best specialist unit.' He stood up. 'Tomorrow,' he said. 'I'm bushed.'

After he had left, they stayed together in silence for several minutes. The theatre area was quiet. Only emergency surgery went on at this time of night and for now there was none. Hospitals were so rarely still like this. Kieron put out his hand. 'Listen, you'll want to see him but not tonight, when he won't have come round. I've phoned in to tell them I have to be off tomorrow but they'll ring me if something urgent blows up. So I suggest I try and find us a hotel, we go there and get a drink and hopefully at least a sandwich, and come back first thing in the morning. And' – he put his hand on hers – 'no strings. Two rooms.'

'I wasn't –'

'I know. Nor was I. Come on, nothing you can do tonight and you need sleep.'

The chain hotel was a mile away. It was clean, comfortable, they had rooms, they had a bar that was still open. Cat felt as if she were swimming rather than walking on solid ground as she followed Kieron to a table. She had put her feelings about Simon in a reserved space of her mind which doctors kept for just this purpose. When you could not deal with something shocking and distressing immediately, you learned early on to park it. But not to bury it. That way, stored-up problems began to fester.

Kieron had brought over two larges whiskies and a jug of water. Late-night food was available until two. He had ordered omelettes.

'OK?'

Cat shook her head. 'I'm all right. I can deal with it. But you have to answer one question, Kieron. It's the most important thing after "will he live?".'

'I'm pretty sure I know that question.'

'All right.'

'Presuming Simon is otherwise fine but he has a prosthetic arm, can he still be in the police force?'

She searched his face and could see nothing there.

'Of course he can. Absolutely. It goes without saying and especially in CID. He could still be uniform, for that matter, but there would be more adjustments and a few restrictions. In CID, not at all.'

'And that's the truth?'

'It will be my call, once the medics have had their say and Simon tells me he wants to stay. He might not.'

'Oh he will. What else would he do?'

'Does he draw with his left hand?'

'No, he's right-handed. But however good he is – and he is good – he couldn't do that alone. He's a cop. It's what has made him who he is, for the last twenty-odd years.'

'He'll still be a cop.'

Their food came and Cat ate hers and finished her drink while she could keep her eyes open.

'I need to deal with a few things. You go to bed. We can have breakfast before we go in to see him, then I'll have to head back to Lafferton.'

'Thank you,' she said, and her eyes filled with tears that she was not expecting. 'I couldn't have got through this without you.'

14

'Of course you could. I'm just glad you haven't had to.' He reached out his hand and she took it for a second, before using her last fragments of energy to get up to her room and bed.

Kieron finished his whisky and sat on, thinking about a Detective Chief Superintendent who had been through mental and emotional as well as extreme physical trauma, and who now had to face a slow, difficult journey to what recovery there could be. He was aware of major advances in prosthetics, of bionic arms that could be fitted up in such a way that they fulfilled orders directly from the brain, to perform tasks almost as well as a natural one. He knew that Serrailler would be at minimal disadvantage in terms of the job. He would be able to use a computer and drive a car as well as be on top of all the aspects of the work which would not be affected at all – interviewing, going over casework, meeting with colleagues, briefing a team.

But he was aware, as he had to be, that Simon was not a straightforward man. He was a fine detective but he had personal issues, perhaps ones he would never resolve, and although in the past they had no impact on his work, they might surface now, when he was at his most helpless, and cause problems. It was impossible to know. All he himself could do was watch and wait, give whatever help and support he could and have neither too many nor too few expectations. He could also make the rest of the Lafferton team aware of the importance of their doing the same.

The bar was empty. He finished the last splash of Scotch, with a lot of water and got up. He hoped Cat was able to sleep.

Cat. She was a strong, resilient, capable woman, a conscientious doctor, a loving single parent. But he had realised early on that she was vulnerable, not only through her children, but through her brother. She knew Simon as well as anyone – better, probably, than he knew himself. She would understand completely how this trauma would affect him, and not in the obvious ways. Physically, he would cope. But there was a great deal more to his recovery than some rehabilitation and physiotherapy. Serrailler would need everyone's help, and above all,

15

he would need Cat and she would give him whatever he asked for and more.

What concerned and preoccupied Kieron, as he crossed the hotel lobby towards the lifts, was whether that meant she would have anything left over, from her brother and her children, for anyone else.

He woke just after six o'clock and could not get back to sleep. The room was comfortable enough but overheated and the windows were sealed. He went out. The streets around the hotel were as dull as the streets of any area bordering on an industrial estate and a motorway. Kieron would have run, which always made boring places less boring simply because you did not have time to take them in, but he had to make do with fast walking because he had not brought any sports gear. He walked for forty minutes, around concrete and metal office blocks, storage warehouses, wholesale units, the car parks which were already starting to fill up. A mile to the right he saw the flat roof of the hospital. He turned back.

Cat was still not up, so he got coffee and checked his phone. No messages. He waited another half-hour, reading the papers, before calling the station. His PA was in but had nothing for him either. He felt oddly restless, as if he should be on the spot to get things started, no matter what they were. He called the duty sergeant.

'Nothing to report, Chief. Couple of RTAs on the other side of the county and all dealt with. One reported breaking and entering but false alarm.'

'Quiet night everywhere then.'

'Pretty much. Just one report, and it's probably nothing. Lafferton. Someone made a bonfire by the old warehouses along the canal. The fire was made like you would do one for Guy Fawkes Night – wood offcuts, sticks, a couple of dead branches. Paper. Wigwam shape. There was a bicycle tyre on top and then they'd poured over half a can of varnish. It was the smell that alerted everyone, quite a few people called in – that and the thick black smoke. Fire brigade got it out in no time and sorted it, but it was peculiar. Who'd take the trouble?'

'Some lunatic. But no damage?'

'Not even close to overhanging bushes.'

'If that's the worst of the night's revels, we can't complain.' As he finished talking, Cat walked in.

'Breakfast. You should eat,' Kieron said. The strain of the previous day shadowed her face.

'Can we go straight to the hospital?'

He made her have coffee but she stood up to drink it. A quarter of an hour later, they were in Simon's room.

He was sitting up, drips and lines everywhere, the machines beeping steadily. He was pale, seemed thinner in the face, but he was drinking from a plastic beaker through a straw.

'One-armed bandit,' he said. It didn't sound like a joke.

'I'll leave you two for a bit, get a coffee.'

But Serrailler held up his hand.

'I know what you've come to say. Let me hear it.' He sounded weary.

'What am I going to say? You tell me.'

Cat looked from one to the other, as if they were two small boys and she had somehow caught them quarrelling when they should be supporting one another.

'Si . . .'

'It's OK. I just need him to spit it out, then he can go.'

It was partly the drugs, partly pain talking, but she knew him, she knew his pride and his fury and knew that, as ever, he would rather have the worst hit him full on and at once.

Kieron sighed, and went to stand close to the bed. He put out his hand and touched Simon's shoulder with one finger, lightly.

'Listen,' he said. 'You've a lot ahead of you. I don't know the half of it and I don't suppose you do either, not yet. But however long it takes, you're coming back. DCS, full-time, as soon as they sign you off. No question, because you're too valuable and there won't be any restrictions on what you do. Do you understand me?'

Simon looked at him for a long moment, then nodded.

'Nothing else to say then. Focus on getting well.'

'Chief.' There was the slightest twitch at the corner of his mouth.

Kieron nodded and went to find the canteen.

Cat smiled. Kieron had got the full measure of her brother. It mattered, and from more than one perspective.

She sat down beside the bed. 'That was a real bugger,' she said, 'the worst luck. They can do the best but infection's always a risk.'

'It's done.'

'Do you want me to go through it with you or would you rather leave it to them? You probably should. They're the experts.'

'You're not my doctor, you're my sister. Let's stick to that.'

'Fine. End of. But you do know –'

'– that you're here for me if I change my mind? Yes, I do know. Thanks. There is one thing though – will I stay here or will they ship me home . . . or what?'

'I don't know, but the chances are they'll discharge you from here once they're sure the infection is under control. The anti-biotics they're giving you are pretty powerful and you'll be taking them for a couple of weeks, but as tablets, so if the surgeon's happy otherwise you won't need to be filling up a bed. But you can't be sent home.'

'Why not?'

'You're resourceful, Si, but you've been through the mill. Being by yourself in the flat straight away won't be an option. The best thing will be for you to come to us. I won't make you stay an hour longer than necessary but I want to be sure you're well before you go home.'

'Yes, Doctor.'

Cat felt a mixture of relief and worry. Immediate agreement to whatever she proposed about anything to do with him was not what she would ever expect.

'Tell me honestly . . . how do you feel? I don't mean pain, discomfort . . . all that, I mean . . . Si, you've lost your arm. Don't dismiss the effect of that on you . . . your mood, your temper, the way you're normally so at ease in your own body. Don't bottle it.'

He stared ahead of him and she could read nothing from his expression. Beyond the room, the usual hospital noises. She had

18

loved her training years working in them but she had never wanted to have a hospital career and felt even more now that she had made the right decision. Patients came and went within days, sometimes hours, there was little chance to get to know them and none to follow them up. She was a people doctor. Neither surgery nor anaesthetics had held any charms for her, partly because of the lack of an ongoing relationship with the patients.

'I won't know how I'm going to deal with this until I find out what I'll end up with,' Simon said. 'And what I'll be able to do. Thank God it's my left arm is all I can say now. Will you pour me some water?'

As she put the glass into his hand, he looked her in the eyes.

'I'll tell you one thing though.'

He held her with his look as he drank slowly. Cat waited, sensing that something important was coming, not wanting to push him, or embarrass him into staying silent. They talked often and sometimes he told her things, very occasionally gave out rare snippets and hints about himself, his feelings, but she was always conscious of the deeply private inner core of him which she would never be allowed to access. She had learned to respect it.

He gave her the empty glass, but as he did so, took her hand for a moment.

'You should marry the Chief,' he said.

One

The last time Serrailler had come to the island, he had dropped down from the sky in a small plane. This time he approached by sea, on the regular ferry which brought him, a couple of other foot passengers and crates of supplies.

Taransay was mole-brown streaked with gold in the sunlight. He had forgotten how small the only village was, a huddle of low-built grey-stone houses facing the water. Behind them, the road out was a pale line for a mile before becoming a track that wound up and around and away over the hill, where there were isolated cottages and a couple of farms. Otherwise, this was empty wild land. A few buildings sheltered in the sandy bays had been turned into holiday lets but once September had gone, they were empty and the islanders closed in for another winter.

He sat on the deck. The sky was soft with cloud, but for once, there was only a breeze not a wind. If you wanted the exhilaration of gales, and to be brushed aside by their force, Taransay, with its neighbouring islands, was the place to come.

As they rode the slight swell coming in to harbour, he had a strange sense of re-entering his old life, as if then he had been another man. It was nearly six years ago and might have been six hundred. He had been young. He had been fit, hale, whole, but he was not whole now, though the physical effects of having lost a flesh-and-bone arm and gained a prosthetic one had been far easier to cope with than the psychological ones. He was haunted by the loss of his limb.

He dreamed almost every night that it was still firmly part of him. He felt diminished even while he was gaining in strength and dexterity and getting used to finding new ways to do old things.

Seagulls formed a noisy, voracious pack following the boat as it turned in and began to nudge its way to safe berth alongside the quay. Simon stood up and stretched and then looked.

One tall man. One only slightly less tall woman. And one small boy. They stood together. The men from the stores and the pub would be down to start unloading, once the *Bright Lass* had tied up and the gangplank had gone down, to let off the passengers. Simon wanted to leap onto the quay. He also wanted to turn his back and hide below deck until the ferry was ready for the return trip.

Douglas had spotted him. Kirsty was waving. The small boy stood, hands in the pockets of his shorts. Looking.

Douglas was first, reaching for Simon's holdall and slapping him on the back. Whatever had happened between them in the past was indeed past, and when Kirsty took him in a close hug, it was natural, it was heartfelt, but most of all, it was friendly, and gave no hint of what had been between them several years earlier. And it did not appear to trouble Douglas a jot.

'This is Robbie.'

The small boy had mud-coloured hair, seal-grey eyes and a strong look of his father. He put out his hand and Simon shook it solemnly, aware of the boy's close scrutiny.

'Can I see your bionic arm?' he said.

'Robbie! What was the last thing I told you before we left the house?'

'Not to ask him about his bionic arm, I know, but it's too exciting.'

'I'll show you. Only not now.'

'Why not now?'

'Because my arm and I are exhausted after a very long journey by a car, two trains and a ferry.'

'OK.' Robbie climbed into the back seat of the Land Rover. 'Only you will show me tomorrow, won't you, when your bionic arm has had a wee rest? You promise?'

'I do.'

Robbie buckled his seat belt with a small smile.

'If it suits you to come and have tea with us, I'll take you to your place later,' Douglas said, turning the old Landy onto the track that climbed steeply uphill. 'Or would you rather drop your things there first?'

'He wouldn't rather do that, he would much rather come to our house now.'

'Robbie, you mind yourself.'

'He's right though. I'd like that first.'

The boy had not taken his eyes off him. He gazed at Simon's left arm and hand, resting on the seat between them.

'Look any different to you?' Douglas asked, gesturing to the landscape.

'Has it looked any different for a thousand years?'

'Oh aye – a thousand years ago there were more people than sheep and crofts to match.'

'It's exactly the same as when I was last here.'

'You haven't seen our house yet.'

But the house, too, looked the same – from the front, a low, cream-washed bungalow with a field around it and the hills behind. Douglas had lived here alone then. But when they got out of the car and walked round, Simon saw an extension, with a dormer above, tucked into the back of the house overlooking the sea.

'We finally finished it last month. You know how it goes up here.'

'See that? Look, Mr Simon, up there – that's MY window. To MY own room.'

'Wow, Robbie, what a lookout! You could spot smugglers and spies as well as birds and seals.'

Robbie's grey eyes widened. 'Smugglers?'

'You'll need a good pair of binoculars of course.'

'Och, I've got those.'

23

'And a telescope would be handy.'

The boy frowned. 'I'll have to ask about that. Anyway, it's a good plan. If you like, you could be my assistant.'

'Ah, Robbie, if only – but you need someone regular and I have to go back in a couple of weeks. I wouldn't be much use to you.'

'Still, while you're here. We could –'

'You could go and change your shoes and wash your hands before tea, that's what you could do, Robbie Boyd. Away . . . go.' Douglas was shifting a bag of gravel which had been left outside the door.

'You've a fine boy there, Kirsty.'

She smiled. 'Aye. And there's another one coming in the spring, but we haven't told him yet. He'll have to be well prepared – he likes to rule the roost here, does our Robbie.'

Simon walked behind her into the house. Kirsty. She hadn't changed. She was still the tall, friendly, careless young woman he had first known six years earlier, had a brief fling with, and taken Douglas's crack on the jaw for his pains. Yet she wasn't. She was a wife, a mother, an energetic member of the small community, all of whom relied on one another, especially through the long hard winters. She was no longer so fancy-free and careless, though she was still friendly, still had wild hair.

He did not wish that he had taken her from Douglas for good. Life on Taransay all year round was not for him and the smallness and inward-looking habits of the island would drive him crazy. He wished them well and was glad they were bringing up their family here, the place needed all the young blood it could get. But he envied them too. Home. Each other. Little Robbie. Another child soon. A steady, settled life.

He pulled off his boots before going into Kirsty's snug new kitchen, with the sea beyond the window and the range sending out a comforting warmth. Even when the sun shone on Taransay stoves and wood fires were needed.

'I'm sitting next to you, Mr Simon.'

'Yes, Master Robbie and you mind your table manners and no cheeky questions or you'll be away to your bed.'

'Can you hold the fork with your bionic hand?'

'Robbie . . .'

'No, it's fine, Kirsty. Yes, I can – I can do a lot of amazing things with this one, but in a few months I'm getting an even more amazing one and then I'll be able to sew on buttons and scratch behind my ears.'

The prosthesis was as comfortable as it could be for now. He had had months of physiotherapy, and there would be more, plus lessons in how to use the state-of-the-art new one. In time, he would be fully accustomed to it, he had been told. It would be almost as familiar, and use of it as instinctive, as his right arm. Almost. He had been told something else. 'It isn't all about the mechanics of your limb,' Alex, the physio, had said. 'Or even about your brain training itself to cope with all the small differences between your own arm and this – which it will. It's about mental attitude. Acceptance.'

'Positive thinking?'

'More a case of no negative thinking. It'll come, Simon.'

And he knew that the process had begun. Physically, it had begun well. The psychological challenge was harder, as Alex had known it would be. He had worked with enough returning military, armless, legless, and all combinations thereof.

'The body is willing. It's far easier to work on than the mind, which often isn't. And that's not my area of expertise.'

He had been more than willing to work with Alex for as many hours as were needed. He had trained, pushed himself, been surprised by his own progress. But when it came to his mental attitude, he had resisted appointments with counsellors from within the police force, and from the rehabilitation team, though he knew he was wrong.

They ate grilled fish from that day's catch, chips, and beans from Kirsty's thriving vegetable garden. Fresh produce was hard to come by on the islands unless you grew your own – and growing your own was not easy, with a short summer, a difficult soil, and a more or less permanent wind off the sea.

Robbie grew very quiet, once the apple crumble had been eaten and the Orkney cheese and oatcakes attacked. He slid down a little in his chair and did not move.

'Right, young man, I know your tricks. If you stay still you'll become invisible. Ten minutes more. Simon, would you have a cup of coffee and a dram?'

The ten minutes passed, and Kirsty pointed at her son. Without a word, he got down and came round for a last, fascinating look at Simon's limb.

'Tell you what, Robbie. After school's out tomorrow, why don't you come over to see me and then I'll show it to you properly and how it works – the lot? It's good you should understand.'

The boy hesitated, then, instead of the handshake, gave Simon a hug, his touch as brief and light as a cat's, and shot away to bed.

Two

Early the following morning, and still cramped and stale after the long journey, Simon set off across the island, climbing the single-track road that led to the hill more or less in the middle. From there, the road descended again, and, because few lived on this side of Taransay, it was stony and narrow, untended.

After four miles of steady tramping, he began to climb again towards the cliffs above the wilder sea. Looking down, he could see a long sandy bay. Gannets and kittiwakes clung to the rock face, occasionally soaring up and plunging back to their ledges again. Ahead, there was only the sea, which, on this side, was never calm, never quiet. The great rollers piled in one after another, foaming in a long white line onto the shore. He could not have heard himself speak above the crashing of the sea and the racket of the birds. But there was no one to speak to.

He sat on an outcrop and looked for a long time. The sky was milky, the air fresh but not cold. And there was a wind. Always a wind here.

He did not know if it was the most beautiful place he had ever visited – perhaps not. But it was closest to his heart now. He loved the solitude, the wildness, the constant shifting of clouds and sea and coarse grass, the rise and fall of the birds. The way it absorbed yet remained quite indifferent to his presence.

The other side of the island was softer, more sheltered, lower to the water, though the gales could still howl and roar, and the sea be rough enough for the boats to be marooned in harbour for days and the ferry crossings be suspended.

Could he live here? All the year round, when it was dark at three for months, in a place where dark meant black? All the year round, when one could be trapped in by the weather for a week or more? Electronic communication was good now, they could contact the outside world as easily as anyone living on the mainland, but that only meant words, written or spoken, flying to and fro across cyberspace, not close human contact.

And yet, he thought, peering down as the sun came out and glanced and glinted on the surface of the sea and he saw the heads of three seals bobbing up close to the beach, and yet . . .

The seals disappeared so suddenly that he looked to see what had startled them and made out a figure walking along the shore close to the water's edge. It was a woman wearing waders and a full-length mud-coloured waterproof, the scarf tied round her neck concealing most of her hair. She walked steadily, taking long strides, looking down at the sand. After a moment, she bent down and picked up something, examined it, and then slipped it into her pocket. A little further on, she did the same again.

A beachcomber, then, and perhaps there were good pickings where the sea left a line of stones and debris as it sucked back. The tide was going out fast, as it did here. The woman walked on. She had not seen Simon. He did not move. Before long, she was out of sight round an outcrop of rocks and the seals had surfaced again.

Three

'One minute.'

'Ready.'

Felix came thundering down the stairs. Grey shorts. Grey blazer with the sky-blue piping that denoted a cathedral choirboy. No cap. Caps had been dispensed with at the beginning of Sam's time at the school.

'Oboe?'

He gave Kieron Bright, his stepfather, a long-suffering look. If he forgot everything else, he would never forget his oboe, the instrument he had taken to so readily that it seemed to have become an extension of his body within a few months.

'And go!'

Kieron's route into the police HQ at Bevham did not take him past the cathedral, but from the first days of his marriage to Cat, he had offered to drive Felix into his early choir practice.

'It's perfectly simple,' he had said. 'It means I have Felix to myself every morning. It gets me into work first thing. It means you don't have to do it, and if it's a bit out of my way, it's a lot out of yours to the surgery. Sorted.'

It made sense, but for her the best reason was not the obvious and practical one. Her husband wanted to bond with her younger son and Felix seemed quite happy with the arrangement – though Felix was happy with most things. He was a contented, settled child who took life as it came, enjoyed what it offered and had barely given her a moment's anxiety.

Hannah, away at her performing arts school, had grown from a troubled child into a talented young girl, who shared Felix's easy-going cheerfulness. Sam, her eldest, was the difficult one.

She watched the car turn out of the drive, her son turned towards Kieron, chatting eagerly, then swore mildly that she had forgotten to remind them that it was her night for St Michael's Singers rehearsal, the first of the new season. Would Kieron remember that he and Felix were home alone for supper?

Kieron would. Her reminder to him would have been redundant. He was Mr Organised, Mr Tidy, Mr Efficient.

He was also the husband she had never looked for or expected to have, after Chris's death. They had certain traits in common, as she had always recognised, but organised was not one of them. Only in his GP's surgery had Chris been that. But his dedication and commitment to the job had been the same, and Cat respected it, along with the fact that often those jobs took first, second and third place, before her. She would not have had it otherwise. Besides, she thought now, going upstairs to put on her make-up ready to face the day, she had often put her own career first and it had not always made for an easy family life. When she had been a GP, before the new regime which had taken away their obligation to do nights and weekends on call, she had been stretched between her patients and her children, and only the fact that Chris had been a doctor too had made it acceptable. When she had been medical director at Imogen House, the Lafferton hospice, she had also been in the middle of conflicting pulls of loyalty and duties.

Now, she was a part-time GP again, no longer a partner. Had it all been the wrong way round? With two of her children away from home for much of the time, and a husband to share her life and the domestic round, she should have been giving more hours to her work, not fewer.

But writing a book on palliative care in general practice was filling the hours she had saved and she planned to write more. Both her parents had been hospital doctors, and had lectured, researched and written. She was following in the family footsteps.

Unlike Si, she thought, pulling the mascara wand out of its container. She must email him later.

And then there was Sam to contact, Sam up in Newcastle, ostensibly to help a friend settle into the university, but more, she suspected, to get away from home and the need to make decisions about his own future – and possibly away from his stepfather, though about that she was undecided. Kieron had said everything was fine between them, but that it would all take a while to shake down. Sam had said nothing.

At their wedding he had been quiet but cheerful enough. There had been only the families and a handful of close friends, and it had been held in the small Lady chapel of the cathedral. She and Kieron had decided from the beginning that she would not be given away by anyone, but that they would present themselves together, as equals. Also from the beginning, her father had said that he would not attend. Simon had not recovered from being at death's door following the attack, losing his left arm and spending several weeks in hospital. He had seemed pleased, but reserved and still slightly shell-shocked. It had been a good day, Cat had had no doubts about marrying again, but was glad when it was over and they could settle down into everyday life, after the few days in New York with which Kieron had surprised her.

She finished her make-up, flicked a brush through her hair again, and left for the surgery, very conscious that she had none of her old enthusiasm for the job. It was not the same. The crisis in general practice had cut deep into everyone's sense of dedication and passion for looking after patients, who, in their turn, had become disillusioned with doctors and the service they received, and, as a result, more demanding and more liable to complain.

She found a piece of paper on her driving seat.

Chin up. It'll be a good day. Love you. K.

He left notes like this, not every day, when she might come to take them for granted, just at random, a Post-it note stuck on her mirror or the pillow, a sheet torn from a notebook, as today, in the car. She slipped it into her bag, smiling as she drove off.

31

As she walked into the surgery, she saw a familiar figure at the front desk. Mrs Coates, eighty-nine and frail, a long-term sufferer from arthritis and polymyalgia, more recently recovered from pneumonia, and with failing sight. She lived alone, had been indomitable, but, Cat thought, had had enough of struggling with life by herself.

'I do understand,' she was saying now to Angella, one of the receptionists, 'I do know how busy you all are. I do know that.'

'So, I've got an appointment with Dr Sanders on Monday week at two thirty. Will you have that?'

Cat did not want to interfere and undermine Angella, but as she slipped past, Mrs Coates turned round.

'Oh, Dr Deerbon, I do understand how it is, but I've been trying to get to see you and you're always so busy, there's never anything available. And it's so difficult seeing a different doctor every time and having to start all over again explaining, although I know they're all very good.'

'I was trying to tell Mrs Coates that you all have her notes in front of you, it really doesn't matter who she sees.'

'I know. May I have a look?'

A quick glance at the appointments screen showed her what she already knew, that she was full at every surgery for the next two weeks, which was as far ahead as patients were allowed to book. Like Mrs Coates, she understood. The new system meant that patients took whatever appointment was available with whichever doctor of the seven. That was fine for the person with a strep throat or a child with a rash – any doctor would serve. But for older patients, or those with a long history about which one doctor knew a great deal, or for the people who felt uncomfortable talking to someone strange, there ought to be the facility for them to choose the GP they preferred.

'Is it about something new, Mrs Coates? You don't have to go into it all here, but just say if you want to talk about something recent or something ongoing?'

Angella was looking furious.

'It's not new, Doctor, it's . . .'

'Can you come back in at ten past one? I'll slip you in then.'

Surgery ended at twelve thirty, but generally overran by twenty or thirty minutes.

'I'm sorry to ask you to come back but I really am packed out this morning.'

'That's very good of you, Doctor, very good. No trouble to come back then. Thank you. I do understand how difficult it is, I do understand.'

'I know you do. I'll see you later.'

The reception area was filling up, the phones were ringing. Angella gave Cat a filthy look. I understand, too, Cat thought. Only too well. But rules have to be bent. She was not going to be bullied into apologising.

She logged on as the first footsteps came down the corridor to her surgery. There were still plenty like Mrs Coates, who needed gentle handling. How many times had she said in practice meetings that the system ought to be a servant but they were in permanent danger of allowing it to be their master?

Four

To s.serrailler@police.gov.uk
From chief.bright@police.gov.uk

Good morning, Simon. Hope all is well on Taransay. Rest up. You need it. But I hope the cop in you is still raring to go when you have caught your breath. We'll find something to ease you back in.

Everything good here.

Kieron

To s.serrailler@police.gov.uk
From sam101notout@gmail.com

Hi Si, still in Newkybroon land. Back Monday and don't ask then what. Gotta make plans, gotta make up mind. Need to talk. When ru home? Last match on Sat. Suppose that's it for you now, cricket-wise. Tough. Mum sounds chirpy. Flixer ditto. Would you even know I had a sister?

Love from Sam

To s.serrailler@police.gov.uk
From cat.deerbon@lafferton.nhs.uk

Hi dearest bro, how is it? Stunning here, 26 degrees today, wall-to-wall sunshine and Felix complaining about having to wear his blazer. Kieron still doing the school run but something has to give surely? How's the arm? Any news on the permanent one? I know you won't want me to mention him, but you're going to have to put up with it – have you heard from Dad? I am pretty sure the answer will be no, and he usually wings me something curt every few weeks and he hasn't since mid-July. Judith is coming down to stay for a few days next week and it will be great to see her but the subject of Dad will be the elephant in the room, as usual, and it isn't easy.

Hannah's school are doing *Guys and Dolls* – she sends excited messages, desperate for a good part. Warning: – we'll all have to go.

Sam due back but not holding breath. He's pretty unsettled. But he seems relaxed about K. They get on fine. God knows what he's planning for this year. His A levels were fine but he seems to be having a rethink career-wise. To what, I have no idea. We can't have that conversation at the mo. He's even mentioned med school once or twice. Until now, it's been police – and, even more, armed police – all the way. And he's never been passionate about medicine, and you have to be.

I used to hope one of the three would carry on the family medical tradition but I wouldn't wish it on anyone now, unless it was their only and complete obsession and then for some rare speciality. Neurologist fine. Facial reconstruction of war victims, fine. Paediatric oncologist, fine. General practice – not so much.

Loads of love. And Phone Home.

C

He was sitting on the end of the quay in the sun – sun which was forecast to disappear that evening, giving way to rain, gales and high seas. It was not always easy to tell how long these might last, but the chances were that when they had eased, the late-summer sun would not return, certainly not with the warmth it still held today. The boat was due in soon, carrying supplies and mail, and he wanted to help unload. He could carry reasonably large boxes and crates but not the heaviest. Not with the arm. Not as he had once done so easily. He had never prided himself on any particular muscular strength, though he had always been a sportsman, and fit. After the physiotherapy he had been subjected to in rehab he was probably fitter than ever but he had been warned not to over-test the prosthetic by lifting and carrying anything too heavy. Later, when he had the new and permanent arm. Later. He had grown used to hearing that. Later. But the physios had been the most positive of people. No. Never. Can't. Those words had not been in their vocabulary.

He slipped his iPhone away. There had been nothing in the emails to alarm him. Sam would get there – wherever his 'there' might be. His sister seemed bird-happy. He had never had any real concerns about her marriage to the Chief from a personal point of view. Because he was still on rehab leave, he had not yet encountered any professional conflict over having his boss as a brother-in-law. Perhaps he never would – not only because they would both go out of their way to accommodate one another, but because he still had doubts about returning to work. How much of a cop could he be? He had been assured the arm would make 'absolutely no difference to anyone or any aspect of the job'. Really?

He let Cat's mention of their father slide past him. Since Richard Serrailler had been accused of rape, and managed to find a defence counsel clever enough to get the CPS to drop the case, Simon had wiped all thought of him from his mind. Their relationship had always been difficult, but that aside, he had no doubt whatsoever that the CPS had made a mistake.

He glanced out to sea and saw the ferry just turning into the harbour. A few people were gathering down there, more would appear. The pub and shop would start stocking up now on extra supplies for the coming winter, using all the storage they had, part of which emptied in the summer season, when the boats came in more frequently. Simon jumped up.

The islanders knew all about his accident, and the loss of his left arm, and there had been many a quiet word or the offer of a drink, but otherwise no great fuss had been made, for which he was grateful. Now, he waited as the boat docked carefully, the hawser was thrown from on board and within minutes the first cartons and crates were being unloaded. Simon and two others started to lift smaller cartons of groceries onto sack trucks and wheel them to the store behind the shop.

'Candles.' The speaker was the woman he had seen walking along the shore on the other side of the island. She was tall, and her blonde hair was tied in a knot at the back of her head. 'You came yesterday?' she said.

'Evening before.' He was finding it difficult to grip the sack truck and manoeuvre it up the slope, so did not want to waste his breath on talk, but she seemed to grasp the fact at once. She did not offer him help, just got out of his way, heaving her own truck to the top.

The unloading, fetching, carrying and storing went on for an hour. The boat was fully laden, and without passengers other than the two-man crew.

Candles. Batteries. Thick socks. Heavy-duty rubber boots. Butane-gas cylinders. Household cleaner. Drums of cooking oil. Salt. Waterproofs. On and on.

Simon stopped to get his breath. He had done a lot of exercise since his accident, but his core strength was still not back to normal and his shoulder ached badly.

'Nearly there.'

The woman was hauling crates off the sack truck into the back of the store, making light of each one. He felt annoyed with himself. He shouldn't be tiring before a woman. That was something that once would never have crossed his mind. Now he was resentful. His pride was hurt.

'That's it,' someone shouted. 'Last to the bar's buying.'

There was a good-humoured rush across to the Taransay Inn.

'Have you met Sandy?' Douglas appeared out of the crush. 'She arrived here not long after your last visit and she's a fixture.'

The woman raised her glass of beer. She was perhaps in her late forties, possibly a bit younger – the wind and weather soon gave those who stayed a winter or two a rough and reddened complexion that added to their years.

'Simon Serrailler.'

'Sandy Murdoch.'

Simon had a large glass of malt to help numb the pain in his shoulder. He had heavy-duty meds prescribed but preferred the whisky.

'How long are you here?'

'A week or two or three. I've no firm plans.'

'Nor had I. I came for a week, a week stretched to a month and that was four years ago, near enough.'

Her accent was not Scottish but she had acquired a slight Taransay intonation, which was a lilt unlike any other Simon had encountered.

'How do you find the winters?'

Sandy shrugged. 'It's the wind can drive you mad. But I like it fine. You hunker down.'

The bar was full and others coming in had damp shoulders and hair. Rain was streaming down the windows.

'And you?' Sandy asked, though she did not look at him. 'You had an accident.'

'Yes.'

'Car smash?'

'No.'

'Ah ha.'

'Let me buy you another.' Simon got up. 'Bitter shandy? A chaser?'

'No, no, I don't drink the hard stuff much. Only to keep out the cold sometimes. But thanks.'

Kirsty had come in and was saying something to Douglas at the bar. 'What can I get you? Douglas?'

'No, I'm away to fetch Robbie, I'm running late and school's out at dinnertime today.'

Sandy waved as Kirsty left, buttoning up her waterproof, hair flying.

'Douglas?'

'Thanks. Just the single and then I have to be away with a roll of fencing to the other side.'

When the two whiskies were pushed over the bar, Douglas topped his up from the jug on the counter. Serrailler made a face. 'Bloody sacrilege,' he said. 'A good malt and you ruin it with your lemonade. I can never get my head round it.'

Douglas laughed. 'Any news?' He had nodded towards Simon's left arm.

'No, it'll be a few weeks yet. They don't tell me much.'

'You going back to work before you get what Robbie calls the bionic arm fitted up?'

'I don't know, Douglas, I just don't know . . . the job's there, they'll hold it as long as I want them to, but that can't be forever.'

'Can you not ease in gradually?'

'I probably could. But do I want to? Go back at all, that is.'

'What else is there?'

Simon finished his whisky and did not reply. It was a question he had asked himself many times, without being able to give himself a reply.

Douglas straightened up. 'Thanks,' he said. 'Looks as if Sandy's kept your seat warm over there.'

'Who is she? Other than a settler. Where did she come from?'

Douglas raised an eyebrow. 'Bit old for you.'

'Get out, I don't mean that and you know it. Just wondered. A newcomer who comes to Taransay and stays . . .'

'Aye, well . . . she's made herself useful from the start. Come to think of it, I could do with a hand with the fencing . . . get it finished in half the time. She turns her hand to most things. Helps out here when it gets busy in summer. Iain says she must

39

have run a bar herself in another life. But it's the fencing for now.' He edged through the crowded bar to where Sandy was sitting.

It was only when he was walking over to the shop to pick up some supplies that Simon thought Douglas could perfectly well have asked him to help out with the fencing. But he hadn't and it made him prickle with resentment.

Five

She wore a headscarf and very few women wore headscarves these days, except the Queen – which is what passed through the desk sergeant's mind as the woman came into the station.

'Good morning. It's Mrs . . .'

'Still. Marion Still.'

Yes.

'What can I do for you, Mrs Still?'

'You know what, Sergeant. Nothing changes. I'm here to see the Detective Chief Superintendent.'

'I'm afraid you're out of luck, Mrs Still – the Super is on extended leave.'

'That's what you told me the last time. You or your colleague.'

'Well, it was true then and it's true now.'

'He's still on holiday?'

'He's on sick leave. And I have no idea when he will be back, but it won't be tomorrow. Best I can do is see if anybody's free in the CID room and can come down –'

The woman burst into tears. Looking at her body, sagging slightly forward, as if she were carrying something heavy, at her grey face, with its deep lines of worry, the sergeant felt real sympathy. He knew why she was here. She had been trying to see the Super for a while now.

'Mrs Still . . . you can sit there a week for all it bothers me, I don't mind, but you'll be wasting your time because we don't know when the Super is coming back. If you won't talk to anyone else . . .'

'It needs to be someone senior, and Mr Serrailler is the best, isn't he?'

The telephone rang, and two uniforms came through the doors with a young man between them, in handcuffs. Mrs Still took a step back from the counter, but made no other move to leave.

And then the Chief Constable's car drew up outside.

There were three ways to deal with someone like Mrs Still, Kieron thought. He could spend the rest of his days avoiding and evading her. He could fob her off onto someone else, with an instruction not to waste too much time on her.

Or he could see her himself.

On the following Wednesday afternoon, his secretary ushered Marion Still into his office at Bevham HQ, to which she had been fetched by a comfortable but unmarked police car. Kieron wanted her to feel that she had been given every possible attention, and a full and proper hearing. He had taken the files home with him and read them carefully. He had also called up a wide selection of press reports on the case, from the day after Kimberley had gone missing to the last time the press had referred to her. In general, as was always the way, media reports had thinned out and dwindled in number only a few months after the event. Kimberley Still was officially a missing person but so were hundreds of others and the media could not keep any one of them on the front page, though the cases of missing children usually got continued coverage.

'I am very grateful to you,' she said. There was tea. There was coffee. There were chocolate biscuits.

Kieron was not sitting behind his desk but in a chair beside hers.

Poor woman. There was nothing else to think about her, as there never was about people who had gone through years of distress, bereavement that was not yet bereavement, alternating hope and despair, who had woken every morning sick to the stomach. He had seen the look in the eyes of people like Marion Still so often. Every copper who had been in the job longer than a couple of years knew the strange deadness and sadness which clouded every spark of life and energy.

'Mrs Still, I have brought myself right up to speed with this case. As you probably know, I wasn't in this force when Kimberley went missing so I had to read it in detail for the first time – which is a good thing. I've brought a fresh pair of eyes to it. I've been able to give it deep thought and perhaps I can now ask some new questions. I hope so anyway.'

'Do you mean you'll start again, try and find out what did happen and where he took her, where he . . . where she is? I know who "he" is, Mr Bright, we all know. It's just that nobody seems to think it matters.'

'Of course it matters. I'm not going to pretend I can solve this, Mrs Still. Please understand. There were a great many people involved in looking for Kimberley, trying to discover what happened to her. A great many man hours were spent over a considerable period of time. Nobody gave up lightly, I can promise you.'

'I know that. I know. I don't have to say how grateful I am again, do I?'

'Of course not. It was, it is, your right. It was owed to Kimberley and to you that we all did our best and then some. What I mean is that, even if there were a new investigation I can't promise you a result. How could I? There isn't any new evidence – not so far as I am aware.'

She put down her cup and looked directly at him, and for a second, he did see something in her eyes. A desperation, and a determination? No. A conviction. A terrible, fixed conviction. He had seen it before occasionally, in the mad and the obsessed.

'Listen, he did it. Lee Russon. I can hardly bear his name in my mouth, it's like a foul taste I want to spit out. He did it. I think he somehow got her into his car and then he drove off with her and then . . . then he did whatever he did. And I know he's in prison for life, only not for my Kimberley. For those others. Those poor girls. You say there's no new evidence but there is evidence . . . there always was.'

'Yes. But when that evidence – and it really wasn't very strong – was put before the Crown Prosecution Service, who are the

43

people who make the final decision, it was found to be too flimsy. They advised that Russon should not be tried for this as well as the other murders because the case was so weak that it would be thrown out. And at that point, Russon might have asked for leave to appeal against the other convictions, as being unsafe, and that could – it's unlikely, but it could – have led to those being overturned and Russon walking free.'

'He did it.'

'I'm inclined to agree with you, having read everything. And the senior investigating officer at the time –'

'Inspector Wilkins.'

'Yes . . . he said that the police were not looking for any other suspect. The presumption was that Kimberley had been murdered, and possibly by Lee Russon. But without finding Kimberley's body or indeed any trace of her at all, Russon –'

'Who lied and lied and lied.'

'Who denied that he'd had anything to do with it – or indeed that he'd ever been in or near Lafferton, let alone on that date – had no case to answer.'

'I don't believe they really wore him down. If someone's guilty, they can be worn down all right – they can be made to confess eventually.'

That was not always true, the Chief thought. But there was no point in saying so to Mrs Still, firmly convinced that Russon was guilty and that someone could eventually break him.

Six

It had been too hot to sit in the garden even in the shade of the trees, but as he turned out into the lane, Richard Serrailler saw that the dashboard gauge showed an outside temperature of 26. At two o'clock that afternoon it had been 30. With luck it would be cooler still by the time he got to the cafe. There were some clouds building in the west, which probably meant a storm later, and a break in the weather.

He would pick up his copy of *The Times*, have the usual cold beer, followed by a second, and then decide if he wanted to eat the *plat du jour* or go home and wait for Delphine, before having a late supper with her on the terrace.

She flicked a smile in his direction as he arrived, but the place was packed, and she was carrying trays of drinks and food in and out, throwing a greeting and a quick word to tables on either side. She would have little time for him now. There was a seat at the far end, just outside the awning. He nodded to a couple of people, shook one man's hand, but then bent to his paper. He liked to be pleasant. Friendly. He liked the French who lived locally, the old men who played evening boules under the horse-chestnut trees, and dominoes on Thursday and Friday afternoons at ancient stone tables. His French was reasonably good. He had spent a year in the country as a young man, and come for holidays almost every year since. And then he had moved out here, renting a small stone farmhouse. He was neigh-bourly to the others who lived in his hamlet, all of them French.

They helped him out if he needed it, he helped back, usually with medical advice – it had not taken them long to learn his profession.

The expat community he avoided. He did not like their clubbiness, their determination to speak English even more loudly than they did at home, their overfamiliarity with the cafe proprietor and the shop owners, calling out 'Delphine! More of the same *s'il vous plais*.'

They had tried to include him when he had been coming here for a few weeks, pulling out a chair at coffee time, so that he could join their extended table. He always smiled and then went to sit alone. They no longer asked, only glanced at him sometimes and, he knew, talked about him the moment he left.

Delphine was twenty-five. He was seventy-four. Some days he flattered himself that he looked ten years younger.

The ice-cold beer was set down in front of him, not by Delphine but by the new young waiter, Olivier. She was sensitive to any suggestion that she favoured Richard by serving him out of turn, and as often as not gave his order to her assistant.

He had learned, after talking to her on visits to the cafe at quiet times, that she had spent three years in London, spoke fluent English though pretended not to, and was as intelligent and good-humoured as she was pretty.

Occasionally he wondered if she would wake up one morning, see him as the older man he really was, and disappear, to resurface later attached to a handsome young Frenchman. He was not in love with her, but he enjoyed being with her, her conversation and her easy affection. Her youth. It was a pleasant arrangement that had lasted almost six months. She earned a relatively poor wage but received good tips and would accept nothing from him. She was certainly better company than his family. Cat was preoccupied with her new husband, her children and her job, Simon had not been in touch with him for a long time. Simon. Had he recovered? Had he retired from the police force? Where was he and who with? Richard would have denied that he ever wondered about any of it. But, when he was alone and had too much time on his hands, he thought about his son, as he thought about his grandchildren. And Judith, his ex-wife. Judith more than anyone.

Delphine brought his second beer, now that many of the diners had been served.

'It's magret, salad and frites. Sorry, chéri.'

Richard disliked duck, which was the mainstay of every restaurant in this part of France.

He made a face.

'The steak frites is good, the langoustines look excellent.'

'Thanks, but I'll have this and go home and wait for you. I'd like that . . . late supper in the warm evening.' He touched her hand.

'I won't be finished until maybe ten thirty, eleven, OK?'

'Of course. I want to watch a programme about post-mortems.'

It was Delphine's turn to make a face, before swishing off to attend to a table of newcomers. Her dark hair was tied neatly back and pinned with a barette, showing off her long neck. She wore black leggings and a loose top, showing off the rest of her figure. She was slender. She was delightful. He sipped more of his beer and turned back to the English news. Everything seemed very far away and of less and less relevance to his life here. His surprisingly settled and enjoyable life.

He sat in the garden, drank another cold beer, watched the moths batting against the lamp, and after a while, fell asleep in the deck-chair. When he woke, it was five to midnight and Delphine was not home. He went inside, checked the phone, looked for her moped in the lean-to. Nothing. He rang the cafe but got voicemail.

He found her sitting beside her moped on the verge, a mile from the house. His headlights picked her out of the blackness. She was leaning forward, her head on her knees.

The bike had a buckled front wheel and a missing fender. It lay on its side, and he managed to drag it towards the hedge before helping Delphine into his car. Her face and hands were covered in blood but she was conscious and, so far as he could tell in the half dark, she had not broken any bones or been knocked out. The bleeding came from her nose and one hand which was badly gashed.

'A car came down very fast on the wrong side of the road.'

'Idiot.'

'Yellow car.'

'You recognised it?'

'Not really. It was over in a flash and I was in the verge and he'd gone.'

'Idiot and bastard. But let's get a proper look at you first. You might need the hospital.'

'No, no, I'm fine.'

Her nose had swollen and was extremely tender but not broken. At the house Richard bathed her face and arms and dressed the gash, which was deep and he thought would need stitches the next day but he said nothing for now, just dosed her up with painkillers and put her to bed in the room that faced the side of the house and was shaded by trees.

'Oh, what about the bike?'

'I'll sort that out in the morning. Now lie down, try and sleep, tell me if the pain gets worse or you get a bad headache. Stupid idiot driver. When you leave England for any country where they drive on the right you don't leave your brains behind. You have to remind yourself all the time – on the right, on the right. He must have been going far too fast round that bend by the recycling bins.'

'Yes.' Delphine had turned her face away. 'Thank you,' she said.

There was something in her voice. He sat on the bed and took her hand.

'What is it?'

'Nothing, nothing, don't worry. I'm just a bit shocked, I think.'

'Of course you are – but it isn't that, is it?'

'Yes, yes. Nothing else. I'll be fine when I've slept.'

'You'll be sore and your nose will hurt a lot, so will your arm. Don't expect to get up and go off to work, Delphine.'

'I'll be –'

'No. You won't be fine. Are you feeling any pain relief yet?'

'Yes, thank you, it's much better. Thank you, *mon chéri*. I think you must have been a very good doctor.'

48

He closed the door quietly, and went to pour a glass of wine. It was still very warm outside. Warm. Still. The darkness touched by flitting ghost-white moths. A screech owl. Nightjars churring.

He was not tired and he thought over what Delphine told him about the accident, trying to construct a picture in his mind. He was uneasy.

His phone buzzed and the screen lit up.

Hi Dad.

Cat, an hour behind in England.

Just finished supper. Hannah rang an hour ago to say she has a part in the new musical, sharing the lead role with two other girls. She's in a fizz of excitement. See you have a heatwave. Here, not. Hope all well with you. C x

He read the message over twice. Cat, her family, the farmhouse. Lafferton. Another planet. Going back was out of the question. He liked his life here. He had Delphine. But he felt strangely unattached, as if his real self and his real existence were as they had always been, at home, at Hallam House, first with Meriel, and then with Judith.

He had often tried to picture himself back at home. The house was still there, let to tenants but his within a couple of months if he wanted to return. The family was there. Nothing had changed other than the usual fact that life moved on, people grew up, grew older, married, died. New houses were built and old buildings demolished. New roads were constructed changing routine journeys. Nothing more. Or less.

He could not go back. Perhaps in a year or two, not now though – he pushed the recollection away if ever it threatened to surface – not when he had almost been charged with rape. Almost. Because, of course, he had not raped Shelley, she had pushed herself at him, and he had been weak and stupid, in a few blurred moments. That was all. The rest had been a trumped-up charge and vindictiveness. He knew that. Others knew it too. Nevertheless, he was still tarred with the 'rapist' brush by those who knew and people had long memories. False ones, but long nonetheless.

He had no idea whether Shelley and her husband still lived in Lafferton but wondered occasionally if he should find out. If they had moved away he could go home from time to time, though he doubted if he would ever want to live in Lafferton again.

He looked in on Delphine before he went to bed. She was asleep, her face swollen and red, her breathing strained through the congested nose. Her gashed arm was outside the covers and blood still seeped a little through the bandage. He touched her hand gently, feeling as protectively towards her as towards an injured child. She stirred slightly, but did not wake.

He lay for some time, taken aback by the feelings her accident and seeing her just now had aroused in him, feelings of great tenderness and . . .

And he did not know. He only knew that this was something unfamiliar, new and disturbing.

Seven

Wookie growled, a low rumble of a growl that seemed to come from his stomach rather than his throat, but he did not stir or open an eye.

Thirty seconds later, Kieron's car turned into the drive. Wookie growled again.

'Silly dog.' Cat had her feet up on the sofa, and had almost finished reading *Flaubert's Parrot*, the book group choice, to be discussed later that week.

'If you'd been five minutes later I could have given you my full attention, only now you'll have to wait because I'm on the penultimate page.'

He came over and kissed her forehead. 'I'm saying nothing. Drink?' She nodded, turning the page.

Wookie went on grumbling. Kieron brought two glasses of wine, put them on the low table, and sat down next to Cat. The terrier got up and moved away to the far side of the sofa, still grumbling.

'When are you going to get used to me and stop growling, Wooks?'

Cat read on for another minute, and then closed the novel.

'Just ignore him.'

'I've lived here for four months and he still treats me like a burglar.'

'Wouldn't make much impression on one.'

'If I snap my fingers in front of him he bares his teeth.'

'Then don't. Hello, you. Went the day well?'

Kieron sighed. 'Too much admin, an overlong meeting with the Commissioner, and a madwoman. No, correct that – an obsessed woman. I feel very sorry for her actually – her daughter disappeared a few years ago, presumed kidnapped, she's sure she knows who did it, so are we, he's in prison for two murders as it is – he confessed to them, but he's adamant he didn't have anything to do with this one. She wants justice, understandably – she wants closure. Impasse.'

'Marion Still.'

'You know about her?'

'She's a patient. So was Kimberley. How did she seem?'

'Fixated. Not overtly emotional.'

'What did you say – that there's nothing you can do?'

'More or less. But I was thinking about it on the way home . . .'

'Russon's responsible, isn't he?'

'It seems likely but I don't know all the details, it was before my time here. I'm going to call up the files and have a look.'

'I had an email from an old med school friend this morning. Luke Renfrew. I used to quite fancy him.'

'Not rising to that. Just don't tell me he's moving to Lafferton.'

'Starly actually, and don't worry, he's gay.'

'Leopards change their spots.'

'Not Luke. His partner's a very rich Italian who has just bought the hotel. He wants to talk to me about a project . . . the least I can do is let him give me lunch there. Old times' sake and all that.'

She shrieked in mock fright as Kieron lunged over at her. It was not evident to Wookie that the lunge was in play.

'Bloody hell!'

The dog had nipped his arm sharply, leapt off the sofa and fled.

'I could die of this,' Kieron said.

'No you couldn't, presuming you've had a tetanus jab. If it starts to throb or gets swollen, I'll give you penicillin but let's put a plaster on it for now.' Cat swabbed the bite with disinfectant.

52

'There's a Dangerous Dogs Act, you know.'

'Wookie is not a dangerous dog.'

He stuck his forearm out.

'He just isn't used to you living here. I'm going to cook supper.'
Kieron followed her.

'And for goodness' sake stop clutching your arm like that.'

'It's throbbing.'

'No it isn't, it's just sore.'

He sat down and looked mournfully at the plaster. 'Anyway, what did this Luke guy who you fancy, say?'

'He didn't . . . just something he wants to pick my brains about.'

'Joining up with your lot?'

'I doubt it, and anyway, that wouldn't be my call, I'm not a partner. Here, top and tail these beans for me.'

'I don't think I can move my right arm.'

'You can move your right arm.' She dumped pan, beans and knife in front of him. 'Meanwhile, you said you had some thoughts about Kimberley Still's murder?'

'Not very useful ones. I'm going to look through the files when I've got time.'

'Which will be when, exactly?'

He groaned.

'Surely there's someone who's got more time than you.'

Kieron had picked up a handful of beans. He put them down again. 'Now you mention it . . .'

'Simon?'

'Simon,' he said.

Eight

The storm had been brewing up all afternoon and by the time the last ferry turned into the harbour the boat was bucking and rising through huge waves, the gale blowing across its bows, so that it had to turn and come back into the dock three times. When they tied up, only the crew were steady on their feet and cheerful.

Sam had never been seasick but this trip had tested him. He steadied himself as he stepped onto the quay, and the ground seemed to surge beneath his feet. He hauled his rucksack onto his shoulders and looked up the slope to where the lights of the pub still shone out. He had not meant to arrive so late. The plan had been to catch a ferry in the early afternoon, but what with one thing and another, including oversleeping, not being able to hitch a lift and then racing for a train just as it left and which turned out to be going in the wrong direction, he had only just made it before they shut down.

'You're lucky. Likely they won't set out at all in the morning if the forecast's correct.'

It was dark and there was no one waiting on the quay. The only other passengers were a man wearing a rucksack, who strode off alone towards the car park, and a party of field trip students, who were climbing into a waiting minibus that would drive them across to the other side of the island and the field centre. The crew were clearing out the boat and making ready to leave. Sam went up the slope to the pub. There were a couple of bikes and a battered Transit van outside. Inside, it was quiet, except for the sound of the gale and two men drinking at the bar. They turned as the door opened.

'Come in and shut that door, laddie, or we'll be swept out to sea.'

Sam had not taken any steps nearer once the door was closed.

'You'll be wanting a whisky maybe, looking as green as you do.'

'I'm fine. Does anybody have a car that would pick me up?'

'They do not, not at this time of night in this weather. Where are you heading?'

'Come on, boy, have the dram on me.' The red-headed man pushed some coins across the bar top to the barman. 'I've seen you before.'

'I've been here before.'

'Go on then . . . Here's to you and a long life.' Sam looked at the whisky. He had never tried it but they were watching him. All three of them. He raised his glass and drank it in two gulps, like the medicine it tasted of, set the glass down and asked again if there was any chance of a lift across the island.

The barman sighed. 'My junk heap's away to the garage with a split sump, the wife rides a bike and you wouldn't want to be borrowing that tonight. You'll be leaving yours here as well, I take it, John?'

The red-headed man slid off the bar stool. 'Aye.'

'Thanks for the drink,' said Sam.

He nodded, then slipped out of the door, letting in a further blast.

'He only lives a hundred yards up the hill. If you're talking about going to the other side, you'll be out of luck tonight. I dinnae have an empty room but you're welcome to sleep on ma couch. You're Simon's young cousin, aren't you?'

'Nephew.'

'I remember. He's about three miles but you can't walk in this.'

Sam looked at his rucksack. He could sleep on the couch a few hours and be up at dawn, when the storm might have blown itself out, but as he was about to accept the offer, wheels slewed

55

up outside and the door was flung out of the hands of the person entering. Outside was a maelstrom of spray, rain and wind.

The landlord let out a roar of laughter. 'Now then, here's the only person mad enough to be out in this, truck or no.'

The woman who came in was wearing a green oilskin, boots, and a sou'wester she tipped off her head, letting water stream off it onto the mat.

She hesitated for a few seconds, glancing round the room and noting Sam and the other drinker at the bar, who now decided to call it a night.

'I need a new gas bottle if you've any left off the last stack, Iain. Damn thing. I'm sure it wasnae empty. I've never used a whole one already.'

Iain laughed. 'You never have, Sandy. I'm forever telling you and now you'll have me out the back in this weather lugging your gas bottle.'

'I'll have half a lager to soften the blow.'

Iain pulled her drink. 'I'll get your gas. Look after this young man for me.' They exchanged a quick look, which Sam took to mean, Keep an eye on him and mind he doesn't help himself to a drink or anything else.

Sandy turned. She gave him the once-over, summing him up, he thought. He felt uncomfortable. 'Sandy Murdoch. Did you come off the last boat?'

Sam nodded. 'I thought I could get a lift from here but no luck.'

'There wouldn't be, night like this. Where are you heading?'

He hesitated. Anywhere else and he would never have told a stranger, but on the island it must be OK. Everyone knew everyone else's business and shared it freely, every visitor was noted and assessed.

'My uncle's. He's at Stane.'

'Simon? Well, aye, now I look at you. You've his good bone structure, though not his colouring – or his eyes.'

'You know him all right then.' Sam looked sideways at the woman. She had a bony face, rough, straw-coloured hair.

'You're not drinking,' she said.

'I'm fine.'

'Well, I won't say I never drink alone but I'd rather have company. When Iain comes back, what will you have?'

'A lemonade?'

'Away with you.'

Sam did not answer and they sat in silence until the landlord came back.

'It's in the jeep and now look at the state of me.'

'Thanks, Iain. A dram for Sam and I'll take the other half off you.'

She ignored Sam's protest, and brought his whisky to the table, along with a half-pint of lemonade.

'That's the way to chase it down,' she laughed, raising her own glass.

Fifteen minutes later, she had got Sam's life history out of him. He had a second whisky, and the bar took on a golden glow. He was pleasantly tired, and suddenly ravenous.

'Right,' Sandy said, slapping down her glass and standing. 'I'm taking you off to your uncle before I have to carry you out of here. And I could, mind.'

Sam felt slightly unsteady but walked with determination to the door. When he opened it, the gale took it out of his hand and slammed it back.

'Hold on there – forgotten something.' Sandy went back into the bar quickly. Sam watched her. She seemed a decent person, someone he felt a sudden burst of affection towards. Whisky seemed to bring out the best in everything.

It was warm in the jeep once the heater was blasting out, making a noise like a turbine over the rattling of the rain on the roof and the wind whistling through the badly fitting windows. Sam thought he would have been happy to travel like this for a thousand miles. His head sang.

'What was all that stuff about?'

'What stuff?'

Sam was trying to get his tongue round the question he wanted to ask her, but by the time he did, he had forgotten it.

The windscreen wipers found coping with the torrential rain too much and just scraped weakly across and back, pause, across and back, pause.

'How can you see out?'

'You get used to this. I know the road.'

Were you born here, Sandy?'

'No. But I love this place, Sam. People come here in June, July and it's all peaches and cream and they don't see it at all. Simon loves it, don't you think? Christ.'

The jeep skidded sideways across the wet road. Sandy righted it skilfully, and they were on the last straight. Sam looked out of the window but could make out nothing.

'Is this far out of your way?'

'Not far.'

They were turning.

'There you are . . . home. Now you mind yourself – it's streaming water and there'll be a slick of mud.'

'Thank you very, very much. It's really kind of you. I'm really grateful. Thanks. Thank you.'

'You're welcome, Sam.' He saw that Sandy was laughing. At him? It annoyed him and he was about to challenge her, standing there in the rain and wind, but then she was backing away, wheels spraying up mud and water, and before he reached Simon's front door he had forgotten what he was going to say.

Half an hour later, after a hot bath, a change of clothes into some of Simon's and the contents of his rucksack put into the wash, Sam sat in front of a mug of tea, watching eggs, bacon and fried potatoes sizzling on the range. Simon had said little beyond the initial 'Bloody hell' as he had taken in the drenched, unsteady figure standing outside. Now, he listened to his nephew's perfunctory but slightly more sober account of his journey. He did not ask what he had drunk, guessing that it had not actually been a great deal.

'What's happened to your hair?' Sam asked suddenly, staring at him as if he had only just seen him in the room.

'Bit drastic?' Simon ran a hand over it. The blond mop, which usually flopped over his forehead, had been cropped very short, showing up the bones of his face and the length of his neck.

'Bit like a convict.'

'Thanks. Just that Geordie can't cut it properly so I'd rather have him get the clippers out. Lasts longer as well. Do you want fried bread?'

'No thanks. Tomatoes though?'

'Sorry.'

Simon put the plate in front of him, and waited until Sam had wolfed down three or four mouthfuls and was pausing to drink. Then he said, 'OK, you've told me how you got here. But why?'

'Well, you know, I was nearby.'

'Nobody is nearby Taransay.'

'Well, sort of. Haven't seen you for a bit. I thought I should.'

'I'm flattered.'

'How's . . . ?' He nodded towards Simon's arm.

'All right.'

'Great.'

Simon left him alone, made more tea and put a ginger slab cake on a plate. Kirsty made them at home and sold them, along with several other bakes, in the store. They went quickly and added a bit to their family income, as did the eggs from the chickens. Life was frugal on the island. Nothing was wasted.

In the short summer tourist season, everyone hoped to make up for a long winter of low earnings. It was a way of life Simon liked but doubted if he was hardy enough to enjoy for long. Besides, he bored too easily for such a limited existence.

They sat opposite one another, hearing the storm still lashing outside. Sam raised his mug. 'Thanks, Si.'

'You're welcome.'

'There is something I kind of want to run past you.'

Simon waited, discounting Sam's casualness of tone.

An uproar of wind and rain surged at the windows. 'I hope she got back to her house OK.'

'Who, Sandy? Don't you worry about Sandy – she's a survivor if ever I met one. And when there's unloading, she does the work of two men.'

'Where does she live?'

'Over the hill towards the shore.'

'With a family?'

'No. On her own. If there's a family elsewhere she's never talked about them.'

'You know her well?'

'As neighbours – everyone looks out for everyone else here. They have to. She's been in for a cup of tea when she's brought over something. Why?'

Sam shrugged and looked away. Simon laughed. 'No,' he said, 'You have to be joking. She's . . . well . . . NO.'

'OK. Your girlfriends are always uber glam, that's true.'

'What about yours?'

'Get off!'

'Ella, wasn't it?'

Sam threw a cushion. 'Listen . . . I was going to ask Kieron about this but then, I . . . I suppose I just trust you.'

'No reason not to trust him, Sam, he's a good man . . . good cop. You're OK with him, aren't you?'

'Yeah, yeah, and Mum's happy so . . . keeps her off my case.'

'Exactly.'

'The police. This SO17 thing I've always had.'

Sam had wanted to be a member of the armed police ever since he, and Simon, could remember. The original plan had been to get a good degree and join the force, fast-tracking into the armed unit as soon as possible. He had been rifle shooting for the past couple of years and quickly become skilled. He had topped the county tables as a clay-pigeon shooter, but refused to have anything to do with killing wildlife. It had been the subject of several heated conversations with Kieron, who could not understand how his stepson could contemplate, as he must, shooting a human being dead, when he would not, on principle, shoot a pheasant. Sam had simply insisted that the two were unrelated. In the end, at Cat's insistence, they'd agreed to avoid the subject altogether.

'I've been thinking . . . maybe reconsidering.'

'About being a cop?'

Sam shifted about. Reached for his mug. Drank. Shifted about again. Simon waited.

'When you left med school halfway through –'

'Less than that. I'd barely finished my second year.'

'OK, why did you? I mean, the real reason?'

'The real reason is the same as every other reason. I didn't want to be a doctor. I knew it before I started but I was . . . oh, I don't know, Sam, persuaded, pushed. In this family, we are doctors. And I wasn't absolutely against it – not till I started anyway. And by then, I knew it was the police I wanted to join not the medics.'

'Did you ever regret it? Think you might change your mind again?'

'Not for a second. I'd have made a rubbish doctor.'

'You can't know that.'

'I do know that. But I wanted to be a cop and I have loved every minute of it. Well – almost every minute.' He touched his arm. 'It was a no-brainer.'

'Right.'

'So, where's your thinking leading you?'

'Can I have another tea?'

'Help yourself.' He had to raise his voice to be heard against a sudden roaring of the wind.

Sam was not inarticulate but he was cautious. He did not commit himself to serious words until he was sure of exactly what he wanted to say, but Simon guessed that he had been thinking hard about this for some time and now only needed to take a deep breath. He would not have come all this way, on a complicated journey, without many a rehearsal.

'I might have changed my mind about the police.' He seemed to be waiting for a reaction but Simon did not make one. 'I kept picturing myself – the life . . . I kept seeing myself like, you know, a piece that didn't fit the jigsaw. The more I went into it, read about the day-to-day, the more I felt like that. Is that stupid?'

'You know it isn't.'

'I'd be letting you down.'

Simon snorted. 'You'd be letting no one down, least of all me. Grow up.'

'I don't want to get it wrong. It'd be a waste of everything . . . so I . . . I might change my mind.'

'Sounds to me as if you've already changed it.'

'Does it? Maybe I have then.'

61

'Much better know it now, Sambo, than a year into your training. Better for you, mostly.'

'Right . . .' He was caught out by a prolonged yawn.

Simon got up. 'Talk more tomorrow. You're bushed. The spare bed's made up but I'll find more blankets – storms like this make the temperature crash.'

They went up the stairs, Sam pulling out wash kit, and the T-shirt in which he always slept, from his rucksack, while the bed was sorted, curtains drawn against the wild night.

'Si . . . I just . . . I mean, yeah, we'll talk about it, only . . .'

'Don't say anything to your mother.'

'Right.'

'As if.' He put his arm briefly round Sam's shoulder, unsure how much he would appreciate the bear hugs he had loved as a boy.

Sam sat on the bed to test the mattress. He tipped sideways to test the pillow, was deeply asleep within fifteen seconds and did not wake until after ten the next morning.

Downstairs, Simon poured himself a small whisky, and settled back on the sofa. He was in the middle of rereading The *Spy Who Came in from the Cold,* but he thought for a while about Sam. If he had been surprised at his decision, he had tried not to let it show. But he had been passionate about joining the armed police for so long, to Cat's lasting concern, that it had seemed a done deal. Nothing else, apart from cricket and hockey – and he was an excellent player at both sports – had ever seemed to interest him. Simon had done his best to put him off, always the way to test the strength of a resolve, but Sam had never wavered.

So what came next? The police force but not the armed division? CID? There was nothing else. Sam was bright and he worked hard but he was no intellectual – an academic career would never be for him, nor would a teaching one, and life in any kind of office would surely drive him out of his skull.

They would have to find Plan B.

Nine

The Burleigh still looked the same country house hotel from the outside, but when Cat walked into the entrance hall she realised that it had had a sleek, sophisticated makeover. The walls were now a putty colour, the carpet taupe, the upholstery various shades of cream and pale grey. The front of the bar was covered in what appeared to be cream leather, the stools covered in the same but darker. The lighting had been redesigned. It was intimate but cool, the Italian influence everywhere.

Luke's partner, Enrico, must have spent several of his many millions on the place, hoping to attract a richer and more international clientele but, location being all, she wondered if he was likely to succeed with a hotel just outside Lafferton, for all that the country was green and pleasant.

'Cat! You look like the spring.'

She saw at once why she had fancied Luke twenty-five years ago. He looked exactly the same, in that he was still slim and more youthful-looking than was decent, his hair was still thick but had greyed a little in an attractive way. And he still had the same charm. He took her hands and kissed her on both cheeks.

'And you haven't forgotten how to flatter. It's so good to see you, Luke.'

'I have a table beside the window. Let's have a glass of champagne to celebrate.'

He led her across the room, which was very quiet. She did not notice him indicating that he wanted to order but as they sat down a waiter appeared with two glasses of Veuve Clicquot.

'That suit came from nowhere but Italy,' she said. It was very pale grey, a fine wool, perfectly cut, worn with a slate-grey shirt and fuchsia silk tie. Cat tried briefly to imagine Kieron in the same outfit and smiled. He was fine in full uniform, but otherwise, the opposite of sartorial. She had been trying to update his wardrobe by small, subtle steps since they were married. Chris had been just the same. Simon, now – he could carry off a suit like that.

'Here's to us,' Luke said. Olives came, and rounds of toast the size of pennies with a dab of potted shrimp and a sprig of dill, a mustard-spoon blob of caviar or a curl of smoked salmon on each.

Cat sighed and leaned back. 'Whatever the reason,' she said, 'this is so good. Thank you.'

'Right, fill me in on the last twenty-odd years, Dr Deerbon. You haven't changed your professional name I presume?'

While they enjoyed their champagne, she filled him in, on the children, Chris's illness and dying, Simon, Kieron. She did not mention Richard – Luke knew of her mother's death from the medical obituaries.

'OK, that's the personal life. Talk about the medicine.'

'That will take until the end of the main course.'

'No problem. I've got plenty of time. You?'

'It's my day off.'

The hotel now had both its old formal dining room and also a brasserie. Luke gave her the choice and Cat looked over her shoulder at the main room.

'Sorry but that would be like eating in a morgue – there's no one in there.'

The Italian brasserie was very comfortable, it felt intimate but the tables were not set too closely together and the menu was written both on a board behind the bar and chalked on individual blackboards which came to the table. They ordered crab and lobster linguine and salad. Fresh warm bread and olive oil came first.

'I know the state of general practice overall,' Luke said, 'but what about your personal experience? Bring me right up to date.'

Cat did, but set out in detail her time in palliative care at the Imogen House Hospice, the short spell as a partner again in a GP surgery, where she had felt undervalued and undermined, to her new job as a locum in the surgery.

'It's good in one way – they're all nice, they're supportive and they include me in discussions and meetings as if I were a partner. But the fact is, I'm not. I pick up the last-minuters, the overbooked patients, the temps. I do quite a lot of phone consultations. There's no continuity, or very little, and I don't often see the same patient twice. The usual.'

'How many hours do you do?'

'The equivalent of three and a half days.'

'Facilities?'

'Not bad. I don't have my own consulting room, but locums never do. It works, in that I get time off to have a bit of life and see my husband.'

'You're not stretched.'

'God no.'

'Nor well paid.'

'No . . . Times have changed. So have doctors.'

Cat stopped talking and ate. The linguine was moist, rich in white crab meat and chunks of lobster, the salad dressed with the best olive oil. She did not want to rush the enjoyment of it.

Luke poured them both more iced water. The jug was topped with lemon slices and fresh mint.

'Let me tell you about Concierge Doctors.'

Bitter-lemon granitas and two lots of coffee, as good as only the Italians make it, came and went and Luke had barely stopped talking. But now he downed his second espresso and leaned back.

'I'm not going to ask you what you think right now – there's a lot to take in, it's complicated, though it actually won't be. But maybe the only reaction I need from you at this point is whether you have any objections to the principle – plenty of doctors are totally against private medicine of any kind, and I respect that. If you are, well, it's been a great lunch and so good to see you again.'

'Chris was totally against it. He'd have made his excuses and left before you were a quarter of the way through. I have never felt like that, though I understood some of his arguments, but with him, pride came into it and there's no room for that, especially the way general practice is now.'

Luke waited for her to continue but she had no more to say. Not today. Not now.

'I need a week to think this over and come up with a response. Is there anything in writing yet?'

Luke reached into his jacket pocket and took out a card. 'All my details are here and the website details – it isn't live of course, it's been mocked up but by a professional designer and it tells you absolutely everything. Trying to be paper-*less* if not paper-free.'

'Thanks. I promise I'll read it very carefully and come back to you – just not until I'm pretty clear where I stand. It's very interesting though.'

'So you're not saying no.'

'I'm not saying anything at all yet, Luke, except that I'd love another coffee.'

The rest of their time was spent catching up on news of fellow medical students, and swapping stories about the parlous state of recruitment and the laxity of present-day training. Cat thought they sounded like her parents when she was in her first med-school years – nothing was ever as good as in 'my day'.

Luke walked her out to her car and kissed her on both cheeks again. 'I can't wait to hear,' he said.

'Well, you'll have to. Thanks for the lunch.'

He waved as she turned out of the gates. She had given him the impression of feeling moderately interested in his scheme but that going onto the website to study it in detail was not an immediate priority. In fact, she was much keener on it than she had let herself appear. She liked what she had heard so far, above all because it presented a possible route out of the professional rut in which she found herself. When she had asked Luke if she could tell Kieron about it, he had been keen that she should. 'Partners are important in this, it affects home life, obviously. So tell him, I'd be interested to hear his views. I hope I get to meet him – never known a Chief Constable.'

Ten

It took Delphine a week to recover, not only from the injuries she had sustained in the crash from her moped but from the shock, which made her afraid of getting another bike.

'You'd better learn to drive a car then, much safer,' Richard said. He had put together a *salade niçoise* and set the table outside under the group of trees in the shade. On the other side of the garden, a hoopoe pecked about for grubs under the hedge. Delphine sat quietly, cutting a slice of bread but not eating anything yet. He poured her a glass of the dry local rosé he had taken to, a couple of bottles of which were always in the fridge, but she did not pick it up.

She sat, her nose still slightly swollen, bruised and scarred, not seeming to want to engage with him. He mixed the salad dressing and poured it.

'What do you think,' he said, 'about driving lessons? You wouldn't have to go far but it would be much better all round. If you're worried about the cost . . .'

Delphine brushed the comment away with a gesture. 'I don't like the car.'

'You're happy enough to go in mine.'

'That's different. I mean I don't want to drive a car. Maybe I get the Velo repaired.'

'It's pretty badly damaged, Delphine, they'll probably write it off.'

'OK, well, never mind. I'm tired of it anyway and it will be very cold in winter.'

'Then you will have to learn to drive.'

She shrugged.

'It won't happen again, you know. There are so few cars coming down here and nobody else is likely to drive so dangerously.'

'It made me very scared.'

'Of course, but you're much better.'

'I do not feel it.'

'Yes, you do, stop being childish. As soon as you go back to work you'll forget all about it.'

'So, how do I go back? No Velo, and even if I learn with a car, it will take some months. Besides . . .' She was looking not at him but at some fixed point at the end of the garden.

'Besides?'

'I don't know . . . maybe I don't want to go back to work there.'

'You should be looking for something better, Delphine. You're a clever girl, you're too bright to be waiting at tables.'

'So, I go like all my school friends to college and end up with a degree and still no better job. We are all working in bars and cafes, you know. Or in the *supermarché*.'

Richard poured himself another glass of wine. The sun had gone down and the air in the garden was velvety, the little anti-mosquito candles glimmering, giving off their acid-lemon smell. A nightjar churred.

He looked at the girl, resting back in her chair, her hair on her shoulders. Yes, he thought. But no. After all, no.

'So, have you any other ideas?'

She glanced at him. 'Oh yes. I could stay here. Look after you.'

69

Eleven

The storm had lessened in fury by late the next morning, when Sam came blearily into the kitchen, to be fed on tea, scrambled eggs and buttered toast. 'I don't need to ask if you slept OK.'

'I died, basically. Thanks for this, Si. I could probably eat it twice.'

'Not until we get supplies you couldn't. I need to go over to the store but maybe we can walk across to the other side then. This place is fine but I get cabin fever after twenty-four hours and it'll be calmer by two o'clock I reckon. Might still be a bit of a blow-up on the top, that's all.'

'Could do with it.' Sam spoke through a mouthful, then continued almost in the same sentence. 'Do you think Mum's OK?'

'So far as I know. Why wouldn't she be?'

'Not sure about her work – she's wasted doing locum stuff.'

'Agreed. Have you talked to her about it?'

'God no.'

'Why not? She listens to you more than you might think.'

Sam shook his head. 'Not my place any more. I used to think I kind of stood in for Dad a bit, you know, and then, well, just for a time after your –' He pointed to Simon's arm with his fork. 'You know, for you. Sort of. Only now, she . . .'

'You know . . .'

'All right, all right . . . now she's got a husband. There any more toast?'

The sky was sable and seal washed together, as they drove towards the quay, the wind calmer but the sea still choppy. They picked up groceries and a paper.

'We'll leave all this here and head out. Want a pint first?'

The bar was half full.

'Ye're here in one piece then?' Iain said, pulling their beers. 'Took a chance on your life in Sandy's jeep.'

'She was fine.'

'She's one of the best, I can tell you that. All right, Simon? The boy's taller than you, do ye know that?'

'Rubbish.' Simon handed over the money. 'Thanks for babysitting him last night.'

'What did he mean about Sandy's jeep?' They had taken a table by the window. 'She's a great driver.'

'Of course she is – and it's a skill, on these island tracks in a squall. He was taking the piss. Plus a dig at women. They're OK but a bit of that goes on.'

'Different world.'

'It is. If we go over the top we'll pass her house . . . down a wee slope to the east there.'

'A "wee slope". Don't stay here too long.'

Simon took a long draw of his pint, without reply. But he wondered. He always wondered. How long would he stay, could he stay, did he want to stay? Was he trying to duck out of a return to normal life, or whatever would pass as normal life with what Robbie called his bionic arm? He was still on sick leave and would be until he had the final prosthesis and was using it easily. Then came the decisions.

Climbing steadily, the wind at their backs, they did not talk but concentrated on the track, which was slippery and stony' but when they got to a spur, they sat on the coarse turf and looked out over the sea. The wind blew the rush of the waves up to them, though the sky was lighter in the distance now and the swell was subsiding. Sam chewed a stalk. Simon tried to lean back on his elbows but the artificial arm did not support his weight and made him unsteady so that he was forced to roll over onto his stomach.

'Is that where she lives?' Sam was pointing to a slate roof just visible below.

'No, that's an empty croft – looks OK from here but it's half derelict. There are one or two on the other side as well. Nobody can make any living to speak of from just a bit of land and a few sheep and chickens. There has to be something else – that's why there are the holiday lets, but of course that's only Easter, or a bit later, until September, and people want all the trimmings now, unless they're walkers and birders – they'll put up with simple conditions so long as they've hot water and something to brew up on. They can't charge much for anywhere that hasn't been tarted up. And they don't go for tarting up much here. That's one of the best things about the place.'

'I've been thinking about medicine,' Sam said, shifting his grass stalk from one side of his mouth to the other.

Simon waited, kept his expression neutral.

'What do you think?'

Silence.

'It's not . . . the thing is, I mean I might. Only different from what medicine you think.'

'I don't think any medicine, you've got to tell me.'

'Pathology.'

'You mean in the labs?'

'No. Forensic.'

'Ah. Right.'

A minibus carrier was coming down the road to the side of them, and as it approached, they saw the field trippers waving madly out of the windows. Simon raised his arm.

'So? Never mind them.'

'OK. Why?'

'Not sure. I like trying to find out things – deductions, you know?'

'That's what I do a lot of the time.'

Sam shook his head.

'Safer, of course – in a mortuary. They can't fire back.'

72

'It's got nothing to do with that.'

Simon sat up. 'Sorry. I'm just puzzled. One, what put you off not just the police but armed police, and what suddenly turned you on to this?'

'It's not sudden. I've been thinking about it for a bit.'

'What – days? A week or two.'

Sam threw his grass stalk away and pulled another roughly out of the clump.

'I'm listening, Sambo, and I am taking you seriously. It's just – a bit of a leap.'

'Haven't said I want to be a big-game hunter.'

'No, but then again, that'd hardly be a leap at all.'

'Ha.'

'Long training.'

'I don't mind about that.'

'You might get into it and decide you wanted to go for another branch of medicine altogether.'

'I might. Probably won't though.'

The sun was lancing through far out over the sea, brightness piercing the grey.

'Come on, we need to move, I'm getting stiff.'

'Race you.'

Sam leapt up and set off all in one movement, running fast over the rough ground. Simon watched him for a moment, then followed. He could still run. He walked ten miles across the island most days. But Sam's particular exuberance and young animal spirits were something he had not felt himself for a long time. He envied him. And he also wondered, as he started in pursuit, if spending most of his days with the silent dead in a white-tiled space was the right future for his energetic nephew.

The sun came out intermittently, but it was pleasant enough to walk. They covered six miles to the far west of the island, mainly in companionable silence. Here, the land rose and there were cliffs, a couple of rocky outcrops offshore, which had been the downfall of many a ship and small boat in the history of Taransay. Gannets, kittiwakes and huge seagulls rose and swirled around, before tumbling back to perch in groups, making a racket with their harsh ugly cries and calls. Sam sat watching them.

'No one lives over here then.'

'No. It's just too steep and it gets the lashing of the winter gales and high seas. You can see the remains of a couple of stone buildings down there. The odd hermit and sheltering sheep farmer stayed in them, I suppose.'

'Someone there now.'

'Can't be.'

'I saw smoke out of that chimney.' Sam pointed. 'Only a wisp though.'

Simon took out his small pair of field glasses and unfolded them. There was no trace of anything.

'Optical illusion. The light here can play tricks.'

Sam shrugged. 'I'm starving.'

They ate the thick ham sandwiches Simon had made, with hard-boiled eggs and a couple of bananas. Sam downed his and an entire bottle of water, before lying back on the turf and falling almost instantly asleep. Simon watched him, his own eyes half closed, but he only dozed. The sun was warm on their faces. Occasionally, a cloud slipped over, shadowing them, before the brightness returned. The seabirds cried. A few of the small, sturdy brown island sheep wandered about on the slope behind them and their occasional bleats mingled with the squawkings and cawing as the gannets and gulls rose and fell. The tide was far out and silent. The waves had frills of white along their edges as they creamed over and back, over and back.

I have everything I could possibly need or want here, Simon thought idly. Why would I go back? Sam murmured a little and was quiet again.

The man who appeared, crossing the path a hundred yards or so away, did not see them, just hidden below the outcrop. He walked quickly, the rucksack buckled tightly to his back. It was small, and did not bulge out. He carried very little. He dropped down and around, following the narrow track that led away in the direction of the main road a couple of miles away, that led to the far side of the island, the village and the harbour. His head was bent, as he concentrated on where he put his feet.

The tracks were both stony and tussocky, making it easy to slip, but he went steadily on, not looking around, not aware of the sea and the landscape and the overarching sky.

By the time Simon registered him and sat up, giving Sam a shake, the walker was out of sight.

Twelve

Thursday was her free day. A farmers' market had been running in Lafferton for less than a year but was already so successful and popular that getting there early was vital. By ten past nine, Cat already had a basket laden with fresh produce – eggs, meat, fruit, vegetables and flowers – and was heading for the marquee in the centre of the square, in which the bakers had their stalls. She would get a steak, kidney and mushroom pie. Kieron often had a Thursday meeting which finished early and sometimes they took the rare chance of going out. Tonight, they were staying in with a bottle of wine and a film. On her own, she would have watched a Scandicrime series but Kieron would not bring work home. 'Would *you* watch *A Day in the Life of a GP?*'

'No, but I watch *24 Hours in A & E.*'

'Not the same thing at all.'

She had finished her shopping but was still wandering between the stalls, before going to the bistro in the Lanes for coffee, when she heard what at first sounded like a low-flying plane roaring overhead, but then, as the noise level increased, was clearly a series of explosions. From the other side of the square came shouts. A scream. Another. And then a huge plume of dark smoke that billowed up and spread. A few seconds later, the wail of the first emergency sirens sounded, shockingly close.

Cat moved fast, down a gap between two stalls and out, the back way to the car park. Others were following her, coming from all sides, running, running, not looking back but now and then glancing up in fear at the spreading mushroom of smoke. Black specks were swirling about in the air now, and touching down on clothes, hair, the ground. Cat brushed one from her sleeve and it left an oily smear. More fell, clinging and making the same marks.

People were leaving the car park in a hurry, driving too fast down the ramps and hooting impatiently at the barriers while tickets were fed in, dropped in panic, retrieved, and everything slowed down. At the end of the street, there was already a jam. Nothing was moving and the sirens were sounding one after another along the parallel road. Cat turned the car radio to local news but there was only a blur of confused music and voice. It was a dead-signal area. She tried calling Kieron but got an answerphone on the direct line, and voicemail on his mobile.

The car in front jerked forward and she pushed on behind it, almost touching bumpers, anxious not to be the one stopped by any roadblock or cordon, but they were clear and she spun out and down a shortcut close to the cathedral, dived out again and headed away fast towards the bypass. By now, fire engines and ambulances were pouring in from the Bevham direction. Ahead, there was no sign of trouble. She tried Kieron again and again got the voicemails. There was nothing yet on the local radio but by the time she reached home a breaking news item was reporting 'an explosion and fire' at a warehouse complex close to the Lafferton canal.

She made coffee and took it into the garden. It was cloudy but warm enough to sit outside, with a notebook and pen. She needed to think about Luke's proposal, to make two lists, for and against, and to work out as much of the finances as she could. Wookie joined her, tucking himself away under her deckchair. It was quiet for over an hour, before her phone buzzed a message.

Major incident. Don't wait supper. Love you x

The centre of Lafferton had been cordoned off and the entire area leading to and along the canal was closed. Ten years ago there had been a number of warehouses, some still in use, as well as others in the process of being demolished and the sites bought for apartment blocks. There had been a couple of working factories near the canal which had been razed but not replaced by other buildings because the council had plans to turn the spaces, banks and towpaths into green park and leisure areas, but promised money had not been forthcoming and nothing had yet been done. The canal areas in particular were still a haunt for drug addicts, winos and prostitutes. The police had an occasional blitz and moved them all on, but they soon returned. The last of the buildings to be in any sort of use were a tyre storage depot and a small paint factory. A fire had started in the former and spread fast. The paint factory had gone up with several explosions, and the job now was to prevent the blaze from leaping the relatively short distance to the smart apartments which had been converted from the old ribbon factory.

Five fire engines had attended, but shortly after the alarm had been raised, there had been an explosion in the cinema and bingo hall complex, in the area of Bevham near to police HQ, which meant all fire engines and crews were needed there. It would take half an hour to get others to the scene from much further away.

Cat watched the television news. The fires were terrifying, black smoke shot with flame billowing up into the sky from the sides of the buildings, threatening streets of houses. More engines arrived. More police started evacuating the immediate areas, and then, as the fires got out of control, further afield. Churches and halls were opened, schools, youth clubs, a dance hall, requisitioned to provide shelter. It was thought that none of the buildings in either Lafferton or Bevham had been occupied but it was still impossible for any checks to be made.

Somewhere behind the scenes, Kieron and other police and emergency teams were coordinating not the response to the fires themselves so much as the wider picture, plans were being drawn up for access to the area the next day or for alternative arrangements to be made for people going to work and school, for traffic movements and for forensics to be on standby.

It was a long night. Kieron came wearily up the stairs just after five o'clock, and fell onto the bed and into sleep in a single movement. Cat pulled the duvet over him and then slept fitfully herself until seven.

Her phone beeped a message received, as she walked into the kitchen.

Good morning. Thank you for being my lunch guest. Great to see you again, looking only maybe five years older and blooming. Let me know when you've had a chance to go into the proposals and we can meet up again whenever you like. You'll have plenty of questions, but I hope your thoughts are all positive. Luke x

She put all thought of it at the back of her mind. She had a full surgery morning and a late-afternoon clinic. If Kieron had not been caught up in the emergencies, she had planned to talk it over with him the previous evening, and now, he came running downstairs buttoning his shirt.

'I have time for a cup of tea if the kettle's boiling, otherwise it's water. Call came in – there's another bloody fire.'

Thirteen

The next day they were walking again. Walking. Climbing. Resting briefly. Walking. Walking. Climbing. Climbing. It was as if Serrailler had to compensate for the loss of his arm by making his legs and the rest of his body work several hundred per cent harder. He had to exhaust himself. Sam did not complain, even though a couple of times he would have been glad to stay later in bed, or even just take a longer rest now and then, but he instinctively understood what this was about – more than the pleasure of the views and the fresh air and the satisfaction of pushing as hard as one could and then some. They had come over to the deserted west side of the island. Nobody lived here. The cliffs were steeper than on all the other sides, and slabs of them occasionally broke away during storms, when the sea battered them until they gave in. Not even the little brown island sheep survived for long here, except during the mild weeks of July and August. There was no house, not even a derelict croft, and the ground was rough and stony, hard even on strong walking boots. The prevailing wind rushed at the rocks. No vegetation or tree could withstand the gales and salt spray.

'You all right?'

'Yeah, but I'm starving.'

'OK, better turn back and head south – we won't find anywhere comfortable to sit and eat lunch this side. Come on.'

Sam's calf muscles were aching, and his face felt burnt by the combination of wind and sun, but he got ahead of Simon and strode on fast, wanting to test himself, as well as show off.

It was another hour before they reached the gentler, easier south side, an hour during which a sudden squall had soaked them, and the sun had then dried them out.

'Here.' There was a huddle of stones where a low wall had once divided the open sloping fields. Sheep were wandering about, their bleating carried on the soft wind. Simon unlaced his boots, got out the food and two bottles of water and they ate in silence, both ravenous now. High above them, the great birds circled lazily. The sea could just be heard but not seen from here.

'I see where we are . . . that's Sandy's place, low down?'

'Yes, we came at it from the other direction so it looks different. Stands out a bit more.'

'That's her jeep. Bloody thing – got no springs at all.'

Simon laughed.

'I need to get back a mallet she borrowed from me. We'll drop down after we're done.'

'Sure you're not seeing her?'

Simon turned on him so angrily that Sam started back.

'Don't be so bloody stupid and if I were what would it have to do with you? You keep your nose out.'

Sam got up and walked away quickly. He had never known his uncle snarl at him, had barely known him even to raise his voice. He had meant what he said as a joke, and he was both hurt and angry. He stood looking up the hill. Something was wrong and he was sane enough to know it had nothing to do with Sandy or his own feeble sense of humour that had caught Simon on the raw. Was it his arm? Pain? A sense of inadequacy? Or something else. He remembered Rachel. He had assumed, probably along with the rest of the family, that Simon would marry her – his mother had been cautious when he had mentioned it once. Sam could see her, standing in the kitchen with her back to the fridge, looking anxious. She had not asked him to keep their conversation to himself but he had known it anyway.

'It isn't Rachel – you know what she's like – she's a wonderful person, she's beautiful, she's fun, she's intelligent – and she adores him. It's him.'

'Why?'

'I don't know, Sammy – not really. He just finds relationships, other than short-term ones, very difficult.'

'Maybe he's gay?'

'I'm one hundred and ten per cent sure he isn't.'

'Nothing wrong if he was.'

'Of course not. Listen, he's just . . . oh God, I don't know.' She had sighed and opened the fridge to get out the salmon she was about to cook. Sam had waited a few more minutes but it was clear nothing else was going to be said.

There was the sound of the wind rustling across the turf, a sound which grew louder or softer but never ceased altogether, and the bleating of the sheep and the monotony of the seabirds' cries. Nothing else. Sam stood still. Simon had not moved.

There should be something. An apology. An explanation. Something.

Several more minutes passed.

'Oh, come on, for God's sake, this is stupid. Let's get whatever you need from Sandy and then we can get home.'

Sam started to move fast down the slope, at one point slipping and righting himself, a few yards further slithering on a loose stony section of the track, and almost crashing down. He did not glance behind him, but he knew that Si was not following. He reached the bottom, and walked on towards the house. He could see Sandy's jeep parked to one side. He stopped. He could no longer hear the sheep and the sigh of the wind was muffled by the slope. The path was still muddy from the night of the storm.

And then there was a scrabble and a bump, as Simon came fast down the track and stopped beside him.

'OK?'

Sam looked at him. There was no point in continuing their stand-off, though he was still annoyed at Simon's overreaction. But he nodded.

'Won't take two minutes.'

They turned into the pathway. 'No bell,' Sam said.

'They don't go for doorbells much around here. Either it's on the latch or you bang.' Sam banged. A chicken wandered towards them across the turf, pecking about.

'She's probably round the back or else along the shore somewhere. She's a great beachcomber.'

There was no garden at the back of the bungalow, just a strip of rough grass and the chicken house. Two more of them were scratching in the dirt.

'Sandy? You out there?'

In the distance, the sheep's bleating. Nothing else.

Simon tried the back door. It was locked. 'Strange. I told you, nobody locks anything. Check the front again, Sambo.'

Sam went. There were no windows at the side of the house. He looked into the jeep again and then he noticed the keys, not in the ignition but in the footwell on the driver's side. He reached for them. As well as the car key, there was a door key and another which looked as if it belonged to a shed. He could hear Simon's voice, calling Sandy. The living-room curtains were drawn back and Sam cupped his hands to either side of his head and peered inside. A table. An armchair. An upright chair. A rug. A standard lamp. A fireplace, with the dead remains of a fire. Bookshelves in an alcove, a couple of them full, the rest completely empty. It was a tidy room, without anything to distinguish it from a hundred others. There seemed to be no pictures or photographs, no personal clutter. The place might have been a holiday cottage between visitors.

Simon came round the side, and Sam showed him the keys.

'We'd better go in. Though my guess is that she's off beach-combing somewhere.'

Simon opened the door, paused, as if he were smelling and sensing the atmosphere of the house, and then stepped carefully inside. 'Stay back a second.'

Sam looked at the narrow stairs straight ahead, the closed doors to the living room and, he supposed, kitchen. The hall was barely that. It had a heavy red wool curtain tied back with a loop. A rubber floor mat. A narrow ledge to the right of the door with an empty pot, presumably for the keys, and an envelope, which looked like a circular.

There was the same feeling of anonymity that he had picked up when looking through the window.

Simon had gone up the stairs and Sam heard his footsteps first to the right, front, and then the back room. In the latter he paused.

'Is she there?' Sam called up.

'No.'

Sam hesitated. He had been told to stay where he was, but almost before he knew that he was going to do so, he stepped to the kitchen door and opened it.

There were two mugs on the table, containing dregs of coffee. A washing-up cloth was draped over the taps. The chairs were pushed in. The range was out.

'Perhaps she's gone away,' Sam said.

Simon was standing in the doorway looking carefully round. He shook his head. 'The jeep wouldn't be here.'

He looked over every flat surface, opened the food cupboard and the one under the sink. Everything was in its place. It was all very swept and clean.

'Two mugs,' he said. 'Odd.'

'Why? People never visit her then?'

Simon shrugged.

'Nothing we can do,' Sam said. 'You'll have to get your mallet another time.'

But Simon did not move, only went on looking at everything, and then went back to the hall, into the living room, upstairs again, left, right, landing. A cupboard opened and, closed. Another. Drawers slid to and, after a second, fro.

'I'm going to take another look outside.'

He seemed to be talking to himself rather than to Sam, who hovered in the doorway, gazing out. A sea fret was drifting up from below, gently covering the landscape, the house, the sheep behind. It left a fine veil of moisture on his shoulders and hair. The wind had died. It felt slightly warmer. The fast changes in weather, temperature, the look of the island, even its colours, delighted him. He thought he heard Simon shout to him but, if he had, his voice was muffled by the fret. After a moment, he emerged out of it, looming through the greyness.

'Can't see a bloody thing of course but there's no one as far as the end of the track.

'Could she have slipped and fallen?'

'Possible but unlikely, I'd have thought. She wouldn't have a reason to venture onto the cliff edge. She walked on the shore almost every day but she took the sloping path from the road. Anyway, there's no point trying to get down there with this coming in. We'll head for the village.'

Sam ran to catch up.

'Stick to me,' Simon said. 'Easy to become disorientated in a fret.'

Sam did not reply, just trudged on, making sure he kept no more than a yard behind. It was miserable walking, heads down, no view, only a dogged pace and the eerie bleating of the sheep from somewhere beyond them, shrouded in the mist.

The fret became denser as they closed in on the harbour, and until they were almost upon it, they could not see the lights from the houses or the pub. There was a din of music and voices as they went in.

'God, the ceilidh, I'd forgotten.'

Simon pushed his way up to the bar, shouldering a couple aside but they made room without comment. The doors of the back room were open and the band and the dancers were going full tilt.

'You've a thirst on you then,' Iain said, glancing up from pulling a pint of Guinness.

'I need a word – has Sandy been in?'

Iain hesitated, then said, 'Havenae seen her but that's no surprising. Take a look through for yourself. I've been here since crack of dawn and I'll be here till crack of the next one.'

He set the black foaming stout on the counter and took a glass down from the row above him in one smooth movement. 'I'll do yours when I've got through this lot and any minute now Lorna will be out with another tray of orders.'

Iain's wife was not normally on hand although they lived on the premises. She was sparing with her assistance and her presence. Simon had barely met her.

'I'll check.' He went in to the packed back room, where the music and dancing were hotting up, but after watching carefully, and checking out those sitting on the benches round the edge, he was sure Sandy was not there. He returned to the bar.

'I need a minute without the music and the blether,' Simon said. 'Can you give me that, Iain?'

Iain paused. 'What's this all about? It's a busy night in here as you well know.'

'Sandy isn't there.'

Iain looked at him, caught his tone of voice. He put a full pint on the counter, then reached up to the ship's bell and rang it long and loud enough for there to be quiet in the bar. 'Just give them the word through there, somebody.'

Within a few seconds, there was silence and a stillness as if they were attending a wake, not a ceilidh. Iain did not ring the bell like that without good reason.

Now he nodded to Simon who stood in the centre of a small space they cleared for him. He was known to them. His history was known. His past history. The job he did. For a short time, he had the floor.

'Just a heads-up to everyone. My nephew Sam and I called on Sandy Murdoch earlier – I had to pick up something – and there was no sign of her or of any break-in or trouble. Her jeep was there. But I haven't seen her for a day or two. Last time was when she gave Sam a lift back to my place two nights ago in the storm. Not unusual for Sandy to be out walking, especially down on the shore, but there wasn't a sign of her when I looked. I'm just a bit bothered. You all know Sandy – if you've an idea that she's maybe gone away to the mainland or whatever, shout out and I'll stop fretting. But Iain here hasn't seen her and she's generally about in the stores or helping out with the unloading. This isn't my patch of course but once a cop . . . Anyway, thanks, back to the music.'

Fourteen

They had been haymaking all day. The warm still air was a whir of dust and noise, coming from the field opposite the house, but they had finished, beaten the rain forecast for the evening, and gone home. The silence was like an alternative noise, so shocking that it woke Richard Serrailler, sleeping through the hot afternoon in the shade. He sat up, and took in the difference around him. The sky had changed, there was a haze in the west, and the air was full of moisture and tiny insects.

He called out to Delphine but she would not hear him if she was in the kitchen. She had looked better in the last couple of days, they had gone to the market together and she had bought a chicken, piles of vegetables, some spices, couscous and herbs, kilos of apricots to make a compote. She seemed to have come to, as if after a long sleep, to have shrugged off the low spirits that had wrapped round her ever since the accident, and become her old, easy-going, happy self. He was relieved. They had enquired about repairs to her scooter which were not as costly as he had feared. The work would take two to three days, longer if they had to wait for parts, but then she could be back on the road. Richard planned to drive behind her the first few journeys, and then she said she would perhaps have another full week off before going back to work. The subject of her staying at his home and looking after him had not been raised again. He was relieved. He liked Delphine, she was pleasant to have around, but he had no desire for her to be here all day every day. He was used to being on his own. He craved the solitude and enjoyed doing as he wished. Not that his habits had changed greatly. He had relaxed a little but he was a man of habit. He was never going to let himself drift into days of unpredictability and idleness.

Now, he went through the open doorway, which had a fly screen covering it, into the cool house.

'Shall we have a cold drink? Iced coffee in the fridge. I'm going for a shower first. Delphine?'

She had probably gone to sleep. He was unsure if her inclination to go to sleep for chunks of the day was a result of the lingering effects of her accident, the heat, or perhaps boredom and mild depression. She needed to be back at work. He did not find moping or low spirits easy to live with. Meriel had been blessed with an equable temperament, so had Judith. Of his children, only Simon had occasionally been the heavy silent presence in the house, though mostly he had taken what Richard had always classed as his sulking, out.

Delphine was not in the bedroom or the spare room, not on the sitting-room couch. He clicked his tongue in irritation, showered, took his iced coffee into the garden, with the *Times* crossword of the previous day – the newspapers arrived a day late – and the latest issue of the medical journal he used to edit and on which he still advised. After half an hour, he allowed himself to drift off to sleep. The shade was pleasing. The sun was moving round.

Delphine would appear in her own time. The last thing he would ever do was go looking for her.

Fifteen

'It's ridiculous, Kieron, you're the Chief and you're behaving like one of the Indians. You haven't had a decent night's sleep for nearly a week, you're trying to do your own job and the job of half your CID. I'm surprised you aren't out with the fire crew manning a hose. What are you trying to prove?'

He had come in just after nine the previous night, grey with exhaustion, poured himself a small whisky, and fallen asleep on the sofa so deeply that after trying to rouse him several times, Cat had brought a blanket and a pillow and made him as comfortable as she could before going upstairs. He had not stirred until after seven, when she was putting on the kettle. Now he was back in the kitchen, having showered, shaved and changed.

'It's Saturday,' Cat said. 'I want to go somewhere.'

Kieron looked doubtful. 'I need –'

'No. You don't need. You need to spend a day with your wife and without your phone.'

'No, I can't –'

'Yes. I will have your phone and I will look at whoever is calling, if and when they do, and if it's the station, take a view.' She reached for his hand. 'Listen, I do understand, you know. Three major fires on your patch, terrible damage – though thank God no human casualties – and the buck stops with you. But not every minute of every day and half of every night, darling. What use are you to anyone if you let yourself get as exhausted as this? I want your company for a few hours. Let's get out into the country and walk – it's not wet, it's not hot, it's perfect. We can drive up to Starly and take the path up to the top. And never mind you, I need the exercise as well.'

Kieron was silent for a moment. 'I'll do you a deal,' he said.

'Sounds ominous and if it's "just let me pop into the station first", the deal's off before it's on.'

'OK, what about, just let me call in first?'

'Hmm. If I time the call and you agree to let me take the phone from you if I hear you say "I'd better come in".'

'That's a big ask. What if the cathedral has been set alight, or the Eric Anderson Comp, or –'

'Then we will rethink. But they aren't going to be.'

'Deal.'

He put his hands on her shoulders. Cat closed her eyes.

'And . . .'

Kieron groaned.

'I want a good lunch out. Not just a sausage roll.'

'Have you tried getting a sausage roll in the gourmet pubs round here?'

The day was perfect for walking and so they took a longer route. Sitting on top of Starly Hill they could see the cathedral tower rising from the flatlands below, the silver curve of the river, the fields of sheep, looking as if someone had taken handfuls and scattered them. Their eerie cries came up on the breeze. But there was nothing eerie about the day or the mood.

I am happy, Cat thought. I was certain I could never be so again, that a general feeling of well-being was the most I could hope for after Chris died. I would have settled for that.

But I am happy.

She put her hand on his.

'Was that the phone?'

She had been as good as her word and taken his mobile from him. It was safely in her jeans pocket and on 'vibrate'.

'No.'

'You would tell me.'

'I would.'

Kieron lay back on the grass, hands behind his head.
'In any case, from up here you'd see the smoke.'

The Oak was another place that had changed hands. It had been old-fashioned, rather dark and uninviting.

'You used to wonder if they fried a batch of chips first thing then just refried them through the day.'

'Not any more apparently.'

'I wonder if Luke's partner has taken this over as well.'

The pub was brighter, smarter, cleaner, with a new menu.

'And new prices,' Cat said. It was early for lunch and they were alone apart from a couple of smartly dressed women having cocktails at the bar. The old Oak would not have known what a cocktail was.

'Has my phone rung? I ought just to check.'

Cat gave him a look. 'Half a pint of prawns and a peashoot and feta salad.'

But they could talk without danger of being overheard and she had his attention because she had his phone.

'Luke's proposal,' she said now. 'I need your take on it because I'll have to let him know soon if I'm on board or not.'

Kieron took a long draught of his beer, and sat back. He was a good listener – like her brother, Cat thought. Two cops.

'You know enough about my job to know that I'm not happy and that general practice is in a mess. Not enough doctors, too many retiring or leaving and not being replaced, an ageing population so more appointments needed, no real time to establish an ongoing relationship with your patients, too much form-filling and box-ticking, too much interference from too many layers of management. Result, dissatisfied public, who can't get a GP appointment for weeks and burnt-out doctors who no longer find their work fulfilling. Luke's idea is to address this by looking at it in a new way. The idea is that three GPs band together and form a practice. If the whole thing works, others would join but three to begin with. We would cover a geographical area – he hasn't worked out the precise logistics but certainly the whole of Lafferton and the surrounding villages within a ten-square-mile radius.'

'So you'd have a surgery in the town centre.'

'No. This is the beauty of it. No surgery. No building. No office . . . except maybe one doctor would have an office in their house for a secretary – there has to be one – or maybe they could work from home. Not clear yet. We would be on call between us twenty-four/seven, and we would visit the patients at home. They wouldn't come to us. We would divide the area.'

'That's a hell of a lot of driving.'

'No more than doctors always did when they made house calls – visits were what happened after surgery or out of hours. Happy days.'

'So you would be on at night and weekends.'

'One in three at first, fewer as we grew.'

'Do the sums work? The NHS is pretty strapped for cash.'

'Ah. This is the nub. It wouldn't be NHS.'

'What, you mean private practice? I thought you were against.'

'Chris would have divorced me for even considering it. But honestly . . . it has to be a better way. For some, all right, I know.'

'How much per visit?'

'It would work on a sub. You join and pay a monthly sum . . . probably around a hundred pounds per patient – paid monthly, quarterly, annually, whatever the individual chooses, by direct debit. That would cover absolutely everything except the cost of the meds.'

'Which could be enormous.'

'Could but usually not – most medicines we give cost less to buy than the price of an NHS prescription, unless you're exempt. It's an open secret. We would always recommend the NHS for emergency stuff and major illnesses – cancer treatments, cardiac bypass, all of that – so people would stay registered with an NHS practice. If you need to have your appendix out, the NHS is the only way and the best way and we'd take on all the post-op.'

Their mains came, fish pies in individual baking dishes, topped with whole prawns. The old Oak had done fish pie, supplied, like the cottage pies, by a food wholesaler and microwaved.

'It's another world,' Cat said, slicing it through to let the heat rise out. The inside was thick with chunks of smoked haddock, more prawns, white fish, mushrooms, in a creamy sauce.

'So is private medicine.'

'I didn't realise you were so against it. So do you think the children should have gone to state schools?'

'No. I think there should be a choice – same with medicine. I suppose I'm testing you.'

'It sounds like medicine for the very rich, but actually, a hundred pounds a month is a supper out or half a dozen bottles of average wine or tickets to something. Not for the poor, no, but affordable for a lot of ordinary people.'

'It sounds as if you're sold.'

'No. Kieron, look, I need your take, and if I think of doing it, I need your support – well, of course I do. You've got to be happy. But I promise you it won't be me out all day and all night . . . we can consult on the phone, by email – it isn't always necessary to visit. Plenty of simple things can be safely diagnosed at a distance, and if there's any doubt at all, then we go.'

'Lot of mileage but you like driving, I know. God, this pie is good.'

The pub had begun to fill but they had a table set by the window in a corner. No one would overhear.

Kieron ate for several minutes, went and got a second beer, and pondered. He had not asked if his phone had rung since they had sat down.

Cat waited. Yes, she thought, it is the same as being with Si. He would have listened and been devil's advocate and then sat silently, working the whole thing through before deciding. Dad would cross-question like a QC and then sum up and pronounce a verdict within seconds and never change his mind. Chris would have . . . No. She would never have put the idea to Chris. His disapproval of all private medicine had been absolute. They had eaten and ordered coffees before Kieron said, 'The only thing that matters to me in all of this is that you should enjoy your job and find it satisfying again . . . and not overstretch yourself. It sounds to me as if this way of working would be right for you, if you think you can make it sustainable. I want to see you as much as I can or why would I have married you? But I want you to be happy and you're pretty conscientious . . . If you're sure it won't exhaust you, I think you should do it. But it's for you to decide, Cat – what do I know about being a doctor?'

'You know about me.'

'I think I'm beginning to.'

'Of course,' she said, 'it may not come off. There's a long way to go . . . lots of hurdles for Luke to jump. He's a doer though . . . he makes things happen, he always did.'

'Good.' Kieron finished his coffee, and as he did so, his phone vibrated in Cat's pocket. Now she gave in.

'Talking of a job being sustainable,' Cat said.

But he was already on his feet. 'There's another,' he said.

Sixteen

'Listen,' Iain said, 'Sandy Murdoch . . .' He went quiet for a moment as if trying to work out how to explain. 'She's great . . . I've nothing against her, you understand, not a thing. But she's just maybe . . . a wee bit strange.' 'I'd never say anything bad about her, she's a good woman, a decent woman, ready to help anyone and she's fitted in, which isn't easy. She's not pushed herself but she's – aye, fitted in. And yet . . .' He was anxious to defend Sandy, that was clear, but against whom? What had people said? Which people?

Simon pushed his glass over for a second pint. 'Where did she come from?'

Iain shrugged.

'Some said Glasgow,' Tommy McDermid muttered into his whisky. 'Some said London. Some will say anything when they ken nothing. She's never told – not to my knowledge. She just arrived one March – what, three years back? Has to be. She'd rented out that house from an advert. Didn't bring much stuff of her own. Couple of packing cases came over.'

'Has she disappeared before?'

'That's a strong way of saying she just hasn't been around for a day or so,' Iain said.

'What would you call it then?'

'She wouldn't have to tell everyone her business, that's all. She's been away a couple of times but there could have been others and why not?'

'No reason at all.'

'You're a cop. You can't help it.'

'Once she said she was away to a funeral in Greenock.'

'She did.' Iain turned to serve the postman, in for a pint at the end of his round.

'Gordon – you haven't seen anything of Sandy?' Simon asked.

'Took a letter and her magazine up there this morning. She wasn't in. No surprise. She goes walking along the shore for miles, she goes over the hill . . . I see Sandy all over the island.'

'But she always goes back home.'

'I wouldnae know what she does.'

'Was her jeep there?'

'It was.'

Serrailler got up. There was only one way Sandy could have left the island and returned to it.

It was an hour before the next ferry left and there was no one on board except Alec, checking things in the cabin.

'You going over? Like a fish pond today.'

'I'm not. I'm looking for Sandy.'

'Ah, I saw her what, last Sunday? She was just there, where you're standing, watching.'

'Watching.'

'We'd a full boat – quite a few for the field centre, quite a few walkers. You know how it is, fine weather. I thought Sandy was maybe waiting for someone, had a visitor, but she just watched the last off and she was away.'

'Has she been over this week?'

'Not with me. Donald was on Monday and Tuesday, with John. I know it was pretty slack. You could ask him.'

'I will.'

'She in trouble then?'

'I hope not but her jeep's parked outside and the house is empty. No one's seen her, she wasn't at the ceilidh.'

'Och, don't worry about Sandy, she's done this before – she holes up by herself somewhere, over the other side. Maybe she watches for the birds, maybe she just likes to live in a cave for a wee while. Wouldn't suit me.'

'A cave?'

'Under the cliff – bit wild out there but it's all right until maybe end of October . . . you wouldn't want to be on your own after that. Nothing much frightens Sandy, but even so.'

Sam drove. He was competent and pretty safe, Simon thought, though still a bit driving-school correct, and he had too tight a grip on the wheel. He'd learn and this sort of trip across the island was invaluable. He had to think fast, read the track ahead. The 4x4 was rock solid but there had been rain, and as they descended on the far side, the road turned to mud. They saw no one, though the minibus was outside the field centre and there were bikes against the wall.

After that, there were no more houses, just some of the old, tumbledown stone crofts and sheep sheds, open to the elements, and an ancient rusting barn. The stunted trees were bent by the prevailing wind.

'No one's been along here recently,' Simon said.

'No tyre tracks?'

'No wheel marks on the side where there's been pulling in to pass.'

'So she comes and lives like a Bronze Age cave-dweller. Or a hermit. Maybe she's religious. Anchorites – is it?'

They were almost on the headland. The sea was navy blue and swollen to a boil, churning about within itself. When they got out, the air was heavy but still. Simon pointed to the mouth of a path that led downwards and they set off, sweeping left, then straight, then left again. It was steep and they had to slither and take hold of tussocks of rough grass here and there to save themselves.

'Don't rush,' Simon said, 'steady . . . one step at a time.'

'No one's been down here. It's not been disturbed at all.'

It took a while to reach first the rocky outcrop and then the beach. They looked up. 'There might be another way back,' Sam said.

'Hmm.' Simon was walking in the lee of the cliff. Sam followed. The tide was out. There were no other footsteps or disturbances in the sand.

There were two caves, a shallow one which they came to first, and which had large weed-covered rocks almost covering the entrance. Simon shook his head. The second was under the steepest area of cliff, and had a sandy entrance. The light showed them the way in for a few yards and then Sam switched on the torch.

'Jesus, the last time I had to investigate a cave . . .'

'What?'

'Never mind. But it wasn't good. This doesn't actually go very far back.'

The walls of rock were gleaming with water, and vivid green weed. And there were no signs that anybody or anything had been here except the tides, ebbing and flowing.

'Nothing.'

'She hasn't been here. And honestly, I wonder if she ever has. You can't see anything, and the tide fills it right up, likely as not. Alec was wrong.'

Sam was in charge of supper that night. Simon stacked logs. It was colder. The cave haunted him, the smell of the wet rock, the seaweed, the sand. The echo. It made him feel unsettled. Uneasy. But he was sure of the reason and he tried not to dwell on his memory of those other caves, set far back into the North Yorkshire cliffs. The stone ledges which the strong torch beams had picked up. The small still figures.

He did not think Sandy had spent any time in the caves here. Why would she? She liked walking, liked climbing over the top and looking out to sea, blown about by the wind. Or going along the beach, peering down to see what the tides might have brought in. Sandy was not a person to hide herself away under the cliffs. He had no reason to be so sure of it but he was sure and he had always followed his hunches, his gut feelings, as a cop and in the rest of his life. He wouldn't change now.

'Any idea how long you're staying?'

Sam gave him a long look. Simon helped himself to the last of the spaghetti Bolognese.

'Maybe another few days?'

'Sure. Then what?'

Sam shrugged. And then he was silent for several minutes, cutting bread, getting out a fresh pack of butter. Simon finished eating. He had lit the fire and it was crackling nicely, not yet giving off much heat. But it wouldn't take long. They would need to have the lamps on soon.

Who does he remind me of? Not his mother. His father then? Yes. Chris had been quiet, thoughtful, occasionally explosive. Clear-minded. Stubborn. Rarely changing his mind. A bit of his father then. Who else?

Simon smiled to himself. Yes, he thought. Like me in some ways. Some of the time.

'Thing is,' Sam said now, 'it's not that easy to get my head round stuff at home. I think Mum sees me as the same age as Felix still and she asks about everything . . . oh, you know. I'm just trying to get it all clear.'

'Sure. Kick me if I start probing.'

'You won't. You don't.'

'Thanks. But if you do want to run something past me, you can.'

'I know that. I don't remember Granny too well now. Was she like that?'

'She was like a mother, if that's what you mean. But no – there were three of us, remember, all the same age. She didn't have time, and she went back to work at the hospital when we were a year old. She was an achiever, our mother. She believed in letting us get on with it, so we did.'

'Was Grandpa the same?'

'Oh God yes. More so. But he was different. He let us think we could do what we wanted and then when we did, he kicked off.'

'He's never like that to me.'

'No. He isn't. I suppose people aren't so tough on grandchildren.'

'I might go and see him actually.'

'What, in France?'

'Why not?'

'Not sure he'd be all that happy if you just turned up.'

'Why?'

Too many 'whys', Simon thought. Like a much younger boy. Robbie. Yes. Because Richard wouldn't be happy if Sam did?

99

Because I would never do that? Because . . . All he had was a hunch, but where his father was concerned, hunches had never been reliable.

'If you want to go I'd email him first – check it out.'

Sam did not reply, just got up and started to clear the table.

Simon went to the back door. The sky was clear and thick with stars. There was no light pollution up here. Any cloudless night was a starry one. It never failed to please him and make him feel an odd sense of rightness. Belonging. No, he didn't belong here. He never would. He could come as often as he liked, it would make no difference.

How had Sandy appeared from nowhere and become part of the island so quickly? She might have lived here all her life. What had Sandy done, or not done, to be so accepted, and how?

It was as still a night as ever it would be. There was always the slight stirring of the grass, the movement of the air; the wind never lay down and slept.

He went out to shut the side gate. If it blew up from nowhere the gate would slam hard, and go on slamming.

When he returned to the house, Sam had gone upstairs.

Seventeen

By six o'clock the tide was going out from the small bay below the field centre, but it was not until after seven that four intrepid swimmers were on their way down to the water, all wearing wetsuits – they had been warned how cold the sea would be. The first two raced ahead and plunged in, following a wave to launch themselves, the next was not far behind, but then Laura Roberts felt her foot come up against a concealed rock and fell sprawling on the hard sand. She lay until it was clear that she had done herself little harm, though she would probably have bruised toes the next day. The others were shouting with laughter, their voices faint against the drag of the waves.

She rolled over and looked along the flat sand, and as she looked, she saw it. She had read about it. The mistakes people made. A big fish. A log. A seal. Part of a boat. She got up and went slowly along the few yards of beach. Slowed as she got nearer. She made herself look. Took a few steps. The tide was going out but a few foam-edged waves were washing over it. Gentle waves. Washing it clean.

She did not remember passing out, only that she came to with Chloë and Angus leaning over her and Ade standing peering down at the woman's body.

Eighteen

Douglas stopped off on his way to pick up a roll of barbed wire that was due in on the morning boat. Simon met him at the gate.

'How long before local police get here?'

He shrugged. 'She's dead so they'll no be in any hurry. Doctor will be first. He's only twenty minutes away in his own boat and it's flat calm. He can get right into the bay. You'd best go over there.'

'I'm not Police Scotland.'

'You're still police, aren't you? There'd best be someone taking charge till ours get here.'

'I'll call them.'

Sam was still asleep when he got through.

'We use the normal services to get over to Taransay unless it's a real emergency. Money's not easy to find for a special chartered boat. Washed-up bodies, no. What exactly are you doing on the island, Chief Superintendent?'

'Rehab after an operation. I'm fighting fit now and I know Taransay.'

'Let me ring you back.'

Ten minutes later, he was speaking to his equivalent ranking officer in the Highlands and Islands CID.

'I'm even more short of folk than usual, there's been a drug-smuggling op coming into the north and I've got no spare pairs of hands. Found-drowned missper goes to the bottom of the to-do list so you're a godsend. Give me your number. I'm heading out in half an hour but keep me posted on this. Any thoughts before you see her?'

'No, but I doubt if she was a suicide. Accident seems the most likely, though she knew every nook and cranny pretty well.'

'Accidents still happen. People get careless, we see it all the time. Meet up with Doc Murray and get his certification and first opinion. He'll bring the body over to the mortuary here.'

He had expected a crowd. There was always a crowd. People came out of nowhere, to hang about and stare and make ghoulish chat. But there were only a couple of young men, who were from the field centre and who were now guarding the body. They had covered it with a piece of plastic sheeting, weighted down with a few stones. They sat cross-legged on the wet and shining sand, like attendants at some primitive funeral.

'Thanks for this. Not the best start to your day. I'm only filling in for the local police until they can get here, and the doctor's on his way.'

'Do you know who it is? There's been someone missing, the local guy said.'

'Yes. I'm just going to take a look. You didn't move the body about?'

They were both standing now. 'No. We didn't touch it only it seemed wrong just to . . . you know, let her lie there like that.'

Simon knelt down and felt the water soak up into the knees of his trousers. He moved one of the lumps of rock and carefully slid the sheeting down a little way.

Sandy. And as he looked at her, he heard the engine of a motorboat coming in fast to the shore.

'OK, guys, you don't have to stay any longer. This is the doc. You might have to answer one or two formal questions later – how long are you at the field centre for?'

'Three more days. You sure you don't need us?'

'You've done brilliantly, and thanks, but you go back now.'

The engine died and the motorboat ground to a halt in the sand.

'Superintendent Serrailler? Ken Murray. Right. What have we?'

Brisk and to the point, efficient, clinical, but somehow also respectful of what was a fellow human being, not just a dead body. Like every pathologist Serrailler had ever met. The doctor got out his bag and unzipped his yellow waterproof and life jacket. He rolled the plastic sheet fully back. Behind them, the tide went out as calmly as it ever did on this coast.

He said nothing for many minutes, inspecting the body first entirely by eye, then with a light touch, disturbing as little as possible. Simon looked on. At Sandy's hands. Face. Ankles. She was wearing a dark-coloured sweater. Jerkin with the collar zipped right up. Black jeans. One boot. The other was missing. Her hair was loose. She had no scarf or hat but those would have slipped off underwater. She was recognisable, but only just. A body which has been submerged and battered about in the sea is not a pleasant sight once it is washed up onshore.

'Dead,' Murray said, straightening up. 'That's the easy part done. Familiar?'

'Sandy Murdoch. She lives on the island.'

'Family here?'

'No, she lived on her own. I don't know much about her. Not sure anyone else does.'

They stood in silence for a second. Murray shook his head. 'It's never right,' he said.

'Fine, I'm not doing anything else here. Help me get her into the body bag and I'll be on my way.'

It was not easy and they had to be careful. The flesh was already loosening. The fingers and palms were wrinkled. But the doctor was expert, his movements assured, he guided Serrailler with only a few words, and the body was on board, strapped down and secured. 'You all right to get back?'

Simon nodded and watched the small boat turn and head east, picking up speed. He saw it almost out of sight before he looked down at the sand, marked and indented slightly where she had been washed up and lain. There was no point in securing the site even if he had the means to do it. The tide would wash everything clean and clear again in a few hours. And it was probably not a crime scene in any case.

Nineteen

The cafe was still full, every table taken by people eating dinner, or just drinking coffee and half-carafes of rosé, smoke blowing up into the still warm night from right and left. Olivier was rushing between tables when Richard caught his sleeve.

'*Nous sommes complets mais si vous –* '

'*Ou est Delphine?*'

The young waiter pulled away and shook his head. '*Pardon . . . je suis . . .*'

The proprietor, Victor, was on tonight, tall, thin, with a built-in Gallic shrug and a surly manner which very occasionally lifted like a cloud away from the sun, to bestow charm, smiles, kisses, handshakes and lively conversation on some favoured customer – always a local. He came down the two steps and glanced over to Richard.

'*Monsieur.*'

'*Ou est Delphine?*'

The shrug.

'Has she been in at all today?'

'*Non.*'

'Has she telephoned or –'

'*Non.* If she is not with you, I do not know where, *monsieur le docteur. Excusez-moi.*'

Richard hesitated. Wait and see if she turned up? Go home?

He walked away, leaving behind the chatter and chink of china and glass and the blue cigarette smoke, into the dark, quiet street to his car. Where was she? Probably Victor knew. Probably Olivier. She had told them – and told them not to say anything if he asked.

He was not worried now. He was angry. Knowing nothing, being told nothing, made a fool of.

He drove too fast through the twisting country lanes to the house.

She was not there. No one was there.

He poured a glass of wine and sat in the garden. Was she coming back? Had she gone off with someone? Why?

And how much did he care? He had been fond of Delphine and enjoyed her company. He had not spoiled her with money or gifts, and she had never expected anything. But he had been made a fool of, and now, he felt that fool. An old fool. No fool like.

He brought the remains of the bottle out, lit the mosquito coils, and with just enough light from the porch, started on the *Times* crossword. He usually did it in the morning, but he was too restless and irritable to go to bed, and disliked sitting doing nothing. He had never been able to do nothing. There had always been work, and later, writing medical papers, editing the journal, his family. Coping with Meriel's death, marrying Judith and, with her, discovering a different life, travelling in the camper van, across America, up and down Europe. He had never expected to enjoy it but he had. Judith. He looked up from the crossword he had not yet begun. What had happened? They should not have separated. She should not have left him. It would have taken some words of apology, some adjustments, but it had not seemed to him that she had wanted to make them.

He poured the last glass. The mosquito coil dimmed and went out, leaving the strange, musky smoke on the air. It was still very warm.

He half woke, hearing a sound – a car in the lane, perhaps passing the house. He lifted his head, but as it was quiet again, went back to sleep, stretched out in the garden chair, deeply comfortable.

In the end, it was not a sound but the sudden chill that brought him up. There was a dampness in the air, as of early morning.

He was stiff, cursed himself for falling asleep, not having the sense at least to stay in the house. There was already a faint dew on the grass as he hobbled inside.

It was a moment, because he was slightly dazed by sleep, before he noticed anything. The kitchen was as usual and he poured himself a glass of water, put some ice cubes into it, locked the back door, and went through to the small room he used as a study. His small Georgian clock was not on the side table, the Royal Doulton jug was not on the shelf, nor the two watercolours by Cotman. His laptop had gone. His Roberts radio. The three silver frames which had contained photographs of his grandchildren. The pictures themselves were scattered on the desk. He opened the drawers. In the top one he kept a couple of hundred euros in a wallet to pay people, take change when he needed it, and in the second the safe box which contained several thousand and a valuable gold pocket watch. He knew with only a cursory look that they had gone. Small items, some of worth, some he was merely fond of, an inlaid mother-of-pearl box, six silver spoons, a locket that had belonged to his mother and then to Meriel.

It was perfectly clear that Delphine had taken what she wanted. All her things had gone as well. Had she acted alone? Had she lied when she had said she wanted to stay in the house here, to be with him?

Did any of it matter?

He picked up the phone. But it was half past five in the morning, Cat would not thank him for ringing her now. What would he say to her? Would he tell her? He felt helpless and unsure and, suddenly, old.

Twenty

'No need to stay too late, Mrs Lee, there isn't anything urgent.'

'I just want to deal with the notes about Mr Barker's will and file it all. I didn't get chance to finish everything earlier.'

He filled the doorway of her office. The building was old, the doorways small, the ceilings low. The firm had been here in Cathedral Close for seventy years. No one would contemplate removal to somewhere more modern and convenient, and the sixteenth-century walls and roof did not prevent their being fully up to date. Too up to date, she sometimes thought but never said. She was fifty-nine but often felt that she should have lived in the 1900s.

'Goodnight then.'

'Goodnight, Mr Dodsworth.'

She would work until six thirty, and then walk through the Close, up via the Lanes, to Silver Street. The restaurant they always met in, Primrose's, was a good place for them because the food was straightforward, the portions not stingy, and because it was comfortable and, above all, quiet, even when it was full. They tried to get the same table, to one side, not in the window but near enough to have a view onto the street, with the cathedral in the background. In the daytime it lacked the atmosphere of the more recently established bars and bistros but after six, they put candles in small glass bowls with lids which had a red tinge, making the whole room feel safe and cosy. There were cushions on the backs of the chairs, and in winter, a wood-burning stove was lit. They had tried a couple of other places but they hadn't been suitable because of the noise. They needed to hear themselves speak without having to shout and then be overheard and draw attention to themselves.

Marion had to talk. It was her life, talking about it, but so few people could bear to listen any more. Her son Tim, living in Newcastle, her brother, neighbours – they were worn down, burned out with listening. They had to protect themselves against it now. It upset them, distressed and troubled and irritated and bored them by turns.

So she clung on to Brenda, who felt it was her duty to allow that. In fact, if it were not for the subject of her daughter, Marion would have been an ideal friend. They got on well, they had plenty in common, everyday tastes and background too. They had even been on holiday together once, to a beautiful bay in Cornwall, and a hotel that looked right over the sea. They liked walking, reading, visiting heritage sites and churches – the weather had been very good apart from a couple of sea-misty mornings but it had cleared by noon each time. But everything led back to Kimberley.

Her daughter-in-law had told her it would make her ill, drive her demented, if she didn't loosen her ties with Marion. But she couldn't just abandon her. She wanted to help. If Brenda could do anything to give her peace of mind, she would, but there was nothing. Only listening. She had managed to create a bigger gap between their meetings, by having this or that prior engage-ment or family commitment, or pleading the need to work late, so it was almost a fortnight since the last time they had had supper together. Her conscience wouldn't let her leave it any longer.

And it must be terrible. Brenda had imagined it enough times, put herself in Marion's place. No one had the right to criticise her for dwelling on it, having it at the front of her mind every morning when she woke up. It was just – wearying for everyone else.

Marion was waiting for her, as always, their glasses of Chablis already ordered. It was quiet at this time – just two other tables occupied. She took a few moments to get out of her jacket, put her bag at her feet, pick up the menu, raise her glass to Marion and take a drink, because she needed to settle, and because she wanted to put off just for a few minutes the inevitable launch into the same subject. Same old. Marion was looking pent-up, as if she had the first sentences ready formed in her mouth and was breathless with the need to let them out. It was never very relaxing.

To give herself five minutes Brenda started on a story of her own, not a very interesting story, about an incident at work when Lauren had slipped and fallen down the steep stairs and lain at the bottom in a heap for several minutes while everyone rushed around, and Mr Dodsworth was showing a client out and didn't know whether to carry on, go back, rush down to Lauren and . . .

'And then she got up and laughed and she hadn't even ricked an ankle. She will wear those stupid wedge shoes. Can you see the specials board, Marion? It's a bit out of focus from here.'

She wanted to keep the subject of Kimberley at bay for as long as she could, so after the menu question, she embarked on last night's *Master Chef* and why the person sent home first should never have left, not in a million years.

In this way, things were moved along until they had their smoked mackerel and country-style pâté in front of them.

'It was five years ago to the day,' Marion said. 'When I went back to the police station.'

The anniversary of the day Kimberley disappeared, though she thought she was the only person who remembered. Brenda clearly had not. As she spoke the words, Marion saw a look flash across her friend's face, a look of – what? Weariness? 'Here we go again'? Embarrassment? She didn't know or care.

'Five years,' she said again. Brenda stared down at her plate.

'It isn't just a day, a date. It's more than that. It was a big shove in the back, you know? I can't let it go. I have to nag and nag and nag until they start again, Brenda. The other day, I read about some murder in the North that had been solved after forty-two years. FORTY-TWO! The man who did it is long dead, but they went on, until they pinned it on him. Well, this is only five years. What's five? Why have they put it away in a drawer and closed it?'

Brenda's eyes remained on her plate.

'I've decided I'm going to see him.'

'See who?'

'I can't bear his name in my mouth. You know who I mean.'

Brenda laid down her knife. 'If it's who I think you mean, Marion, you can't. You just can't.'

'Yes I can. I know which prison he's in.'

'No, that's not the point.'

'He murdered my daughter. We know that.'

'Well . . .'

'I thought you were my friend. I thought you were on my side.'

'I am. But this is different. Listen, yes, the police think he killed Kimberley, and yes, we all know that he probably did, but they didn't have the evidence. That's a fact, Marion, and you can't deny it. There is the probability, if you like, but there's no proof. Besides, what good do you think it would do, going in there and confronting him? What do you think you'd achieve?'

'Get him to confess.'

'He never would. He never has and he never will.'

'I could make him.'

Brenda reached out a hand and put it on Marion's, which was holding a fork and shaking so that she could neither use it nor put it down.

'No,' she said, 'put that out of your mind. It's going to eat away at you and you don't need it.'

'I didn't need my daughter murdered, I didn't need him to get off scot-free.'

'Hardly. He's in prison for life.'

'Only not for Kimberley.'

'I don't understand what difference that makes. If he confessed tomorrow, what difference would it make? It wouldn't –'

Marion's eyes were full of tears but they were angry tears and her voice was angry, bitter anger suffusing every word, though she spoke quietly.

'No,' she said, 'it wouldn't bring Kimberley back – do you think I don't know that? But it would be a resolution. I could die knowing it was settled.'

111

Brenda sighed and looked down at her plate again, at broken bits of toast and small smears of pâté. At a tomato and a sprig of parsley and a slice of lemon. The restaurant was filling up now. The pink-shaded lamps on the table, the smell of wine and grilled meat, the murmur of conversations, the air of comfort, of people enjoying themselves, the general sense of well-being seemed to shrivel and sour as Brenda sat silent, and Marion's tears continued. How could they carry on for the rest of the evening? What would they talk about now this impossible thing stood between them?

'There's another thing,' Brenda said, because it had just occurred to her and, in occurring, had come to her rescue. 'You wouldn't be able to see him because you don't just turn up at any prison for visiting hour, you have to apply, and it isn't the prison authorities who have to grant the application, it's the prisoner. They can choose to see you or not. It's their decision, Marion, not yours, not anyone else's.'

'That can't be right.'

'Well, it is right. I happen to know it.'

'I'll apply then.'

'And you honestly think he'd agree to a visit from you? Come on.'

'He ought to. He ought to be made to.'

'Nevertheless. I know he's a prisoner but he does have a few choices left and this is one.'

Marion started to cry in earnest now, ugly, unchecked tears that made her gulp and catch her breath, her nose ran and her face flushed, and still she went on crying. Brenda saw that the waitress was standing a few yards away, about to take their empty plates and not knowing whether to move forward or step back. Frozen with confusion and embarrassment.

Twenty-one

'I need your help,' the voice said, but it came over as 'If feed shelf . . .'

'Who is this speaking?'

'Sheevon.'

'Hold on, let me walk up the slope a bit, it's sometimes better there.' Serrailler did so, but when he put the phone to his ear, there was only a hissing sound and then abrupt silence.

'Effin mobile signal.'

Sam said from the doorway. 'I made some coffee.'

'Great, thanks. God knows who it was, I couldn't make any sense of it.'

They sat down at the kitchen table. Sam had put out the pot of coffee, milk and a plate of Kirsty's chocolate brownies, dropped off at the front door by Douglas just after dawn.

'She likes feeding me up,' Simon said. 'Thinks I'm too thin.'

Sam looked at his plate and said, 'She's pretty. Really.'

'She is. And a delightful woman and safely married.'

'Safely?'

Simon didn't answer.

'You mean if she'd been free she'd have been a threat to your safe single life?'

'No.'

'You'd have done OK.'

'Living up here? I don't think so.'

'You always skip sideways.'

'Does *your* mobile work here?'

'There you go again.'

'I'd better go over to the pub, see if anyone's left a message. You coming?'

'Bloody hell, it's like living in the 1950s. I got a signal on the top road the other day . . . well, half a bar.'

But Simon was on his way to the door.

'It was probably the doc,' Sam said, whisking the car keys away and climbing into the driver's seat.

'That's why I want to pick up any message now. I can drive with this arm, you know. Don't you feel safe with me any longer?'

'Yes, I just love driving this. You feeling insecure, being disabled?'

'Fuck it, Sam, sometimes you push it too far. No, I feel perfectly normal. I've got a very clever fully functioning arm, thanks to the brilliant prosthetic engineers, and in a month or two I'll have one so state-of-the-art I'll be able to pick up a pin in my fingers. I do not feel insecure, I feel bloody lucky. They saved my life, so what's an arm?'

'Between friends.'

'Watch it!'

A sheep had wandered across the road within a few yards of them. Sam braked, swerved and skidded, righted the car and continued.

'Would he be able to tell if she drowned herself?' he asked after a silent couple of miles.

'Not sure . . . certainly he will know if she died of drowning, which she almost certainly did – that's the easy bit. Other factors come into play when recording a suicide verdict – known state of mind, any note or other communication left to anyone, things like coat pockets full of heavy stones to weight herself down . . . but I'm no medic. What do you think?'

Sam shrugged. 'You knew her, I didn't.'

'True, but you were very possibly the last person to see Sandy alive, so if she was in a state of mental distress . . .'

Sam looked at Simon in shock. 'Do you think that's likely? That no one else saw her after she dropped me off that night?'

114

'It's possible, Sambo. She lived alone, it was late . . . and a filthy night. No one would be likely to call then . . . maybe the next morning, who knows, but when it was first noticed she hadn't been around for a bit someone would have said if they'd been to the house that morning.'

'Jeez. What will happen?'

'If you were thought to be the last person? Nothing, except you may have to give evidence at the inquest. Don't worry about that – it'll be short and formal and the chances are the coroner will return a verdict of taking her own life by drowning.'

'They might think I'd killed her.'

'Why on earth would they think that? You mean you might have left me once I'd gone to bed, walked through a storm and a howling gale to a house you didn't know, gone in and . . . and what? Knocked her on the head and dragged her down a steep path to the sea, in pitch darkness? And what would your motive have been?'

'OK.'

But even so, Sam remained silent for the rest of the way.

Iain gave a short laugh. 'If I were a betting man . . . Do you want the phone before or after the drink?'

There were half a dozen in the bar. Sam slipped over to a far table.

'In case you're wondering, it's everyone – there's been damage to the mast or some of the usual nonsense. Mobiles are nae use out here, they really are not. You've had three calls, all wanting to leave messages, or wanting me to hike off and find you, as if I'd the time.'

'Sorry, Iain. I'll have a pint of Cluny, and Coke for Sam and what you're having.'

'No need, thanks all the same. There's Lorna off the phone now, away and grab it before someone else does. Here.'

He held out half an envelope with names and numbers.

Dr Murray. Kieron. Richard.

He started with the pathologist and got voicemail. Left a message. Richard? He couldn't think of a Richard. He rang Kieron.

'Chief Constable's office.'

'This is Simon Serrailler. I got a message to call the Chief.'

'Ah, I'm sorry, he's out at the meeting, he has a dinner this evening, and I've no idea what he wanted you for, I'm afraid – he didn't tell me anything.'

'Right . . . thanks. Will you tell him I'll ring tomorrow? No point in him calling my mobile, the whole island's off signal. Or he can email me. That seems to be working.'

'I'll do that. Thank you.'

He went back to Sam, who had finished his Coke, got another, and was flipping through the *Sun*.

'Rubbish paper,' Simon said.

'Sure is. Get everyone?'

'No one.'

'Simon,' Iain shouted across. 'Doc's on the phone again.'

'I take it you're still in charge,' the pathologist said. 'You know about the business over on the mainland?'

'I heard they can't spare a man. Some drug-smuggling. But I'm fine to hold this end. Do you have any results for me?'

'Aye and one or two surprises. Can you get over here?'

'Next ferry leaves in twenty minutes, I'll catch that. Where do I come?'

'I'll meet you.'

Dr Murray was waiting on the jetty when the ferry docked, in the usual battered jeep relied upon by those who had to get about and no fuss, in all seasons and weathers.

They drove about a mile and then parked in front of a Victorian building which looked like a school but was in fact the old cottage hospital. That had been transferred, along with the local primary school, to a modern building to the west of the town.

'We're the path lab, the mortuary and the records office, and behind is the procurator fiscal's office. We've been pressing for more space and modern facilities for years but we're no likely to get them. Come in.'

They had reached the entrance via a short flight of semicircular stone steps and now walked down the inevitable cream-painted corridor, with high sash windows set along it, to a pair of doors declaring 'No Unauthorised Entrance'.

The usual mortuary smell. Disinfectant and chemicals of a very particular kind. Formaldehyde. And something else. The smell of death which nothing could ever stifle or disguise. And yet Serrailler knew that it was not really there. Death in here had already been sanitised, rendered neutral. Death had been wiped clean, distanced from its former self, which had been life, and plunged into the maelstrom of that huge change in its every molecule. Death was not death here. And yet it was not life either. Death was a medical matter, an anonymity, an object robbed of personality and status. Death had been taken over and dealt with.

He had never found the pathologist's theatre of work alarming or repellent. In some ways, he found it rather beautiful, in the way that all ritual was beautiful. There was always respect, always formality. Rules were adhered to, routine followed. There was never any place for informality, for creativity, for making it up on the spot, for diversion. A post-mortem had a pattern, and a shape. A form.

Murray had sent the assistant out. 'We've no but the one,' he said. 'Yesterday I had three. Small boy went under the wheels of a sheep transporter. His dad's.' He shook his head.

Never let anyone say these men grow callous and cynical, that they have seen it all and can no longer feel anything, that they are medical automatons, that each dead body means as little to them as the last and the one before that.

'I knew them. This is it – you live in a small community. You suffer with it.'

He shook his head again.

'You can stand over there if you prefer.'

'I'm fine.'

'Surprising how many policemen aren't. Right, Peter.'

Serrailler watched as the mortuary assistant wheeled in the sheeted body. He and the doctor slid it onto the examination table and then Murray beckoned Simon closer. He first rolled the sheet down to reveal the face and neck.

Sandy looked as they all looked. Wiped clean, as if death had taken not only the breath which was life but the person, the personality, the essence, leaving a blank, for all there was still a face with features, and those features spelled her name.

It was Sandy. But Sandy was no longer there.

'Still the same ID?'

'Yup. That's her.'

'Right. Let's turn, please.'

They turned, so that Sandy was now lying face down. The long hair had been cut and the head shaved. But it was the neck the doctor pointed at.

'See there?'

Simon bent over, looked. Whistled softly.

'Not suicide then,' he said.

What he saw was a wound where a bullet had entered. It was precisely placed to kill in one.

'Do you have any idea of the type of gun yet?'

'Not exactly, but of course it wasn't a rifle or the head would have been blown off – and rifles are the only legitimate guns owned by the islanders. It could be a Glock but I'm not a ballistics expert. I've emailed pictures, I'll get a firm ID from Glasgow, maybe tomorrow if I'm lucky. I presume that will tell you more.'

'No one has hit her while meaning to take out a rabbit. This is a revolver.'

'Which means the killing was deliberate.'

'And probably carefully planned. I doubt if anyone on Taransay owns that sort of lethal weapon – if they do, they'll have kept it well hidden. But why would they? Any other injuries?'

'Nothing serious – some scrapes and minor cuts on the hands and head – bumped against a rock or whatever. Body was dead when it went into the sea.'

'I have been on the island before now – know it quite well, so far as any incomer ever can – and I can imagine brawls – I've seen a few on a Saturday night. But it's a close community . . .'

'They all are and no worse for it.'

118

'No. And I can't imagine anyone who would murder Sandy. She was popular . . . bit of a loner but she pulled her weight, she'd become part of the island. Why would anyone kill her?'

Murray looked at him in silence for a moment, then gestured to the assistant to help him turn the body over and take off the sheet.

'This didn't entirely surprise me, given one or two other features, but it may come as a shock to you.'

Sandy. Still unmistakably Sandy. Dead. Lying on her back.

His back.

Twenty-two

To s.serrailler@police.gov.uk
From chief.bright@police.gov.uk

Hope it's good with you and at least better than here. Serial arson on the menu and counting. As you're in the quiet, crime-free land of sea and sky, I'd be grateful if you could open this up and let me have your thoughts. The mother wants the case reinvestigated. I am attaching a Zip file of everything re Kimberley Still's disappearance and ongoing. Also, background to Lee Russon ditto. This has had to go on the back burner as we're short-handed and the arson plus the usual is occupying everyone. No time for cold cases but Mrs Still doesn't know that.

It's pretty clear to me Russon did abduct and murder Kimberley, pretty certain we'll never prove it. But if there's anything in here, might just be worth our while interviewing him again. But early days. When are you back? All well here, fires aside. Cat has something new – she'll tell you. May not work out. I'm ambivalent. Is Sam still there? No word for a few days.

All best, K

Twenty-three

He had sent Sam a text saying that he was liaising with the local police – such as there were – and discussing his own position in what was now a murder inquiry. He'd be back on the last ferry, and meanwhile, Sam should pick up something for supper from the shop – eggs and frozen chips easiest. It was hit or miss whether he'd get it with the terrible reception.

He had not told his nephew about the further complication.

The police were stretched thin dealing with the drug smugglers.

'We've no bodies to spare you,' the DI Simon met had said. 'I've the official OK to leave you as SIO on this one – anything you can find out pass it over. Can you do the usual interviews – where last seen, who with, anything unusual reported and so on? We'll have to rely on you to progress everything and we'll send someone over as soon as we can. But I'm afraid you're on your own for the foreseeable. OK with that?'

Simon saw the DI glance at his arm.

'Fine,' he said.

He would go home, shower, change, then to the pub, and ask Iain if he could set up a mini-inquiry room in the snug, which was little used except on busy Friday and Saturday nights. He could ask questions there for the next few hours, as locals came and went, try to build up a picture – though he was pretty sure it would be more of a faint sketch. Once he had talked to the landlord and whoever came in first, he knew the others would turn up in the course of the day.

*

Loud music came through the open window of the spare bedroom.

'Drop it a bit, Sam.'

Sam did. Just.

'Thought you were out helping Douglas.'

'Didn't feel like it.'

Simon stopped on his way to the bathroom. 'Not the way you usually are.'

'No, well. What happened anyway?'

'Tell you about it when I've cleaned up. Have we got anything to eat?'

'Eggs. Bread's a bit elderly.'

'Can you make a start?'

Sam didn't move.

The water flowed cold, then boiling hot, before settling for lukewarm. It was one of the trickiest things, taking a shower. Baths were not much easier. Simon looked at the top of his left arm, from which no arm now grew. The skin and flesh had healed, but even though the prosthesis fitted well – far better than those people had had to put up with until the last few years – there was still the inevitable chafing until it all hardened and toughened. He had to clean it and rub creams into it morning and night. But the angry redness had faded. It was settling down.

He remembered every time he looked at it how lucky he had been, how he had got away with the loss of one arm, instead of his life. He had been in pain, he had been frustrated and angry and tired of it, but he had never once asked why. 'Why me? Why this?'

Because there was a clear answer. It was the people struck down by random illnesses, not attacked by deranged criminals, who were haunted by that question. As a cop, even in CID, he put himself in the line of fire every working day, they all did. Given the level of danger out there it was only surprising it didn't happen more.

It took time to make sure his arm was thoroughly dry. If it wasn't he was asking for trouble.

Sam was whisking up eggs and frying tomatoes when he finally went back downstairs.

'Good man.'

'Sorry – no bacon or anything. I'm toasting the bread.'

'That's fine.'

Nothing else was said until they sat down, the food in front of them.

'OK,' Sam said with his mouth full. 'So?'

Simon told him, about the bullet hole first. The easy bit.

'I knew it. I mean, I didn't but . . . it was just peculiar. Didn't you think?'

'Of course I thought. I'm a policeman. I'm CID. It's what I do all the time. With any dead body, it's always a possibility – sometimes a very remote one, sometimes barely one at all, because all the evidence points in another direction, but it has to be in your mind. With Sandy though – it wasn't my first or even my second possibility, I admit.'

Sam had put down his knife and fork and was looking at him. 'Who the fuck? WHO?'

'No idea, for now. Possibly it's a why before it's a who.'

Sam shook his head. 'You'd think this was the safest place on earth, this island.'

'And you'd be pretty much right, in terms of violent crime. This is way out of the norm.'

'What do you know about her? Sandy? Did anyone know anything?'

It was Simon's turn to stop eating. He hesitated. Strictly speaking, this was unethical, but his nephew had taken to Sandy, and Simon was genuinely interested in his reaction to the news that Sandy had been a man. He had no idea what it might be. Surprise, surely, but after that . . . shock? Disgust?

What he would never have expected was laughter. Sam stared across the table and for a split second there was no reaction at all, but then he let out a shout of laughter, and punched the air.

'Bloody hell . . . good for Sandy . . . that'll stir up the Wee Free. Bloody HELL! Alexander not Sandra . . . and thinking about it, you know . . . well, I barely met her – him – just on the journey here and it was focus on the weather and my state . . . but looking back, it figures. Yup. Never cross your mind, Si?'

'No.'

Sam was still chortling as he finished his plate of eggs and toast, but then stopped quite suddenly and went quiet. 'Only . . . Sandy was murdered. Doesn't really matter, does it – who or what, man or woman . . . someone shot him. And not by accident instead of a rabbit. I mean – sod it. No one should have their life ended that way.'

'No.'

They sat, thinking, going over it, trying to make sense of it. It was a quiet night. There was always some wind on Taransay but it was so faint now it could barely be heard down the chimney and the window catches did not rattle, the curtains hung still.

'Oh, and I thought I'd be moving on from here, maybe tomorrow or the day after.'

'Going home?'

'No. Maybe join up with a couple of friends in London – least that's where they were last I heard.'

'London,' Simon said. 'What to do, Sam?'

'You know . . . meet up.'

'Just meet up?.'

Sam looked puzzled.

'And when you've met up? What then?'

Silence.

'Have you got enough money to get to London?'

'Oh. No. I thought . . .'

Simon stood up and collected the plates. 'Well, you thought wrong, Sambo. You couldn't even be bothered to get out there to give Douglas a hand again and he could do with it, Kirsty's sick every day at the moment, she can't do much to help until she's over it. So don't expect me to put my hand in my pocket for you to doss off to London.'

'So I've got to stay here then?'

'No. Did you get return ferry and train tickets when you came here?'

'Er . . .'

'Thought not. OK, I'll give you money for your tickets back. And I mean, back to Lafferton. Either that or stay here and work.'

He had never spoken to Sam like that – he had never needed to. Sam wasn't lazy or a sponger, he had always been an eager, active, cheerful boy, but he was not a boy any longer, he was a troubled young man who was unsure where his future lay or what step he wanted to take towards it. Perhaps he should have gone easy on him, even though he was not a soft touch for money to join whoever in London.

Iain was happy to have him set up in the snug, and there were five regulars drinking to whom he could talk first, including Douglas, but also Fergal Morne, whose farm was the nearest occupied dwelling to Sandy's cottage. Fergal was deaf, son of a father and grandfather who had also sheep-farmed in the same place, and who also had been deaf. He was married with a daughter, whose hearing was perfect, and dreaded having another, for fear it would be a boy who might carry the gene. Fergal wore hearing aids though they still left him listening to the speech of others as through a wall of cotton wool. But he was good at reading both lips and expressions.

'It was a big shock, Sandy . . . big shock. Never thought she'd do that to herself, I tell you. Good woman – good neighbour, though I never went inside the house, no once. She came to us.'

'Did she talk about herself, Fergal? Before she came here – you know where she lived, what she'd done, family, all of that?'

Fergal's face registered that he was listening, taking in what Simon said, working out the questions but slowly, carefully, and it was only when he had thought that it became animated again.

'No. She said nothing, ever. Very private woman, Sandy . . . though I never grasped that she'd any secrets, anything bad, you understand? She went out a fair bit. She'd walked the length and breadth of Taransay many a time. Saw her down on the beaches or across the top. Aye, she was fit and active.'

'When did you see her last?'

'Maybe four days ago. Day the last storm brewed up.'

'Where?'

'In the stores, and then she was driving her jeep homewards and we passed – you have to stop for one another, you know how it is – we waved. Nothing else.'

'How did she look?'

Fergal shrugged. 'As usual.'

'Did she always go off on her own, over the island?'

'All the time. I used to think she'd nine lives, she was always scrambling down the cliffs and setting up a rock fall or coming back fast to outrun the tide or something of that nature. Wild woman. Aye, Iain said she'd as many lives as a cat. Only she ran out of luck.'

'Did she have any visitors?'

'We didnae watch her house through the net curtains all day.'

'I'm sure you didn't but you must have been aware of any visitors.'

'No, I wasn't . . . which doesn't mean there were none, you ken?'

'Sure. Was there anything different about her last time you met? Did she seem worried about anything . . . a bit preoccupied maybe?'

'Not that I noticed. But we didn't stop to talk much.'

'Fine. Now if there's anything at all you can remember, however small, let me know, will you? It might be important, Fergal – people don't always realise and they dismiss some little thing. Anything you remember that seemed . . . not quite as usual, not right, about Sandy, her house, her vehicle . . . anything. Don't feel awkward about it, and never think you'll be wasting my time or anyone else's.'

'There's nothing. But I'll do as you ask, I'll certainly do that.'

And so it went on. No one had seen or heard anything or anyone. Nothing out of the ordinary, nothing rang a bell . . . it was all the more strange because the island was so sparsely populated and yet so close-knit. No matter that they lived scattered around, they looked out for one another and everyone knew what went on. But about Sandy – nothing.

126

Only one thing came up, but although he racked his brains about it, Serrailler could not for the life of him work out why it seemed in some way significant. But it did.

Derry Muir delivered everything there was to deliver round the entire island – stuff that had been ordered from the store or off the ferry, mostly to those who could not come to the quay and collect it themselves, maybe because they were too old or infirm or their vehicle was out of action. Derry had not known Sandy any better than the rest, because she always fetched her own stuff, but they had chatted in the bar, and once, a month or so ago, Sandy had helped to tow his van out of a pothole near her house. She'd asked him in for a mug of tea and they had discovered a mutual passion for curling. Derry and his wife both took part, travelling to competitions between different leagues on the mainland, and Sandy said she had lived in Canada for three years in her early twenties, and discovered the sport there. They had talked about it until Derry had been an hour behind, and after that, he had called and taken her some curling magazines. He had even suggested she come with him and Monica one time to watch and even start playing again. Sandy had been non-committal.

'I don't see how it could have to do with anything – the curling. Or Canada.'

'Neither do I, but thanks, Derry. It could mean something.'

But what the hell that was Simon had no idea, though it stayed in his mind and he gnawed at it over and over. Because there was nothing else. No visitors to Sandy. No vehicles. She had always come and gone at strange times, so seeing her walking across the moor or the beach at nine in the evening or clambering down the cliff path as dawn broke was not regarded as unusual. She had been her familiar self. The last time anyone in the village had seen her had been on the night of the storm, when she left the pub with the inebriated Sam, to give him a lift home. And so far, it still seemed likely that Sam had been the last person to see Sandy before she was killed.

Twenty-four

Cat had made a risotto and gooseberry fool. There had been a bottle of New Zealand Sauvignon and then Kieron had left them together while he went into the den to watch a crucial football match. He and Luke had got on well in the end, though Cat had noticed with an amusement she kept to herself that Kieron had begun the evening by being his most formal self and had eyed Luke's suit and richly coloured Missoni tie with some suspicion. But once he had satisfied himself that Luke had no interest in his wife whatsoever except in the way of good long-standing friends, nor she him, they had discovered plenty of things in common, not including football, and Cat had sat back and listened to them.

But Luke had come to talk business to her. She had invited him home because she wanted him to meet Kieron outside the less relaxed atmosphere of the hotel or a restaurant. And home was the best place to talk about work and the future. She made coffee and Luke opened his iPad on which were a draft website, brochure, financial forecasts and legal disclaimers and conditions. He handed it to Cat and then leaned over, picked up Wookie from his seat on the end of the sofa, and put him on his lap.

'Careful – he bit Kieron the other day.'

'This isn't a vicious dog, this is a little pussy cat.'

'And you're a stranger to him. Kieron's one of the family.'

But she saw that Wookie had settled down, curled into a ball and gone back to sleep. Luke was stroking him.

'We provide high-quality, personal general practice delivered to your home in a caring, professional and discreet manner.

We choose to care for significantly fewer patients than traditional general practitioners, enabling us to spend that extra time understanding you and your medical needs. As a practice member, you will have unlimited access to the advice, support and reassurance of your own private doctors 24 hours a day, every day of the year.

We provide all that you would expect from your GP, delivered in a convenient and timely way. Whatever your health needs may be, we're here to help.

We're a completely independent service covering Lafferton and its surrounding areas. We've restored the traditional 'doctor's house call' to the forefront of personal family medicine, rekindling that often lost relationship between doctor and patient. You and your family will always be cared for promptly and professionally by experienced local doctors whom you know and trust.

Our practice has been developed to focus completely on the health and well-being of our members. Enjoy a completely new approach and discover how medicine can be delivered in a caring, convenient and responsive way.'

Cat looked up.

'How much do people pay?'

'I want to keep this as reasonable as possible . . . we'll save a lot by not having a bricks-and-mortar practice. We employ someone to do the office work, but there won't be an office . . . we travel everywhere, see everyone in their own home. No surgery overheads.'

'How much?'

'Individual membership around £100 a month, couples £150, family £175 no matter how many so long as they are related and live in the same house.'

'Do they remain registered with an NHS GP?'

129

'We would recommend it, because of emergency hospital admissions and so on. Once you've left the system it's not always easy to get back in.'

'How big an area would we be covering?'

'Depends. There would be three of us initially and we'd divide it quite simply according to where we start from. You'd consult by Skype, email and phone as well – not everything needs a visit but we'd go if the patient preferred it – a lot of older people probably would.'

'And those with new babies.'

'And some would want to see a female doctor. We'd try to oblige but it won't always be possible.'

'Emergencies?'

'If we're called at 2 a.m. because someone on the other side of the area has chest pains or fallen downstairs, obviously they should call an ambulance and we'd tell them that. No private A&E, as you know.'

'What about palliative care?'

'To be discussed. That's where your input will be crucial.'

'Luke . . . I haven't said I'll do it.'

'Yet.'

'I've thought about it and talked to Kieron – not that he's remotely clued up about anything to do with medicine, other than being a hypochondriac. But it would impact on our time together.'

'My guess is that you'd have more of that.'

'Possibly. But I'm only a part-time GP at the moment so I'm here evenings, weekends – that would change.'

'It won't be going back to the old days of being on call, Cat – we didn't do email and phone consultations, and if patients demanded a home visit at 2 a.m. for a hangnail, we were legally obliged to go.'

'My patients weren't often so unreasonable. But there are other things . . .'

She set down the iPad and was quiet for a while. Luke continued to stroke Wookie, who was snoring softly.

She knew that the idea was a good one and knew that it would be perfect for her. She had always liked home visits.

They gave her time to get a full picture of the patient, to listen to them, to assess things more calmly. She would like being free of a packed surgery with ten minutes per appointment and panic if one person had to take twenty. She was happy driving, she agreed that many consultations could safely be made over the phone, on Skype or by email when there was also the backup of a visit if it then seemed necessary. Having fewer patients on the list meant giving them more time and attention, and she would be free of the admin that was the bane of every GP's life.

'But . . .' Luke said.

'Chris would have divorced me for even thinking about it. He would say it was totally unfair and unjust that people who could pay would get access to better medicine, that money shouldn't talk . . .'

Luke went on stroking Wookie. He said nothing. He simply waited.

Cat had not cried for her first husband, father of their three children, for a long time but now it was impossible to stop the tears. She had a vivid picture of him, curled up on their bed, her arms round him, dying of an inoperable brain tumour, too young, with too much still to give and enjoy, too much love and life.

Luke put his hand over hers. 'Don't worry. There's no hurry, you need to think it through. And I understand – I knew him too, remember. Chris was a fine doctor and he had principles he never wavered from . . . The thing is, Cat – this isn't a question of things for the rich that the poor can't get. A friend of mine runs a private practice like this – they were the first. And yes, they have some well-heeled patients, but they also have people who use some of their pension money, or their savings, because they want consistent reliable care. General practice is in crisis for all sorts of reasons, we know that, and especially as people get older they want peace of mind about their health. More ordinary people can afford this than you might think. £1,200 a year . . . think of that in terms of a holiday. I'm not doing this to get rich – I'll be happy if I can eventually earn what I've earned in the NHS. I guess you would be too.'

Cat blew her nose and got up to make more coffee. At the sink, she splashed cold water onto her face. She would go on thinking Luke's plan through. There were the details, the small print. There was Kieron's input. All of that.

But she knew. She already knew what her answer would be.

When she returned to the sofa, the old cat Mephisto had come in and was pressed against Luke, purring, and Wookie was still firmly settled on his lap. Kieron put in a brief appearance to get a beer at half-time and ask if anyone else wanted one. And as he did so, Cat had a strange and quite unexpected sense of finally letting Chris go, and, with him, so much that she had been clinging to for so long – and that it was with his blessing.

Twenty-five

Serrailler put Sam on the ferry and went across to the pub. It was just after six and the bar was empty. Iain was changing the optics.

'If you're wanting the snug again, that's fine – Tuesday's always quiet. Can I get you a dram? On the house. It might be for all the wrong reasons but you've brought a few folk in, and when they're parched after talking to you, they've come through here.'

'Not just now, thanks . . . I'll maybe take it from you another day. I'm glad you're empty, Iain. There's something I need to ask you.'

Iain looked at Simon oddly. 'Not me,' he said. 'I've only a rifle and it's fully licensed, and in any case, when do I ever get the time to go shooting?'

'That wasn't what I was going to ask. Though she could have been shot with a rifle of course.'

'That makes no sense. You know what a person looks like after that. Whoever found her . . . whoever saw her first . . . they wouldnae have been in any doubt. But you hear me, Simon . . . I'm very sorry for it. Maybe some out there in the world deserve it, but not her. Not Sandy.' He had wiped the bar counter clean but still went on pushing the cloth to and fro. 'And you're no further forward? You've no one in mind?'

'I've just been asking questions – and getting some useful answers.'

'In what way do you mean useful?' Iain turned and took a double malt. 'Your health,' he said, and downed it. Simon was surprised. He had never seen Iain take more than a few sips from a pint, kept on the side of the bar and lasting him all evening.

'Did you ever have any thoughts of your own about Sandy? Where she came from, her life before here?'

'Who didn't? We've all got a past. People learn not to ask too many questions. You'll know that yourself.'

No, Simon thought. They didn't ask newcomers direct questions because they did their best to find out in other ways. They watched and listened and talked among themselves and put two and two together. But so far as he knew, no one had made five out of this one – or even the correct four.

'You never noticed anything about her? Didn't you once think she was, I don't know, a bit different?'

'Well, of course she was different. You met her, talked to her . . . she wasnae like anyone else on the island because she wasn't an islander. But she was always willing to lend to hand. She came in here several times a week, she helped with the unloading, she'd give anyone a day's work who needed it, and never accepted anything but a joint of lamb for the freezer or a home-made cake, maybe. She'd talk to anyone in here, friend or stranger, she'd have a joke, she'd have a dram, she'd come to the ceilidh and she'd come to the quiz. She never went to the chapel but she'd dance at a wedding and wet a baby's head. She was as near one of us as can be without being one of us. I tell you, Simon, I'm as upset about what happened as I would be if it had been one of my family. And it's not just that she's dead. It's knowing she was shot. That's what's shaken me. Shot dead.'

It was the longest speech Simon had ever heard the man make.

And now he was going to shake Iain again.

'You should keep this to yourself for now.'

Iain stopped what he was doing and looked across the bar and there was something in his look Serrailler couldn't interpret . . . a challenge, a defiance? Why would that be?

The wind was getting up again, blowing against the side of the building, the west wind that would rise and rise and might not die down for a week or more. They both listened to it. But Iain was watching his face.

In four words, Simon told him.

Twenty-six

'I want to speak to the Chief Constable please.'

'I'll put you through to his office.'

Did they know it was her? Did they have some special police way of seeing who was calling, even though she knew how to screen out her number? Because it was barely a split second before 'I'm sorry, the line's engaged, can you call back please?'

'No, I'll hold on.'

'It could be a long time, they're very busy this afternoon.'

'I don't mind. I've nothing more important to do. There isn't anything more important, actually.'

There was the usual jingle that went on a loop. Not proper music. Just a stupid jingle. Then a recorded voice, thanking her for holding and then telling her how many road accidents were caused each year by drink-drivers and then more jingle, and then explaining that she should not dial 999 unless her call to the emergency services was indeed a genuine emergency but instead to call . . .

'Line's still busy, I'm afraid. Do you want to continue to hold?'

She waited twenty minutes before the secretary spoke to her and then of course Mr Bright was out all day and she would take a message but she had no idea when he would get back to her, perhaps someone else . . . ?

She put the telephone down, and as she did so, something happened. Instead of going with the sense of disappointment and of being brushed off that usually overwhelmed her at these moments, Marion felt a strength and a new determination rising in her, at the same time as an entirely new idea formed. Why it had never struck her before that she could and would do this she did not know, but she wasn't going to waste time on those ruminations. It didn't matter. It had occurred to her, flashing like a brilliant light, and she acted upon it.

'Newsroom.'

'Oh. I'm not sure if I have the right . . . I want to speak to someone who'll come round and talk to me. I've got . . . well, I suppose it's a story only it probably isn't news. Not new news, if you follow.'

'Right. Maybe if you tell me what it's about briefly, I can either carry on with it or put you through to the right person. Who am I speaking to?'

'Mrs Still . . . Marion Still . . . mother of Kimberley Still.' A beat. But why should she know?

And then, 'Kimberley Still . . . Excuse me, there's no good way of putting it . . . the Kimberley Still who went missing and could have been murdered?'

Her name was Dorcas Brewer and she was at Marion's house in Mountfield Avenue within the hour. Marion had made tea and put out the fresh ginger cake she had bought at the new bakery the previous day.

'It's very good of you to come so quickly. I hadn't expected that.'

'You sounded worried.'

She was an exceptionally tall young woman, with very short hair dyed pink. But it had been well done, Marion thought. It suited her. It didn't look common, as she had always judged brightly coloured hair to be, it looked smart. She wore an orange trench coat. Pink and orange? But that looked good, too.

She didn't have a notebook, she had a mobile phone which would record their conversation, and when they first started, Marion found that it inhibited her. She kept glancing at it, wondering what her own voice sounded like, wondering if she had just said the wrong thing. But the girl was very relaxed and friendly without being too pushy, she drank two cups of tea with sugar, ate a slice of the cake and helped herself to another. That made it so much better. Her sort of girl might have asked for black coffee and looked at cake with disdain.

'Just talk to me,' she said, leaning back in the armchair.

'It was this morning, when I rang the Chief Constable – Mr Bright, I don't know if you've met him – he did see me once, and I suppose I've to be grateful for that. He's a very busy man, I understand that, and he wasn't even in the job when Kimberley . . . yes, he saw me and he said he'd look into it all again.'

Marion poured herself another cup of tea and drank half of it before continuing. The reporter just smiled and waited, not asking endless questions, not being impatient. It was reassuring. It helped.

'But nothing's happened of course. I've tried to phone him twice since that day and this morning they kept me on hold for twenty minutes and I still didn't get to speak to him. I know, the police are all busy but it isn't any good just fobbing me off. I know he's in prison but he isn't in prison for Kimberley's murder, is he, and that's what matters to me. Can you see that, Miss Brewer?'

'Dorcas. Of course I can.' She leaned forward, hands on her knees, and looked Marion not only in the face but in the eyes. And her own eyes, deep brown eyes, were warm with sympathy. 'They have things they call "cold cases" – perhaps you know about them. They're often part of TV crime dramas – all it means is that a crime was committed some years ago and was never solved but they have run out of leads and –'

'Ideas.'

Dorcas smiled. 'In a word. They stop working on those cases but they don't close the book . . . they can't until they have someone to arrest and charge and that person is found guilty. Even if the person is dead, they can still be found guilty, and the case can be closed.'

'I wish he were dead. That's a terrible thing to say.'

'Is it? It seems highly likely that he murdered your daughter, Marion. I'd probably say the same. I can only struggle to imagine how it's been for you all this time. Of course the police have got a lot of work and they have new cases every day – but they don't actually have many murders. They have a duty to solve this one. How long is it – four years?'

'Nearly five.'

'Time for them to open it up and look at it again. A lot's happened since then.'

'Like what?'

Dorcas looked vague but still said, 'New techniques for examining evidence,' which impressed Marion Still.

'But what can we do . . . what can you do?'

'I think calling the police to account, reminding them about Kimberley, bringing everything to the full attention of the public all over again – all of that will actually do a great deal. They don't like to be wrong-footed, you know. They certainly don't like any sort of bad publicity and who can blame them? So here's a chance for them to show us they are going to pay more than lip service to what the Chief Constable said to you . . . let's shine some fresh daylight onto this.'

'I'LL NEVER REST UNTIL I GET JUSTICE FOR MY KIMBERLEY'

Mrs Marion Still tries to put on a brave face and she gives me tea and a slice of delicious ginger cake in her bright, immaculate semi-detached house in a pleasant part of Lafferton. There is a clock with a smiling sun face on the mantelpiece and cushions with 'The Cat Sleeps Here' and 'Beware Flying Pigs' on the comfy sofa. Mrs Still wears a blue cardigan and her hair has been freshly set. But when I look into her eyes, I see sadness, and next to the clock there is a photograph of a pretty girl whose own face is full of life and laughter.

'Yes,' her mother says, taking it down and handing it to me. 'That is my beautiful Kimberley. Who could have taken her life? Who could have done such a thing?'

Yet even as she asks the questions, she is certain that she knows the answer.

'She was murdered by Lee Russon,' she says firmly. 'He is in prison for the murder of two other girls and the police know he killed my Kimberley as well, everybody knows. But they say there wasn't enough evidence.' Her expression is angry, even though her eyes are brimming with tears.

When I ask her if she thinks the police did enough after Kimberley's murder, she says reluctantly, 'They worked very hard, I'm sure of that. They all did and of course they got Russon for the other killings, didn't they? Maybe they think that's enough – I mean, he's in prison for life so . . .' She pours us both another cup of tea and I look again at the photograph of her daughter.

'But what I'm asking is, why can't they start again? Why can't they look back, go over the whole thing? I know it's done, I've read about murders being pinned on the guilty person twenty or thirty years later, when something new has come to light. And that's been when they haven't even had anyone in mind as a clear suspect. Well, they've got one now, haven't they?'

I ask her if she wants revenge – and who would blame her for that? She fidgets with a corner of the tray cloth, but she says that it isn't a question of revenge.

'It's about justice . . . I want him to confess what he did, and if he won't, I want them to show him they know – that there *was* enough evidence, they just didn't find it.'

Who does this determined but broken-hearted woman feel is to blame for the fact that after five years no one has reopened the case?

'I don't know whose responsibility it was then so I couldn't say.' She hesitates. Until this moment, Marion Still has spoken quietly but now her voice rings loud and clear. 'I only know whose responsibility it is now. And that's the present Chief Constable. Mr Kieron Bright.'

She flushes, with anger and with pain, as she tells me that she has seen the Chief Constable in person and pleaded with him to reopen the case against Lee Russon.

'He was very pleasant,' she says without any irony. 'We had a cup of coffee, he couldn't have listened more carefully. But since then – nothing. He's done nothing.'

Has she tried to talk to Chief Constable Bright again?

'Oh yes. I've tried. I just get fobbed off. He's never there, they can't put me through. I was on the line twenty minutes yesterday. I asked for him to ring me back but of course he never did.'

She now despairs of anything happening. 'He's not interested,' she says to me, 'it was before his time. He doesn't see what it's like for me. I suppose I can't blame him.'

But I am well aware that she does. I can understand why. I would be asking the same questions.

Why do the police not reinvestigate the murder of lovely, bright-faced Kimberley Still, aged 24, who had everything to look forward to? Why do they not look to see if there is any new evidence, of whatever kind, against the man they must surely know killed Kimberley? Mrs Still says quietly that it is probably all down to money. 'They say they don't have the resources. That's terrible, don't you think? That justice is all about hard cash?'

She shows me out. In the hall, there is another photograph of Kimberley, this time as a laughing, pigtailed little girl of nine, dressed as Dorothy from *The Wizard of Oz*, at the Lafferton Jug Fair.

'She won first prize,' Marion Still says. And touches her finger gently to the photo. 'And let me tell you this. I won't leave them alone. I will pester and pester the police and anyone else to do with it. I won't rest until I get justice for my Kimberley.'

She means it.

Twenty-seven

Full house. Saturday afternoons usually were when it wasn't raining. A lot of the buggers couldn't be bothered in bad weather.

He'd got a table up against the wall, so that was a bonus. Only one next to you to listen in and this pair wouldn't, they were too busy having their own set-to and the set-to had been clocked. Any minute, the nearest warder would be over and warning them. What was the point in visiting and then starting up a row the minute you sat down?

He looked across his own table. He didn't have a missus. One less to worry about. This afternoon, Dave was here. Russon had four brothers. Alan never came near and Jim was on a container ship halfway to South America, so it was always either Lewis or Dave.

They said this and that for five minutes. 'Have you seen Dad?' 'How's the kid?' 'What are the Hammers messing about at?' 'I brought you some of your toffees.'

Then Dave said, 'I got something else,' and started fishing about in his pocket. He'd been searched, they'd opened the sheet of newspaper and shaken it, but papers and magazines were OK, not much you could hide in them unless you taped a packet inside somewhere, but Lee didn't do drugs and he didn't believe in having them for barter. A few things he thought were wrong, and drugs came top of his list. No one had ever got round to asking why murder was all right and coke wasn't. No one asked him much about anything.

Now Dave took the folded page out and handed it over. Lee looked at him.

'You can read it now if you want.'

'What is it?'

'Stuff about . . . you and that . . . Kimberley girl. Kimberley Still.'

Lee's expression went absolutely blank. He pulled the folded sheet towards him, and folded it again, and then again. Flattened it and put it in his trouser pocket. The warder was looking over. Lee pulled the paper out again, spread it, waved it at him. Turned it over. Turned it back.

The man switched his attention back to the pair next door.

The room was warm and smelled of people's bodies. There were kids, babies with dirty nappies and older ones with bags of cheese and onion crisps. Lee half closed his eyes. His brother leaned forward, elbows on the metal table.

'Remember Ash Alamba?'

'No.'

'Yeah, you do.'

'No.'

Dave sighed. 'Right. Don't matter.'

'What?'

'If you don't know who he is –'

'For Christ's sake, you've got to talk about something, so talk about this Ash guy.'

'Nicked a Jaguar and wrapped it round a tree and himself with it.'

Lee shrugged. 'It happens.'

'You want anything before the bell goes?'

'No.'

'You might. When you've read that paper.'

The couple next door suddenly kicked off so loudly that they stood up and the man turned the table over, shoving it towards the woman. Warders jerked to life, then the time bell went off.

Dave got up. 'Look after yourself.'

Lee rolled his eyes.

It was only after lock-up that he could sit down at his small table to spread out the newspaper page. He pulled open the bag of assorted toffees Dave had brought as well and which had twice given him painful visits to the prison dentist. He could only chew on his right side until he got the latest filling done but he put two rum and butters into his mouth at once and turned to the paper. It was still noisy out on the landings. Not that prison was ever quiet, just as it was never dark. Things like that got to you more than you'd expect and Lee Russon expected quite a lot. He was a lifer, which in his view was the punishment. There shouldn't be rubbish conditions and having to put up with crap like being locked in your cell three-quarters of the day because there weren't enough staff and being fed pigswill. And having lights boring in your face and metal doors clanging and boots going up and down metal staircases when you were trying to sleep. You had a right to sleep.

One thing he didn't mind was being on his own. For the first three years inside he'd shared with various other men, brain-dead, or druggies, or the sort that wanted to talk all day and half the night, the sort who wanted to get you involved in stupid schemes. He was happy with his own company – in the absence of the company of young women.

He liked reading. History. Napoleonic Wars. Third Reich. 1914–18. Early aeroplanes. World War II aircraft and missions. All of it. He could order up titles in the prison library and they'd try and get them. Mostly they did. He was studying as well – psychology and business. He'd more or less picked them with a pin out of a list and he didn't think he'd last much longer with psychology. It wasn't just difficult. It was a load of crap. Business studies weren't crap, they were useful. When he got outside again . . .

He never ever let himself think that he might not. That life would mean LIFE. It wouldn't. He was attending counselling sessions, he was able to prove that he no longer had fantasies about not only the company of young women but of raping and strangling them. The sessions were interesting. He began to get where the person who saw him was coming from and then he began to work out how he could give him what he wanted, and with understanding, and fathoming how it all worked, a plan was slowly forming. Slowly meant slowly. You couldn't barge at these things without any thought. You thought and thought, slowly, carefully and in detail, and you made your plans accordingly.

He spread out the newspaper page Dave had left him. Local lad getting gold in the Invictus Games. Kebab van owner selling horsemeat. He thought that's what they all did. A couple of fires in derelict buildings – arson suspected. Road closures. Bicycle accident. School given star ratings by Ofsted. Fucking hell, what was all this rubbish? Only the arson sounded fun. Made him wonder if one of his old cellmates was up to no good again. The way he used to describe how the flames went up in a big whoosh.

Then he turned over the page and saw it. Spread right across the middle.

'I'LL NEVER REST UNTIL I GET JUSTICE FOR MY KIMBERLEY.'

Her picture. Her daughter's picture. His bleedin' picture. The steep bank behind the canal. The overhanging scrubby bushes.

He could feel his own rage move up inside his body, like bubbles being pumped faster and faster through a tube, pulsing harder, strengthening. The rage started in the pit of his stomach, went up through his chest and into his throat and neck and head, swelling out and heating. If he checked in the shaving mirror he would be red in the face. His eyes would be bloodshot. The doctor had told him he had to control his rage or it would control him.

'Finish you off,' he had said. 'You will explode. Simple as that.'

He'd been given a sheet of breathing exercises, a list of twenty calming phrases. If he felt the rage so much as stir slightly in his toes he ought to reach for them.

He did the breathing stuff now and it made a bit of difference. He didn't want to explode. He'd always had a way out before, of course. He had been able to lance the rage like a boil, by doing what he did.

No chance here.

He took the sheet of paper and tore it, across and across and across, tore it into bits the size of confetti. His stubby fingers were sore, he put so much force into the tearing.

He threw the bits into the bin.

He cursed Kimberley Still's mother and the reporter and the paper, in the foulest words he knew, muttering them aloud so that they might be more effective. He would have yelled them at the top of his voice but that would have brought someone running.

But then, he reasoned, nobody would take any notice of her, not now, any more than they ever had. She could do what she liked, bleat, complain, write letters, get reporters round, even go on the bloody television. It would make no odds. They weren't going to reopen the case. Why would they bother? They had him anyway.

He had told them he hadn't done it plenty of times. Others. The two he was in for. Yes. But he'd said until he was blue in the face he was not confessing to Kimberley Still. No way. What difference would it make to him? He was banged up in here, he wasn't going anywhere, life meant life and they couldn't add to that, they'd no more idea than anyone else how long 'life' would be. He could 'explode' tomorrow, couldn't he?

He calmed down. Calm and peace. He could feel the last of the rage blowing away out to sea.

And then the idea came to him. He knew what he could do.

Twenty-eight

Richard Serrailler had never been a cook, or indeed any sort of a housekeeper, but he liked things to be orderly, and he enjoyed good food. He longed for a home-cooked dinner, and company for eating it. He missed Delphine, though he despised her for what she had done, continuing the relationship with her old boyfriend while staying in the cottage with him, and finally robbing him.

He felt morose. He could not focus on anything for long. He went for solitary, dismal walks and drank too much wine in the evenings.

It was on the day he caught himself pouring a third glass of Sauvignon at lunch that he knew he ought not to stay alone any longer.

The drive through France to the ferry port could be done in a day but he took the slower roads rather than speed down the toll motorways, stayed a night in a small hotel in the Dordogne and another in Normandy. He walked about the villages, sat at cafe tables in the evening sun, ate well, and felt a relief that he had made the decision to return. His only concern was where he could stay – Hallam House was let and the tenants had another couple of months there. But he felt lighter of heart than he had for a long time. He liked France but he did not belong there, any more than the rest of the expats he watched gathering in their groups in this or that cafe every day. The difference was that he knew it. He had never planned to see out his days there but Delphine had put a brake on future plans.

He sat on until the lamps shone out from the bars and cafes around the little square, enjoying a small, carafe of red, thinking that Cat would be pleasantly surprised when he turned up at the farmhouse front door. He wondered if he would see Simon, from whom he had not heard for some months. His son disappointed him. Even the third triplet, Ivo, was now married to an Australian nurse. They never saw him but he sent regular emails and photographs. He seemed in many ways to be a closer member of the family than Simon.

The waitress came to clear the tables. He offered her a drink but she was finishing in five minutes, she said, and ready for home. She smiled. And *'peut-être mon mari n'aime pas que j'accepte. Mais merci, monsieur, vous êtes très gentil.'*

The music was turned off inside the cafe. He got up, a little stiffly after the long drive, and went to walk round the village before going to his hotel.

It was clean, quiet and comfortable, but he slept badly, waking several times and having strange, flickering dreams, and when he woke he realised that he had been shivering and sweating. He showered and walked out to find a pharmacy, where he bought paracetamol and throat lozenges.

By the time he was on the road again, after three strong coffees and a croissant, he felt better and decided if he was getting a cold, he would be able to stave it off until he arrived back in Lafferton.

Twenty-nine

He sat at the desk and the short queue of book borrowers shuffled slowly forward. Between them, they brought back twelve books and went off round the shelves to pick more. Lee Russon stamped and wrote down names and put the books on the trolley to re-shelve at the end of the session.

He liked books. Well, some books. He also liked this room because it was quiet and orderly and there was something about the atmosphere, as if, for the time being, and only in here, thoughts of anger and violence and revenge and drugs and drink and desperation faded a bit. It wasn't true that nothing and nobody could get to you in here but it felt true. It was chapel for those who didn't do God.

A couple of men were sitting down to look through books, a third was standing reading. Two came in. The blind bloke who came for his Braille books that had to be specially ordered and reserved. And Gerry.

Anyone thought twice and then again about getting across the prison officer called Gerry Moon. He was six foot seven, worked out in the gym two hours a day, had never been known to crack a smile. His reputation went ahead of him.

He changed with one of the others, Normanton, another misery. But there were always rumours about Normanton, involved in whatever drugs were being passed round, and SIM cards.

Gerry Moon was down hard on drugs. He had a nose for them, a sixth sense, and when he found them, the prisoner's feet didn't touch the ground, Moon would have him by the scruff of the neck straight to the governor. The governor loved Moon.

Normanton went out. Moon looked round the room. Everybody was suddenly deep in a book, head down. Moon folded his arms and stood by the door. Lee put a couple more books on the trolley. Nodded in Moon's direction.

'Checkout, please.'

'Taking these?'

'Thanks, and I think I'll have that back, the one I brought in, there . . . think I'll read it again.'

Lee took the Dick Francis off the trolley and handed it over. 'Got another four or five of his though.'

'Read them all.'

'Tried Lee Child?'

'He write about racing?'

'No. But they're great reads.'

'I'll just have this for now.'

One by one, they checked out and left, books under their arms. Two more came in. Gave Moon a look.

'Just checking these in, don't want any more thanks.'

'You? You never stop reading, what's up?'

'Being transferred Friday. Silverdale Open.'

Moon had stepped forward. He was listening.

'Good on you, mate. See you then. Best of luck.'

Two were left, one head down to a book laid flat on a table. He had barely looked up since he had been there. The other was running a finger along the spines of the History shelf, not seeming to read any of the titles, just running to and fro.

'Ten minutes,' Moon said.

'Yes, boss. I'll just get these out.'

Russon took the trolley and began to put books back in their places, slowly. The finger-runner went on doing it. The reader at the desk turned a page. Lee put back a copy of *The Name of the Rose* in the Crime section. Hesitated. Moved it to Historical Fiction. Hesitated again. Waited. Moved on.

150

Andy McNab, ever popular. He reached Fantasy Fiction. Terry Pratchett. Some couldn't read him, some couldn't get enough.

'Guards! Guards!' He read the title out loud with a short laugh. Paused. Then without glancing round, swift and sure with practice, he took out an envelope from his pocket and slipped it between the pages of the book. Set it back on the shelf. Moved on to the last two books, re-shelved them and returned the trolley to its place behind the checking-in table.

Moon was still standing there, arms folded.

'TIME.'

The two readers scuttled out. Russon signed out of the staffing rota with the date and time, and followed without glancing at the prison officer.

Moon waited until the room was empty, before going over to the book containing the envelope, and extracting it. He folded it, put it into his pocket, switched out the lights, left and locked the library door.

He only lived a couple of miles from the prison and he always cycled. That night, as he did every so often, he posted Lee Russon's envelope in a letter box, on his way home. His remuneration would come sometime later and would not be traceable.

Thirty

'Simon?'

'It is.'

'My God, you have a signal – or have you left the island?'

'Who is this? You're very faint – the line isn't good.'

'Kieron.'

'That's better. Sorry. Morning, Chief.'

'I think you can drop that, we're not on duty. How are you?'

'OK. In the thick of something, which started off by being just sad but probably routine and turns out to be sadder and definitely not routine. Interesting.'

'I'm calling to ask how you're getting on with the Kimberley Still files. It's warmed up a bit on that front.'

'I'm afraid I've not done much . . . this other thing has got in the way and I've had Sam staying with me, as you probably know.'

'Isn't he there now?'

'No. Went two days ago.'

'Went where?'

'I thought to you. No?'

'Not as of this morning.'

'Oh Christ. Well, don't say anything to my sister.'

'As if. He's probably just taking the scenic route. Any chance of getting into the files soon? It would be good to know what your thoughts are, see if anything comes up that looks wrong.'

'I will. Not a lot more I can do here. I've talked to everyone on the island and drawn a blank.'

He cooked himself a fresh mackerel with mashed potatoes and tinned peas, fresh vegetables being in short supply now. While the fish was baking, he sat at the kitchen table with a glass of Malbec and went over everything he could remember about Sandy. That she had in fact been 'he', and a completely unaltered 'he' at that, had surprised him, as it seemed to have surprised Iain at the pub. Sandy had never dressed up much, but when there had been a ceilidh she had danced as a woman, and looked and dressed as a woman entirely convincingly. He tried to picture her now. She had never worn make-up but that was true of most of the island women. Her hair had been a slightly dry-looking blonde, not apparently dyed. She had been tall but not exceptionally so, and she had had no mannerisms that he recalled that pinned her especially to either sex. But then, you saw what you expected to see. What had her features been like? The only image he could call to mind was of her dead, on the beach, and then when he had seen her on the pathologist's table.

He had looked down at her and seen the Sandy he had remembered. Yes. Her. The features had been . . . what? Neutral? There had been no noticeable facial or bodily hair, unusual for a female, but when he'd mentioned it, the pathologist had said there were traces of oestrogen in the blood, which indicated that Sandy had been taking female hormones. Nothing else.

All he had was a name. Sandy Murdoch. For Alexander? Alexandra? The whole name could have been a fake. She had had a slight Scots accent but had that been as a result of living on the island or of being Scottish?

He had absolutely nothing to go on.

He took the potatoes off the boil. Any day now, Police Scotland CID would arrive and take over the case. They had the resources to find out more about Sandy, but it wouldn't be easy. And when they did, might they be near to discovering who had killed her and why? He would hand over everything he had found out, which was precious little, and they would get on with it, and he had no problem with that, except that he had liked Sandy, what he had known of her, and he felt a personal, rather than a professional, desire to find out what had happened to her.

After he had eaten he went to the Kimberley Still archive files which Kieron had sent and which he had barely glanced at. They had been scanned and zipped, but once he had opened them, he saw that they would take him many hours to read. He cleared his mind of everything to do with Sandy's murder, made a fresh pot of coffee and settled down.

He finally went to bed at three the next morning, and only then because his eyes were raw after reading on-screen for so long. He was still going over details of the case as he fell asleep and the moment he woke, to a gale and heavy rain lashing down on the cottage, it filled his mind again.

He needed to get back to the computer but he was conscious that he was in more pain than usual from his arm socket. He had breakfast, did his twenty minutes' hard exercise routine which he had evolved for days of seriously bad weather, took painkillers and read the incoming news and messages. In just over a month he would be at the clinic to have the permanent prosthesis, in which a new arm would be bolted onto the remaining bone. He had been told that when it was fully functioning, the advantages would be many and the difference between it and his old, living arm much narrower. He was withholding judgement but he smiled at the thought of visiting Taransay again to show the bionic arm and its magic properties to young Robbie.

The gale howled like a banshee. There would be no ferries in or out today but he had plenty of supplies. For now, too, he had an Internet signal and in any case, he had downloaded the Kimberley Still file.

John Wilkins, who was senior investigating officer when the girl disappeared, had retired and moved to Spain. Reading carefully through his reports, Serrailler became more and more uneasy. Yes, many of the right pieces had been put into place straight away but he quickly formed the opinion that Wilkins had stuck to his view, that Kimberley would probably turn up, for far too long. True, she was a young woman of twenty-five and the clock was not presumed to be ticking down as quickly if she had been a child. In those cases, the window during which the child could still be alive was small and focus on that possibility was intense. After forty-eight hours the chances of a child being found alive shrank rapidly, partly because they were unlikely to have disappeared of their own accord. Kimberley might well have done so.

The investigation had focused firstly on the immediate areas of her workplace, SK Bearings, and her home. But then the SIO had sent patrols out beyond Lafferton, to anywhere in the surrounding villages and the countryside around a young woman might conceivably have been gone – or been taken. He had also clearly had a passion for leaflets, which had been handed out in so many places it seemed unlikely that anyone in Lafferton had failed to receive one. The other works buildings adjacent to SK Bearings had been searched, more leaflets spread about.

As he read, he scribbled every so often in the notebook on the table beside him and the notes were sometimes underlined, they became more frequent, the underlinings and question marks and capital letters spreading like a rash.

> Work colleagues.
> Public areas adjacent.
> CCTV.
> Taxis in nearby rank.
> Vehicles inc motorbikes.
> Fiancé.
> Home life.
> Neighbours.
> Other relatives.
> Regular evening activities – classes. Leisure.
> School.
> College of FE.

The gaps in the investigation process, small gaps and gaping holes, were too obvious. And all the time, Wilkins had been assuming they were searching first and foremost for a girl who was alive and who had been abducted and was being held or, more likely, had gone off somewhere.

He broke at noon, and looked out of the window. Great banks of fast-moving cloud and rain were sweeping across the landscape but the wind had veered slightly so that the weather was no longer hurling itself directly at the cottage.

When he returned to the computer, he skipped forward to read not more police but newspaper reports, and primarily those local ones in which friends, work colleagues and family members had been sought out and asked to give their opinions, feelings, fears.

'I can't believe she's gone off by herself.'

'Kim would never do that, she just wasn't a girl who would skip off on some train or bus out of the blue.'

'She was always perfectly happy. She liked her job, she was very happy with Rick, they were starting to talk weddings – whyever would she go off?'

'Someone's taken her, of course they have, but the police seem to think they're going to find her alive. I just can't see it.'

'She had Rick, she was probably just going to meet him. Of course she wouldn't get off with another man, just on the spur of the moment like that.'

'Surely to God someone somewhere saw her . . . surely someone saw *something*.'

'Grown-up people don't just evaporate in broad daylight in the middle of a busy town.'

The national press had picked up on the dissatisfaction with the police investigation. DCI Wilkins had issued a bland, jargon-ridden statement and things had continued for a further week. By then, Simon was feeling a mounting frustration. He had to remind himself that the case was five years old, that everything had changed, most of all the personnel involved. SK Bearings had closed down, he knew that from a more recent investigation of his own, and the site was now a small shopping complex, with offices above. Two lanes led to the cathedral, one to the main square, a side road led to the fire station and opposite that was St Michael's Park and the children's playground.

Another factory next to SK Bearings, which had made cheap children's clothing, had closed the same year and been demolished and a couple of blocks of flats stood in its place.

Simon sat, drinking a mug of tea and going over the whole area in his mind. He knew it well. He had gone through the lanes and side streets almost daily on his way to and from Cathedral Close, where he lived. He had eaten at his favourite Italian restaurant at the end of Dulcimer Street more times than he could remember, had bought milk and newspapers and other bits and pieces from the solitary all-purpose corner shop left in Lafferton, had used the Adelaide Road Park as a cut-through at the end of a run.

He vaguely remembered Mrs Marion Still, but he had only had a cursory knowledge of the case. Now, as he went through everything slowly, sometimes scrolling back and rereading, making his notes, he was catching up. Within twenty-four hours, he would be as familiar with its every detail as if he had run it himself. Except he would never have run it so badly.

The interviews with Kimberley's mother, fiancé and work colleagues were done by various members of the investigating team and on the whole they were fine, though Serrailler would have pursued one or two lines of questioning further, and that of Rick, the fiancé, was perfunctory. Her immediate boss at SK Bearings, Wendy Peak, had confirmed that she was an excellent worker, a girl liked by all, and added that if anyone in the place had problems or 'a wild streak' which might have made her run away, Kimberley Still was absolutely not that person.

The young woman she worked with closely, Louise Woods, had said simply, 'She never said anything to me about going off, and I think she would have.'

Eventually, the SIO had had to turn his attention away from the focus on finding Kimberley alive. Dead ends were everywhere. The search for her had extended well beyond Lafferton, to the old airfield, to two quarries, to barns and stables and a boarded-up farm and a recently closed pub. Woodland, moorland, waterways had all been searched without a trace or even a mistaken identity.

Only then did Wilkins put out an all-media plea for urgent information, with photographs of the missing girl and the solemn statement that 'we must now face the strong possibility that Kimberley will not be found alive. But even if she is not, we must and we will leave no stone unturned in our search for this young woman, about whose safety we are increasingly concerned.'

The rain had stopped, though it was still blowing a gale. But that might be the status quo for days. Simon put on boots and a heavy outdoor jacket and headed for the hills that led eventually to the single-track road across the island from west to east. He walked fast, he climbed steadily, he had his head down against the wind, and he went over and over the case of Kimberley Still. The Chief had said it was probably 'stone cold'. But already, even without having read the last third of the archive, Simon knew that it was not. Before even addressing the possible involvement of Lee Russon and any possible case against him, he knew the whole investigation needed to be reopened.

Thirty-one

Sam could think of better uses for the cash Simon had given him. So he had hitched lifts for the first two legs of the way back, defying every warning he had ever been given, but the lifts had been fine, both in lorries, one from Glasgow to Birmingham, from where Sam had walked some miles, until he found the next one heading south. Each time, he had slept in a comfortable enough bunk at the back, eaten in transport cafes and at roadside pull-ins, and talked a certain amount to the drivers. He had then been stuck for another lift for almost a day, before getting himself within ten miles of home. From there, only vaguely aware that it was five thirty in the morning, he had telephoned his mother.

'You smell feral,' Cat had said on meeting him. 'Have you eaten?'

'No.'

She sighed and drove on to the next service station, where Sam ate a double full English breakfast and she bought a paper, had coffee and did not try to chat.

Sam seemed to have grown taller in the weeks since she had seen him, and his face was thinner. He was indeed feral, his hair needed cutting with shears rather than scissors and he had a rather patchy beard. But he was here, safe, well, sitting opposite her and she did not now mind at all that he had got her out of bed before first light.

'How's Simon?' she asked when his plate was finally empty and he was on his second mug of strong tea. Sam leaned back and gave a sigh.

'That was great, thanks. Si . . . he's OK. I think his arm bothers him a bit. He didn't say so but you know.'

'He's due to get the new one fitted soon. Apart from that?'

'Well, he must have told you about the woman who turned out to have been murdered, not a suicide.'

'He never has to go far, does he? Is he actually investigating?'

Sam filled her in and talked about his own involvement with Sandy, but she was quickly aware that his eyes were red with tiredness and cut him short.

'Tell me in the car. Or when we get back.'

As she pulled out to join the stream of motorway traffic, she saw him rest his head back. A minute later, he was asleep and slept until they arrived home.

There was an unfamiliar car in the drive and Kieron came to the front door as he heard them.

Sam was still rubbing his eyes and stretching, while Cat was beside her husband.

'Your father's here,' he said.

Thirty-two

'Russon?'

He was creosoting one of the fences along the five-a-side area. The bloke doing it with him hadn't spoken a word since they had started, not in answer to questions or of his own volition. He was skanky, with moles on his head and an oddly sallow complexion. Whenever he encountered someone new, Lee Russon liked to chat to them. He couldn't contain himself. Where do you live? Are you married? What was your job? Have you got kids? What telly do you watch? Play pool or billiards? Footy? Like gardening? Curry? What car did you drive? Anything that came into his head. Sometimes they stuck it out for a bit, nodding, grunting, but usually they answered and came back with their own questions and then they were on different terms altogether. Not friends. You didn't make friends in here, not in the proper sense. Couldn't happen. But you had to get along and this was the way. Only the odd one wasn't having any of it and today, that was the bloke who hadn't even offered his name.

'Come on, I've got to call you something.'

No answer.

'Can't just say "Hey, you".'

No answer. But then, 'Don't talk to me.'

The one thing you always, always needed to know – or he did – was, what did you do? What are you in here for? Once in a blue moon somebody would come in and you knew, because you'd seen their picture on the telly or in the paper, and then you knew everything. Mostly, though, you didn't.

He didn't recognise Skanky and his wasn't a face you'd forget.

Men didn't always want to say why they were here but it was surprising how many couldn't wait to spill it all out, and when they did, there were two things. Whatever they'd done, it had never been their fault, and they'd been allocated the worst brief in the country. Diabolical.

After that was out of the way, they seemed to loosen up. Lee had a knack of listening, making them feel at ease with him, so they gave him all the detail. When they'd done that, they were his.

'Russon? Governor wants to see you.'

Not what he was expecting. His illicit postbox via Officer Moon could not conceivably have been discovered. He knew it. Moon would never – more than his job, his future prospects, his . . . no. Not that.

What else was there? He was very careful not to break petty stupid rules, because it was the petty stupid rules that got to everyone, made them so mad they broke them out of frustration, because they couldn't help themselves and that way they lost privileges, their parole was set back – if they were ever entitled to parole. Russon was careful. Kept his head down. Kept his powder dry for the serious stuff.

'What's it about?'

The officer shrugged. He walked quickly. Inside the building, doors unlocked. Corridors. Upstairs. More corridors. Up more stairs. Windows up here. Barred of course, but still, windows you could see out of. Well, a bit.

Unlock. Lock. Stairs. Short corridor.

Stop outside a door.

PRISON GOVERNOR.

An outer office. Small. Green plastic-covered bench. Desk. Computer. Swivel chair.

Nobody sitting there.

Inner door.

The officer pointed Russon to the bench but stood himself.

There was total silence for ten minutes by the office clock.

*

The governor, Claire McAlister, was a woman in her fifties, with very short hair, and what Russon's mother would have called a boot face. She wore a navy-blue suit and a pale blue blouse. The suit jacket hung over her chair back.

But she did not have the manner that went with the boot face. She was quietly spoken, she seemed calm, she looked him in the eye.

'Good morning.'

'Morning, ma'am.'

A laptop was open on the desk in front of her and she glanced at it, but just once.

'In case you're worried that you've been brought in here for a reprimand, you can relax. But I thought it best to see you because I have had a slightly unusual request. Mrs Marion Still.'

Her eyes did not leave his face and he found it difficult to meet them.

'Do you know who that is?'

Russon nodded.

'Have you ever met or spoken to Mrs Still?'

'No, ma'am.'

'Have you had any communication with her at any time since being in this prison?'

'No, ma'am. There's . . .'

'Yes? Go on.'

'There'd be no reason, would there?'

'Nevertheless, Mrs Still has put in a visiting request.'

'You . . . I beg your pardon?'

'You do look surprised.'

'Of course I'm bloody surprised. Sorry.'

'Why do you think she is asking to see you?'

'No idea. It's . . . it's just mad. What could . . .'

He did not often find himself confused or at a loss for words but he had been so thrown by what the governor had said that his head seemed to be subject to a great pressure which was making him hot, and unable to think straight or focus.

'Just let me recap. I know you were charged with the murder of Kimberley Still but that the case –'

'It was thrown out. The CPS threw it out.'

163

'For lack of evidence.'

'Which there wasn't any of because I didn't do it.'

Claire McAlister was silent for a few seconds, looking down at her desk.

Then she met his gaze again. 'How do you feel about this, Lee?'

She was known as the governor who believed in giving prisoners the option of being called by their first or last names. Lee had ticked the 'First name' box when he had arrived. How did she remember this? Because she had looked it up before he came in, stupid. Still, she'd bothered to do that.

'I can't get my head round it.'

'You don't have to accept, you know. I can reply saying that you are refusing the request to visit and I do not have to give any reason. Nor do you. But if you do agree to see her, we need to talk for a bit longer.'

'I just . . . Jesus. It's . . . I said. It's thrown me. I don't know.'

'I tell you what. I don't have to answer straight away. We can leave it until tomorrow. Please think about it carefully. If you want to decline the request just tell the officer on duty at lunchtime tomorrow and he will get the message to me. But if you decide that you will see Mrs Still, then you ask him to find out a time when I can see you again. It will be in the afternoon, I have meetings out of the prison until two. Does that seem to you the right way of going about it?'

'Yes. It . . .' He shook his head. 'It's just mad. But OK, I'll do that.'

'Think it over carefully . . . reasons for and against. Then we'll go from there.'

'Yes, ma'am. Thanks.'

She nodded. 'Thank you, Lee.'

He had another hour of creosoting the fence. Time to think. Skanky had gone. Russon picked up his brush and dipped it into the sticky brown liquid and started to stroke the wooden paling carefully, down and up, down and up. It was a blue-sky day. The creosote got into his nostrils and at first he had liked it, as he had always liked the smell of new glossy magazine paper or turps or size, though it began to cloy and then to sicken him, after a while.

But he was preoccupied not with what he could smell but with what he thought. Thought and felt. And the first thing he did was try and bring that newspaper piece to mind, in which the mother had talked to the reporter about 'justice for my Kimberley'.

That had only been a week earlier. Why the thing suddenly seemed worth looking into again God knew. Nothing had happened. No one had found out anything. *He hadn't done it.* By this time, he believed himself. He had convinced himself. He hadn't done it. He had done the others. Not this one.

He jabbed the brush hard at the fence panel. What? Of course he'd done it. Nobody else knew but he knew. What was this? He could hide from everyone, everything, but not himself and why would he bother? He wasn't talking.

She had asked for a prison visit. She wanted to come here, sit down opposite him, see him, look him in the eye and talk to him. What about? About Kimberley, what else was there? But what about Kimberley? 'Did you kill her?' 'No.' End of.

He didn't have to agree. He could say no, tomorrow, get the word to the governor, and that would be that. Nothing would be heard of it all again, and if the woman asked to see him a second time, then he would refuse her a second time, and a third and a hundredth.

But if he saw her?

He was not used to having problems bother him, mainly because, inside, any problems that arose were the straightforward sort that just got dealt with. He ate and said nothing, and the problem revolved like a Ferris wheel inside his head, and when he went to play pool, his moves were mechanical and that got noticed and he had to start lying about the dentist.

The Ferris wheel went round and round.

If he saw the woman.

If he didn't.

If he . . .

If . . .

He tried to read, and a new Michael Connolly ought to have grabbed and held him, but the Ferris wheel got between him and the printed pages.

Lights out and he watched it go round until he thought he'd smash his own skull in to stop it.

But then he decided. It stopped. His head felt normal again. And then he didn't understand why he hadn't done it from the start, because he knew himself, he was all right, he didn't have to say or do anything he didn't want to, ever. Christ, he ought to know that by now.

He went to sleep, not gradually, in an anxious, drifting way, but off, bang, his mind settled.

Thirty-three

'DI Lynch, Police Scotland. This is DC Goode.'

Graham Lynch, red-headed, very tall and Aberdonian dour. Andy Goode was none of those things and his handshake with Serrailler was firm, his expression friendly, interested. Lynch might be interested, but he was clearly a man who played his cards close to his chest.

'Come in. I've the kettle on, or there's a coffee machine.'

'No thanks.'

'A brew of tea would be great . . .' Lynch gave his junior colleague a hard look. Sod you then, Simon thought, you can sit and watch us both drink tea and eat our way through the shortbread.

'I've come to release you from any further involvement in the case of the woman, Sandy Murdoch, dead, believed murdered. I have to thank you for your assistance while Police Scotland was undermanned in the area dealing with urgent matters, and to formally assume responsibility for the investigation.'

He sounds like a bloody robot, Serrailler thought, and the junior knows he is one. He deliberately avoided DC Goode's eye as he set down the teapot and mugs.

'Sure you won't?'

'Sure thank you.'

Serrailler joined them at the kitchen table. There had been no small talk, no preliminaries, no light touches. This was official and even tea was out of order. He sensed that the DI did not feel comfortable in the cottage, would have far preferred to sit in a police station, which Taransay did not have.

'I have read your report and the report of the pathologist. I don't think there's anything to add.'

'How do you see the investigation proceeding?'

'You're leaving it in capable hands, Chief Superintendent. We'll obviously follow everything up.'

'I'm sure you will. But listen, Inspector, we know that this was neither accident nor suicide, so it's a murder inquiry and once the islanders find that out, they will be pretty shaken. Sandy Murdoch was well liked, she'd become a member of the community. People were upset at her sudden disappearance and then the finding of her body but murder would have been a million miles from their thoughts.'

'What exactly are you trying to tell me?'

'Just –'

But just what? Simon thought. Just go carefully. Just be respectful. Just be tactful. Just . . .

'Nothing.'

The fact that he had taken a dislike to the DI did not mean he doubted his competence, and even if he did, it was nothing to do with him. He was out of it. He would like to know if they ever found out the identity of Sandy's killer but he had a suspicion that in the end the case would go down as 'unsolved' and remain open. Perhaps for years, perhaps for good. But he could not have said why he thought it.

He worked on the Still files for the next three days without much of a break. The longer he spent on them the more holes he found in the original investigation and the more unanswered questions came up. He wanted to finish and then go over the whole thing again, filling out the notes he had made.

But on the third night, with the gales still battering the house, he woke at three o'clock, and at once his mind was full, not of Kimberley Still but of Sandy Murdoch. He lay on his back, his right arm behind his head, hearing the window latches rattle and the floorboards creak and groan and it was as though the time spent working on another, quite different case had freed some portion of his mind to think about Sandy. He was well aware that the case no longer had anything to do with him but he was certain that the pair who had taken over would put the whole thing on the back burner, once they had brought themselves up to speed.

It was not who Sandy was, she or he, which was exercising him. It was the bullet wound. Plenty of islanders kept rifles but it was not a rifle that had killed her. It was a revolver – the sort of gun which, since the Dunblane incident, was virtually impossible to get hold of. Criminals in major cities might have access to them but no one on Taransay, surely. Why would they want, say, a Glock pistol? You didn't go after rabbits with one of those.

So, either the weapon had come onto the island with a stranger, been used to kill Sandy, and then gone away with the same person, or . . . or there was someone on Taransay hiding one away. This was so unlikely that Simon dismissed the idea and turned to thinking about an incomer. There were the students at the field centre. There had been a man seen getting off the ferry with them but walking away alone. Had he been the same one Simon had seen on the top road? He tried to focus on the figure in his memory. Walking boots. Rucksack. Cap. Wax jacket. All dark green and khaki, blending in with the background. Average height and weight. He had had no glimpse of the man's face. Nothing had stood out except that he was a stranger and walking across the island alone. But people did that. Hikers, birders, archaeologists, who visited for a day or a week, and left. The man had not stayed at the inn and there was nowhere else.

But he had almost certainly gone and trying to trace him was a needle-in-a-haystack business. You bought a ticket for the ferry at the quay. It was possible to book online but nobody did so except during the peak few weeks of summer. Nobody asked for a name, ID, a passport any more than they did when you boarded a train.

He turned over. Let DI Lynch and his sidekick find the man.

He slept through the wind and rain until after seven o'clock and as he woke he was still thinking about Sandy and the gun and the stranger and the oddness of the whole scenario.

169

Twenty minutes later he was driving up to Douglas and Kirsty's house. The kitchen smelled of frying bacon and Robbie was struggling with his shoelaces.

'Dad wears boots all the time, and slippers in the house, I never ever see him in a pair of laced-up shoes,' Robbie said, pink in the face with bending over. 'Can you tie laces Mr Simon?'

'I can. Let me –'

'Even with your bionic hand you can?'

Simon hesitated. He was wearing pull-on boots. Because until he not only had his new prosthesis and was practised in using it, doing laces, picking up small objects and performing fine finger-and-thumb tasks was impossible. The previous evening he had automatically gone to lift a heavy fallen branch out of the way, and dropped it on his foot, because there was no muscle power in his prosthesis. And when he was caught out like that, it made him flare up, swear at himself, curse the inanimate objects that defeated him. And now he was being challenged by a four-year-old over tying shoclaces.

'No, Robbie. You're right. I can't. I can't help you.'

It seemed a huge and significant failure and it sickened him.

Kirsty simply handed him a mug of tea. 'Bacon on toast?' She gave him a close look.

'Douglas is out back but he'll be taking Robbie to school . . . if it's him you wanted.'

'Yes.'

'Sit down, enjoy your breakfast.'

'You didn't ask if I'd already had it.'

'I can tell you haven't by looking at you, and even if I'm wrong, who turns down a second one, in this weather?'

Robbie had bent over again and said nothing more, but as Simon took a mouthful of tea, he leapt up. 'I've done them, I've tied them, I've tied them!'

Kirsty gave a great, warm smile. 'Come here, let me look.' Robbie stood on one and then the other leg, raising each shoe to show.

'Clever wee boy, you can tie them and you'll never forget it again. Well done, Rob.' She put out her arms to hug him but he ducked away, and fled from the kitchen. Kirsty laughed. Her face had rounded out and she showed her pregnancy well.

'You're looking bonny,' Simon said. 'Everything good?'

'It's fine, thank you. I'm a lot happier now I'm no so sick every day. What about you?'

He nodded, his mouth full of hot bacon. He thought he might well not be on the island for much longer, and he did not want to tell her. He would tell no one, just get on the ferry and wait for it to return and spread the word that he'd left, with a heavy rucksack and a holdall.

Kirsty sat down opposite him with her own mug of tea. 'Next time you come,' she said, as if she knew what he had been thinking, knew that he was soon off, 'you'll have a new arm, we'll have a new bairn and they'll have found out who killed Sandy Murdoch.'

'Who?' Douglas came in through the back door. 'Robbie? You've ten minutes.' A shout from above.

'He tied his own shoelaces.'

Douglas looked at her and smiled. 'That boy!'

Simon saw the look that passed between them, a look of pride and delight. And love. He felt a chip of ice settle on him.

'Morning, Simon. What can I do for you?'

'I wanted a talk but you've to get Robbie to school. Maybe I'll come by another day.'

'Is it anything I can help with?' Kirsty asked.

He hesitated. He had no idea, but to stay a bit longer in the warm kitchen, with tea and bacon, was appealing.

'You might. I just don't know, if I'm frank. I'm probably flying a kite.'

'Fly it. Robbie, have you your bag and your recorder and your gym shoes?'

Robbie slipped out.

'When's the new one due?'

'February. No doubt it'll be blown in on a force eight.'

'Boy or girl?'

'No idea. You don't get scans every other week here. With the early one it was too soon to tell, and besides, we'd maybe just like a surprise.'

171

'It's a boy,' Simon said.

'Oh, you're the expert, are you?'

He laughed. But Kirsty was the mother of boys. It seemed obvious to him and he had no idea why.

Douglas and Robbie whirled out in a chaos of bags and coats and boots and shouts and churning wheels and they heard the jeep rattle off up the track.

'More tea and bacon now?'

He leaned back in his chair. Was this what he really needed? Wanted? This life here. He could work at cold cases. Distance detective. But Kirsty would not be part of the deal and who else was there on the island? Possibly others but he hadn't made it his business to find out.

Perhaps he would ask her. Kirsty would know.

She had put the kettle back on and was setting herself a plate now. 'I can't settle to a calm breakfast while all that's going on.'

'And now I've come to disturb your peace.'

'Aye, but I'll cope. So – what's this all about?'

'Sandy Murdoch.'

'I thought you were off that now.'

'News travels fast.'

'As you should know.'

A look. He knew what it meant. She knew.

He explained. 'Kirsty, I've been going over and over it and I know what they'll do. Yes, it was a murder, yes, they'll investigate as they are duty-bound to do, but they'll take their time. Sandy had no relatives we know of, nobody has come forward, and without that, it will go slowly through due process. Of course they'll be back over here and asking all the questions I asked but meanwhile . . . I barely knew her but I have an itch to get this sorted because there's something, something . . . it's either the stranger who was seen getting off the boat and then walking across the top paths, in which case –'

'No chance.'

'Very little . . . remember Jill Dando's murder – that beautiful young television presenter, gunned down at her own front door by some random man who was never found. No motive, no gun, no killer. Nothing. It's like that, only Sandy wasn't famous,

172

so no one from the press is over here, there's nothing to interest anyone. Listen. I'll tell you what I can't stop turning over. She was killed with a revolver. Not a rifle. And who in God's name would have that sort of gun on Taransay?'

She sat in silence, drinking her tea, looking out of the window. Thinking. Simon did the same. But he had no hope that they would come up with any answers.

'Who would have had a gun like that for some years? Kept it?'

'And ammunition.'

'What kind of a person?'

'A criminal. Someone who'd been part of a gang.'

'A policeman?'

'Impossible. If you're an officially armed officer, the checks on taking guns out and handing them back are done for one incident at a time and one only, and on the rare occasions when a cop like me, say, has to carry one – and you have to take proficiency tests frequently – the same would apply. They don't just hand you a gun if you ask for one.'

'So who else?'

'Ex-military – but again, they don't just get to have one and put it in their back pocket.'

'So when would they carry one?'

'In wartime. On military ops. And in training. But then they are checked in and out.'

'Isn't that machine guns?'

'Depends on who they are, their role, rank, the circumstances. Of course this only applies to the UK – you go to the Middle East, Russia . . . But this is Taransay, Kirsty.'

'Yes.' She got up and took the last two rashers of bacon out of the pan. Toast from the range.

'One each.'

They sat and ate in silence. Guns were in front of them. Guns and bullets. Guns and bodies. None of it seemed relevant to where they were. The sun had broken through for the first time in over a week, and the sky was suddenly blue and brilliant over the sea. The wind had dropped.

Kirsty sighed.

173

'Does he enjoy his school?'

'Yes. But there are too few of them. It worries me. I don't tell Douglas but Robbie needs more – more friends, more challenge.'

'What will he do later?'

'Off on the ferry, either every day, or Monday to Friday. They stay on the mainland – the school has no boarding itself but they stay with families, that's not a problem.'

'You'd miss him.'

'Of course, but it's what Douglas did, it's what everyone did, and what's the alternative for us? Mainland life? No.'

'I'd better go. Thanks for . . .'

Kirsty looked up at him. 'You said war? In wartime?'

'Well, yes, but I'm not talking about ancient weapons left over from 1945 or even 1918.'

'I know that.' She was frowning.

'What?'

'Maybe I shouldn't . . .'

'Yes,' Serrailler said. 'You should.'

'It might not be relevant.'

'Let me be the judge of that. Kirsty?'

She stood and walked over to the window. Came back. She seemed anxious. But it was better not to push her, better to wait and let her work it out and hope she would make up her mind correctly. Whatever she had to say would not be trivial but he could not see at this point how there might be anything at all which would help him.

Then she sat down again and said, 'Iain.'

He said nothing.

'He's been here twenty years near enough. He met Lorna on the mainland and brought her here. I don't know how . . . we don't see her much and I've never got to know her well but I sense she isn't happy, and that she hasn't been for a while.'

She poured out more tea for herself. It was lukewarm now, the dregs of the pot, but she drank it anyway.

'Douglas . . . he ought to be telling you this himself. I don't know.'

'Would you like me to ask him when he gets back?'

'No. No, he won't mind. He's told no one else but me . . . Douglas keeps things to himself. On the other hand, he can't be the only one – you know Taransay. He saw Iain with Sandy once or twice.'

That took him by surprise. No need to ask if Douglas was sure, no need to say anything.

'But I know that doesn't mean . . . well, why in God's name would he shoot her dead?'

'Yes. And how?'

'You said . . . wartime. People had those guns in wartime. Soldiers.'

Kirsty had seen Iain and Sandy. Had they really been having an affair? Iain was always at the pub. Sandy had always been alone. And Iain had a wife. Plenty of other people were out and about over the island but Iain never seemed to be. But if it had been true, Iain would have had to cover up his own shock and distress and he had surely done so successfully. Yes he had been upset but so had everyone. And you did not leap from vague suspicions of an affair to accusations of murder.

There was the sound of the jeep outside. The front door banged.

'I'll make fresh tea.' Kirsty got up without meeting Serrailler's eye. It was clear that she was not going to carry on their conversation.

'Not for me, thanks. I've work to do.'

'When's the arm-fitting?' Douglas asked. 'Robbie's desperate to see you tie your shoelaces.' He put his arm round Kirsty who leaned against him.

Simon went. If he had not had so much on his mind, he would have felt excluded, for all the bacon and tea and toast and talk.

175

Thirty-four

'Sam, be a love and see if your grandfather wants anything, would you? Tell him I'll be up in a minute.'

'I went last time. Get Felix to go.'

'Felix is doing his maths homework.'

'OK, OK.'

'And stop sighing.'

Sam sighed. Cat leaned on the kitchen table and took a deep breath. It had been a difficult day. She had told the partners at the practice that she was leaving, though not until the new year. When she had explained why, both had told her she was mad and that the whole new enterprise was both unethical and doomed to failure. The surgery had been overflowing with people who could have treated themselves or gone to a pharmacist, but one small child had been brought in with a temperature of almost 104. It had measles, the mother had a new baby, and did not 'believe in' vaccines. The child was now critically ill in Bevham General and the baby might well have caught the disease too. With luck and appropriate, emergency treatment, both should recover, but it was not a given. And her father was at home, ill, though with what she was not sure, refusing to see any other doctor, cantankerous and difficult. Kieron, having had to let him in and make him comfortable until she had returned, had opted out. He had cheerfully, willingly, taken on Cat's children and treated them as his own. Her father was another matter. Cat did not blame him in the least. But he was seriously ill, he had nowhere else to go, and . . .

'Blood is thicker than water,' she said aloud, and went to pour a glass of wine. A rack of lamb was in the fridge and the steamer was stacked with freshly prepared vegetables, a pan with peeled potatoes in water. She felt a spurt of guilt at having sent Sam upstairs, when he had already done all this, and unasked.

'He wants you.'

'Sam . . . thanks for getting all this ready.'

'I can't cook it.'

'Time you learned. But for now, this is great. What did he say he wanted?'

'You. Now. Kieron in tonight?'

'Yes. Supper at half eight.'

'That's hours.'

'Don't start making a pile of toast to be going on with. Bag of crisps and that's it, or you won't want your supper. And take off your jacket or you won't feel the benefit of it when you go out.' He dodged the flying dishcloth and took his crisps off into the den.

Richard was a poor colour and thin in the face, puffy under his eyes. She could hear the sandpaper sound of his breathing from the doorway,

'I'm going to take your temp and listen to your chest.'

'I need the lavatory but I'm not feeling steady enough on my own.'

'Sam would have helped you, Dad.'

'And you won't?'

'Of course I will. I just meant there was no need to send him away. Come on.' She turned back the bedclothes.

He was very hot, his skin dry. When he got back into bed sweat was running down his face.

His temperature was too high, and, ignoring his arguments, she listened to his chest carefully.

'Any pain?'

'No.'

'Sure?'

'I'm tired. Ache a bit. It's influenza obviously, Catherine. Get me some paracetamol and a whisky and I'll sleep it off.'

177

'Paracetamol yes, whisky no, and you have pneumonia, Dad. You should be in hospital.'

'Rubbish. If everyone with a touch of pneumonia took up a bed . . .'

'All the same.'

'I am staying here, you're a competent doctor, more experience than whatever junior houseman I'd be blessed with. It'll be viral. I don't need antibiotics.'

'Hmm. I'm going to send a sputum sample off to the lab in the morning and then we'll know. You should eat something . . . egg whisked in milk with a spoonful of sugar.'

He snorted.

'Nutritious. Easy to digest. I'll get you a jug of iced water as well. Hopefully, your temperature will go down with the meds and you should sleep. I'll leave your door open tonight.'

'Will you kindly stop treating me like a small, mentally defective child?'

'What I can't fathom is how you drove up through France, crossed the Channel, drove here with a sky-high fever without collapsing.'

He turned his head away.

Kieron sent a message to say he would be very late, and Felix had taken himself to bed with his book. So she and Sam ate together, without much conversation. When she tried to bring him gently round to talking about his future he blocked her, and retreated to the den after filling the dishwasher.

Cat slipped into Richard's room. He was asleep, his breathing poor, but he was cooler. She touched his forehead which was clammy and put the bedclothes back over him but he threw them off again. She had never nursed him. She could rarely remember him being ill other than having the occasional cold. Her mother had been the same, and toughness gave no quarter for those less robust. As children they had been sent to school through most ailments other than a clearly infectious rash. 'You'll feel better when you get there and if you don't they'll ring me.' In those days, though, school rarely rang. You were put on a hard camp bed with a single blanket and a bucket beside you in case you were sick, and the school secretary looked in on you with brisk, cheerful encouragement now and again.

She smiled now, remembering the smell of Dettol and floor polish and the feel of the rough grey blanket under her chin.

She stood for several minutes looking at Richard, listening to his breathing, feeling nothing but a detached, medical concern. He had behaved in a way that had shaken her and made her feel ashamed. She also felt that she not only did not know him, but never had.

When Kieron came in she was asleep and he did not disturb her. What woke her was the sound of Richard coughing, retching, struggling to get his breath.

It took forty-five minutes for the ambulance to arrive.

Thirty-five

'I'll have the pâté again. It was very nice last time.'

'I don't know . . . I might go for the pickled herring.'

'We always called them rollmops.'

'Yes.'

'Only thing is, they can give you awful indigestion.'

'That's the onion.'

'Yes.'

'And after that the chicken and mushroom pie. The pastry's always so good.'

'I don't know.' Marion stared at the menu and nothing made sense and she didn't want to eat any of it.

Brenda set down her menu and put her hand on her friend's. 'Come on, we're here to have a good meal and a chat and we always manage that, don't we? Just take a deep breath.'

'I don't think I can eat.'

'I know what I'm going to do. Waitress . . . we'd like another two glasses of the Chablis please.'

'Oh no, no, Brenda. I –'

The Chablis was the most expensive, which was why Brenda chose it, going on the principle that it had to be the best. Large glasses.

'No, Brenda.'

Brenda ignored her and went back to her menu. The wine was brought.

The second glass made a difference, and quite quickly. Marion relaxed.

'You see? I'm enjoying this. Now then, are you sure about the herrings?'

'Not really. I think I might join you in the pâté.'

'You won't regret it. And then?'

'I do fancy some fish though. The plaice perhaps?'

'I always think plaice is a dull sort of fish. What about pan-fried hake with chorizo and spinach?'

Marion took another sip. The menu suddenly looked enticing. 'I'm spoiled for choice. I'll have the lamb shank – redcurrant gravy, carrots and peas and mashed potato.'

They handed the menus back to the waitress. It was as usual in the restaurant, not too busy, not empty. They timed it exactly.

'There's something I want to ask you,' Marion said. She drank again and this time it was for courage. 'Will you come with me?'

Brenda took off her reading glasses and set them by her side plate. But she said nothing. Their starters arrived, the toast wrapped in a napkin. They took up knives for spreading and squeezed lemon juice and ate and did not meet one another's eye. They drank their wine almost to the last mouthful. People came in. A couple sat next to them. Four took the window table. They had to lower their voices.

'Marion, I can't come. To start with, I'm at work. I don't have a reason to go, they wouldn't let me in, and I'd have nothing to say to him. Besides, it's . . . I think it's wrong but you seem to feel the need to go and I won't try and stop you any longer. But I can't come.'

'No. I see.'

'You'll be fine. He can't do anything to you, the place will be full of guards.'

'It's not that. It doesn't matter, Brenda. I will be fine. This pâté's different. Not quite as nice as last time.'

Thirty-six

The book was *The Da Vinci Code*. Very popular. 'Load of old bollocks.'

'Really got into that. Didn't believe in any of it, mind.'

They had two copies and one was out. He put the second back on the shelf, letting his hand stay on it for a second or two.

There were a couple of people reading at the tables, heads down.

Only four minutes before closing time. Nobody would come in now but Russon hovered by Fiction A–E just in case.

The two-minute buzzer went. Both readers got up, set their books back and left together.

Russon went to the door, Moon went to the shelf.

And out.

Moon took the slip of paper out of *The Da Vinci Code*, pocketed it, switched off the lights.

And out.

Thirty-seven

'You could do this professionally,' Kieron said. Sam had stuffed the chicken breasts with cheese and herbs and wrapped them in bacon, fried mushrooms and tomatoes slowly together and served it all with jacket potatoes.

'Ha, no thanks. Though this was . . . quite satisfying.'

Kieron poured himself a glass of wine. Cat was at choir, Felix in bed early with a cold and an old and beloved Roald Dahl, for comfort.

'So not cordon bleu then.'

Sam shook his head but said nothing.

'Tell me to mind my own business.'

'No, only first it's Mum, then Si, now you. And the answer is I just don't *know*.'

'I'm not getting at you, Sam. To start with, you make up your own mind about your future, and equally important, I would have no right to do so anyway. But I'd like to think you could use me as a sounding board if you need one, and if I can help as well, that would be good. But if you'd rather not talk about it at all, fine, we'll talk about something else.'

'Such as?'

Kieron ate in silence for a few minutes, then drank, then looked at Sam.

'I would be interested in your take on something actually. Because I'm baffled – the rest of us are much the same. And anyone's view from the outside might be useful.'

'A police thing?'

Kieron nodded.

'What help would I be?'

'I've no idea. I just thought it would be worth throwing it in your direction. You're not involved, you're a civilian, you've not – well, so far as I know – thought about this before – fresh mind.'

'OK. Throw.'

'How much do you know about the fires in Lafferton?'

'What, the arson attacks? If that's what they are.'

'They are. A completely accidental fire – you know, electrical fault, someone leaves a cigarette burning – is a pretty rare event. So this many in one area . . . they're deliberate. There are other pointers too – the fire people are quite certain. All you need to know is that these are arson attacks. So – any suggestions?'

'You mean how or why . . . ?'

'I mean what type of person? Motivation? Background?'

'What is this, some sort of test?'

Kieron laughed. 'Absolutely not. If you want to be tested for the police force you go the usual route. No, we just need all the help we can get.'

'Run me through the fires – just in brief.'

Sam leaned back. He had never been asked a question of this kind and he wasn't sure where to begin. But he saw that it was not straightforward. And that it was interesting.

'OK, to start with, it seems likely that most of these things are done by men. I don't know why I think that, maybe I've just read newspaper reports. Am I right?'

'Overwhelmingly, arson is a male crime, yes.'

'So in a way that makes it clearer. Or maybe not. Mentally deranged?'

'Ah, that begs a huge question, doesn't it? Would any totally sane, rational person keep setting places alight? Well, obviously not. After that though – what's sanity, what's madness?'

'OK, someone with a grudge. Maybe, if they're setting fire to, say, betting shops, then they've lost a load of money, or they think they've been cheated. Or, they're just pissed off and broke.'

184

'Possible. A grudge . . . revenge. Yes. It's a clear motive. But in the Lafferton fires, each one is different, in a different place, different type of building. There's no pattern.'

'Could still be a grudge, maybe against businesses. Capitalism?'

'Yes. But none of these are existing businesses – thankfully – they're derelict or unused commercial buildings, and in a couple of instances the fires have been in the open air. An empty car park, the towpath.'

Sam got himself a Coke, and poured Kieron another glass of red, thinking all the time. It was like the best sort of logic puzzle with an added psychological element. Except there seemed to be nothing logical about it that he could see.

'He just likes fire. Starting it and watching it blaze. I mean, I can see that.'

'So can I, up to a point. I can enjoy making a bonfire of fallen branches and dead leaves and old boxes, finding the right cold, clear day and then whoomph! But I'm not damaging anyone or anyone's property and I wouldn't want to do it very often.'

'True. Still, the same holds, doesn't it? You love doing it. You love seeing the results. And one of the results is getting the fire brigade out, watching all that.'

'Yes. And it's all down to you.'

'Power then.'

'Yes. Just that?'

'There isn't a pudding by the way. There are some apples and bananas.'

'Thanks.'

'I guess . . . the thrill of starting a blaze and watching it take hold is kind of a turn-on?'

'Now there you are spot on – arson is very often considered by the psychs to be a sexual crime.'

'Only by the psychs?'

'Who am I to disagree with them?'

'But?'

'But I don't believe that's always the answer or at least not the whole answer.'

185

'So . . . it's a male. Age? Could be any, though maybe not over seventy?'

'Why?'

'You have to be fit and agile. Good at getting away.'

'Seventy isn't ninety.'

'Maybe not married or with a partner. All that going out by yourself at weird hours . . .'

'Possibly. Not conclusively.'

'Loner?'

'So many criminals are – excluding gangs and drugs. But this sort of thing, yes, very likely.'

'Local. He isn't going to come a hundred miles. He could do it nearer home.'

'Local because of . . .'

'Local knowledge.'

'Exactly.'

'So, a Lafferton bloke. How does he start the fires? Not just matches.'

'No. Petrol, either petrol-soaked rags or the usual way we all start a fire in the grate – newspaper, kindling, firelighters, only a whole lot more than we need and then he douses it with petrol. Adds old paint cans. Varnish. Anything. None of which are hard to get hold of.'

'He'd smell of them.'

'Good point.'

'So all the more reason why he's single or else he has some-where to dump the clothing he wears for doing it.'

'Where?'

'Anywhere . . . empty house, old shed, even down by the river or the canal.'

'How does he get from the fire to there and from there to home?'

'Bike. Or he runs. Easier to slip in and out of back alleys and back gardens. Which means he doesn't come too far.'

Kieron reached for a pad and pen. 'So what have we got?'

'Male. Single. Bit odd but maybe not totally bonkers. I mean, he's cunning, he can plan. Local. Age, what, twenty to fifty? That's a big field. Something else . . . have people at work

186

or wherever noticed he's interested in fires, maybe in these fires – you know, looking them up on the Internet news, in the paper, watching for them on TV? I mean, he wants a result, doesn't he? He wants to be sort of famous, even if it's only in his own head.'

Kieron finished his wine and got up to clear the table. 'This has been great, Sam, it's very helpful. It's got a lot of dead wood out of the way and cleared my mind.'

'Yeah, but it's not you, is it? You're the Chief. You're not CID. You're not leading the case.'

'No. But I have to be on top of it, like everything else. This isn't just one incident which would probably whizz past me, you're right. This is ongoing and it could easily get worse – and we need to be ahead of him. Which isn't easy.'

'Do they suspect anyone yet?'

'No. Which is the big problem. There's no one even on the radar. So it may be just a case of vigilance on the part of the patrols rather than clever detective work.'

'Is it often like that?'

'Varies. Do you want a coffee?'

'No thanks. You mean, often patrols catch criminals by chance?'

'By chance, occasionally, but not usually. It's generally based on something – a tip-off, CID work, everything's different. That's why police work is so interesting.'

'Not sure I'd like just swanning round in a patrol car for hours.'

'"Swan", isn't the term I'd apply, Sam. It has its moments as well.'

'I think I'll go out and see if anyone's about.'

'About?'

Sam gave him a look from the doorway. 'That's right.'

He was not late back. None of his friends were in town. He met someone he vaguely knew from school and a posse of his friends, but after an hour, he realised with a shock that he had nothing at all in common with them. They wanted to get pissed and behave in as juvenile way as they could manage.

He had driven in, so half a lager was his limit, and the jeering because he switched to Coke was enough to send him home.

Kieron had gone to bed. Cat was emptying the dishwasher and finishing up the red wine Kieron had left. She did not ask where he had been.

'Kieron said he'd sent you a link to a couple of things he thought might interest you. I went from choir straight to the hospital.'

'How is he?'

'Not very well. They've done everything – CAT scans, X-rays, bronchoscopy – thoracic medicine wasn't his own speciality for nothing. The consultant was one of his old students.'

'It's who you know, as usual.'

'Sometimes. Anyway, he has pneumonia and he should have been treated earlier – the congestion on his lungs is bad. They'll get on top of it though – he's pretty fit generally for his age.'

'Bet he's giving them a hard time.'

'Oh he is. Gave me one as well, come to that.'

'It's not your fault.'

She laughed. 'Switch the lights off and all that when you come up, Sambo.'

She gave him a quick hug and ruffled his hair to provoke him, as she went by.

To sam101notout@gmail.com
From chief.bright@police.gov.uk
Thought these two might interest you. K

One link was to a forensic psychology journal and an article about arson. The second was to a couple of university degree courses in criminology. He filed the first to read later and did not plan to do more than skim the second but ended by going upstairs and investigating several prospectuses on his iPad. He was still reading when he fell asleep with the light on after two o'clock.

Thirty-eight

Marion had not been sure if she could drive safely when she first got into the car. She was shaky, her palms were damp, and she seemed unable to focus properly, the edges of buildings seemed blurred.

But it was better once she started and the first few miles, out of town onto the bypass and then towards Bevham, were fine, because they were so familiar and she could drive without thinking about where she was actually heading. But then it was all new to her. Satnav took her left and right, round roundabouts to this or that exit, over crossroads, then 'continue on for four miles', and she gripped the steering wheel, as if she thought it might come away from its fixing. She was usually a perfectly relaxed driver, and competent, but she did not feel so now, she felt as if she was a danger to everyone, and also, as if somehow people could look at her through the car windows and know who she was and why she was on this road.

The signs began, several miles from the prison. They could have read Recycling Centre or Hospital or Crematorium but they didn't. And when she took the last turning down a short road, they were white on black. HM PRISON LEVERWORTH.

She stopped at the side of the road and got out. She was going to be sick. She took gulps of the cold air. Her chest tightened and she felt dizzy again. Several other cars passed. She leaned on the car door.

After all this, she would have to give up and turn back. She couldn't face it. Face him. It wasn't the prison itself that worried her. The prison was nothing. She wasn't going to be attacked or challenged. Ordinary people were on their way, other women. Children.

Him.

Lee Russon. The last person on God's earth to see Kimberley alive, she knew, and the only one to see her dead. She knew that too.

She heaved and spat out phlegm onto the grass.

Why had she insisted on doing this? What had possessed her?

The letter had told her she would be searched and she had thought that it wouldn't bother her – it was necessary and she had nothing to hide. But it did bother her, it made her feel she had a number not a name, that she was unclean and exposed. Zap, up her and down her, went the sensor in the prison warder's hand, front and back, and then hands, and turn round this way, now to the right, thank you. You can go through.

She had brought nothing. There had been a list of what could and could not be taken into the prison but it had never crossed her mind. Now, she saw women with magazines and sweets and bars of chocolate and felt guilty. Mean. Which was ridiculous.

There was a lot of noise, metal chairs being scraped back on the bare floor, screeching, children's voices, and then their footsteps as they filed in through a door at the back. She stared down at her hands in her lap, at the Formica tabletop, and the floor, at her feet. She could not look at any one of them, not try and see him, watch him walking towards her.

There was a smell, floor cleaner and something else she could not identify. Sweat? Fear?

The chair opposite her was pulled out and she saw a body blocking the light from the window behind. Hands on the table. Hands.

'Good afternoon,' he said. 'Marion.'

190

She noticed the hands. Squared-off nails. Clean. Fat stubby fingers. Hairs down the backs like furred creatures. The hands. How had he killed her? With his hands?

'It's all right.' He spoke quietly. 'I'm not going to bite. I'm very glad to see you, actually. Marion.'

She drew a sharp breath and glanced up quickly and he was looking straight into her face, her eyes; she could not have avoided his stare.

The face was flabby. There was a shadow on the jaw and chin. The hair was greying and short. There was nothing interesting or surprising or unusual or remarkable about the face. You could have seen the face anywhere. The eyes were pale. Grey-green, with streaks, like the streaks in marbles. Pale. Small piggy eyes but staring, staring. Not blinking, not leaving her face. He smiled. He had poor teeth. She looked away.

'Thank you for visiting, Marion. I appreciate it. Can't have been easy.'

Smile.

'Listen, I know why you have. You don't bother me, I'm glad you're here because I can tell you to your face. Look at me, Marion.'

She looked.

'Thank you. I'm not a monster, Marion but I know I did what I did and I'm being punished for it and that's only right. Not good but right.'

He did a tattoo with his fingers on the tabletop, drumming them and drumming them, faster and faster, but he did not take his eyes off her face. Then he stopped abruptly.

'I want you to listen to me, Marion, because we won't get this chance again, you won't come here again, I know that, and why would you? I have to take my chance. Listen.'

Russon leaned forward so suddenly that in pulling back she almost tipped her chair over. She could see the guard out of the corner of her eye, looking in their direction.

'I did not kill your daughter. I did not kill Kimberley.' He was almost whispering, his words hissing out between almost-closed teeth on a stream of bad breath. 'As you are my witness, Marion. I have done bad things, though I am not a bad person. Never mind how I came to do them, but I did. Only you hear this

191

because it's the plain truth. I know what you think and I know what you believe, and do you know what, I don't blame you for that, because in your shoes I'd probably believe the same. Only I am telling you now and I am telling you straight. I did not kill your daughter. And you have to believe me, Marion. You'll get no rest until you do.'

And then Lee Russon smiled.

A few miles from the prison she saw a roadside diner. It smelled of cold fried food and there were a couple of van drivers sitting on the red plastic benches. They did not glance in her direction. She got a mug of tea and a slice of coffee cake. The tea was strong and hot and fresh, the cake dusty with fondant on the top.

Traffic swished past through the steady rain that must have begun when she was in the prison.

She could not get Russon's eyes or his face or his voice or his hands or his clothing, anything about him, out of her mind. It was like a poster pinned up, and no matter what she looked at, it came in front of her eyes.

She had gone to confront him. She had gone to demand he tell her the truth, confess to Kimberly's murder. Say where he had dumped her body.

Instead, he had taken the lead. He had not seemed troubled. He had said he had not killed Kimberly, almost as if he was saying he had not watched the TV news the previous night, and by looking at her out of those pale eyes, had insisted that she believe him.

Did she? She sipped the tea, which was so very hot it scalded her tongue but revived her. Did she?

Yes. Somehow or other, he had convinced her. He had more or less admitted to other terrible crimes, but wanted her to know, from his own mouth, that he was innocent of the murder of Kimberly, and had no idea what had happened to her, and certainly not whether she was dead.

She pulled herself up. No. He had not said he had no idea what had happened to her or that he knew or did not know if she was really dead. He had said he had not killed her. But in that case, surely he would have told her he knew nothing about her disappearance at all?

He had not said that.

Her brain spun round.

She sat for nearly an hour, finishing the mug of tea and ordering a second, even eating the sawdust cake, going over everything Lee Russon had said to her, but when she eventually left she was no clearer in her mind, no further forward.

Nothing had been gained and, oddly, she had somehow been made to feel as if she were the one guilty of something. She had come away from the prison with this vague sense of guilt, but other than that, she had come away empty-handed.

Thirty-nine

Kirsty had followed him outside as he had left that morning and said five words to him, quietly, as if she had finally made up her mind that if it had anything to do with Sandy's death, then she had a duty to speak. If it had not, no harm would have been done. And she knew Simon. He would tread carefully, not barge in, shouting it out, challenging, asking questions.

He woke just after four. The gale was roaring across towards the house. The last thing he had done before he went to bed had been to repeat those five words to himself. Then he had read a couple of chapters of an old Evelyn Waugh favourite, and gone to sleep. The words would sink down into his unconscious. He would know what to do, if anything, in the morning.

He knew at four o'clock and knew also that he wouldn't sleep longer. He got up and made a pot of strong coffee, took a notebook and wrote down a list of single words. Then he showered, read his emails, and opened up the Kimberley Still file.

The gale had blown itself out quite suddenly, as it sometimes did here, and the clouds had scudded away, leaving one of the occasional brilliant, brittle days of late autumn. The sea was edged with foam as the tide came sweeping in.

It was only just after eight when he reached the pub, but smoke came from the chimney. Lights were on.

Should he go in now, even though Lorna might be about, or wait, and risk the first ferry coming in with a delivery? He needed to catch Iain alone and keep him like that for a while. What his reaction would be to the things he had to say, the questions he needed to ask, it was impossible to guess.

He waited in the car until he saw movements through the window of the pub. If Lorna was there Simon had an excuse in mind for arriving so early, but when he tapped on the door, the man opened it himself, held it wide, and was obviously alone.

'Morning, Simon. I canna get you a dram but there's a brew of coffee on.'

He seemed unsurprised to see him there so early.

'Thanks – that'd be great. I've been on the other side trying to get a signal.'

He took a table in the far corner.

Iain brought two mugs of coffee, sugar and milk, and sat down, which meant Simon didn't have to ask him to stay.

'It's a great time of the day, you know, from five or so till half eight. I get a load of stuff done but I do it on my own without anybody bothering me.'

'Ah. Sorry, Iain.'

Iain waved him away. 'It'd never be you.'

'Is Lorna not up this early?'

'Lorna's away to Glasgow with her family.'

He put sugar in his mug. Did not meet Simon's eye. Simon waited calmly, sipping the hot coffee. It was a technique, he knew that he was using it, his interviewing cap on.

Iain still did not look at him. 'Ferry's not for another hour, you know.'

'I know.'

'So you're not going aboard.'

'I'm not.'

'How much longer are you staying here?'

'I'll be off soon. I'm nearly done.'

'Done?'

He went on with his coffee and did not answer, knowing Iain would be forced to bring the subject up soon.

195

Because there was no wind, a rare thing, the pub and the world beyond it seemed very quiet. The tide was out. No waves crashing onto the quay.

Iain was staring hard at the tabletop.

He would do what he always did, count slowly to a hundred, then break the silence. But before he had reached twenty, Iain was on his feet and to the door. He bolted it and drew the blind halfway down the near window. When he turned, Serrailler saw that he was crying.

'Take your time,' he said.

The man hesitated as if he would go behind the bar and take a dram from the optics, but in the end, he just sat down again and went back to staring at the table.

'You were seeing Sandy?' Serrailler said.

Iain nodded. 'You know how it is. Lorna isn't here much. We rub along, I won't be lying that we were miserable, it wouldn't be true. But Sandy . . . great company and . . . interesting. I thought about her a lot and then we talked a lot, you know, in here after we were closed, early mornings. Like this. And she could talk to me . . .'

'Did Lorna find out?'

He did not answer.

'All right,' Simon said, brisk now, pulling things together. 'What happened, Iain?'

'How much . . . do you know?'

'About Sandy? Everything. Well, and in another sense, nothing. But the important thing.'

'Aye.'

'I saw the body.'

Iain wiped his eyes with the back of his hand. 'Aye.'

'Do you want to tell me from here?'

Silence.

'We've a bit of time, I'm not pushing you. But someone will be here before long and you'll have to open up.'

They sat on. More silence. Too much silence.

'When did you find out?' Simon asked.

Iain shook his head.

196

'Did she refuse to sleep with you? When it was clear that you wanted to? Did she tell you or . . . ?'

'She'd no choice.' He made a strange sound in his throat. 'I still cannae believe it, you know? I still . . . I can't understand how I didn't know.'

'Why? I didn't know Sandy as you did, but I saw her quite a bit, we had some talks. I didn't guess. Nor did anyone else. She was she.'

Silence.

'Did it make you angry?'

Silence.

'Understandable if it did. You would have felt betrayed.'

Silence.

'Did Lorna find out?'

Silence.

Simon paused before, in a swift change of tack, he leaned across the table and said, 'Where did you get the gun, Iain?'

Nothing. Then Iain looked up at him, tears streaming down his face, his mouth working.

'You have to tell me,' Serrailler said. 'You won't live with yourself if you don't, and what's more important, if you don't, I can't help you.'

'Why should you help me?'

'You tell me.' He got up. 'I don't care what the hell the time is – you need that dram.' He took two from the optics, though he was not going to touch his own, and went back to the table. As he did so, he glanced out of the far window. No one. The sky had clouded over.

Iain drank his single whisky in one.

'What are you going to do?'

'That depends on what you tell me.'

'You'll shop me. It's your job.'

Now it was his own turn to be silent.

'How do you know? How did you find out?'

He waited.

Eventually, Iain said, 'I was in the army. Bosnia. You were meant to hand in your gun, of course, but I didn't, like plenty

197

of others. You'd be surprised. No good reason except you never feel safe, you never want to be without one again. It stays in your head. Jesus.'

'Twenty years then.'

Iain nodded. He had not looked up, not met Simon's eye once.

'It just stayed there, in the bottom drawer of my old desk. Locked drawer, I'd never take risks. I never forgot it was there, it was what made me feel secure. Not that there's any danger on Taransay.'

'You have a rifle as well.'

'Two, and a full licence, and they're locked away in the gun cabinet, all legal. But a rifle's a different matter. As you know.'

'What happened? You got angry.'

'Yes. But – no. I was angry with myself for being a fool, angry with her – him – for making a fool out of me . . . all of that. Upset. Plus I didn't understand. I still don't. She knew full well what she was doing but she let it go on and she must have known it'd come to a head, she was going to have to tell me. So why?'

'She liked you. She wanted to be with you. I don't think she meant to make a fool of you at all, Iain. People can make a relationship work in this way, though it takes time.'

'Maybe.'

'Did Lorna find out?'

'She did and she didnae. She asked me questions, she watched me, she thought there was someone, something. But she never found out the truth.'

'You sure?'

He shook his head. 'No. How can I be? I'm no sure about anything much any more.'

'Except for the fact that you shot Sandy Murdoch. You went to her house, with your gun, you knew what you were going to do, this wasn't a red mist coming over you when she told you, it wasn't hitting out at her in fury and distress and knocking her to the ground, so that she fell and hit her head. You planned it.'

'I suppose so. Sounds so fucking callous.'

'It was.'

Now, Iain did look up.

'What's going to happen to me?'

'Where's the gun now?'

'In the sea. I threw it . . . I threw it over the cliff. After her. And don't look at me wi your copper's face, it's God's truth.'

Serrailler was taken aback for a moment. 'Your copper's face?'

'That's gone. The gun. That won't wash up.'

'No.'

'I asked you what's going to happen to me.'

Simon was silent for a while. Then, the sound of tyres outside and the doors of a vehicle slamming.

'I don't know,' he said, 'and that's God's truth too. I know what ought to happen. I know what the law says.'

Iain shook his head again.

'I'm going home. I'm going to think it all through. You understand this isn't mine any longer, it's Police Scotland now. I have no say.'

'What difference would it make?'

Simon stood up. Someone banged on the back door. 'You OK to get that?'

'Day has to start.'

'I'll come in tonight, Iain. Ten or so.'

'Lorna gets back tomorrow.'

'Will you tell her?'

As he went out to answer the door, Iain said, 'That's for me to know.'

Forty

He hadn't heard anything but someone had slipped the paper into the crack of the door. There was no letter box. He had no letters. No address. He didn't exist. He hadn't existed for nearly two years.

Thin cheap brown envelope. Nothing written on the outside. He looked at it, picked it up and turned it over.

He left it and went to make tea. When he came back and before he could think about it and start asking himself questions he couldn't answer, he slit it open and took out the sheet of paper. There were four lines, typed.

No signature.

He had two reactions, one following quickly after the other. A spurt of excitement. Then fear.

The excitement was real and as strong as he had ever felt but the fear as strong, too. He didn't need to go through the possible dangers, the possible consequences if things went wrong, they leapt out at him, almost smacked him in the face. But so did the excitement. The anticipation. The overwhelming sense that this might be the best, what he had always been leading up to, planning for without knowing it.

The last line was. *Will be in contact. Till then stay out of the way.*

Forty-one

Simon did not go back to the cottage. Instead, he drove to the north of the island, the wild side where few people came, the sheep did not graze, there was nothing but a scrape of soil and starved grass on the hard rocky ground, treacherous scrambles down to the shore, and the wind. But, from here, there was an incomparable view of endless sea meeting sky, changing and shifting from greys to blues, dark to light, the surface ruffled and ribbed by the movement of the air. He sat on an outcrop and looked out. He never came here with his sketchbook because there was nothing to draw. Pencil and ink could never convey the constant movement and there was not enough detail, though he had often picked up stones, strangely bent twigs and grasses, and sometimes bones, to take back and work with.

After sitting for a few minutes watching the sea, he began to think, calmly and methodically, going over what had happened from the time Sandy had gone missing, to the moment he had driven away from the pub just now. All his old skill at taking a case apart piece by piece, in consecutive detail, came into play. Kirsty had said five words. 'Iain was in the army.' From there, it had been straightforward, but Iain's confession had been vital. His having been a soldier twenty-odd years earlier did not mean he had either kept a gun or killed Sandy and the business of finding out the truth would have been left to Police Scotland.

But Iain had admitted to murder.

The next thing Simon had to do was notify the DI, and then either arrest Iain himself or wait until they arrived on the next ferry to do it themselves. It made little odds. Iain would be taken to the mainland. Simon would be asked for a full report, after which he would have nothing more to do with the case. Again. And after that, Iain would never return to Taransay but most likely be sentenced to life. The waves were coming in across the bay, from the west. Simon watched their rhythm, as they rolled back upon themselves, over and under, over and under. It helped him work out what he was going to do.

Which was nothing. Nothing at all. The law demanded that he make one call. Justice demanded that. Or did it? Yes, Iain was guilty, and yes, he himself was duty-bound as a police officer to pass on the information he had been given. But nothing would bring Sandy Murdoch back. Why had he come to the island and stayed here? Had his family rejected him? His friends? Society? Simon realised that in working out what had happened for the last half-hour, he, or his subconscious at least, had also worked out the solution to a puzzle, while he had slept or walked or listened to Iain.

He watched the waves and the scudding sky and the changing shifting light on the horizon and on the surface of the sea. He made up his mind.

He had always believed that the day he forgot that he was a human being first and a cop second – or at the very least, a cop at the same time – was the day he should quit. He hoped that he had never forgotten it, either in mind or in action. The human being was pretty sure what he should do now and the DCS did not disagree – he remained neutral. His conscience was untroubled.

He walked back across the tracks to his car, enjoying the stretch and the space, thinking of everything else, now that he had made up his mind – thinking of Cat and Sam, his father, the hospital appointments to come, his future as a policeman and what difference his injury would make to it – though Kieron had assured him that there would be none. He thought about

Kirsty and Douglas and Robbie. About when exactly he would leave Taransay.

The cottage was cold when he got back but he would not make up a fire and stoke the range until he had made the one call.

'Iain?'

Pause.

'Are you all right?'

'What do you think?'

'Have you people there?'

'A couple but I'm out the back. You coming over? Or will it be the others?'

'I think this is down to you, Iain. Not to me. I've only your word for all of it – I've nothing else, no evidence, no proof. So this is what should happen. You should be the one to tell them. Ring them. Speak on the phone or get them to come over. And tell them what you told me. It's not my case now, it's theirs. You talked to me as a friend, not as a policeman, and I'll be gone in a couple of days. But my conscience is clear on this. It's for you to spare everyone a long investigation, and the island being in the spotlight for months, it's for you to make it clear and simple. Which it is. You owe it to yourself, and even more, you owe it to Sandy. You owe me nothing. Think about it but not for too long. It's your call, Iain.'

He had made his decision. Now he had to live with it, something every cop started learning from his first day.

There was just one other thing. Nobody, so far as he was aware, knew about Sandy, and although it was not Simon's job to broadcast the news to the entire island, he thought he ought to tell her.

'Kirsty?'

'Hi, Simon. Everything OK?'

'There's something you should know but it's for you to keep to yourself, at least for now. You'll know if the time comes when you have to tell someone else.'

'For God's sake, you're worrying me now.'

'It's about Sandy.'

203

'What's happened? What have you found out?'

'That Sandy was Alexander . . . she was a man.'

'What? What are you saying? I don't believe you.'

'I saw the body, Kirsty. Who knows if Sandy would ever have chosen to tell anybody on the island . . . maybe, maybe not. She was taking hormones but no other form of treatment so far as the pathologist could tell, though there'll be more info from the full report. I just wanted you to know . . . you can help if it all comes out.'

'Help? Sandy's beyond help now.'

'Yes, but it's about softening the blow of it. You don't know how people will react.'

'Same way as they react anywhere. Some will accept it, some won't, but it will surely come as a shock to them – though maybe it's easier now.'

'How?'

'They don't have to react to her face, think what to say, all of that. Because whatever they thought it would have been difficult, strange. Aren't you surprised yourself?'

'Very. It had never crossed my mind.'

'Well then. I have to go, the soup pan is going to boil dry. I won't say anything.'

He was sure of that.

Now, there was only the house to pack up, which would not take him long. He would send the owner a message, leave the key and money for cleaning, and catch the late-afternoon ferry.

He spoke to no one, saw no one, and when he arrived at the quay, there were only half a dozen field-centre students waiting, huge rucksacks and canvas holdalls bending their backs. They wore bright padded jackets and looked cheerful – and, Simon thought, not more than fifteen years old, though they were all postgraduates. He had glanced at the pub and seen the lights on and Iain's tall frame behind the bar.

Douglas and Kirsty's house was not in view from here. He sent them a mental farewell. They would not be surprised at his leaving abruptly. They knew him well enough by now. Robbie might ask a question, but if he did, it would probably be about the bionic arm. The ferry gangplank went down. Simon nodded to Alec, holding the rope, but he was focused on the job, and barely returned the greeting. No one else saw him leave Taransay.

Forty-two

'Dr Deerbon? Hello, it's Sister Odone, from G Ward at Bevham General. Now don't worry . . .'

They always said it. She remembered saying it herself.

'Is he worse?'

'Indeed he is not, he's doing very nicely, we're very pleased with him.'

Yes, Cat thought, and I can imagine his expression if you told him, 'We're very pleased with you, Dr Serrailler, you're our star patient.'

He would respond with a grunt and a frown, and when she saw him next, tell her he was sick of being patronised by nurses and doctors young enough to be his grandchildren.

'Are you coming in to see him today?'

'I am, probably early this evening.'

'Can you make it before four?'

'I can try – why?'

'Because the good news is, you can take him back home with you.'

Richard looked grey and the sides of his face seemed to have caved in. His eyes were sunken into his skull and Cat noticed for the first time that he had a slight tremor. In a week her father had aged ten years.

'I'm not sure he's ready to leave hospital,' she said to the registrar, trying to sound as if she were asking him not telling him.

'I wouldn't feel justified in letting him take up a bed any longer.'

'He isn't "taking up a bed" though, is he? He is ill and using one because of that.'

The registrar shrugged.

'I know full well what bed blocking is.'

'The point is, Doc, he's in a privileged position.'

'How do you make that out?'

'Well, obviously, he's staying with you so he has not only a daughter to look after him but a GP to boot. How many old people can claim that?'

Cat wanted to slap him. She also knew better than to start an argument.

'I'll put his things together.'

'He has meds to wait for.'

'What meds?'

He listed them.

'Right, I can prescribe all of those for him, which will be a lot more efficient than waiting for a couple of hours for an overstretched pharmacy. One less patient for them to get round to.'

'This hospital's pharmacy is excellent and if you have a complaint –'

'I don't. They are always, always overstretched. Can you get me a copy of his notes please, Dr Girling?'

'I'm afraid I can't, it's strictly against patient confidentiality, as you ought to know.'

'All right, will you give my father a copy of his notes please? He is a doctor too, as I'm sure you know.'

His bleeper sounded. Cat thought they were both relieved.

'You'll have to ask the nurses. I'm wanted elsewhere.'

It was after seven o'clock by the time Richard had been discharged, waited in a wheelchair in the entrance until Cat had found her car, pulling an overstay penalty sticker from the windscreen. Richard was unsteady and it was difficult to make him comfortable. Twice she had to stop and help him when he had a paroxysm of coughing.

She had never been so glad to see the farmhouse lights on and smoke coming from the woodburner. Kieron was not in, but when she called, Sam came and helped his grandfather indoors, Felix carried both his bag and hers, and between them, they made him comfortable in bed. He complained about the car, the seat belt, the roads, the bumps in the drive, the stairs, and only stopped when the coughing took over again.

She did not reply to his grumbles, because she was used to them and could take them in her stride, but she minded that he was curt to the boys, and by the time she got back into the kitchen, she was not far from tears, of frustration and tiredness rather than any misery.

'Mum . . . come with me.' Sam held out his hand to her. They went across to the sitting room, and Sam moved the armchair closer to the fire.

'Sit down and don't move. I'm coming back.'

Felix reappeared, looking worried, gave her a quick hug and vanished again.

'Here. You need this.'

Sam had a Coke for himself in one hand, and a large gin and tonic in the other. He had sliced the lemon and hooked it over the side. There was ice.

'Sammy, you are the best thing. Probably the best ever.'

He smirked, and hid behind the Coke bottle. Cat took a long drink and closed her eyes. For now, she could not feel more content.

A shout from upstairs. Sam jumped up. Another shout. But Sam waved at her to sit down again.

What to do? What to do, what to do, what to do? Richard would recover, unless something unlikely happened. He was a fit man, physically young for his age, and although he had been seriously ill, he had not been at death's door. She was unworried about him except in so far as she had no idea what she could do about his longer term future, even assuming that he would let her have a say about it anyway. The old house would be vacant again in a couple of months and he would want to return to it. Maybe he would want to go back to France and stay there. Selfishly, Cat thought it would be the best thing for her and the rest of the family, even for him – for a time. But then would come the inevitable problems, the emergency trips out there, the issues about selling the house . . .

She had been involved in plenty of discussions with relatives about what should be done with an elderly patient, been witness to the emotional blackmail, the distress on one side or the other, while she had tried to be both helpful and impartial. It had never been straightforward, never been easy. Now it was her turn. If Judith had stayed, things would not have been so difficult, but she was not wishing any of this on her. Judith had had more than enough to bear. They were in touch, mainly by email, and with cards and presents for the children at Christmas and on birthdays, and there was nothing but affection between them. Richard was never mentioned. He had not been mentioned since Judith had left him.

The room was quiet, the fire burning low. She had finished her drink. From upstairs she could just hear Felix singing in the bath. She closed her eyes again and turned her mind to the new job. She was in the final stages of signing the contract with Luke. She was going back to practising patient-focused medicine. But she could still hear Chris's disapproving voice. She would be treating the rich, she would be betraying the NHS which had trained her, she would be neglecting those who needed her most but could not afford to pay, all of this and more. She woke in the night sometimes and his voice was there, nagging her, reminding, goading, causing her to have anxious doubts. It was the one thing he had been unmoving and unshakeable about.

She came to as she heard Sam calling her and Kieron's car pulling into the drive.

Richard was propped up on three pillows, he had a jug of water and a glass beside him, a book, his spectacles and a box of tissues to hand and a disgruntled expression. Sam had given her a look and shot past her out of the bedroom as she came in.

'Dad? How are you feeling? It looks as if Sam has thought of everything.'

'Do I need to take anything?'

'Yes, the antibiotics in half an hour. I'm going to listen to your chest.'

209

'Thank you.' It was the first time he had allowed her to behave like his doctor without either complaining or criticising.

'You still sound pretty creaky. And there's a bit of a wheeze. Did they give you salbutamol?'

'I'm not asthmatic.'

'Not exactly but your chest is tight and it will ease that. As you know, of all people. Do you feel like eating? I'm doing omelettes and vegetables and there's a baked apple.'

'I couldn't eat.'

'Did you eat anything in the hospital?'

He screwed up his nose.

'I know. Anyway, this will be quite different and I'll only give you a few morsels. Would you like some ice in the water?'

'If you please. I don't know why it didn't occur to him.'

She let the remark go.

Kieron turned round as she went into the kitchen.

'Hi, darling – sorry, I was upstairs.'

'Sam said.'

'I wasn't expecting to have him back but there you go. Supper in half an hour. Are you in now?'

'Yes, thank God. Longest most pointless meeting of the police complaints committee on record, at the end of which both complaints were dropped. Waste of bloody time. I'll have a quick shower and change.'

He sounded tired and edgy, but meetings, of which he had too many, never brought out the best in the Chief Constable.

'Hold on a second, love . . . will you take this up to Dad?'

Kieron hesitated. Frowned. Then he took the jug of ice without a word.

Something else, then, Cat thought. Something bloody else.

Forty-three

By the time he reached Bevham, very late in the evening, Serrailler was aching, hungry, thirsty and longing for a hot shower. Every connection had been delayed or else the train had been cancelled, he had stood for three hours in a packed carriage, and there had been no buffet car from Glasgow. Why had he not spent money sensibly and got a flight down? The rail fare had cost him almost as much.

He had planned to get a cab to the supermarket, buy food, and then collapse into his own flat to catch up on washing, sleeping and eating for a few days. But it was almost eleven o'clock, there would be no heating on, and he had a sudden need, which he knew was pathetic but which he gave into without a fight, to be looked after.

There were no taxis on the rank and when one came after twenty minutes the driver was disgruntled at having to take a fare in the opposite direction to his own home. He looked at Simon as if he might mug and rob him en route. At the very least, he would make the interior of the cab smell. It was only after Serrailler handed over thirty pounds before he got in that he agreed to start. He tried to call Cat but his phone was out of battery. That didn't worry him, he had a key to the farmhouse, but knew he would not need it. They were never early to bed. He would get his supper and whisky, the hot shower and a long sleep.

After he had rung the bell twice, someone shouted from inside, before the bolts were drawn, and Sam opened the door, on the chain.

A series of expressions went across his face from surprise to alarm to pleasure. But he said, 'Listen, they're in the middle of a mega-argument and Grandad's here . . .' Simon dumped his bags in the hall. He heard voices from upstairs, slightly raised but not sounding especially angry.

'I'll get you a drink,' Sam said.

'Any cold leftovers? Nothing on any of the bloody trains.'

Sam hesitated. 'Sure.' But he didn't make a move.

'What's up?'

Sam shrugged. He looked as if he were aged seven and caught out in something.

A door slammed above. A moment later, Simon heard his father's querulous voice.

'I'd better go up.'

'Maybe not,' Sam said, looking even more embarrassed.

'Can you just drop a hint at whatever this is all about?'

But Sam was saved by the sound of footsteps on the stairs.

'And what the hell are *you* doing here?'

Cat was slightly flushed, her hair dishevelled where she had been rubbing it with her hand, something she had done since childhood when angry or upset. Simon's own tic was to push his hair back, from where it flopped onto his forehead. At this moment, they looked as alike as they ever did, which was not very much.

'Sorry.' She went to the cupboard and took down a bottle of whisky. 'You?'

He nodded. 'I gather Dad is here.'

'Christ.' She sat down at the table. 'And I know what he's like, and I am not desperate to have him here for the foreseeable either, given the way he behaves, but he is still quite ill, he couldn't be alone in the house even if it weren't let, and the hospital needed his bed. Well, of course they did, seeing as they assumed I would be doctor, nurse and dutiful daughter. Ignore me.'

'No. I'd feel the same and say worse. And I guess Kieron isn't happy?'

212

Cat drank her Scotch. 'We haven't had a single argument, let alone a row. Not one. Of course it had to be Dad who broke the duck, didn't it?'

Simon went behind his sister, hugged her tightly, took his whisky.

'Yes. On the other hand, what did he expect you to do – put him in a nursing home?'

'He feels . . . oh shit, you know what? Let's talk about why you've popped up here out of the blue. What happened?'

'Nothing. Time to come home.'

'You can have Hannah's room if you want to stay tonight and don't mind pink fluffiness . . . only . . .'

'I don't want to queer the pitch – I can go to the flat, no problem.'

'Which will be cold and cheerless. Do that tomorrow. I'll help you, I'm free in the morning. But not for now, I'm bushed and I'd better settle Dad down. Are you going to look in on him?'

'Maybe. Listen, this is just something and nothing, isn't it? With Kieron?'

'What about me?' he asked, coming into the kitchen. 'Where did you spring from?'

'It's complicated. How are you?'

Kieron hesitated, then looked at Cat. 'I'm sorry.'

She shook her head

'No, I was out of order. He's your father, of course he has to be here, for a time anyway.'

'I wasn't thinking of it being permanent, Kieron, I couldn't stand it any more than you could.' She reached out her hand. 'But it's fine. He does this to all of us. Always has, probably always will. Did Sam go upstairs?'

They sat round the table, not chatting, not comfortable, all of them tired and frayed at the edges.

'You staying, Simon? You're welcome of course.'

'Just tonight.'

They had another drink. Simon made himself an omelette. Cat went to see to her father, and then to bed.

'He's a bugger,' Simon said after a few minutes. Kieron nodded. 'Don't hold back, say what you want about him. I have.'

But Kieron shook his head. 'You think you've got something on the Still case?'

'I think so. It was a cock-up, essentially.'

'All right. Tomorrow's full, but let's have an hour on it first thing Thursday. You have to convince me that I should allocate some of the budget to reopening a case and the budget's tight, as ever. Tighter. These bloody fires have stretched us.'

'Still happening?'

'Not for a while. Which is what is bugging me of course. Arsonists don't just stop, you know that, and they don't go to the other side of the country to start up again either, they like their home patch. Familiar territory. He's out there planning something and how the hell can we stay ahead of him? We can't. There's no pattern to it.'

'No sense to it.'

'Not to us. There will be to him. We've got an exhumation tomorrow night as well.'

Simon raised his eyebrows.

'I know. An exhumation is a rare event and we get two in eighteen months. It was one of yours actually. The woman found in the stables?'

'Yes. That was natural causes though.'

'Maybe not. You want to come?'

'I'm not operational yet.'

'No. Just a thought. Get you back into the swing.'

'I'll tell you something, Chief —'

Kieron frowned.

'No, this is a work conversation, so, Chief.'

'OK — tell me what?'

'I've been in the force one way and another for twenty years and I have never attended an exhumation. Still, given their rarity, you could say that of most of us.'

'Time to tick the box then, Superintendent.'

Forty-four

'I don't feel like coming out, Brenda.'

Brenda stood her ground on the doorstep. 'I know. You said on the phone. So I knew I'd have to come round and prise you out. You're coming. If you don't feel like the usual place we could go somewhere else – that brasserie's supposed to be very nice and we've never been. Wednesday's always quiet.'

'I'm sorry. I feel . . .'

'I understand. Honestly. You feel like putting your head under the duvet and never getting out of bed again, you feel everyone is going to be staring at you and talking behind their hands about you, you can't make the effort to wash and change and do your hair. I know.'

'How?'

They were in the sitting room now. Marion was looking exhausted, leaning back in the chair. It was cold. It was dark.

'It isn't surprising . . . doing what you did was brave.'

'Foolhardy, you said.'

'As well. But it's taken it out of you. You'd been a bag of nerves beforehand, all that waiting and strain and then seeing him . . . But please come. If you don't I shall have to go home and eat out of a tin because I haven't got anything else. I look forward to our evenings.'

It was the right tactic, of course. She'd known Marion would respond to being made to feel sorry for her. She had a perfectly good pair of lamb chops and a box of vegetables in her kitchen, there would not have been any tin. But needs must.

Marion stood up. 'We can't have that,' she said. 'I'll be five minutes.'

They went to the brasserie in the Lanes. It was quiet, and Brenda headed for a window table.

'Could we sit at the back, Bren? Would you mind?'

'Well, no, only in the window we can see what's going on.'

'There's nothing going on at this time of night.'

'There are people going by, the shop lights . . . it's a nice table.'

Marion did not move. The waitress hovered behind them holding large menu cards.

'Oh all right, you decide where you want to be.'

The table was in the corner, out of sight.

'Are you OK, Marion? I was hoping it would cheer you up to come somewhere different. Thank you.'

Marion stared down helplessly at the menu. 'Such a lot . . . it looks so complicated.'

'No. Ignore all that on the right column, that's breakfast. Ignore along the bottom, that's the children's menu. All right? Now, left . . . top block is starters, then fish, then meat, then veg dishes . . . puddings underneath. On the back it's all the drinks. Nothing complicated about it, is there? . . . Oh, Marion.' She put her hand out quickly. Marion's eyes were full of tears, her face bleak and anxious.

'What is it? I shouldn't have pushed you into coming out. Aren't you feeling well?'

'I'm all right.'

'It's this business over the prison visit.'

Marion wiped her eyes. 'I'm just being weak.'

'No. That's the last thing you're being. Listen, shall we have our glass of wine? Would that help?'

It helped. They ordered their food and some colour came back to Marion's face.

'I'm sorry,' she said. 'I've felt terrible, if you want to know, ever since I went to see that Russon. I've never been this like

216

before, I don't know what's happening to me. I've woken up feeling sick, I've been dizzy, I'm frightened of . . . of things.'

'What things?'

'Things that aren't frightening. I go off to sleep and wake up with my heart pounding. I keep thinking there's someone – something – in the house. I keep checking the door locks. 'She paused as the waitress brought their food. 'Am I going mad? Maybe it has nothing to do with him. Maybe I'm just going mad or getting dementia.'

'No. You're not. Anyway, that isn't how dementia starts. And I don't think this is how going mad starts either.'

Marion pushed a piece of fish around her plate. It was beautiful fish, sea bass, and she couldn't eat a mouthful, her throat seemed to close over when she tried.

'I'm sorry.'

'Just drink your wine and don't worry. Nothing's going to happen.' Brenda ate her own crab linguine. It was delicious and she felt greedy, swallowing anything in front of her distressed friend.

They left within the hour.

'I'm sorry, I am so sorry,' Marion repeated. 'You won't want to be bothered to come out with me ever again now, I've spoiled it all.'

'Now listen, here's the cab rank, you're not struggling on buses tonight. He can drop me off first. And don't argue.'

But she was too tired and frayed. The taxi ride was short and Brenda waved at her own front door until they had turned the corner.

'How much do I owe you?'

But Brenda had paid for them both, thinking of everything. That was friendship and kindness and Marion felt ashamed of herself for being such a miserable companion, for wasting good food – for having gone out at all. She wouldn't make the same mistake again.

The taxi drove away as she opened her own front gate and saw her house staring at her out of dark, blank windows. Those on either side and opposite all had curtains drawn tightly, with the television flicker behind a couple of them. She walked up the path. It was too quiet.

Someone had tried the front door. She could tell. The key felt odd in the lock. The door yielded too easily. It was usually a bit of a jiggle and a shove, and really, she was the only one who had no trouble with it.

She pushed it open onto the hall and stood back. A dark silence. A car went past and she half turned, thinking to flag it down, get help. Or she should go next door. The Masons were quite private but perfectly nice and she knew that John would come round and check everything for her.

She hesitated inside the hall for a moment, then backed out, and went quickly down the path.

'There's nothing at all, nobody here, and to be perfectly honest, Marion, it doesn't look to me as if anyone has been inside.' John had come at once and gone in ahead of her. 'Nothing looks disturbed – only you know if any valuables have been taken, of course. Come and look all the way round with me, check everything.'

She did. Nothing. No one had been inside the house, nothing was missing, or even moved out of place. She sat down abruptly on the edge of the sofa.

'I'm so sorry,' she said.

'Here, don't be daft, you did the right thing, I'm only glad to set your mind at rest. I have done that, haven't I?'

He had, definitely, she said. Nobody had been into the house.

But he hadn't. There had been something odd about the door lock. She should have asked him to check that, how stupid. She was stupid. She dared not go and try it again and she could not go back and ask him to return. She sat on the very edge of the sofa for a long time, still with her coat on, her heart beating too fast, knowing that no one was in the house or had been, knowing that she had been into every corner of it with John Mason ahead of her, and seen nothing unusual, heard nothing, felt, smelled, sensed nothing. No one.

She got up. Drew the curtains tightly. Put her coat on the hook. Unlocked and relocked. Bolted. Checked every window bolt.

She went upstairs and did the same, without turning on any lights and only washed quickly and then got into bed, in the

218

dark, and lay in terror, her mind seeming to be on a roller coaster which suddenly dropped a thousand feet and then swept up again, swirled round so that she felt sick and dizzy and the dark room went round. Round and round. She kept her eyes open, then shut them, and still the room went round. Round and round.

STOP.

She sat up in bed, wide awake because she had heard someone cry out, though, coming to, she realised she had heard her own voice. She switched on the bedside lamp. Everything was quiet. A nightmare.

But then there was a sound, from somewhere downstairs, a creak or a movement, and she switched off the lamp again. It was ten past three by the illuminated travelling clock. Ten past three, when no one was awake, there would be no comforting lights on, even the street lamps were dimmed down now, for energy saving. She reached out her hand for her phone and heard the sound again, louder, and started so much she knocked the phone onto the floor. It fell beyond the carpet edge onto the wooden boards, with a crash that must surely wake them next door.

She sat shivering, though it was not cold. The sound again. Not a creak, no, a scrape or a bump, coming not from the window end of the sitting room below her, but nearer the door that led into the hall and then straight up the stairs.

She leaned over, picked up the phone and, as the face lit up, saw the list of most-used numbers, with Brenda's at the top.

It rang for a long time before the voicemail clicked on, but as it did so, Brenda's voice cut over it.

'Hello? Who is that? Wait a minute, I need to switch on the light.'

'Brenda, please . . .'

'Marion? Is that you? It's the middle of the night, what's wrong? Are you all right?'

'No, there's someone downstairs, I can hear sounds, I'm quite sure.'

'Then ring the police, don't waste time with me. You call them on 999 now and then ring me back?'

The sound was different now. A faint bumping and tapping and somewhere at the back of the kitchen, though it was hard to be exact. She tried twice to get the phone number right. Her fingers slipped and her eyesight seemed to be blurring as she looked at the screen. She took deep breaths to calm herself, but they made her more anxious so that when she came to speak, her voice wouldn't work for several minutes. But they were patient, they kept on asking what service she required and in the end she managed, but when the police came on the line she could only give her name and address before bursting into tears.

She sat huddled in a chair, her arms tightly round herself, waiting, waiting, and there were no sounds at all now, everywhere inside and outside her house was deathly quiet. She didn't care. She needed someone.

Fifteen minutes later, two women police officers had arrived, gone round the entire house, the garden and the houses along the row on both sides, and reported nothing at all.

'It could have been a fox or a cat, even a badger,' one of them said, 'they're everywhere round the back gardens at night, you'd be surprised, and badgers especially can make quite a noise. Anyway, there isn't a fox or a badger out there now – we didn't even see a cat – and there's certainly no sign of human activity. Please don't worry, Mrs Still, you can't be too careful and you did right to call us.'

'I feel such a fool.'

'Well, please don't . . . it's the middle of the night, you're here on your own and you heard sounds. Of course you were alarmed. Always ring us, we'll come and do a thorough check – it's what we're here for, so don't hesitate, will you?'

They would not have a hot drink, a call came for them and they were on their way. The patrol car went up the road and the house was suddenly quiet again. Quiet and still and empty.

'Brenda?'

'I was just going to ring you – are you all right, Marion? Have the police come yet?'

She told the story that was hardly any story at all.

'They were very thorough. I felt so stupid.'

220

'Will you stop saying things like that? Listen, would you like me to come over and stay with you? I can easily get a taxi, they work all through the night.'

'No, no, I'm fine. I feel quite all right now they've been and found nothing. They said it could have been a fox in the garden bumping about and trying to find the bins. An urban fox.'

'It isn't that I think there was anyone outside your house, it's that I know how bothered you get and how frightening it was. It's this Lee Russon business, Marion, you know it is, and I'm not surprised. If it hadn't been for that you'd never have thought twice about it. You'd have picked up the poker and gone out there yourself.'

Marion laughed. It was true. She had been unnerved by the whole prison visit and who wouldn't be?

'I've got to pull myself together. I don't need you to come and stay, I just need to get my head straight. But thank you, Brenda, you're a good friend and I know you meant it.'

She had locked and bolted the door after the police had left and she checked it again. Then she went back to bed, where she told herself sharply that she was perfectly safe, that nothing had happened or was going to happen, and that she was going to sleep now and stay asleep until it was fully light.

Surprisingly, she did, so that she did not hear the patrol car come back, stop as one of the officers got out and took a quick look round the outside of her house again, front and back, and then drive off.

In the morning, she went into the garden and made sure nothing had got in under or through the fence or by the side gate, and that there were no animal or human prints. And there were not. She replied to John Mason, who called out, that she was fine. 'I must have been hearing things.'

Only the echo of a small voice in her head told her that yes, she had been hearing things. She had.

Forty-five

He opened his eyes on a chain of pink fluffy lights strung across the end of the bed and his sister standing over him holding a large steaming mug of coffee. He sat up and groaned.

'This bed was not made for a policeman of six foot three.'

'Bloody lucky to have a bed at all, let alone hot coffee, the state of this house. Felix fell down the stairs but he's fine, gone to school, Dad's complaining that it hurts when he breathes, and Kieron went off in a bad temper. Come on, take it.'

'Thanks . . . you don't have to wait on me as well.'

'I needed to talk to someone sane and rational.'

'Tell you what, I have to get back to the flat this morning but why not escape this evening? – I'll take you out to supper. We can talk properly.'

'God, that sounds good. I'll have to check everyone out but yes, please. How's the arm in the mornings?'

'Not bad. There'll probably be an appointment waiting for me to go and have the new one fitted. Only got to learn a whole new set of rules and regs for that and I'm a full functioning human being again.'

Cat looked at him sharply. 'You've never been anything else. You do know that, don't you? I'm not minimising what losing an arm means, Si, and you had a major trauma, it's bound to have affected you in every way, mentally as well. And don't look at me like that. But you've never been anything other than Simon, whole and intact.'

'Yes, Doctor.'

'I'm serious.'

He pushed back the narrow duvet which was sprinkled with tiny sprigs of pink flowers.

'Oh, and you left your phone in the kitchen and it's been buzzing. Here.'

Not thinking there could be anything urgent, as he was not at work and unlikely to have important messages from anyone else with whom he was not already staying, he did not open it. He showered, repacked and took his bag downstairs to the kitchen before cooking himself and Cat scrambled eggs and bacon.

Then he looked at the screen. Three missed calls, all of them made this morning, between six thirty and half an hour ago. All of them from Kirsty.

He did not call back. He sat staring at the phone for a moment, then put it in his pocket as Cat came through. He knew how to set something aside, shut a mental door on it, how to leave it be and not open the door again until he was ready to give it his full attention and deal with it. He had compartmentalised things all his life. He was an expert. It was the way he had always coped with problems and complications, in his work and his personal life.

'Thanks, bro. I owe you.'

He poured her coffee. 'Tell me about this new project.'

Cat shook her head. 'Tonight. I've got a mountain of stuff to deal with and I want a nice calm time to explain it all. You OK?' She knew him inside out. She knew how he coped with bad news, issues that he could not address at once, things he wanted to duck. A certain blank expression came over his face and she recognised it now.

'Sure. I need to get some supplies. Any chance of a lift over?'

'I've got to see to Dad first. Sam's still asleep. Did he sleep for three-quarters of the day when he was with you?

Simon shrugged. Sam. His visit. The island. Those things were behind the closed door.

'Wait half an hour. Dad's chest isn't right yet but it's improved a lot. He's weak as a kitten and raging about it but I'm not

223

worried. I'll take him some breakfast. He's got the paper, the radio, clean sheets, and a book called *Do No Harm,* about brain surgery. He'll manage.'

'How long before he can go home?'

Cat made a face.

'Kieron doesn't like him, and he doesn't like having him here, partly because he regards him as a criminal who managed to get off on a technicality but is still guilty.'

'Kieron's right.'

'I know. But his motive for wanting Dad out of the house is pretty shabby.'

'What?'

'It might reflect on the office of Chief Constable.'

'For fuck's sake!'

'Quite.'

'Catherine . . . where are you? I can't find my spectacles.'

A couple of hours later, Cat had dropped Simon at his flat with the supermarket shopping, he had switched on the heating and thrown out 90 per cent of the waiting mail, the unasked-for catalogues and circulars, and filled the washing machine, fiddled with the kitchen blind where it had come loose, chucked out a pair of walking boots which had served their time and should have been left behind.

In the end, unable to find any more displacement activity, he checked his phone again. Taransay was far away. But still near. Too near.

A text message.

Iain has gone missing. Can you ring me? K.

He had missed that and another voicemail as well.

Simon got up and walked to the window. It was grey, slightly misty. The mighty nave of the cathedral loomed to his right, the houses of the close looked small, a line of pretty dolls' houses with trees spaced evenly between, well-mown grass verges on either side. He stared down. And in front of him was the bar of the pub, empty and silent, and Iain beside him, knocking back his whisky, his face seamed with distress. Iain.

He should ring Kirsty now, discover if anything more had happened, even if Iain had returned, causing concern but nothing worse, after having gone out walking to clear his head.

If he had not returned, then he had taken the late ferry and gone to the police. Simon had given him the chance, and then left, without speaking to anyone. Iain trusted him. He knew this was something he ought to do. He had killed Sandy Murdoch. Simon knew it but no one else in the world.

If he had not been personally involved he would have rung Kirsty back straight away, found out what was happening and done or said whatever he could. But he was involved. He had been the investigating officer, appointed by Police Scotland, and continued to investigate even when he had handed over the case. So far as he knew, that had been a technical offence but not a hanging one, and besides, who had known?After that, though, and once he had even had suspicions about Iain, let alone talked to him, he knew full well that he should not have kept anything connected with Sandy Murdoch to himself. For giving Iain warning, for not passing on information, for leaving the island without reporting anything about the matter – for all or any of it he could be disciplined, and even dismissed from the force. Or he thought that he could. Police Scotland was a separate authority, independent of the rest of UK policing, and he was not under their jurisdiction, though he was when he had been authorised to take charge in the early days, when Sandy had gone missing and after her body had been found.

He did not feel guilty, morally, about how he had treated Iain, and Serrailler had never set much store by technicalities.

He could ignore Kirsty's message. Nothing would happen and it would not matter or have any consequences, other than possibly damaging their slightly uneasy friendship.

But he had been involved and he was responsible for making Iain talk. The least he could do was follow up. At one time, he would not have thought twice about it, but he was aware that he had changed – and who knew if that was temporary?

When his phone rang, yet again, he did not look at it. He went out for a run along the towpath, came back via the brasserie, drank two black coffees and read the papers, which they kept hanging on the wall attached to long sticks, as in Paris. He booked a table for his supper with Cat. He went shopping, bought a pair of black shoes and a pale blue cashmere sweater. The men's shop was a few doors along from the Lafferton bookshop. There were several new titles he had stored in his mind from recent reviews, which he wanted to check out, and he was low on the sketch pads he used and which the shop had always stocked, probably especially for him. He knew full well that everything he did was a diversion but when the phone buzzed in his pocket, he still did not reach to take it out.

The bookshop door was open but there were no other customers and he made straight for the 'New Titles' section.

As he did so, someone who had been putting books on shelves approached. 'Can I help, or are you happy to browse . . .' She stopped. Stopped speaking. Stopped moving. Stood frozen, several books under one arm.

'Oh.'

And he had forgotten too, and was also frozen, head half turned towards her, shaken as he rarely was, stumbling over some phrase or other, the muscles of his mouth seemingly paralysed.

In the end, he managed 'Rachel . . .'

She did not move. Perhaps neither of them would ever have moved or spoken again, for neither knew what to do or say, how to react, caught up in a turmoil of feelings, anxiety, confusion. Embarrassment. But two customers came in together, one wanting to exchange a book, the other asking for the cookery section, so that Rachel's attention was taken up.

Simon slipped quickly out of the door.

'Coward,' Cat said. They had met at the door to the brasserie, and, when she had noted that he looked bothered, Simon had told her why, as he would have told no one else at all. They were shown to what he had asked for, a quiet table, which was at the back and dark.

'Is there anything nearer the window? Even in the window?'

'There is, you can have table five on the left but it won't be as quiet, and you did ask –'

'It's fine, thank you, much better.' He gave the waitress one of his most winning smiles.

'A large glass of Sauvignon Blanc, New Zealand if you have it, and a large vodka and tonic. Thank you so much.'

She brought a candle under a little domed glass, a jug of iced water and the menus, and was rewarded with another smile.

Cat gave him a sharp look. 'What was all that about?'

'I don't like sitting over there . . . should have thought.'

'Why?'

He shook his head. 'Dad been all right?'

'No, he's been a complete pain, but Kieron's in this evening, he won't mess him about. He always calls for Sam first but Sam's gone to rifle club so Dad is stuffed. Si, please don't tell me you had failed to remember that Rachel owned the bookshop.'

'I sort of did, but not as I went by and thought of something I wanted. I just went in. Doesn't matter.'

'Does matter.'

'Forget it.'

'Si . . .'

'Listen, that's not important, I need to ask you about something. And I mean "you" only.'

'Understood. Hold on.'

Their drinks came, the glasses ice cold. The waitress looked at Simon only as she talked through the specials of the day.

'Thank you. We're not in any hurry.'

'That makes me so mad!' Cat said. 'Like I'm invisible. I wish you wouldn't flirt with every damn woman in sight.'

'I didn't.'

'Of course you did, you always do. Right . . .' She raised her glass. 'Now. Ask.'

'Tell me about this new job.'

Cat set down her glass of wine, reached over and took his hand. 'Si – stop this. Stop changing the subject, stop drifting off. Yes, we will talk about my job whenever, but it's not as important as that right now *you* are going to talk to *me*.'

He was about to put an olive into his mouth, but instead he lowered it back to his plate and stared at Cat. She read as much

227

as she could into his expression, saw distress, even anger but also, and she had never seen it before in him, a sort of despair. A giving-in.

'Have a drink. Take a deep breath, and tell me.'

He drank. He looked out of the window. A few people walked by. The jeweller's shop window opposite sparkled and gleamed by the light of the old-style street lamp.

'Where do I start?'

'Anywhere. Doesn't matter.'

'There are things I don't need to bother with – stuff that happened on Taransay, police stuff.'

'All right. I don't think it's police stuff that's bothering you.'

'No.'

'Rachel?'

He shook his head. 'It caught me out, that's all. If I'd known I was going to see her I'd have been OK.'

'Would you?'

'I think so.'

'It wasn't properly resolved though, was it? You ran away.'

His face darkened.

'Yes, you did. Come on.'

He finished his drink and asked for a glass of wine.

'Listen, forget Rachel for now because I think that's a side issue, it just added to the mix, but will you let me talk to you as a medic? Isn't that what this is about?'

He was silent, looking at the table. The fresh drinks came, and their food. He still did not look at her.

'I'll take that as a yes. You haven't dealt with what happened to you. You had a major accident, a trauma, an awful time in hospital, and then again, you lost an arm. You've had to cope with a temporary prosthesis and now learn to use the permanent one. You scuttled off to Taransay and got involved in police stuff before you were fit and ready – no, this isn't a criticism, that's you, it's what you would always do. But it all adds to the initial stress. And now you're back, you've got some work on for Kieron but you're not properly operational, there's the whole business about Dad . . . your life is a lot of loose ends, Si . . . unfinished business. Not all of which can be neatly tied up and snipped off, so it's how you sort it all out and cope with it. And it's hit you after a bloody awful journey back. Seeing Rachel didn't help. You are suffering from PTSD and why am I not surprised? You're not to blame, not in any way at all, and you know that perfectly well, but you have to attend to it, because if you don't, it will come back to bite you and it will be worse. Listen to me. I know what I'm talking about here.'

'I hear you . . . but – I've had plenty of unpleasant experiences in my time . . . some minor, a few worse – not many cops haven't. You learn to deal with them. When I started there was no help, no one to talk to if that's what you needed – now there's more. But I've always coped. I've always got through on my own and this won't be any different.'

'Tough guy, right.'

Cat took a few slow breaths. She knew how easily she could become angry and frustrated with Simon's attitude, how that would push him further back into his shell of denial. She took up her steak knife and carefully sliced the sirloin, looking down at her plate not up at him. There was a beef and ale pie on his, the pastry golden and with a small hole out of which savoury steam spiralled like the old advertisement for Bisto. He did not touch it.

'I'm not ungrateful to you, you know. I just don't need any sort of talk therapy. I can cope with it. I've got my own way.'

'And do you feel as if your own way is working?'

'Yes. Or rather, yes it will.'

'Same old Simon. Always so sure of yourself.'

'Don't talk to me like that.'

'What, like a doctor with a patient who refuses to take advice and do the best thing to help themselves get better?'

Simon stabbed his pie, then cut a segment of pastry and set it aside.

'In the absence of a waxen image,' Cat said.

They ate in silence for a while, Simon refusing to meet her eye, Cat trying to get her confusion of emotions under control. How much easier if her brother had indeed been only a patient, for whom she felt concern but no strong feelings.

229

'I understand that because it's me it's harder,' she said in the end. 'When you go to the prosthesis unit they may well have someone they can refer you to.'

'I don't need referral. Can we talk about something else? Kieron maybe.'

She sighed. Ate more. Drank more. Gave in. 'What about him?'

'Are you two all right? Seemed a bit of an atmosphere when I turned up.'

'Oh, nothing, a spat. As I said – Dad doesn't make things easy. I think Kieron's worried I might announce that he has to live with us permanently.'

'And does he?'

'No, he bloody doesn't. I don't owe him that. No, it's fine, we're fine.'

'You don't wish you hadn't married him?'

'Good heavens no. What gave you that idea? Every married couple has spats, you remember how Chris and I used to blaze up every so often – far worse. And he's good with Sam, and Felix just rolls on in his own sweet way, no matter what or who. This is great steak.'

'One thing . . . do you see Rachel much?'

'No. She isn't in the shop full-time, she's got a couple of staff and I don't go in there often. I bumped into her a few weeks ago – we went for a quick coffee and promised it would be lunch next time, but there hasn't been a next time.'

She was not going to question him about it. Whatever his feelings still were or were not for Rachel, he was never going to tell his sister. He never did. Over the years she had become expert at guessing, but this time she doubted if even he knew what he felt for Rachel, because of everything else that had overtaken him, and because Simon dealt with such things by ignoring them. That or burying them in some deep dark pit that formed part of his inner self.

'Your phone keeps buzzing.'

'I know. It won't be important, I don't have any work on – at least not till I see the Chief tomorrow.'

'Work isn't the only thing in life. The message could be anything.'

230

'No,' Simon said. 'It couldn't.'

'What do you mean?'

But he only shook his head and carried on eating.

Half an hour later, he had put Cat in a taxi home and started to walk down the medieval lane leading to the Cathedral Close. The walls rose on either side of him and the lamps sent a buttery light up the stone. He stopped. The mobile had vibrated inside his jacket again and it suddenly seemed cowardly that he had been evading for so long whatever message Kirsty had for him. Talking to Cat had cleared his head. It usually did.

He took out the phone.

No luck reaching you. Did you get my messages? No sign of Iain. Police here but v stormy so no major search poss. Ring me? x K

Shit. He went slowly down the lane holding his phone but he was not there, not in Lafferton, not beside the cathedral. He was on the island, in the pub, seeing Iain's grey face and anxious eyes, working out in his own mind what to do. So he worked it out, he gave him a chance to turn himself in. Instead . . .

Instead what?

Shit.

And now he would probably have to leave a message or a text and on it would go. Communications with Taransay were unpredictable in the best of weathers.

'Hello?' Douglas, loud and clear.

'It's Simon. I've been away, I've just picked up Kirsty's message about Iain. Is she there?'

'She's upstairs with young Robbie, he's no sleeping so well.'

'She messaged me about Iain. Is there any news?'

'No. I don't know a lot about any of it, just that he hasnae been seen for a while.'

'Will one of you ring me if there's any developments? My phone's back on now.'

'Aye.'

'Thanks, Douglas. You all well?'

'We're fine.'

Douglas was a man of few words. He rang off.

*

Simon was a good sleeper but that night was different. He stayed up until late, going through the Kimberley Still files again, noting down things that should have been covered by the original investigation but apparently were not, trying to work out a more careful, detailed timeline. The longer he went over it, the more small but crucial omissions he spotted. Unless there were reports missing, which was possible, things had been left undone which might have given vital information. In particular, time had elapsed when men had been deployed to chase what he thought was the SIO's red herring, and other lines of inquiry had been left dangling.

Simon knew that the Lafferton force had been going through a bad patch at the time, with disorganisation, personal vendettas and a weak Chief Constable who had taken early retirement. It had been his replacement, Paula Devenish, who had sorted everything out with impressive grasp and determination, but the extensive fallout had not been cleared up for some time.

He worked until half past one, and all the time Iain was also in his mind, almost a presence in the room. He knew that if and when he turned up, Kirsty would let him know yet he dreaded the call. By now, if Iain had gone to the mainland to give himself up to the police, the news would have been out. Simon doubted if that was what he had done. He had most likely caught a train to somewhere or other unconnected with his present life – gone to old friends, or simply lost himself in a big city, perhaps Glasgow. And there, eventually, he would be found. But how long might it take? Iain was an odd, closed and now very troubled man. Simon was unable to put him or his disappearance in a mental drawer and lock it, as he usually did with matters he could not, or did not want to deal with immediately.

He went to bed and slept fitfully, hearing the cathedral clock chime the hours – three, five . . . and then he crashed out, and only woke to the sound of his phone beeping insistently on the bedside table.

Kirsty's number.

'He's been found. Over in Kenneth Mackie's old barn.'

Simon's stomach dropped down a deep shaft, to crash at the bottom when she said, 'He hanged himself, Simon. Nobody can think straight. Nobody can understand it.'

But he understood. He made coffee and stood at the window looking down the Close, empty for now, too early for people walking through or coming to work in the offices on either side.

When he had decided to give Iain time to think, and not to arrest him and hand him over to Police Scotland at once, Simon had known that he was in fact offering him an escape route. He could have taken the next ferry and disappeared. He could have handed himself in but why, seriously, why would he do that when he had other, and, from his point of view, better options? The third way had been at the back of Serrailler's mind. Had he expected Iain to take it? He closed his eyes for a moment. He could not answer his own question.

And now, the end result was that Iain was dead and no one would ever know who had killed Sandy Murdoch unless he had left a letter of confession somewhere, had told someone else – which was unlikely – or Simon owned up to their conversation. Morally, ought he to do that? Legally? Technically, as a police officer, he supposed that he should. But what good would that do? It would bring neither Sandy nor Iain back and how would the knowledge help Iain's wife, or any of Sandy's relatives who might surface?

Of course he would say nothing. He would bury the information within himself, as he buried so much else that was painful or uncomfortable. He would have no conscience about it. If anyone could have been harmed as a result, if justice might have been served and Sandy's murder avenged, he would not have hesitated. He would have been on a plane to Scotland.

There was only Kirsty. She knew nothing for certain, he had told her nothing. But she had been the one to reveal that Iain had been in the military and from that everything flowed.

Kirsty.

If she rang, he would listen to what she said, but if she didn't, he would leave it be and he guessed that she would ask the same question he was asking himself – what good would it do to anyone to bring it out into the open?

Forty-six

They had given out gale warnings, with the potential for gusts up to 80 mph. Marion Still had shut the doors and windows firmly and put the bolts across, but just as she was going upstairs, she thought of the bins and the garden bench. The bins were housed in the side passage, to which there was a gate, shared with next door, whose dog could push it open.

She sighed, put down her mug of tea and book, and went to check. The side gate was firmly closed, so that even if the wind blew through its slats, the bins could not be blown away. But the bench was flimsy. She had switched on the outside light but the bulb had gone. She went back for her torch. The bench was pulled out from the wall, beside the flower bed. She was looking at it, wondering if perhaps she should put something on top of it and if so, what, when she heard a slight sound behind her.The wind had not yet got up to a serious extent but the trees were moving about among themselves and she heard a gate slam somewhere down the road. She stood very still, the torch beam directed down at the bench. Nothing. She waited a minute longer, then shook herself and turned to see if there was anything at all she could put on top of it to anchor the bench down. There was a pot by the kitchen door. Perhaps that.

The sound she heard then was like someone clearing their throat softly. Or coughing. Or . . .

She rushed to the back door, pushed it open and slammed it behind her. She leaned on it and locked it and drew the bolt.

She knew it had nothing to do with the wind, the rain, foxes, badgers, cats . . . it had been a human sound though she knew she would find it hard to convince anyone else.

'Police, how may I help you?'

'They're outside again.'

'Can I have your name and address please?'

It was a busy night, they said, there had been two major road traffic accidents and the weather was starting to cause problems across the region, they would be with her as soon as they could.

Her tea had gone cold of course. She went into the kitchen. The curtains were drawn, and the back door had frosted glass so she put on the kettle and waited and there were no sounds. No sounds.

Her hands were stiff, though it was not cold. It was hard to lift the kettle and pour her tea and then to switch off the light. She went back into the sitting room to wait. After a while, she heard the wind getting up at the front of the house. A gust and then silence. A stronger gust. But then nothing. Silence all round, front and back.

She ought to call again and cancel the request, because when the police turned up, not only would she feel stupid, they might charge her with time-wasting. Or refuse to come out to her again. Perhaps they would fine her. Could they do that?

The phone ringing made her jump and spill her tea. For a moment she did not answer it, fearing that it would be the police to cross-question her, but then, it might be Brenda, who was always sympathetic.

There was only silence. She gave the number. Waited. Gave her name.

A faint sound, like the wind.

She ended the call quickly.

It was another forty minutes before they came, two young men this time, fresh-faced, one with a beard, genial, friendly. 'Now then, Mrs Still, I gather you've been hearing things?'

235

The same routine, quicker this time, out into the back, torches sweeping round, one trampling the flower bed, the other lighting the fences on either side.

'Anybody out there?'

'Show yourself if you're out there, come on . . .'

'Cats, Mrs Still.'

'Or foxes.'

'Could be, could be. No sign but they're cunning little beggars. Pretty sure it isn't people though.'

'I heard a sort of cough.'

'A cough.'

'As if someone was clearing their throat.'

'Might that have been a neighbour, out emptying the bin or having a quick smoke?'

'No.'

'Well, there isn't a sign of anyone now. What's over the fence, Mrs S?'

'A bit of scrub, a path to the garages. Then the backs of the houses in Albemarle Road.'

He looked at his colleague and shrugged. 'Quick over the fences and off?'

'If there was anyone.'

'We'll drive round Albemarle and take a look, see if there's any sign. But honestly, Mrs S −'

'It's Still.'

'I think these noises you thought you heard were animal not human. If I were you I'd go to bed. We'll make sure everything's locked up and then just don't worry. But if you do hear anything again . . .'

'I know, don't hesitate to call you again.'

'Exactly.'

'Thank you, you've been very kind.'

She did as they had said, went straight to bed, not even making a third lot of tea. She felt limp as a dishcloth, but whatever it was they had said or done had reassured her and she had only been reading her new copy of *Good Housekeeping* for five minutes before she was too tired to focus and switched off the light. Even the 70mph gusts failed to disturb her.

236

Forty-seven

Moon was off on holiday and it was a busy night for the phones. Russon waited twenty-five minutes. Men turned their backs, changed their position several times, worried that those behind them in the queue would hear, and he worked out that if the next one stood too close, then yes, he could hear, enough anyway. Most of the conversations were domestic and not worth listening in on but he had more important things to say. He had to be careful. Still, he was used to being careful.

There was a weirdly good mood in the air this Saturday night. It happened, like a bad one spread like poison gas, and everybody got a face full of it and snarled and shoved and then something kicked off. Nothing would now. It was as if they'd all been given a couple of pints with chasers. Not a bad idea.

'There you go, mate.'

'Cheers.'

Dave took too long to answer, given they'd fixed the time. People behind you got restless when you were hanging on without speaking.

'What you messing about at, Dave?'

'Sorry, got tied up.'

'Yeah, right. How's things?'

'All right. Donna's got a bad back again but she's going to –'

'Fuck off. *Things*.'

'Thought I'd wind you up.'

'Well, don't.'

'OK, OK. Listen, I can't go there again. Well, not for a bit. That's twice she's called the cops out.'

'They see you?'

'I'd hopped off, I was watching from the van. They went inside, had a chat, came out and poked about a bit, torches going this way and that. No chance of seeing me. I don't know what they get paid for.'

'So why aren't you going back?'

'Just think next time they might be a bit more thorough.'

'You're joking.'

'You're not the one prowling round her back garden in the dark.'

'Too right. I'm in here.'

'Sorry, Lee, only I just think it'd better be left for a week or two.'

'One week.'

'That's Donna shouting me, I'd better go.'

'Never mind Donna. You heard me.'

'I heard and I know what you're going to say next – if I don't, you'll cut the money off.'

'Too right.'

Dave sighed. 'OK, only I've got to be careful.'

'I thought you already were.'

'Got to go. You doing all right, anyway?'

'Great thanks, Dave. I'm great. Talk next week.'

He went away from the phones wondering how he came to have such a wuss of a brother. Dave was weak. If Lewis had been on it would have been different, but Lewis had taken off a roof and broken his leg. All he'd got was Dave.

He went into the TV room to see what was on, which was some rubbish film. Both pool tables were in use and there was a queue for them. He kicked the door hard as he came out but all that got him was a sore foot.

At home, Dave watched the kettle boil and wondered how he could tell his brother he wasn't going to hang about the back garden of old Mrs Still any more, payment or not. It wasn't as if Lee gave him fistfuls of notes. It was a stupid game, and one

238

of these nights he would get caught, the cops would be having a slack shift and decide to do a more thorough search about, or else she'd come out and see him and have a heart attack and die on the spot and then what was he supposed to do? Lee said the reason was just to put the wind up her a bit but how was that going to stop her talking to the paper about Kimberley? It wasn't. When he'd pushed a bit, his brother had said if he went on doing it a few more times it might make her move out, go and live with her sister or something. Why did he want that to happen? He wouldn't say.

The kettle clicked off.

No, he'd made up his mind. He wasn't doing it again. It was stupid and he got cold and Donna asked where he was off to this time of night. He made the tea.

He'd write a note, just saying it was off and to forget the money, he didn't need it – though he did. He never asked where exactly Lee got it either, though it wouldn't be legit, he'd been into all sorts of dodgy things since he was twelve years old. He didn't handle it himself, of course, not now he was inside, someone, Dave didn't know who, did all that for him. There was probably a mint stashed somewhere. Enough to have paid his brother a lot more for hanging about old ladies' gardens at night.

Forty-eight

'Morning, Simon. Come on in. Katie, no calls unless very urgent.'

People who assumed that the Chief Constable had a massive space, with mahogany furnishings, deep carpet and its own espresso machine, would not have recognised this utilitarian room with a veneered office desk, metal waste bin, standard-issue computer and no coffee equipment. The view was of the station car park and the side road.

'Any news on the arm?'

'Another couple of weeks. Right, I have the Still files all loaded onto here and my notes alongside. I'm afraid there's quite a lot to be looked into, but it boils down to some slapdash policing, not enough focus on the routine detail, not enough follow-up where it was strongly indicated . . . and in my opinion, the SIO concentrated too much on one area and ignored the parallel investigations that should have been taking place – at least in his own head if nowhere else.'

'I've read the outline but I didn't have time to go over it closely, so talk me through.' Kieron leaned back in his black leather chair – the only non-standard–issue item in the room. 'Katie will bring us some coffee in a minute.'

'Right. Kimberley Still, aged twenty-five. Lived in Mount field Avenue, Lafferton, with her mother, Mrs Marion Still. Father deceased some twelve years earlier, one married brother who was working in Canada at the time of her disappearance and is now in Newcastle. Kimberley had a serious

240

boyfriend who was likely to become a fiancé any day – at least he said so, and Kimberley had talked about it to her friends so there's no reason to doubt it. He was out of Lafferton for four days over the time she disappeared, on a course in Basingstoke. All verified. Kimberley worked at SK Bearings, had done for three and a half years. Regarded as an excellent worker, keen, never late, rarely ill, not any sort of a time-waster. They thought a lot of her. On Wednesday 3 June, she clocked into work as usual at eight thirty. She mentioned that she wanted to go into town to exchange a pair of shoes she'd got in the wrong size and she also said she hadn't brought anything in for her lunch so she might get it in town. In the summer she often took a packed lunch and ate it in the Adelaide Road Park, either with a workmate or on her own. She clocked off at a quarter to one – she had an hour and a quarter off. She was the first out that day and her colleague Louise Woods said that she hadn't actually taken the shoes with her – they were still in her locker when it was searched, in their box and carrier bag, receipt enclosed. So maybe she forgot them but most likely she changed her mind about going into town. It was a fine warm sunny day, perhaps she thought she wouldn't waste it in shops. But after she left her workplace, alone, nobody there saw her again. She didn't come back after lunch, or again that day, which was very unlike her and she didn't ring in or even text anyone she worked with. It was remarked on quickly, and just before they clocked off at five, Lousie took it upon herself to ring Marion Still, to ask if Kimberley had come home because she was ill. She hadn't and Mrs Still hadn't heard anything from her since she left that morning. By seven o'clock that evening the alarm was raised. Mrs Still had phoned everyone she could think of but there was really nobody Kimberley would have gone to, or with, except her boyfriend and he was away on his course – Mrs Still apparently knew that already but she checked to make sure. There was no chance that her daughter would have gone anywhere without telling her and especially it seemed totally unlikely to everyone who knew her that she would simply have decided not to return to work after lunch.

'We then get the police visits and when Kimberly had failed to come home or get in touch with anyone at all by the next morning, the inquiry moved up several notches. A team was set up and the case was regarded as a missper. The usual lines of inquiry were followed up . . . everyone at SK Bearings was interviewed, Mrs Still gave a list of her daughter's friends that she knew of and who were not work colleagues, leaflets were rushed out and distributed in the town centre, in shops Kimberley was known to visit sometimes, the paper shop where she often bought a magazine and a drink if she was going to have her lunch in the park. The local paper ran the story with a photo of Kimberley the next day. All the usual. It was well covered in the routine sense. But the SIO decided that as there was no sighting of the girl and as it seemed wholly out of character for her to disappear of her own accord, she must have gone with someone, either voluntarily – which idea was dismissed pretty much off the cuff – or under duress. The DCI put out an appeal on television. He was convinced, he said, that the girl was being held somewhere and could well be still alive.'

The door opened on Katie with a tray of coffee and biscuits. Mugs of freshly brewed, Simon was pleased to notice, and chocolate biscuits.

Now, a couple of months after Kimberley disappeared, the same thing happened in the Devon and Cornwall police area. Petra Blake, aged twenty-three, from just outside Exeter, went missing on her way home after an evening out with some friends who were celebrating a birthday. It wasn't very late – Petra left first as she had some things to do at home – her parents were away on holiday and there were two dogs to feed and so on. She was on her own for the week so she wasn't reported missing until the next day when a neighbour heard the dogs barking and howling non-stop, which apparently they never did. They went into the house with a key they kept and found everything as normal, the dogs starving and no sign at all of Petra – she clearly hadn't been home the previous night. Usual search, nothing. But her naked body was found bound and gagged, a week later, in a gully on farmland twenty-odd miles away. She'd been strangled . . . no sexual assault though, which was unusual.

242

Of course the similarities with the Kimberley Still case were flagged up and we liaised with them, they had access to whatever we had. But it was all circumstantial at that point. A month later, Avon and Somerset also had a missing girl, Annabel Perkins, aged twenty-six, a nurse who had gone missing as she walked from her flat to go on early duty at the hospital – not far. She was known to have left at seven twenty-five – her two flatmates vouched for that. One was a nurse, the other a physio, at the same hospital but neither was on early shift like Annabel. Again, going A WOL was regarded as totally out of character. She had split up with a long-term boyfriend a couple of weeks earlier, though quite amicably, so not likely to have arranged to meet him or any other male. But she had occasionally walked in to work with Chris Maynard – the boyfriend – who lived nearby and was a junior doctor. He was interviewed but had an alibi. Annabel's naked body was found buried in a shallow grave, in dense woodland about five miles from the hospital. Again she'd been tied up and strangled, but no sexual assault. Clearly that case and the one in Exeter had been linked quite quickly. Incidentally, no clothes belonging to either of those girls were ever found, though there was extensive searching in both cases. But Lee Russon was caught on CCTV in the case of the Bristol girl, Annabel Perkins. He drove a dirty white Ford van and one of those was seen by two people around the hospital area the morning Annabel disappeared. He was tracked down and interviewed but it was all too vague at that point. When Annabel's body was found, however, they got his DNA. It was also found on the body of Petra Blake. There were similarities between both these cases and the first one, our Kimberley, but her body wasn't found, of course, and still hasn't been. Dead end. No case to answer, so Russon went down for the two others and we have an open file.'

'But this has to be sexual. Was everyone really satisfied that there had been no sexual assaults on the two bodies they had?'

'Apparently. The pathologist in Exeter was killed in a car crash not long after but the junior and the attendants were still there and all the notes. Seems cast iron. Same with the Bristol girl.'

243

They drank their coffee and refilled. Kieron leaned back in his chair, arms behind his head, thinking. Simon scrolled down to see what came next, because he had the feeling that so far he had failed to impress the need for the Kimberley case to be reopened.

'The next thing I come to is what seems to me really significant . . . with such a gap in what should have been full and detailed inquiries – so much so that I went back over it all twice, and then checked that there were no pages of the reports missing – there weren't.'

'You're convinced about this, aren't you?'

'Yes. I have no interest in manufacturing a case where there isn't one, or in wasting our limited resources. There's an argument that whether he killed Kimberley or not, Lee Russon is doing life anyway and his sentence can't be added to. This may be just pandering to Mrs Still's quite understandable feelings, to no great purpose.'

'He could have his sentence added to, at least on paper. And it would prevent any request for parole or early release being heard. I don't want this to be a vendetta against an earlier investigating team, that's all.

'Neither do I. I have no personal quarrel with anyone.'

'All right . . . let's get to the heart of it.'

As we know, Kimberley hadn't made herself a packed lunch on the day she disappeared. There is a record of the owner of the corner shop near the factory being asked if he recognised her photograph and he did – he said she would buy a drink, a paper or a magazine from him, occasionally something more – fruit, some crisps maybe. On this day, he – his name is Chan – was not in the shop at all, he had to take his wife to the hospital for an appointment. A note was made of this, and another, that a return call should be made to check with the two people who were helping out – one in the morning, one from half past one. There is no record of this having been done. The shop closed last year and it's now a taxicab office.

'However, an officer did go to the park. It's very popular with mothers and toddlers – there's a duck pond – with office people in the lunch hour, and with those just using it as a shortcut. There are also a number of older people who meet there or who just go alone on fine days, to sit on the benches. There's been a recent problem with its use by druggies – evidence of needles and paraphernalia – and with the occasional rough sleeper, but those don't happen in daylight or hardly, and they haven't been pursued.

'Leaflets about Kimberley were handed out to people in the park on a couple of days and people took them, and said they would have a think, but only two said they recognised her. One was an old man who was dozing on a bench and said he might have seen her, though he often nodded off. As the officer was talking to him, a young woman came up – she'd been handed a leaflet too. She thought it was probably Kimberley who had helped her when her toddler ran down towards the pond.

'The girl had a double buggy with a baby in it as well and she was in a panic trying to get the buggy brake on and go after her boy. Apparently Kimberley had jumped up from her bench and run across – grabbed him just in time. The mother – Natalie Stoker, twenty-seven – had, of course, been extremely grateful and they had had a brief chat. The problem was that she came into the park most weekdays and couldn't be sure if this had happened on the day Kimberley went missing, which was a Wednesday, or the day before . . . possibly even on the Monday. She said she would think hard about it. Perhaps she did but so far as the files show, no one went back to interview her again. Her name and address are noted but that's all. And then there was the elderly gent – Stanley Barnard. He had taken a leaflet and said he was in the park often and thought he recognised the photo. For some reason either he wasn't questioned further or there is no record of it. Perhaps he was another they were going to get back to but didn't.

'Anything else?'

'That's enough to give me a reason to try and find both those people and reinterview.'

'Just about.'

Simon drank the last of the coffee, and as he did so, the Chief's phone rang. He raised an eyebrow and answered, listened, said, 'Thank you. Give me a moment, Katie . . . Message from Cat. She said to tell us she was on her way to Bevham General with your father. She thinks he may have had a heart attack but it could be pleurisy. She'll let me know.'

'Shit. I'd better go up there. I've nearly finished. Let me just come to what I think needs looking at more closely. As far as I could find out, nobody went back to see the young mother and nobody reinterviewed the old man, on that day or any other. By then everyone was being spread out on searches and the park was ticked off.'

'So – what would you hope to find at this stage?'

'The young woman and the old man . . . and put out a press call asking again for people who used that park to think back, look at the photographs of Kimberley, try to remember. But they were two who definitely recognised her only days after she disappeared. Why did no one go back and talk to them again?'

'Yes, they should have done so, as a matter of routine checking, I agree. But still – it's five years ago, populations change and shift. What chance of finding those two and getting any helpful info at this stage?'

'Not a lot probably but that isn't a reason for letting it go again.'

The Chief stood up. 'I have to meet the Police Commissioner in quarter of an hour. I want to think about this and I'll come up with a decision for you tonight – come round and eat? No idea if Cat will be there – but can you let me know about Richard? I hope things aren't as bad as they sound.'

Simon was closing down his laptop, and as he did so, he looked quickly across at his brother-in-law. 'You don't care for Dad, do you? No, it's all right – nor do I much.'

Kieron did not reply.

Forty-nine

Cat looked grey with exhaustion. Richard was tied up to tubes and machines.

'Hey. Thanks for coming.'

'Listen,' Simon said, sitting down at the other side of their father's bed, 'you go home. You don't have to stay with him. I'll take over.'

'I was waiting to see the consultant.'

'Who might come now or never. What's your take on him?'

They both looked at Richard. He was asleep, pale and miles away somewhere. Nowhere. But Cat lowered her voice.

'Not good. His breathing worried me but the chest pain might have been cardiac. They did an ECG when he first came in and it was all over the place. He was in and out, don't think he knew what was happening.'

'So, what next?'

'Not sure. If it's pleurisy then meds – if it's an infarct, they'll have to see what the damage is and go from there.'

'Why haven't they found out already?'

'Because they've been up to their eyes . . . Dad's a priority but the scanners are banked up. He's on oxygen and a morphine drip. If anything threatens, they'll leap on it, don't worry.'

'Meanwhile, you can't stay here all day. Go home, have a rest. I'm coming over for supper – the Chief and I have to finish off what we started this morning.'

'You know . . .' Cat was rubbing the edge of the sheet between her thumb and forefinger. 'I think Kieron would be glad if . . .' She looked at her father.

'No, Kieron wouldn't. But he doesn't want him living in his house. Your house. That's all.'

'All.'

'I know.'

'At the moment, that's the only place, once he's out of here again. I can't send him somewhere to be on his own. He couldn't possibly cope.'

'Nursing home?'

'That would be temporary as well. And you know how fiercely he would resist any sort of "home" at all.'

Simon looked at his father. His cheeks had sunken down, his colour was bad. He looked suddenly very old.

Cat said, 'You could . . .'

'Absolutely not. Besides, he couldn't get up the stairs.'

Cat shrugged.

'And I'm not there – he'd be just as alone as he would in some sort of sheltered flat. Kieron has to lump it for a bit until Dad's better and ready to get on with his own life again. Which he will, you know he will. I mean, how much does Dad being with you actually impinge on Kieron's life?'

'It takes me away from him.'

'Tough.'

Richard stirred slightly and mumbled but did not open his eyes, and after a moment, was quiet again.

'When do you start the new job?'

'Not for a while, I'm still doing locums, and working the contract through with Luke also takes up my time. I can't run home every time Dad wants a cup of coffee.'

'Is Sam any help?'

'Yes, but he can't be expected to stay at home to look after his grandfather. Listen, you go . . . I will too as soon as I've seen someone and got up to speed with all this.'

'Medical opinion – which way is this going?'

Cat looked at Richard for a moment. 'All things being equal, I think he'll be fine. Not yet. But he's tough.'

'Good.'

'You?'

'Well, I'm always fine. You should know that.'

He left before she could challenge him.

Fifty

The house was wonderfully quiet. Cat let Wookie out into the garden. She ought to take him for a walk but she felt so drained of energy she ducked out of it. Sam would take him later. He liked walking. Mephisto was sleeping in a tight ball inside an empty grocery carton in front of the Aga, something he did for longer periods as he grew older.

She could not remember the last time she had had the luxury of the house to herself. She drank a glass of milk and ate a banana. Upstairs, Anne Tyler's novel *A Spool of Blue Thread* was on the bedside table. It would be at least an hour before anyone else came in, an hour during which Cat could dive back into her book. She took off her shoes, jeans and jumper. Lay down. Pulled up the duvet.

An overwhelming weariness came over her, as if she had a chloroform pad over her face, so that she read less than a page before she slept.

The afternoon ticked on, the sun moved round, the silence in the house was as thick as felt.

She woke from a dream about Chris, who was in the room, shaking a thermometer and looking at her with disapproval, to find Kieron standing by her.

'You poor love. I haven't known you for very long, as things go, but I have never known you sleep during the day.' He sat down and took hold of her hand. 'Are you feeling ill?'

'No, no, I'm not ill, I was just totally wiped out. Someone hit me with a lorryload of bricks. What's the time for goodness' sake?'

'Whatever – doesn't matter. Now, Simon is downstairs and he and I are going to cook supper. How about I run you a bath and bring you a drink, so long as you're really not ill? When you feel like it, come down and we'll have everything under control. You will be putting your feet up. Oh, and the hospital rang – your father hasn't had any sort of cardiac incident, but he does have pleurisy and his left lung is being X-rayed again tomorrow. You can ring them if you want to. He's on new meds and they want to keep him quiet. Apparently he is finding that difficult. All right?'

Cat looked at him as he spoke. His long face was full of concern. She noticed a few grey hairs that she had never seen before, in his otherwise dark wavy hair. She felt guilty that she had dreamed of Chris, while knowing she could not have helped it, but perhaps the dream was a wake-up call that she was still clinging to threads of the past and neglecting, or at least paying too little attention to, what she had now.

'You are a saint. I'm going to say yes to all of that. And thank you.'

He smiled with real pleasure, as if she had given him something precious, and she saw that he had been worried and wanting badly to do something for her, give her something.

'Right – bath first. Then glass of wine? G and T?'

'Perfect,' Cat said. 'G and T please.'

'Mum?' Sam's voice and then his footsteps came loudly up the stairs. 'Can I come in?'

'Hey, Sambo. You look very pleased with yourself.'

'I am. I've got a job.'

Kieron had been heading downstairs but stopped. 'Is this just for your mother's ears?'

'No, no, you're fine.'

'What sort of a job?'

'I'm now a hospital porter at Bevham General, if you don't mind. I start next week.'

*

251

A couple of hours, and grilled salmon steaks and broccoli, raspberries and cream later, Felix was asleep, Cat went back to bed to read, Sam to his room to watch *Game of Thrones*, and Kieron and Simon took over the kitchen, the remains of a bottle of Shiraz between them.

'I didn't have a lot of clear thinking time today what with one thing and another, but I used the journey from HQ to go over everything you told me. Two things. You are on full salary anyway, but still officially sick, so there's no problem with you carrying on with your own reinvestigation of the Still files. For the time being though, I just haven't got the resources in terms of bodies or money to give you much help. But I can suggest that where you do need someone else to do some legwork or back-checking – you can't do everything yourself – you take anyone from CID who isn't deeply involved in an ongoing case, borrow them for a day maybe? If at any point you come up with a cast-iron reason for me to let you have more, I will look at your request very seriously. But for now, I'm afraid that's it. You've got carte blanche from me, to go anywhere, talk to anyone, without having to report back until you feel you must. It's the best I can do.'

'All right, thanks. I had hoped to be a bit further forward today but what with Dad . . . Anyway, I have narrowed it all down and I know exactly what and where I need to zoom in on tomorrow. There are some gaping holes. I know it's never possible to follow everything up and do a repeat, but this was hot for, what, twenty-four, thirty-six hours, max? After that, trails go cold. On the other hand, they never disappear completely. I'm pretty sure there are people who were never interviewed or only cursorily, and who – always assuming they are still around – should be talked to again. The time-consuming bit is finding them and that's where even a few hours of help would be good at this stage – tracing names and addresses, finding out whether people have moved, and if so, where they've gone – it's so much easier now but it still takes time. Any chance of some civilian help?'

'I doubt it. They're as stretched as the rest of us.'

'OK. I have to find enough to make it important you put some resources into this. If I do . . .'

252

Kieron nodded and poured the remains of the wine into their glasses.

'While we're on this,' Simon said, 'have you had any more from Mrs Still? She wasn't going to ease off on the pressure, last you told me.'

'Not exactly – but she applied for a visiting order to see Lee Russon, and got it. She went to the prison last week.'

'Bloody hell. Surprised he accepted. Has she been in touch since?'

'Not a word. I only know because I got an email from the prison governor, just a notification.'

'Brave of her, or foolhardy?'

'Bit of both.' Kieron got up. 'I want to watch the recording of the Formula One. Interested?'

Simon was not. Most sports other than cricket left him cold but especially motor racing.

'I want to dig into the files a bit more. I'm going to get a full reinvestigation out of you if it kills me.'

But before he could even turn his laptop on, Cat had come into the kitchen with Sam behind her, talking loudly about his job.

'Mum thinks I'm mad.'

'Not at all. Mum thinks it's fine – for now. And that you won't know what's hit you once you do your first night shift.'

'Great idea, Sam, and with luck in a couple of years or so, you'll get promotion to mortuary attendant.' Simon ducked as his nephew lunged at him.

'I don't want to doss about, I don't know which way I want to go yet, I thought everybody would be congratulating me.'

'Well, I congratulate you. Very enterprising, Sam,' said Kieron. 'No point in going to uni until you're sure you know what you want to study, no point in launching into any career at all until you've made up your mind completely. Because both medicine and the police aren't play jobs, as you well know. Meanwhile, being a hospital porter will show you what it's like from the inside and there's great camerarderie. You'll enjoy it. Coming to watch the Formula One?'

'Right.'

Cat sat opposite Simon. 'I love my husband,' she said, 'and I am willing to try and share his interests but there is no way . . .'

'Nor me. Are you really OK about Sam?'

'I was a bit taken aback. It's a dead end.'

'It's not for life, sis.'

'I know. And Kieron's right. He got up off his backside and did it for himself. I have no cause for complaint.'

Fifty-one

She was wearing a smart red jacket and grey skirt and about to open the front door, when Serrailler got out of his car. She hesitated, looking at him. Lights were on in the downstairs rooms and the curtains were not drawn.

'Mrs Stoker?'

'Yes – my husband's in the house.'

'That's fine. You're the one I'd like to talk to.'

'Who are you?'

He took out his warrant card. 'Simon Serrailler, Lafferton CID. Can you spare me a few moments?'

'If it's about the speeding fine . . .'

'Nothing to do with that. Could I come in?'

She had opened the door and called out so that a man and a young boy came into the hall.

'This is a police officer . . . he wants to speak to me and it isn't about the speeding ticket.'

'All right. Can I see your ID please?'

They were standing in the hall. From the room at the back came the sound of a children's TV programme.

'Come into the sitting room a minute. Only I can't give you long, Greg gets them home and gives them their tea, but he's on nights this week – he does safety investigation with the railways.'

It was a pleasant room, with no sign of children's toys and general clutter. The sofa and armchair were upholstered in pale duck-egg blue, the carpet a deeper version of the same shade. This was kept for the grown-ups.

'I'm sorry to call unannounced, Mrs Stoker, but I took a chance you'd be at home.'

'Well, you're lucky – I leave at a quarter to eight and don't get back till now.'

'What do you do?'

'I work for the council – the town clerk's department. Can I ask what this is all about please?'

'About five years ago, a young Lafferton woman called Kimberley Still disappeared. She had left her work at SK Bearings at a quarter to one, and she didn't go back at the end of her lunch hour. She wasn't seen again.'

'Oh God, I remember that. Someone spoke to me about it. I said I thought she was the one who gave me a hand when Daniel had went running towards the pond and I had Lauren in the buggy. That girl chased after him and got him back. I remember it so clearly – I was so grateful. It all happened in a flash, you know how it is, he could have fallen straight in. But I told someone all about it at the time – they came round the park with leaflets – and I said it could have been her straight away.'

'Did you go to that park often?'

'I did. It's lonely when you have two little ones – there are often other mums and kids there and always someone to chat to. It can be a long day, you know.'

'Do you remember if you'd seen Kimberley Still before? Was she often in the park?'

'Oh help . . . it's a long time ago. I wasn't even sure at the time.' But I think she came sometimes – quite a few people would come and eat their lunch sitting on one of the benches. That was a lovely summer.'

'The day she ran after Daniel – can you possibly remember if it was the Wednesday of that week?'

'Was that the day she went missing?'

'Is there anything that would help you remember? I know it's difficult. Anything that marked it out as a Wednesday? Did you always go somewhere else or meet someone on a Wednesday, which you would have done that day?'

256

She stared at her hands, thinking. But she'd been asked before, a few days after, and she hadn't remembered. Why would she remember now?

Then she looked up quickly. 'Wednesday's market day in Lafferton,' she said.

'Yes. Is that significant?'

'We walked through the market and Daniel wanted one of those metallic balloons someone was selling. I said no and pushed on so he got in a strop. He was still in a strop when we got to the park . . . I think that was why he got out of the buggy and started to run to the pond. I think it was . . . it might have been. But that could easily have been another day. I am sorry.' She was. Her face was downcast, her eyes troubled on his face.

'Have they – has she been found?'

'No. I'm afraid not.'

'It's such a long time ago. Are you still looking for her? It's great if you still are, I didn't think inquiries went on so long.'

Simon got to his feet. 'They don't usually . . . we're just following up some new leads. Mrs Stoker, if you remember anything else – especially something that might make you sure it was that Wednesday that you saw Kimberley Still – please ring me. This is my mobile number, ring me at any time. And even if it seems trivial to you, or a bit vague, it might not to us. Tell me anyway. And thanks for seeing me – I wouldn't have disturbed you if it wasn't important.'

On the doorstep, she said, 'I hope you find her, I really do. I will think hard because she was so nice. She was so nice.'

Fifty-two

'Mrs Still? This is Dorcas Brewer from the *Gazette*. You were kind enough to speak to me about your daughter a few weeks ago.'

'Yes, of course. Hello.'

'Can you spare me a few minutes?'

'Of course. Did you want to come round?'

'I'd like to but this is something I have to get in today – though another time would be lovely, thank you. I'm actually doing a twice-weekly diary at the moment, under my name. It's catching up on local events and people, looking back on things that have recently been in the news? For example, I don't know if you read about little Jensen Brownsword? He's the six-year-old who's been fighting an awful cancer and they've been desperately searching for a bone marrow donor?'

Everything Dorcas said, Marion thought, sounded like a question because her voice rose up at the end.

'Well, we heard yesterday that a match has been found and it looks as if they'll be able to get Jensen into hospital and give him the bone marrow next week? It's very hopeful, and local people raised a lot of money for Jensen so it's quite a news item. That sort of thing, you know? And I thought I might do a paragraph about Kimberley, just as a reminder?'

'There's nothing new though – at least, I haven't been told anything by the police.'

'Then let's remind them . . . give them a shot in the arm. I like to follow up on stories, people don't forget. Can I say you're still anxious for the police to reopen the case?'

'Of course . . . and I am. Whether it would do any good or not I have my doubts.'

'I think it always does good to keep up the pressure, Marion. OK, so if you're happy? Nothing we didn't cover when we met, nothing you need to worry about. But let's keep it in the public eye, all right? Maybe just give me a word about how you are at the moment? Help me colour it in?'

'Not any different, really.' She hesitated, wondering whether to mention her visit to the prison and immediately decided against it. 'I'm still waiting, I'm still hoping and praying. Life goes on, of course it does, but I miss Kimberley dreadfully. I'd give anything and do anything to know what happened to her.'

'That's great, Marion, thank you so much. It'll be in tomorrow's paper.'

It was.

Fifty-three

He had not expected the same luck with Stan Barnard as he had with Natalie. There had been no record of his address or age in the files, just his name, but it was the only one listed for Lafferton, and he was apparently still at 53 St Mark's Road seven months ago.

The small terraced houses in the grid of streets known as the Apostles had mainly been bought by young couples over the past ten years, updated and extended, but one or two were still lived in by people who had gone there in the 1960s and 70s when they were first married. They had liked where they were, brought up families in them without feeling the need, or having the spare money, to enlarge them, and you could tell them at a glance. Number 53 was clearly one. There was a small privet hedge, a painted gate, a short path up to the front door. The curtains were drawn and the sound of a television with the volume turned up came from the back.

Serrailler knocked hard on the brass lion's head. It gleamed in the light from the street lamp and the doorstep had recently been whited. Nothing spoke more clearly of an older, house-proud inhabitant.

'Wait a minute, wait a minute, let me find the . . . Who is it?'

'Detective Chief Inspector Serrailler, Lafferton CID.'

'Oh my heavens above. But how do I know you are? Anybody could say that, couldn't they?'

'If you come to the window of your front room and pull the curtain back I'll show you my warrant card and my face.'

'That's fair enough, fair enough. You come to the window then.'

After peering as closely as he could, the man let the curtain fall and came back to open the door.

'Come in, sir. Come in. I didn't mean to sound suspicious.'

'You should.'

The small hall was as it must have been the day he moved in. The staircase had been boxed in, the ceiling was Artexed, the radiator panel was painted dark crimson. In the front room, the fireplace had also been boxed, in the 1960s Simon guessed, and the wallpaper had decorative columns and borders in the same pattern but different colours. There was a china cabinet with massed figurines on the top shelf, trophies and cups below.

'Sit down, please sit down, sir. And what can I do for you? I don't own a car, I am too old to have to pay for a TV licence, so I'm at a loss really.'

'Neither of those. Firstly, can I just make sure – you are Stanley Gordon Barnard?'

'I am certainly. And my late wife was Gwendolen Mary Barnard but she passed on a long time ago now – nearly eleven years. So I am the sole resident.'

'I want to ask you about something that happened around five and a half years ago, Mr Barnard. I know that's a while but I hope you can help all the same. Do you remember having seen this young woman at any time?'

Stanley Barnard must have been in his late eighties. His hearing was aided by large earpieces, he was a man who had been tall but who had shrunk in old age, with bent shoulders, and his eyesight was poor. He took some time to find his spectacles in their case, take them out, polish the lenses and put them on. Simon doubted if he would recall anything but the moment he took the newspaper photograph he said, 'Yes! I certainly do remember and I remember very clearly. I was very upset when I read about her disappearing and then do you know, only the other day, I read something in the paper again

261

and it brought it all back. I was upset again to think she'd never been found. That sort of thing destroys your faith in humanity, sir. She was a lovely-looking young woman. Lovely. I didn't have daughters only the one son and he went before the wife, cancer, but I can still imagine what it must be like to lose a young daughter like this. I certainly can.'

He took off his glasses and wiped his eyes, shaking his head as he did so.

'Do you have any news of her then? Though I must say it's taken long enough for you to get round to me. I don't know why, you had my name and address. I don't mean you personally, sir, I don't recognise you – it was a much younger policeman I spoke to at the time.'

'When exactly was that, Mr Barnard?'

'Well, at the park, the Adelaide Road Park. You know the park?'

'I do. So did you see the girl – Kimberley Still – at that park?'

'I told the young policeman.'

'Mr Barnard, it was, as you say, a few years ago and I wasn't on the case, I'm just picking up the threads and looking into the files. So would you mind starting from the beginning?'

'I go to that park almost every day and I have done since my wife passed away . . . winter and summer, except if it's pouring with rain, there's no enjoyment in that. I don't mind the cold, you can wrap up and the park's quite sheltered. So I'm there most days, usually late morning or early afternoon – the children come out of school at half past three and then there's a lot of them in the park with their mothers and their friends, playing around. We get the babies in the morning more, the babies and toddlers, I love to see them and hear them chatter. Some of them know me and wave to me or say hello, though I don't encourage them at all, that wouldn't be right, they don't know me – I would never give them anything, sweeties or anything, but I wave and say hello if they do. I go mainly for someone to chat to, really, and there are plenty of those, plenty of us regulars. She was a regular, the young lady – at lunchtime only, and sometimes with others, sometimes on her own. She brought her lunch. A lot do that. So, I'm gener-

262

ally in the Adelaide Road Park at some point of the day. I take a paper, I buy a cup of tea from the corner, though the best one shut down, you know, so I get it from the big coffee place. Only I get tea. Sometimes a bit of cake but not always. That's how I recognised her straight away, when her picture was in the paper.'

'Do you remember when you last saw her?'

'I do, I remember very well.'

'That's good news . . . would you tell me about it?'

Barnard sat up suddenly. 'I apologise, can I offer you a hot drink? I know you won't take alcohol but a cup of tea?'

'No thank you, I had a coffee just before I came out. But thank you all the same.'

'I wouldn't like to think I hadn't so much as offered. Still . . . now then, that poor young woman. I said I was in Adelaide Road Park most days – still am, still am – and this day I remember because there weren't so many about, only a young mother with a pram pushchair thing came in, and all of a sudden I saw her little boy start running towards the pond. Well . . .'

'I've just been to talk to her and she remembers that too.'

'You have? Good, so that will back me up, show I'm not making things up.'

'I would never suppose that you were, Mr Barnard.'

'Stan. Are you allowed to call me Stan?'

'I certainly am.'

'Now, this little chap – if I'd been quicker off the mark I'd have jumped up and been after him but I wasn't so near and the young lady – that young lady in the paper – no sooner saw it than she was after him and grabbed hold of him just as he got to the edge of the pond. You don't realise how fast they can go and the poor mother was beside herself, she was trying to anchor the pushchair thingy and go after him, it's a big load being a young mother with two little ones, you know. I see them every day. So, they stood and chatted for a minute, I can see them now. But the mother gathered herself up and left, probably worried he'd do it again, and that lass – Kimberley – yes, this one here – she was just sitting down on the bench again and getting out a paper bag with her lunch in when he

263

came through the gateway at the side just nearby and went up to her and spoke and they went off and in a bit of a hurry too.'

Simon sat forward. 'Just a moment . . . you said "he" – did you recognise the man?'

'No, no. Never seen him but I did watch them go and I think he had a car parked outside so maybe he was a friend – maybe she had to go somewhere urgently. I wouldn't know.'

'Can you describe the man?'

'Oh dear. Well, my memory isn't so good –'

'Your memory is excellent, Stan. Just think back – go over the scene in your mind. Close your eyes if that helps and take your time. It's surprising what you can recall if you give yourself a chance.'

The old man did exactly as he was told – he was of a generation who obeyed the police automatically, Simon thought, and he found it both touching and slightly disconcerting, but he almost held his breath, willing his memory to surface, as Stan put his head back, closed his eyes and was still and silent.

'I can recall a bit but it isn't very clear, I'm afraid.'

'Never mind – just tell me as much as you can.'

'Not tall and not bald and not old but not young either. That's too many "nots" for you, isn't it?'

'No, it's fine.'

'Not hairy – I mean to say, not a beard or anything like that. No glasses. Now I think he had no jacket either but I couldn't swear to that. He might have had a jacket. It was a sunny day but maybe I'm just making that up – I had a jacket on, I know that. But then, I always do, rain or shine.'

'If he wasn't bald, can you have a guess at the colour of his hair?'

Stan closed his eyes again briefly, but then he shook his head. 'Not coming,' he said. 'Could have been anything, but then again, if it had been down to his shoulders, say, like some of these young chaps, I'd have remembered that, wouldn't I? Or if it had been like yours, colour of wheat in the sun . . . do you have Scandinavian origins?'

'Not that I know of but people often ask. You say the man went up and spoke to Kimberley Still – are you quite sure that it was her, not some other young woman?'

'I'm quite sure of that because so far as I can remember there weren't any others – there were one or two older ladies, but unless I'm very mistaken, which I am not . . . no, it was her, because it caught my eye, you know, having seen her before.'

'Did she appear to know the man?'

'That I couldn't say. She might have known him . . . she might not.'

'But she got up and went out of the park with him?'

'Yes, and in quite a hurry, as if she'd been told something was urgent, if you follow me.'

'Yes. So she went willingly?'

'It seemed so.'

'There was no question of his forcing her to go with him, or of her being at all reluctant?'

'Not as I remember. It was all quick, you know, not any talk or arguing.'

'Did you see if he had a car and if she got into it?'

'No, I couldn't see anything once they'd gone through the gateway.'

'Did you hear a car drive off?'

'Well, you couldn't, could you? I mean, that is a nice little park, it isn't full of people making a noise or anything, but it is in the centre of town, I don't think you could hear just the one car. No.'

'Mr – Stanley, why didn't you tell all this to the police when they interviewed you?'

'They didn't. That's to say, they were in the park handing out these leaflets and I looked and said I thought I recognised the young woman, I thought I might have seen her that day but it could have been a different day, of course it could – he took my name and address and said they might need to talk to me again. But they never did.'

'Are you sure? They didn't phone you asking when you'd be at home?'

'I don't think they took my phone number. I don't think they did but of course I could be wrong about that . . . it is quite a while ago, you know. I'm surprised at how much I have remembered to be honest with you.'

'I'm impressed at how much too. Now one question more and this really is very important . . . this day, the day you saw Kimberley in the park, the day a man walked up to her and spoke and she went away with him – was this the last time you saw her, in the park or anywhere else? Or might you have seen her again?'

'I definitely didn't see her again. I know that much because I was there all that week – it was beautiful weather after that day, we had lovely warm sunshine, the place was quite busy especially at lunchtimes, and for some reason I looked out for her – no, no, I didn't do that, but I noticed that she wasn't there – there are a few people I see regularly, we even chat, we know each other and I'd miss them if they weren't there for a few days. Dare I say they might even miss me. I didn't chat to this young woman, I'm not even sure if we ever passed the time of day. But I know I didn't see her again and it wasn't many days after that the police were round with their leaflets and then I saw it on the local television news. No, that was the last time.'

'Have you any idea why the police didn't get in touch with you – even come and find you in the park and talk to you?'

'No. Thinking about it, maybe they should have done but I didn't really . . . I suppose they must have had other, what do you call it, "leads"?'

'And you didn't think to go to the police station yourself and speak to someone about it?'

There was a pause. Stanley Barnard's face clouded over and when he looked up at Serrailler next he had tears in his eyes. 'This is terrible. I should have done that, shouldn't I? I suppose I just didn't think it was important. I don't know. I should have done though. I should have realised and done my duty. Have I done her harm? Is it my fault?'

The photographs of Lee Russon Simon pulled up from the files when he got home were mugshots but there was enough for him to check off Stanley's list of negatives – not bearded, not fair-haired. He checked with information from the two murders for which he was now serving life and found his details. White, stocky, not tall. None of it got him very far, only enough for Simon not to eliminate him altogether at this stage. Why the original team hadn't followed up on Stanley Barnard he was at a loss to understand. 'Leave no stone unturned,' his first DI had said almost every day, 'and no pebble either.' The first stone was CCTV.

Ten minutes later, he was pulling up at the side entrance to the park. The gates, both here and at the front, were closed at six o'clock. There were no CCTV cameras. He walked down the road, alongside the high hedge that surrounded the park. Opposite the entrance were two blocks of flats, set well back and with parking areas in front and, in one case, at the side as well and this block also had security TV. He crossed over. Privately owned cameras were often dummies, especially on single houses, but this one looked real and seemed to be switched on, in that there was a green light blinking steadily.

He walked along to the main park entrance, which had tall stone pillars on either side and imposing wrought-iron gates, the originals, dating from the turn of the last century, and here a CCTV camera was placed to cover both the entrance and the main path. The children's playground at the far end, which was surrounded by high wire-mesh fencing, could be seen clearly under the street lights and there were cameras on the posts, positioned to view the playing area and equipment.

He walked back. There was little traffic here at this time in the evening, though cafes and bars were open and busy a few yards away.

If Kimberley Still had left with a man by the side entrance, as Stan Barnard claimed to have seen, there was a very slim possibility that the pair could have been caught on the camera outside the flats. If it was real and active and less than ten years or so old, the footage would be digital and the chances of picking up a recording, even now, were good. A warrant to view could be obtained.

Simon supposed that, unless he could now persuade the Chief to give him some help, he would be in for hours of looking at old CCTV images, something he had not done since he was a rookie detective constable. But he had a hunch that it would prove worth his while, that he would find something. There was no record in the case files of any camera searches having been made by the original investigating team, which meant either that indeed they had not been made or that someone had forgotten to write up the notes. Either omission was, in his view, a clear case of professional negligence.

Fifty-four

'Sis?'

'Hi – just a heads-up. I'm on my way to the hospital.'

'Now what?'

'They're discharging him. Don't ask.'

'Oh help . . . You're taking him home with you?'

'Where else?'

'While I've got you, I had a call from the rehab people – they want to fit my new prosthesis and give me a couple of days' intensive training but do I really need that, do you think? I'm just at a breakthrough point in this cold case.'

'You'll definitely need some time with them – this prosthesis will be more sophisticated than the one you've got now which doubtless means more complicated. It's going to talk to your arm's computer via Bluetooth.'

'Wouldn't a day cover it? I can always contact them if I come up against a problem– or you can help me out.'

'No, I can't, Simon, I know next to nothing about it. It's a highly specialist area, as you should know by now. Why not tell them you'd find it difficult to spend two days there just now, ask them for their opinion? Si, I've got to go, I'm in the hospital car park and of course there are no spaces. Let me know what happens. Come round tonight? Dad would appreciate it.'

No, Simon thought, Dad sure as hell would not.

But he went, partly in case he could catch Kieron, partly out of guilt, but also because he had caught himself once or twice lately feeling an unfamiliar bleakness at being alone in the flat he loved so much, probably because he was in it too much just now, so that it was no longer a blessed relief from the job, which he loved but which was so often frenetic. He had time to work up the drawings he had done on Taransay, yet whenever he opened the sketchbooks, he felt an ennui. His gallery was nudging him but he had stalled them. There were evenings when he found nothing he wanted to read or listen to and could find only crime shows on television, which annoyed him because they so often got the procedures wrong.Yet when Rachel had moved in with him, he had not been able to cope – not with her so much as with someone else in his private space.

'Midlife crisis,' Cat said, handing him a gin. 'I've had several. You need to get back to proper work.'

'This case is proper work.'

'Are you getting anywhere?'

'Yes.' He pulled a kitchen chair out and straddled it.

'You will go up and see Dad?'

'Soon.'

Cat glanced at him. He wanted to talk to her. She could always tell.

She took the dish of chilli from the fridge and put it in the oven, set the timer and then picked up her glass. 'Come on, let's be civilised for once.'

The evening light came into the sitting room, gilding the far wall. Cat opened the windows onto the garden a crack. It was just warm enough.

She sat down and sipped her drink, leaned her head back, closed her eyes. Waited. Said nothing. That was the way you had to be with Simon.

A blackbird was madly singing from the holly tree.

'I was wondering if I should move,' he said and at once got up, took both their glasses and went into the kitchen to refill them, so that she had time to take in what he had said and he did not have watch her immediate reaction.

'Move as in job or home?'

'Home – wouldn't want a new patch – not for now anyway. Probably never.'

'Why?'

Simon shrugged. 'It might have had its day.'

'You love it. Always have, always will . . . least I thought so.'

'I still do – in most ways.'

'I think this is part of your coming to terms with what happened. Moving house won't change everything.'

'I know that.'

'Right, what are you tired of – the view from the windows?'

'Never.'

'No. The space – the way you've arranged it? All that.'

'No. I might refresh but I wouldn't want to change anything.'

'Lack of an outside space?'

'I'm no gardener, and anyway, I can come here. Or go away.'

'Lonely?'

'I'm perfectly self-sufficient.'

'You think you are.'

'Here we go – knowing me better than I know myself.'

'Sometimes. It would be OK to admit to being lonely. It's in order. People are.'

He shook his head.

'Not being at work all day and occasionally half the night makes a difference. The time I broke my leg I nearly went round the twist being here on my own for most of the day, for weeks on end. I was close to inviting the postman in for coffee, just to talk to another human being. It's understandable, Si.'

'Yes.'

'Where would you move to?'

'A cottage maybe . . . village near here?'

'Roses round the door?'

He threw a cushion at her. Cat was about to catch him off guard by saying a name, but before she could, Kieron's car came up the drive and Richard shouted from upstairs and, simultaneously, banged hard on the floor.

'I knew I shouldn't have left that bloody walking stick by his bed,' Cat said. A moment later, Kieron put his head round the door. 'Didn't know you were coming,' he said. He looked tired and drawn. 'Sorry but I'm not going to be sociable. I've had budget meetings the entire day and a migraine to finish all. I'm off to a darkened room.'

Simon followed him as far as the hall. 'One quick question.' Kieron stopped.

'I'm at breakthrough with the Kimberley Still case. Can I have extra manpower for twenty-four hours?'

'Have what you want,' the Chief said.

Fifty-five

'Dave.'

'What do you want? I'm just getting ready to go out.'

'Nice. Wish I could say the same.'

'You all right? Your voice sounds funny.'

'Got someone's phone.'

'Whose?'

'Never mind. You've got to go up there.'

'I can't, we're –'

'Go up there. Put a note under his door.'

'I'll do it first thing, Lee.'

'You'll fucking do it now.'

'Or else, oh yeah, there'll be an "or else".'

'There will. Now listen. Write "Thursday 6th".'

'That all?'

'No. Give him the address.'

'What's happened anyway?' Dave asked.

'You should know. And you remember the "or else", because if you don't do this and do it tonight, there will be be an "or else", Davie. Man of my word, me.'

'I'm your brother, Lee . . .'

But Lee had rung off. And Dave wasn't stupid. He knew his brother too well not to believe him. Knew what he was capable of.

'Got to nip out,' he called to Donna. 'Back in ten.'

273

He was in the car and off before she could stop him – not that she'd bother. She never asked questions because she wasn't interested in the answers.

He didn't really want to know what Lee was up to either. He just did as he was told when he was told and every now and then, took some money. It seemed to him that he couldn't be blamed for anything he didn't know about, and if asked questions, he could tell the truth.

He drove along past The Hill, took a couple of left turns, then skirted the new housing estate and up towards the quarry. Two miles. Three. Sharp left down a narrow track between trees, cursing the potholes. Through an open gateway. Along another track which was barely suitable for any vehicle at all. Stopped in a circle of rough ground at the end and from there he went on foot.

At first he thought the place was empty but then he saw a thin string of dirty yellow light under the door and as he reached it, heard a television, crackling and hissing for lack of good signal. But it did the job of hiding the slight sound as he folded the brown envelope lengthwise, pressed it as flat as he could, and slipped it into the door jamb. The noise from the television continued without a pause.

He crept for the first few yards, keeping his head down, then ran to the car and drove away. He didn't know what Lee was up to, didn't know what the message he'd delivered meant or who he had taken it to, only knew the place itself. Lee had never referred to anyone by name, never would, and that was fine, he didn't want to get any more involved. He stuck by his brother because they had always been the closest and because, no matter what, blood was thicker than water, but that didn't mean he was happy with the things Lee had done – quite the opposite.

The message in its folded envelope stayed in the door jamb all night, the noise of the television turned up to its loudest having blotted every other sound. It was only early the next morning, because he was always up by six, that he spotted it, read it. And laughed.

Fifty-six

The new DC Simon had borrowed had been in Lafferton CID since the week of his attack. Fern Monroe had come in on the fast-track scheme after having taken a degree in criminology, and at twenty-three was enthusiastic, brainy and abrupt and clearly thought that she was rather above spending hours trawling through CCTV footage.

'How long is this going to take, guv?'

Simon bit his tongue. She was young, a rookie, she hadn't had the shine rubbed off her yet. She'd learn.

'I am hoping less time than you might expect. A note was made on the Still files that all local authority CCTV cameras were ordered to tag their recording for that day. You know about tagging?'

She did not, he could tell by her expression. He could also tell that she would die rather than admit it. Well, he was going to cut her some slack. Just not too much.

'Oh yes.'

'So run through it for me.'

'Certain cameras are marked out.'

'Not quite.'

'Sorry, no. I meant certain times.'

Serrailler leaned back. He knew that he would be fairer to her than many a senior CID officer, and that if she did not mend her attitude quickly, they would be unforgiving. They were not bad people, not unkind or impatient, and they had all been at the bottom, at the beginning. But there was still some prejudice against fast-track graduate entrants to the police and someone was always ready to trip them up and make fools of them. If he said nothing now, things would get worse and quickly.

She sat looking at him coolly through tortoiseshell glasses.

'DC Monroe, listen. You have been a DC for a few months. Fine. You cannot have experienced everything – or even very much – and you can't know everything. There is absolutely no shame in saying so. There are plenty of things I still don't know. Same applies to every single officer in this station. So, let's start again. Do you know exactly what a tagged day means in terms of CCTV recordings?'

'Probably not, comprehensively.'

'You mean "No"?'

She met his gaze defiantly and did not look away. 'All right.'

'You mean "No"?'

'Yes, guv.'

'OK, got there. Now you're going to find out and it's very simple. It isn't something you'll come across every day though it isn't a rare occurrence either. Let's take this particular case – the disappearance of Kimberley Still, nearly five and a half years ago. How familiar are you with the case?'

'Not at all.'

Serrailler opened up his laptop. 'Here – this page and the next – read it and get up to speed. I'll get the coffees in. Black? White?'

'Tea, Earl Grey, black. The machine does have it.'

He was waylaid by a couple of people wanting to greet him, and by the time he returned to the room as large as a cupboard that he had purloined for the viewing, DC Monroe had brought herself up to date on the cold case.

'There are quite a few things that ought to have been done as routine that I can't find any reports on.'

'You could say. That's why we're here.' He set down her plastic cup of tea.

'Thanks, guv. I owe you 90p.'

'On me. What about tagging?'

'Got it. So we're hoping to find that every local authority CCTV record taken on the third of June was frozen, as it were

276

– tagged. It should never be erased, whereas even with digital they do eventually have to erase some data from way back. I was just getting up the LDC stored files.'

'Good. Find the date and see if they have all been tagged as requested.' He drank his coffee and watched her fingers speed, concentrating hard. She was clearly an expert and they had never had enough of those. He had watched too many stubby fingers poke and jab ponderously at keyboards.

'Here we are . . . it looks as if the tagging worked. Now we just need to find the relevant cameras – there'll be a database. Shall I access it?'

He noted that she did not say 'try to'.

Three minutes later the information was on-screen, the relevant cameras narrowed down to four.

'We can rule that one out,' Serrailler pointed. 'That's in Victoria Street, at the back, away from the park. This one is at the main gates – probably doesn't concern us for the moment.'

'So, it's these two – 245 and 248?'

'Can we look at the tagged day only?'

'Third of June . . . we should be able to – that's basically why it's tagged – never to be deleted.'

'Right – can you find the date? It's in white on the top above the pictures.'

She found it.

'This is saving so much time. Glad I'm in expert hands.'

She gave a very small smile.

They started to go patiently through all the images for the day on which Kimberley had gone missing, starting at midnight and one second. There was nothing at all until three, then an urban fox and a cat. Nothing again. Slowly, they caught up with that day, frame by frame, with delivery vehicles, people cycling and walking to work, children going to school, postmen, more delivery vans. Plenty of quiet patches – this was not an especially busy area at any time. They got to four in the afternoon without any sighting of any car near the side entrance to the park. The camera was pointed just away from the pavement.

'Someone could have stopped a car in this area – here to here – and this camera wouldn't have picked it up. You can just about make out people going in but no full-on shots. If we're going to see anything it will be on the camera at the entrance by the block of flats. That might catch the road and the kerb as well or it might not. It'll be someone's law that we're trying to get a sight of activity in the one small area not covered by any camera at all.'

But at the camera's date and time of 3 June at 13.11, they got lucky.

'Look, guv.' Fern Monroe had pressed pause.

Serrailler leaned forward. The image was not good – they never were – but Fern had paused at a frame which showed a man and a woman come out of the side entrance to the park and cross the road.

'Go back.'

She ran back to where a car came down the side road, paused and then turned slowly into the entrance to the flats. They watched it park, and what looked like the same man get out. He took the short walk in reverse and entered the park.

'Freeze that please. Enlarge?'

'It will make it less clear.'

'I know – I need to get a better idea of his height and build. There – stop. Russon is white, around five ten, full head of hair, stocky but not fat.'

'Looks about right but his face isn't visible.'

'Shoot forward to where he goes into the park.'

Four minutes and twenty-two seconds passed without sight of him, though three other people came out of the park and one went in.

'There.'

The man came out again, hurriedly this time with, on his left side, so turned away from the camera, a woman, probably five inches shorter. They crossed the road, towards the block of flats, walking more quickly still. Up to the car. Another frame and the man was opening not the driver's door but the offside rear. He had the woman directly in front of him, so close that there was little view of her between him and the open car door. The next frame had to be moved to and fro several times because the movements were fast and jerky. The woman seemed to have

278

got into the rear seat, the man slammed the door, went quickly round, got in and reversed, wheels spinning, and then was away left and out of sight of the camera.

'Bingo,' Serrailler said.

'But is it him?'

'I think it could well be, but this on its own isn't enough of course.'

'That's as clear a picture as I can get. If I pull it in closer it'll just blur.'

'Go back to where we first pick up the car.'

'Ford Focus, I think,' Fern said. 'Light colour. Older model.'

'Driver's clearer but still not identifiable enough – I'd put money on this being Russon. It would help in court but it isn't conclusive.'

She moved on and stopped again. 'Ah – thought so. Number plate.'

'Well spotted . . . not quite all of it. Let's see if we can improve on that.'

But all the subsequent views of the car showed less. Simon made a note of the best they had, which lacked the first letter and the last two numbers.

'That's almost certainly a Y.'

'No . . . J.'

'You don't usually get a J at the end. Y is common.'

'We need to keep them both for now. Can you try and track this down please? ANPR should find it for you in a trice. Email me what they come up with.'

'And then?'

'Nothing else today – we struck gold early on but I may need you later, if nothing more urgent comes up.'

'Famous last words but it's quite quiet at the moment, guv. Where are you going?'

Simon hesitated, partly because it could have been regarded as an inappropriate question from a rookie DC to a Chief Super, but mainly because something occurred to him.

'I need you to get info from ANPR first, and if it's helpful, it might be interesting for you to come with me. Good experience for you to sit in.'

279

'On what, guv?'
'An interview in prison.'

He left the station straight away. He was still officially on sick leave and the last thing he wanted to do was breathe down the necks of CID. Fern Monroe would get any information about the car in double-quick time – she was keen and efficient, and he could work with her, so long as she didn't forget that she was in her first job.

He walked round to Adelaide Road and took the side entrance into the park. It was a dull, cold day and there were not many people apart from two mothers with toddlers, duck-feeding, and a few of the elderly regulars. Stan Barnard was not among them. Serrailler went to a bench halfway round, and then walked briskly back – it took him just over a minute. From there across the road to the block of flats was half a minute. It was very little time for anyone to notice the man and woman, whoever they were, leaving the park together, but Stanley Barnard had and it had taken more than five years for them to find that out.

He walked down through the shopping arcade, and out in the direction of the cathedral, adjacent to the Lanes. He had wanted to buy a new book about Leonardo da Vinci, which the bookshop would get for him in a couple of days if it wasn't already in stock.

He almost turned towards it, then stopped. He wanted the book but not urgently. He was fabricating a reason for going in there, tantalising himself with the chance of seeing Rachel again. But why? And if she was there, what would he say to her?

No.

Instead, he made a call to the prison, requesting an interview with Lee Russon that afternoon. An hour later, DC Monroe sent him an email.

Not enough info on car number plate to recognise categorically but they came up with 24 close enough to be worth pursuing based on what we have. Am checking now. Might be a slow job?

But by the time Simon arrived back at the station he found that she had easily eliminated half of them as being nowhere near a match for the car make and model, and two others because they had been recorded as off the road and destroyed.

'Leaves me with ten, guv.'

'Take each one and go carefully. I'll look as well.'

Five down, she stopped. 'Look at this . . . it's all the numbers we can make out clearly. It's the right car. Light colour. But nothing is coming up under owner, tax or insurance info. Just blanks.'

Simon thought for a moment. It felt right. They were near. Nearer than near. But there had to be more.

'Speed cameras?' Fern said.

'Good call. Find every one within a radius of ten miles and focus first on the west side – Starly Road. Then look for those at the bypass end. Black Earl Grey tea?'

'Thanks, guv.'

The machine was out of china tea so he went down to the canteen. There was a queue, at the end of the shift, but while he was waiting, Fern Monroe burst in through the doors, calling as she came. 'Guv – got it. I've got it!'

Serrailler frowned as odd people stared round, and turned away from her until he had got their teas, before taking them across to a window table on the far side.

'Guv –'

'DC Monroe, I know this is on police premises, not a public cafeteria, but even so, best not shout all our secrets to the entire force.'

She looked annoyed but sat down and took a sip of her tea. It was boiling hot but she appeared not to notice.

'So – what have you got?'

'There are three speed cameras within two miles of the park on the Starly side – the first was out of order on that Wednesday, but the second camera picked up our car, pretty certain it was him but he wasn't speeding. The third camera is in Gulliver Road.'

'Runs along the top of the park.'

'Yes – the camera is on the straight, before you get to the left-hand turn into Waterloo Way which leads to the side of the park and that block of flats.'

281

'Well known for speeding – people going away from the town centre, using it as a bypass, which it isn't, it's a residential road – wide though, and often there are cars parked on both sides.'

'Our car was caught on that camera speeding towards the turning, which he took a bit fast. This time, the camera got him full on and also as he was speeding away from it. It clocked him and he was issued with a ticket. I've asked for a copy and note of address and when it was paid.'

'If it was paid.'

'Well, yes. The result won't be as quick as the ANPR was though – separate department and not fully digital at this date.'

Serrailler drank half of his tea and then looked across the table. 'Good work, DC Monroe. This is what you need to have – attention to detail, perseverance – plus never lose sight of the big picture, and never ignore your hunches. Just don't rely on them, to the exclusion of all else. Sermon over. Finish your scented tea – we're off to Leverworth Prison.'

Lee Russon had been notified in advance that he was to be interviewed and immediately asked for his solicitor. The request had been refused but now they were in the small room with him – Serrailler across the metal table, DC Monroe on a chair against the back wall some yards away – he asked again.

'You don't need your solicitor, this is a talk. You're not under caution, you are not charged with anything, you can refuse to answer any of my questions, and you are free to go at any point – just ask.'

Russon was leaning against the back of his chair so that it rocked. He had his arms folded across his chest and a sneer on his face.

'All right, then, no worries, I haven't a clue why you're here but I haven't done anything – haven't really had a chance, have I? So I'm fine without the legal team. Who did you say you were? I don't remember you.'

'No, we haven't met. Detective Chief Superintendant Simon Serrailler. This is Detective Constable Monroe. She is sitting in but not taking part. Is that all right with you?'

282

Russon shrugged but gave Monroe a quick up-and-down, before looking away.

'I want to talk to you about cars, Lee.'

'Try a garage.'

Simon ignored him. 'Specifically, cars you have owned in the past ten years. Specifically, one car, but let's go through them.'

'As if.'

'Sorry?'

'Had a lot of cars, me.'

'How many is "a lot" – over ten years? Try to be exact, if you can.'

Russon closed his eyes and tipped his head back. He stayed like that for several minutes and Simon did not nudge him, did not speak, just waited.

'Twelve. Fourteen. I dunno.'

'That seems a lot.'

'Does it? Why does it?'

'I know some people like to change their cars regularly, especially if they buy new and have a sort of rolling deal, exchanging every two years. Is that what you did?'

'Don't take the piss.'

'So what did you do?'

'Bought. Sold. Normal I'd say.'

'Maybe. All right, you bought a banger, drove it into the ground, tarted it up and sold it to some monkey, bought another –'

'You accusing me?'

'No. Just saying what probably happened.'

'Fat lot you know.' Russon swung his chair fully upright suddenly, bumping against the table as he did so. He leaned on it and stared at Serrailler. 'That it?'

'I've hardly started.'

Russon rolled his eyes.

'What was the last car you owned?'

'Still on cars, are we?'

'We are.'

'Can't remember.'

'Try hard.'

The man spread out his arms.

'OK, let me help you. Colour – black? Silver? Blue? White?'

'I had a black car. And a white van. I had a maroon car. I had –'

'Which were you driving on the third of June 2009 . . . when you were caught on camera speeding in a thirty mile per hour area and issued with a ticket?'

'I never got a ticket.'

'The camera never lies, Lee. Which car?'

'Told you. No idea about speeding and tickets. Wasn't me.'

'Which car did you own on and around that date? Come on, don't mess me about, You know.'

Russon tipped his head back and closed his eyes again. 'Time goes slowly in here,' he said. 'Not that you'd know. It's a very, very long time ago.'

'But nothing much has happened during that time. It was your last car, wasn't it? So you'll remember.'

'My last car, was it?'

'It was.'

'Which car was that?'

'Oh, you tell me. Make and model. Colour. Registration number.'

'Bad memory, me.'

'It was a beige Ford Focus, wasn't it?'

He shot the question out quickly and saw the flicker of surprise on Russon's face before he closed his expression down.

'Registration beginning APW . . .'

'I told you, I had dozens of cars.'

'On that third of June you only had one – a beige Ford Focus. What happened to that car, Lee?'

'How should I know? Five years ago and I've been in here, no cars in here.'

'Did you dump it? Did you set fire to it?'

'I don't know what you're talking about. I'm fed up with this, this is getting boring.'

'You left the car outside the block of flats in Waterloo Way. You crossed the road and went through the side entrance into Adelaide Road Park. Not long after that you were seen emerging by the same route with a young woman, aged about twenty-five, who I believe to have been Kimberley Still.'

Russon sat bolt upright, his hands gripping the table. 'Hang on, hang on. "You were seen"? By who? Who saw me with whatever her name was, who says they saw me?'

'I can't tell you that, Lee, but you could tell me.'

He watched Russon weighing everything up, as he stared down at the table. He could continue to say nothing, know nothing, remember nothing – plead innocent. He could give the wrong answers, or partially wrong. Or he could give out the information. Serrailler knew he was now trying to work out exactly what that would mean and what would happen next. He could make a shrewd guess but, depending on what he had actually done with the car, he couldn't be sure what Serrailler himself knew, and if he knew anything troubling, then how, how?

He looked at the copper. He didn't know anything – or nowhere near enough. He'd picked up a few bits, God knows how or why, but that wasn't a problem. Keep his head, that's all he needed to do. Give away nothing.

'The car, Lee?'

'Can't remember.'

'Just the colour will do for a start. Just give me the colour.'

'Can't remember. Maybe black?'

'Try harder. Or the make?'

'Can't remember.'

'Bit careless to get a speeding fine on that day of all days.'

'Didn't get one.'

'When?'

'When you said.'

'When was that?'

'Can't remember.'

'Where did you take her, Lee?'

A split-second pause, before the man closed down again. But there had been the flicker of shock in his eyes.

'What did you do with her?'

'I don't know who you're talking about.'

'Where did you take her in the blue Mondeo?'

285

'It . . .'

'Yes?'

'Nothing.'

'That was it, wasn't it, a blue Mondeo? That's the one we've got a note of.'

The man was biting his lip, holding himself back, wanting to say 'No, I never had a blue Mondeo' but forcing himself not to, wanting to show Serrailler he was talking out of the back of his head but not doing it.

'Or was it the Ford Focus? Sorry, my mistake. Yes, of course. You took Kimberley over to the Ford Focus when you got her out of the park – we know that for sure. Where did you drive off to? Pretty fast, wherever it was. Did you get another speeding ticket, Lee?'

Russon stood up. 'I've had enough of this. I want to leave now.'

'All right – just tell me it was the Ford Focus and I can tick that off the list.'

'What list? What are you talking about?'

'My list. We've got the car, we can have that confirmed, just thought it would be helpful of you to tell me as well.'

'What do you mean, you've got the car? How can you have got the car, there's no way –'

'No way what?'

'I want to go. If you don't let me out of here I'll have you.'

Serrailler stood up calmly and walked to the door, opened it, ushered Lee Russon out to the waiting warder. 'Thanks, Lee. You've been very helpful. I may need to talk to you again.'

There was a silence from the corridor, and then footsteps away. Serrailler turned back into the interview room.

'Great,' he said.'Excellent. He's got the wind up. He doesn't know what I know, and he's worried. Let him sweat. Come on, Monroe – you can tell me your thoughts on the way back.'

Fifty-seven

It had made Lee Russon angry and for a few minutes it had worried him, but when he got back he had calmed down, told himself that in spite of some of the questions, the cop did not know anything worth knowing – definitely nothing that could lead to the truth. But the reason they were raking through the cold files again was obvious. They ought to have better things to bother about than reading interviews in the paper with the Still woman, trying to stir it all up.

Mrs Still. He couldn't stop smiling.

In the shack, everything was ready and all he had to do was pass the time until dark. He found an old *Wordsearch* magazine under a pile of newspapers and did the few puzzles that he'd missed, only that didn't take long. He was good at wordsearch. Very, very good.

So he did the only other thing that would help him pass the time; drank two cans of Strongbow and went to sleep.

'Marion?'

'Hello, Bren, how are you? I rang you yesterday but you weren't there.'

'No, I was out for the evening with Clive and Vicky. The pub quiz evening. Anyway, I was just calling because I can't do Thursday as usual, so could we make it Friday? I thought we might try the new Italian place, it looks really nice, we walked past it last night. How would you feel?'

'Yes, nice idea. Why not? It's good to try out somewhere new and I like Italian so long as it isn't pizza. Always gives me heartburn.'

'It's that pastry-bread base. Can be quite soggy. But they have lots of other things, I stopped to look at the menu. Shall I book us a table for seven?'

'Would you? That's kind. Everything all right with you?'

'Oh yes, but the other thing I wanted to ask was if you'd had any more problems with noises out in your garden at night? Because if you have, you do know you can always come and stay here, any time, you only have to just ring – the bed's always made up.'

'I know and that's so kind of you as well. But actually, it's all been quiet, thank God. Not a whisper. I think it was a fox out in the garden myself. I read in the *Gazette* that they're becoming a real problem in towns. They don't know what to do about it.'

'I hope they don't start putting poison down.'

'Yes, but what else is there? They wouldn't shoot them in a town, and people have had them walk through patio doors into their houses. It's no joke. They spread all sorts of germs and illnesses as well.'

'Make sure yours stay out in the garden then.'

'Oh yes. I have to go, the oven timer just pinged. But I'll see you Friday, Brenda, really looking forward to it.'

Dave went down to the club at half six, got a pint, and ticked his name off on the sheet. He was fourth. He wouldn't drink more until after the games were finished, it upset his focus, and this wasn't just a friendly, this match was important. He saw a couple of the others over by the bar, and went to join them. They were smart – clean shirts, clean jeans or trousers with a crease, hair brushed and gelled. They were pumping themselves up. So was he. They were going to win.

He raised his glass. They replied.

'Here's to us,' Dave said, 'and wiping the floor with them.'

'Cheers, Dave.'

They were focused. They were ready. That's all any of them were thinking about.

Fifty-eight

'Have a glass of wine, Dad? It won't clash with any of your meds.'

'I am well aware of that, thank you.'

'Or a Scotch?' Kieron held up the bottle of Famous Grouse.

'Don't you have a malt?'

'We do. Laphroaig?'

'Too peaty for me. I'll have the Grouse.'

Kieron shot Cat a look as he reached into the cupboard for a glass. She knew he was biting his tongue and who would blame him? Her father had always been irascible but since being ill he had become downright rude – to all of them, except for Felix, who was his favourite, the apple of his eye, the one who had done no wrong since the day of his birth, and who never said more than half a dozen words to his grandfather.

'Water or soda?'

'Splash of water. No ice.'

'How are you feeling, Richard?' Kieron asked as he set the drink on the table beside him.

'Tired but otherwise pretty well, no thanks to the poor treatment in my old hospital – wrong drugs, not given at the right times, awful food, registrars aged thirteen and consultants never to be found, and the standard of hygiene has plummeted. Do they not teach it any more?'

'The trouble is that years ago, cleaning was outsourced to a private contractor, who inevitably got the contract with the lowest bid, and if you do that, you have to cut corners to make any profit at all. They pay their staff the minimum and there are too few of them to do a decent job. What do you expect?' Cat was sitting on the sofa with a glass of Sauvignon balanced on the arm and Mephisto and Wookie on her lap together. 'And you and I probably looked thirteen to the older patients, when we were junior doctors.'

'Don't try to humour me.'

'Perish the thought, Dad.'

Richard swirled a mouthful of whisky round, savouring it, but then said,'By the way, I hope not to impose on you for too much longer.'

'Of course you're not imposing, you've been very ill.'

'But recovering. Now – the house is let to these perfectly acceptable tenants for another month, and if he gets an extension to his research post, they will probably want to renew. I'm happy with that because I won't want to return there. Too big and too full of the past. I've been thinking about getting somewhere else.'

'A smaller house?'

'No. Do you remember the old maternity hospital, Ascot Court?'

'Just about. Didn't it become a private nursing home?'

'Yes. Awful place. They shut it down and rightly. It was empty for a time but I read in the *Gazette* that it's been bought by a developer and is being converted into luxury flats – just eight of them and exclusively for those over sixty.'

Cat stroked Mephisto's back slowly. What should she say? Not leap at the idea, not condemn it out of hand. Take the lead from him.

'You'd want your independence, Richard,' Kieron said. 'No forced social gatherings.'

'Certainly not. Unforced might be a different matter. I would want one of the two larger ones – garden flats. It has very pleasant grounds, as I remember. I went on calls there once or twice. I'll probably buy one straight away. I won't sell Hallam House for the time being. I thought you should know my plans.'

'It sounds good. And not too far from here.'

'Nor too near.'

'I'm surprised you've felt up to thinking about it at all.'

'Reading a newspaper and thinking wasn't beyond me, Catherine.'

'Clearly not.' Cat stood up. 'I'm going to put the vegetables on. Have another whisky, Dad.'

'Thank you, no. Perhaps after supper.'

She went out to the kitchen feeling elated. Trust her father to have said no word at all about contemplating his next move, just when the worry about his being with them for good had become serious and Kieron had started muttering threats.

Kieron. She heard Sam come up the drive at the same moment as Kieron's mobile buzzed from where he had left it on the kitchen table. She picked it up, cursing, and took it through, colliding with her son. 'Hey, Mum. So, guess what I've been doing today? The mortuary run.'

Fifty-nine

It was fine. It was great. It had worked out. As always, he had wanted to stay back and watch, see it all unfold, get the buzz, enjoy the happy ending, but this time he couldn't. He knew better than to take the risk. He had some sense, didn't he? He was buzzing though.

And then it happened, on the way back, climbing over the high gate at the back of four houses down, onto the waste ground behind. He'd done gate climbs, and much harder, much higher, a hundred times and this wasn't difficult and then his foot had caught and he hadn't time to save himself, just gone hurtling over and landed badly, one leg under him, arm splayed out. The pain had been terrible and he'd yelled aloud, couldn't stop himself. Then he'd blacked out.

First off, he didn't know where he was or why or who was talking to him. They kept asking his name and he could smell the smoke, and the pain in his leg and ankle was worse. There was a lot of noise from nearby, voices, engines. Yellow and orange spurts and flares behind his eyes and in the sky.

Something was put over him.

'He's not going anywhere.'

He remembered then, but it was no good because he couldn't move and because of the pain. He had to get away and he couldn't get away, and after a long time and a lot of smoke, the voices again, and the faces looking down on him, asking his name.

'Can you hear me, Barry? You're in an ambulance, on the way to hospital.'

They had put something over his face so he couldn't reply but they kept on asking and then, 'Squeeze my hand if you can hear me, Barry.'

Squeeze.

'Is your name Barry Grove? Squeeze my hand.'

Squeeze.

There was something wrong, he knew, something that should have happened. Or shouldn't. Or was going to. Just that he didn't know what. It was there in his mind, hovering about, but it wouldn't come clear. Something was wrong. Something.

Her father went to bed straight after supper, leaving Cat to clear up while Sam and Kieron watched Chelsea versus Spurs, and, as neither of them supported either team, they could enjoy the match without tensions arising.

She was still getting over her surprise at Richard's announcement, and as he had gone upstairs, Kieron had given her a thumbs up, with a grin. Her father had always been a man to make his own decisions, and to be brisk with those who tried to change his mind. But she would not dream of trying to do so. He would enjoy a totally different life in the new flats, might or might not make any friends, but in any case would be safe and not too far away if he needed any of them.

'Everything's working out then,' Sam said, coming in to fetch a beer for Kieron and a cake for himself. 'Except Grandpa doesn't think I should be a porter.'

'Has he said that?'

'Yes. I think he feels it reflects on him.'

Cat snorted.

'Thing is, nobody much remembers him now.'

'Sam – do NOT tell him that.'

'As if. Whoa, sorry, Kieron. It's OK, I've got them.'

'Update. The fire was in Mountfield Avenue. It was pretty certainly arson and they think they've got him.'

'You don't have to go, do you?'

'No. They'll brief me first thing. Come on, Sam – I have a hunch Spurs are going to walk this.'

'Nah . . . luck, that last one, pure luck. Yours are all over the place.'

They had set up a rivalry where none had existed, which, for them, was probably the whole point of watching a match. Cat smiled to herself.

They had dosed him up but he was aware of being pushed along corridors, through swing doors, and then X-rayed, aware of the young doctor telling him his break was very bad and did he give his consent, would he sign the form, why had he said 'None' when asked for his address, and 'Nobody' for name of next of kin?

He said his name again. Nothing else. There was nothing else. Someone put a paper close to his arm and he signed it. He remembered the man wearing a green sheet and a mask rubbing something on his arm and then he remembered nothing.

Sixty

It was ten past seven in the morning but the Chief had to be in London by eleven.

'Update, Simon. Mrs Still was pronounced dead at the scene . . . she didn't stand a chance. She'd locked and bolted every door and window after the scares she'd had about noises outside, so she would have been overcome by smoke and then the fire took over very quickly. Place is pretty much gutted. We have Barry Grove in hospital – he's been operated on for breaks in his leg and ankle and we can't talk to him yet but someone's waiting till the medics give the green light. We know it was him, he had traces of the accelerant all over him, and his footprints are in the soil of the flower bed under Mrs Still's window. But more to the point, he's a known arsonist – he went to prison for it a few years back when he was living in Bevham. What we want to find out is who set him up – because someone did. He'd started plenty of fires before but never anywhere near residential property or people. This was new. So either it was the culmination of a lot of practice runs or someone knew what he did and paid him. He's in a bad way so my guess is he'll crumble at the interview.'

'This is Russon.'

'We just have to prove it. Meanwhile, I read through all your notes – you got pretty close on the CCTV ID – good work, Superintendent. And no doubt you could get further if you had the speed camera stuff analysed, but honestly, do you need to do that now? I don't think so. Because whatever you found to corroborate that it was Lee Russon walking out of Adelaide Road Park with a girl who was pretty certainly Kimberley Still, without any material witness and without a confession, you and I know that this wouldn't persuade the CPS to reopen the case and bring Russon up for a new trial. But if he did get this Barry Grove to set Mrs Still's house on fire and Grove names him, we've got him that way.'

'And if he doesn't?'

'We cross that bridge. I think it's very likely he will.'

'Agreed.'

'So, what do we do? We can't charge Russon with arson of course and there'll be no paper trail. Grove gets charged anyway – murder almost certainly but he might get away with manslaughter if he claims not to have known there was anyone in the house at the time – been told it was empty, all of that. Doesn't matter.'

'My guess is that he'll sing. What's he got to lose?'

'This case was reinvestigated because poor Mrs Still never let it go. Understandably. But she's dead. She wanted justice for her daughter, proof that she was murdered by Lee Russon, and her body found. That's what we wanted – case solved, file closed. But Russon is serving life. If the arson and Mrs Still's murder are pinned on him, he is never going to get out of prison alive.'

'So why pursue him for this? Yes, you're right. I don't like it though.'

'Nor do I, but police resources are finite. If he was still out there of course we'd pursue it. If this guy in hospital so much as breathes Russon's name you go back there and this time it's under caution, he'll have his Brief with him but you still ask him again about Kimberley.'

'Russon won't talk,' Simon said. 'Ever. Why would he?'

'It's bloody frustrating, I know – you got very close.'

He called Monroe as he was leaving the building late that afternoon.

'We can't go any further.'

'But listen –'

'We know it's the right man, we know we've got the car and placed him at the scene at the right time, but it would never stand up. CPS wouldn't buy it as cast-iron grounds and new evidence for recommending a retrial, and as you know, nobody can be tried twice for the same crime unless there is "compelling new evidence". It's a dead end. But you've done excellent work, and thanks very much for your help.'

'Oh.'

'I know. Unfinished business – you have to get used to it. Sorry. It's bloody frustrating.'

'Right. Well, glad to be of some help anyway.'

Simon heard the flatness in her voice, knew her disappointment at what, at the moment, seemed like time wasted. But on several fronts, it had not been. They had, as the Chief said, come close. Now, maybe the arsonist would sing and they could link him to Lee Russon. Or maybe not.

And then there was the island. That was unfinished business too, and the police would not be able to close that file either, so long as there remained the faintest possibility that one day they might turn up something. On that basis, it would remain as yet another cold case.

He felt drained suddenly. His shoulder ached. In a couple of days he would have the permanent prosthesis fitted. His bionic arm. Robbie would want to see that in action, give him tests – 'Pick up a pin with it. Now hold that jug and don't drop it. Now wave to me. Now twist your hand round.'

He smiled. Would he ever go back to the island? Probably not. Some things were best left.

Kirsty rang him gone eleven o'clock that night. 'Is it too late? Had ye gone to bed Simon?'

'Never before midnight, if then, but I'm surprised you're still up. Are you all right?'

'Aye, more or less – I don't sleep so well now with a footy game going on under my ribs, and Robbie has been having nightmares.'

298

'Nice to talk then. Poor Robbie . . . my mum used to open the window and throw the nightmares out. She said they went galloping away across the sky.'

'That's a great notion, I'll give it a try. Listen, I just wanted to give you an update.'

'About Iain?'

'Well, of course once they knew about the hanging everyone's had their own theory, but nobody knows for sure about him and Sandy – Lorna never said anything and she's gone now.'

'Gone for good?'

'Aye . . . she never really liked it here and she couldn't run the pub and stores on her own. The pub's closed. There's an idea of taking the stores over as a community thing – because it'll take a while to get someone new, if we ever do.'

'Community pub too?'

'Maybe. That's a bit of a bigger enterprise. We'll see. The thing is, news got out about Sandy. Everyone knows.'

'How the hell did that happen? Who talked?' He could not imagine any of those officially involved saying a word out of turn.

Kirsty sighed. 'Letters. Something official-looking arrived, addressed to "Alexander Michael Murdoch".'

'Gordon.'

'He said he had to open it to get a return address. He started by asking if anyone knew if Sandy had a brother or even a husband, but it turned out to be something medical – gave the game away.'

'And he told everyone.'

Kirsty was silent.

'Not sure he shouldn't be reported for that,' Simon said after a moment.

'Och, no, you wouldn't, Simon, you –'

'I wouldn't, no. There are one or two things I could be reported for too.'

'Yes.'

'And how have people taken it?'

299

'After the initial shock . . . not so bad. This is a tight little island. Sandy had become part of it when not many outsiders do. She was liked. She pulled her weight. I should say "he" but I can't . . . I can't think of Sandy as a man, I just can't . . . it's sad she didn't feel able to tell us.'

'Yes, it is sad, but I wouldn't worry about it. Life goes on, life takes over.'

'It has. It's hard but we've just to get on with things. I'll have to go, Robbie's shouting out again and it's only me he wants when he has these dreams.'

'Don't forget – throw them out of the window. Look after yourself and your boy, Kirsty.'

'Boys. I had to get a scan as they thought there was a problem – there isn't but it showed another boy.'

'Your three boys then.'

He smiled to himself as he tidied round before going to bed. Three boys. Kirsty might have thirteen and she'd probably take it all in her stride. It was what they had to do on Taransay, take things as they came and deal with them, because life was too full to do anything else. They had known Sandy as a woman and that was how they would always think of her, so long as their memory of her survived. And if she had still been alive? Well, Kirsty was right – gradually, they would have just accepted him and got on with that too, and if the odd one found that difficult, they'd have kept it quiet. But he thought that what many did not understand was that finding it difficult for a time, having to learn how to take it, did not mean disapproval or concern. It meant, like so many things, that it was all a matter of time.

Barry Grove woke again to find two cops at his bedside and his leg stuck up in the air and held in some sort of sling. It wasn't hurting, just now, but it had and he knew that it would again, and then they would give him more of the stuff which made his brain spin off into fairyland. He had to sort things out before that happened.

'Can I have a drink?'

One of them poured him a glass of water. The young one. There was an older, fat one who he thought would be the hard one. Didn't matter. He drank. Then he said, 'I want to tell you about it.'

'Good,' the fat one said.

Barry Grove began to sing like a canary.

Sixty-one

'How does it feel?' Cat asked. They were sitting outside in the pub garden under a heater, having a glass of wine before going inside to eat. It was a quiet Saturday evening, too late for ramblers, too early for the supper crowd coming out from town. She had not seen Simon for almost a month, though they had talked and messaged each other, because she had been finding her feet in her new job, at the start of Concierge Doctors, and he had been away, and then easing himself back into full-time work again.

'Good.' He lifted his glass, turned it round and round by the stem, set it down, moved it to and fro.

'Can you pick up a pin?'

'Haven't tried but probably. It's amazing actually. And fits perfectly.'

'Prosthetics have come on very fast – it's probably the only thing we can thank foreign wars for.'

'Hmm.'

'Ascot Court have nearly finished the conversion and Dad's flat will be one of the first ready. He's started sending for paint charts and furniture catalogues.'

'Never having done such things in his life.'

'Always left it to the women. He's a reformed character.'

'Don't you believe it.'

'Exactly what Kieron said.'

They talked on as the sun moved off the garden, about Cat's work, his, Sam's plan to share a flat with a nurse and a junior doctor from the hospital.

'He's happy as Larry, Si. He loves the hospital, loves the job, loves the porters' cameraderie, loves being independent . . . but he can't stay there forever.'

'He won't. He'll gradually work out his real future – and I wouldn't put money on which way he'll jump, but meanwhile, he isn't dossing about at home, he isn't spending time wandering uselessly round the globe with a backpack – what's not to like?'

'And Kieron's happy – by Christmas he'll soon have me in the house to himself.'

'Plus Felix, Hannah, on the rare occasions she gets home, Wookie and Mephisto.'

'Bit worried about Mephisto actually . . . he's not himself. Sleeps most of the time and isn't out half the night any longer.'

'He's – what – eighteen?'

Yes.' She shivered. 'Let's go in and eat.'

Over whitebait, he told her about Kimberley Still, her mother, Lee Russon. But not about the island, not about Sandy Murdoch and Iain. Not about his feeling that he did not want to go back there.

Calves' liver and roast salmon.

Cat wanted to ask him about Rachel and did not.

'The gallery was asking if I have enough for another exhibition,' he said.

'Have you?'

'Maybe. But I want to do some more portrait drawing. I'm quite keen to do Felix.'

'Why Felix?'

Simon laughed. 'Because he has such a quirky, interesting face. This calves' liver isn't as good as they used to do at Dino's.'

'Nostalgia's a sign of old age.'

'But it's pretty damn good all the same. Are you and Kieron OK?'

This was the way it always had to be with them, chat and then the quick lunge. This worked.

'Fine. You asked that before. Listen – it's never going to be the same, bro. I know that. The arrow only strikes home once and my once was Chris. But I can't stay alone forever, I love Kieron, he's a good man, he's been fantastic with the kids and we get on. Yes, it's been bumpy with Dad but when wouldn't it have been? I didn't mean to get married again – I was never looking for it and I never expected it, but I'm very glad he came along. You're OK with it, aren't you?'

'With him as him or him being the Chief?'

'Both.'

'Got used to the second and it's fine – better than I expected actually. Him as him is all right too . . . like you. No, I'm good with it all. Never thought I would be but I am.'

He looked up at her, a direct, warning look. Don't ask, it said. Don't ask.

She didn't ask.

He dropped her at the farmhouse, where the lights were all on, but didn't go in, just waited, watching Cat wave briefly and close the door.

Home. The Close was quiet, the lamps casting their tawny rings of light onto the cobbles, lights on behind curtains or in porches of the houses that were lived in by cathedral clergy and staff, dotted between those that were offices and dark now.

There was not a soul on foot.

He parked and turned for a moment, to walk back down the avenue. It was cold. He looked, as he always looked, at the tower and the nave end of St Michael's Cathedral. He had often tried to draw it and always given up. It did not need an interpreter, or any copied image. It was itself and perfect, and he would never attempt it again. But he suddenly remembered the face of a very old, bent man he had seen a few days earlier, going in through the west door, a timeless but very individual face such as Dürer might have drawn and made a mental note to look out for him, and ask the man if he would sit to be sketched. He was more used to drawing objects and creatures, of which he did not need to ask permission. This was a new direction and he felt the old excitement spiking through him.

He ran up the stairs two at a time. Opened the flat door. Switched on the lights and looked first. At the white sofa and chairs, the elm floorboards, the white walls, the huge, curtainless windows with their long view down the close, the paintings, the tall, full bookshelves. He smiled slightly, with pleasure.

He went inside. Home.

He closed the door.

From *The Benefit of Hindsight*
Chapter One

Carrie wanted to stay out longer. She had nothing else to do but she did not want to go home. She had come out of the newsagent's in a churn of anxiety about what she had found out, what was happening, and until she had processed it in her head, she could not walk into the house and face Colin.

There were cafes on either side, new and smart, old and comfortable, but all full. Someone bumped into her, someone else almost tripped her up. A man sat in a doorway on a piece of old matting, with a dog and a mug of coppers, and spat on the pavement. Her hair was damp from the drizzle, as were the sleeves of her coat and the handles of her tote bag.

She felt a surge of panic, and the need to move, to get away, though it was herself she really wanted to get away from. She went down the side street towards the cathedral, past the great west door and into the new visitors' centre which had opened just before Christmas, to equal choruses of delight and disapproval. It was cool and beautiful there, a calm place, like the ancient cathedral itself, and there were only a few people in the refectory. Carrie got her pot of tea and a cheese scone, and went to the far end of the cafe, beside a glass wall through which she could see the tiled space beyond. She closed her eyes. She did not come to the cathedral to pray, she had no particular belief, though sometimes she spoke aloud to someone, someone who might be listening, and if there was no one and she was only talking to herself, it still helped.

Perhaps she would not have to tell him, she thought, spreading butter on her scone, perhaps he would work it out for himself. No. Colin was incapable of working anything out except the figures he saw on his computer screen from early morning until late at night, the white electronic arrows moving up and down.

A woman came into the refectory, took a tray, gave her order, the sort of woman who usually came in here, a volunteer who manned the shop, or sat behind the new glass counter giving out information and leaflets, or arranged the flowers. No, not flowers, Carrie remembered that the flower arrangers came in as a group, three or four of them, clattering their trays and talking cheerily. A lot of the people who helped out in the cathedral and this visitors' centre were cheery.

She pushed some crumbs around her plate with her forefinger, and pressed them together to form a ball.

Then the swing doors opened again and there was bumping and shuffling and voices. Two young women with pushchairs. They came down the aisle towards her, and settled down at a table with a lot of fuss and chat and coat removing and chair scraping. The refectory was noisy because all the surfaces were hard. No one had thought of that. Every cup and saucer clattered, cutlery clashed, the sudden noise of the coffee machine muffled speech.

She came here for peace and quiet, a place where she could be safely herself, and sooner or later people and their racket always drove her away.

One woman had gone to the counter, the other sat with the children. A baby was on her lap, its arms jerking up and down like the arms of a string puppet, not yet within its control. Carrie did not want to look at it. She looked at it.

And then she saw the other child. It had not been taken out of its pushchair and it was turned slightly to face Carrie. She did not know how old it might be, only that it was not a baby. Children like that could be any age.

Children like that. It was still but not asleep. Its lolling head was too large and it wore a bib into which it was dribbling. Its eyes did not focus. Its face was the colour of dough.

The woman was bringing over the tray of drinks and as she set it down on their table she looked at the child and her face broke into a smile and seemed to blaze up at the sight, as if she had been bathed in sunshine. The look was joyous, a look of delight. But most of all, a look of love, unconcealed, all-absorbing.

The child saw nothing, only moved its head a little, as it dribbled and its eyes rolled up and round and up again.

Carrie left, almost knocking over her chair, startling the baby on the lap. But the child in the buggy was not startled. It seemed to be unaware of every sound, every movement around it, every person.

Outside she leaned on a pillar and felt her heart race and lurch and her mind spin and nausea rise up in her, like a creature springing out of water deep down, and she retched, but nothing came out of her mouth except an ugly sound, so that a man walking past flinched slightly, before quickening his step. She took in gulps of air which tasted of rain.

Somehow she had to find her car and drive home and, eventually, talk to Colin, tell Colin, make Colin angry or shocked or miserable. Frightened, perhaps, as she was. Her fear was deep-rooted and powerful. It was absolute, certain, real, the fear of her worst nightmares and waking terror. A fear that was growing inside her.

She had plenty of time to think about what she was going to say. She made shepherd's pie with three vegetables, peeling, chopping, mashing, making gravy, process after process which was soothing. She baked apples, stuffing the cores with brown sugar, raisins and ginger, which took more preparation, so that she would be even calmer. But of course it was no help at all, she did everything slowly, mechanically, and all the time the lines she had to speak were being rehearsed in her head, over and over again, and with them came the questions–what would he say, how would he react, would he be silent or angry, shocked or irritated, or perhaps even disbelieving? No, there would be no reason for that. Why would she lie to him about this of all things?

The scene in the cathedral refectory played itself out again too. The two young women. The baby with jerking hands. The one in the push-chair. The way it had been and would be forever, and yet still, the mother had given the child such a look of blazing love. So that could happen? It was possible, was it?

But Carrie could not believe it.

The table was laid and the supper ready when, as he always did, apparently knowing the moment by some sixth sense, Colin came out of his office, where the monitors would sit by themselves, scrolling through their eternal rows of figures, their flashing panels of red or green, occasionally remaining calm for moments, before going into a dance of non-stop manic moves and then a brief panic. She had sometimes gone in and glanced at the three screens and felt panic in turn. It was infectious and yet she did not understand any of it, did not have any idea what the frenzy meant.

'Good?'

'Very good.' Did he know that he rubbed his hands together, like a man in a cartoon about greed? Was it greed, or just satisfaction with his job, a day's decent results? She never knew. The money came in, was stored away somewhere, in more rows of numbers, moved out again, increased, decreased. How much money?

He went into the cloakroom to wash his hands, which was the signal for her to start carrying supper into the dining room.

'Careful, Carrie, it isn't properly on the table mat.'

She shifted the hot dish a millimetre. Colin reset his knife and fork exactly parallel to one another.

'Profitable day?'

'Very. The markets have been going crazy, all over the place.'

'So that's a good thing? I never understand it.'

'You don't have to. It just means I can dip in and out making quick profits and locking them in, making more, locking them in too.'

When she had met him he had been about to leave the City hedge fund he worked for and set up on his own. They had moved out of London and were renting this house until they found one he thought was worth buying. She would have been happy to stay here. She liked it, the house, the garden, the park beyond which belonged to a large estate. But he said it was not an investment. It was pointless, bad financial management, to rent for any length of time.

He ate neatly, taking small mouthfuls. Carrie ate nothing, though she pretended to, even putting food into her mouth, but she could not swallow it because her mouth was already full, of the thing she had to tell him.

'Sorry . . .' She went into the kitchen to get rid of it.

'No bones in shepherd's pie,' Colin said.

Back in the dining room, she sat down again. He had taken four carrots and they were arranged on his plate in order of size, though to her eye there was little difference between them. He was hesitating. Which end should he begin to eat from? Once he had decided, he was committed.

'I'm having a baby,' Carrie said, and the words seemed to blurt out of their own accord. She had not meant to tell him just then.

There was a long and terrible silence while he stared down at his plate and she sat very still and the nausea rose again, filling her mouth.

'The worst is that you didn't tell me and now it's too late.'

Colin had paced round the room like a zoo animal, sat down again without looking at her, paced again, sat down again. Gone into his office to check his screens and come out, shaking his head.

'I can't focus, I can't concentrate, this is all I can think about. Why didn't you tell me when you first found out? We could have done something.'

'I was frightened of what your reaction would be.'

'And now?'

'It was unavoidable.'

'We said we would never have children, I couldn't cope with children and you certainly could not.'

'Why "certainly"? Why do you say that?'

'Because of the way you are with all of this. Because of . . . Listen, when do you have to see a doctor or go to a hospital or something?'

'I don't know. I don't think I can. I'm afraid of what I'll find out. You know that.'

'That's in your head. It isn't fact.'

'It is.'

He paced round the room again. Round and round.

'What are you going to do?'

'Nothing.'

'Yes you are, you're going to have a baby.'

'That. Yes.'

'Dear God, after all we said. You should have been more careful. Why weren't you more careful?'

'You could have had the vasectomy.'

'I trusted you.'

'This is not only me. It's you. It's both of us. I'm not taking all the blame.'

'You have a neurosis, a phobia, whatever, about having a deformed child . . . handicapped – I don't know what one is supposed to call it these days. I simply do not want any child. It isn't going to have problems, it will be fit and healthy and living in the house, and I can't face that.'

'Why? If you believe it will be fit and healthy.'

'Because it will intrude on my life . . . I need to think about this. I need to go away to think about it.'

'Why go away? Why can't you think here?'

'I won't be able to work.'

'Take a break from work.'

He stared at her.

She got up and started to clear away the dishes.

'Leave that. Sit down. We have to decide what to do.'

'Nothing. There's nothing we can do. It's too late for . . . to get rid of it. Far too late.'

'Are you sure about that?'

'I don't think . . . I couldn't do that. Kill a child.'

'But at the beginning . . .'

'This isn't the beginning.'

'No.'

'When will it be born?'

'I'm not sure.'

'All right.' He stood up. 'I'll help you clear the table. I can't go back to work now.'

He came round to her. Put out both his hands. Carrie took them. 'If this is what happens, it happens.'

'I won't be able to cope with a child who isn't right.'

'That's all the nonsense in your head. Forget that.'

'I can't.'

'You can and you will.' His eyes did not flicker away from her face. She had always believed him, believed him when he said she should marry him, that they would work perfectly together, that it was the right thing for her, no one else would ever have married her, plain and awkward as she thought herself to be, she had been amazingly, miraculously lucky really. But she could not believe him about this because it was simply not a question of belief, but of knowledge. She knew the baby had something gravely wrong with it, so that nothing he said to try and reassure her, convince her, could possibly make any difference.

She followed him, with the loaded tray he was carrying, into the kitchen.

Fact was fact.

SUSAN HILL'S SIMON SERRAILLER MYSTERIES

THE BENEFIT OF HINDSIGHT
978-1-4197-4358-0
$27.00 hardcover with jacket
"Beautifully told, Hill's gimlet eye
and steely prose remind you how
fierce she can be."
— *Daily Mail*

THE VARIOUS HAUNTS OF MEN
978-1-59020-027-8
$16.00 paperback
"Masterly and satisfying."
— *Ruth Rendell*

THE PURE IN HEART
978-1-59020-085-8
$16.00 paperback
"Realistic, gritty, and gut-
wrenching crime fiction . . . Hill has
mesmerizing storytelling ability and
[a] gift for making characters and
situations come alive, and the result
is an outstanding read that will stay
with readers long afterward."
— *Booklist*, starred review

THE RISK OF DARKNESS
978-1-59020-290-6
$16.00 paperback
"Hill crime novels are engaging and
gripping reads." — *Strand* magazine

THE VOWS OF SILENCE
978-1-59020-442-9
$16.00 paperback
"Will haunt you long after
reading . . . terrific and engrossing."
— *Washington Post*

THE SHADOWS IN THE STREET
978-1-59020-684-3
$16.00 paperback
"As every Trollope reader knows,
English cathedral towns can be
hotbeds of viciousness and vice. And
so it is in Lafferton, where Susan Hill
sets her thoughtful mysteries. . . .
Elegant."
— *New York Times Book Review*

THE BETRAYAL OF TRUST
978-1-4683-0065-9
$16.00 paperback
"Beautifully written . . . Hill is giving
us a timeless panorama of life and
death in an English town, one in
which a murder investigation is only
one drama among many."
— *Washington Post*

A QUESTION OF IDENTITY
978-1-4683-0712-2
$16.00 paperback
"Chilling . . . twisted. The darkest
entry in an elegant series."
— *New York Times Book Review*

THE SOUL OF DISCRETION
978-1-4683-1299-7
$16.00 paperback
"An atmospheric page-turner."
— *San Francisco Review of Books*